The Urbana Free Library

To renew: call 217-367-4057
or go to *"urbanafreelibrary.org"*
and select "Renew/Request Items"

Aftermath
Stories of Secrets and Consequences

A 2012 Main Street Rag
Short Fiction Anthology

edited by
Rayne Debski

MINT HILL BOOKS
MAIN STREET RAG PUBLISHING COMPANY
CHARLOTTE, NORTH CAROLINA

Library of Congress Control Number: 2012944334

ISBN: 978-1-59948-384-9

Produced in the United States of America

Main Street Rag
PO Box 690100
Charlotte, NC 28227
www.MainStreetRag.com

CONTENTS

INTRODUCTION

When you step onto an escalator at a shopping mall, somewhere in your subconscious you know certain things are going to happen. You will pass static displays of merchandise, inhale the scent of indoor tropical plants, and reach a particular floor untroubled by your ride on the moving stairs. Forget about certainties when you read the stories in this volume. The escalator might suddenly stop, causing your heart to lurch because the person behind you is someone you haven't seen since a disaster twenty-five years before. Or the stairs might change direction, carrying you back to a time of such family strife you lost your voice. There is the possibility that nothing will move, that you will be stuck where you are with people you've harmed by your good intentions. Or the railing you're gripping will slip away when your father appears on the opposite staircase holding the charms you've stolen for his ritual to avenge you.

The theme of this volume is secrets, those things that are intentionally withheld, not widely known, or not understood. But the stories are about more than that. They are about ordinary events—a bus ride, a walk to the cinema, a business conference—where people are unexpectedly forced to confront experiences and relationships they thought were buried. They are about what happens when men and women hold back truths not only from one another, but from themselves. They are about children and adults so desperate to maintain a pretense, they don't recognize the dangerous truths others keep hidden.

The people in these stories ride the errant escalator until they come to what George Oppen so beautifully describes in his poem, "Image of the Engine":

There hovers in that moment, wraith-like and like a plume of steam, an aftermath,
A still and quiet angel of knowledge and of comprehension.

Step onto the escalator. Enjoy the ride.

—Rayne Debski, Editor

LEGEND

John Struloeff

This is a story I've told only twice—first to the state police and federal officials, and second to my mom and dad. I never told it to the newspapers. I have never told it to a therapist or my wife of nine years. People have warped it and exaggerated it into twenty dead and wolves circling and hell-fire shooting through the mountains. But I know what really happened, and it haunts me like nothing else in my life. I was chosen by God to witness something, but I do not understand why.

Early in the morning the Saturday after my high school graduation, I had my father drive me up the fire-road as close to the peak of Nikolai Mountain as we could get. All I had was my backpack stuffed with gear—sleeping bag, pup tent, matches, rope, and other camping gear, though I realized I had forgotten my flashlight when I was hours into the hike. There had been no bear or mountain lions on Nikolai since before I was born, so I did not bring a gun.

All morning and into the early afternoon I followed abandoned roads and old animal trails along the ridgeline towards Tower Peak, which was the highest point in the area at 3,680 feet above sea level. On the map there was a spot near the peak called Spirit Lake. No one I knew had been there. I thought a two or three day camping trip into virgin territory would be a nice graduation present to myself. Maybe it would help me see my future more clearly.

When I spotted the sliver of granite they call Tower Peak, I stumbled upon a fresh elk trail and took it for the last mile up a long stretch of hill, crackling my way through dead, twisted branches, the air slightly humid but cool under the large Douglas fir and red cedars. I emerged onto a smooth grassy embankment, the sun warm on my skin. The grass here was a tangle of yellowed stalks and strong green shoots, buzzing with flies and grasshoppers. I stopped for a moment to catch my breath. The air carried the deeper smells of the lake, the decay and slick, wet mud of centuries of rainfall and dripping forest. Just ahead was a thin stand of fir trees where the ground leveled, and through the scattering of trunks I could see the lake, spreading like rough, blue glass, its surface a rich color, as if the sky had fallen into the water and melted. It was my vision of paradise.

Two boulders stood near the lake's edge. The earth between them looked recently chewed up as if animals had been sleeping there, maybe a herd of deer or elk. I sat down, leaning against one of the boulders, then closed my eyes. The dried moss on the boulder crunched against the base of my neck. I fidgeted for a moment, then opened my eyes again. The sky was clear, a light blue that was almost white, and the air smelled of blooming dandelions and the moist wood of fir trees. Cranes were out in the middle of the lake, wading in a shallow spot. I felt incredibly alive.

A few hours later I awoke and hopped down the bank to kneel at the water's edge. In my backpack was a collapsible fishing pole—a graduation gift that I had been anxious to try out—so I peered into the shadowy water for the silhouettes of fish jetting around.

But instead something bright caught my eye. I looked up to my right, across the lake and just above the tree line. It was a small white plane, silent, floating smoothly downward toward the water. There was no engine noise. It was a single-prop plane like a Cessna, and it continued gliding, the nose angling sharply downward. Then it was over the water, its white reflection rippling quickly across the water's surface below the plane's belly.

It struck violently nose down, blasting water into a fountain. Metal groaned as the fuselage stood on end, the tail high in the air. Then it fell forward and hit the water upside down with a dull smack. Water cascaded, popping down onto the metal like hail.

An electric shock passed through my body. I felt the urge to yell, but no one was around for miles.

The plane was a good fifty yards out. I waded into the water, looking for any movement, doors opening, people splashing. Nothing. A few moments more, still nothing.

I dove in.

The tail of the plane was deep in the lake, pale in the green tinted water like the belly of a fish. The front end was half exposed, angled in the air. One propeller stretched above the water. A wheel was suspended about a foot out, the other a dark shadow just beneath the surface. It must have landed on the high point where I'd seen cranes wading.

"Holy shit," I said. I wasn't a good swimmer, so I was tired, almost too tired to go on, but I felt time evaporating quickly for whomever was inside. Near the engine I glimpsed a side window. I took a few deep breaths and rolled under, squinting against the sting of the water.

A few feet away was a handle, and I made my way to it. Blood pulsed in my ears. I put one hand on the plane while I pulled with the other. There was suction behind it, and then a burst of bubbles crackling the water above my head. The door opened wide enough to see in. I was running out of breath, my lungs convulsing every few seconds. There was a person near me, the face hidden—only a pale neck, hair covering the face and lilting with the movement of the water. I grabbed a piece of clothing and pulled, but something had snagged it.

The muscles in my chest burned, so I pushed away and kicked my way to the surface, bursting out of the water, gasping. Moving to the tire, I held on with one hand while treading with the other, then I took a deep breath and dove again. The door was ajar, and the body had not moved. I ran my hands around the seat until I located the seat harness and the buckle. I released the harness and grabbed the person's clothes and pulled hard. The body moved slowly sideways. I could see blood on the person's face, thin streamers like spit near the temple. I grabbed the cloth firmly and pulled myself out, hauling the sagging weight of the body. The pressure to breathe was incredible, and my throat felt like it would burst and let the water rush in. After I surfaced I could barely keep my head above water. I had to keep my legs and free arm working furiously as I inched my way to the engine where I let my legs drift down, hoping to find the bottom. My foot landed on solid rock, and I stood, chest deep. I reached with both arms and pulled the body towards me, managing to get the person's head above water. It surfaced, short dark hair sodden with water. A woman. Her eyes were closed. Her face was smooth with water, supple, more unconscious than dead. I rolled her on her back to keep her face above water. To my left was a black shadow beneath the surface, grass stubbling through the surface around it. I waded towards it, working to balance myself on the uneven bottom until the water was shallow, less then a foot deep. I dragged the woman there as quickly as I could, then knelt and listened to her mouth, then her chest. I pushed on her chest once. Water gurgled in her throat. I pushed again, forcing more water out of her mouth, then listened at her chest. No sign.

A vague image came into my mind: two people in the plane as it went down. Seconds ticked with heartbeats. I swam again to the doorway and pulled myself in. The inside was very dark. Pieces of paper were floating around. A fish slid along my leg, cool and slick, making my heart thump like a hammer against my chest. I reached out with my hands. I felt something soft and cold and gripped it. A hand. I almost lost control then—I had the urge to get out of there and never return—but I grabbed it, intertwining the fingers with mine, and pulled. I gripped the woman's seat and pulled past it. The body seemed to be free moving, though heavy. I just kept going without looking back, pushing out the door, kicking, doing a one hand crawl, concentrating on the convulsive pressure in my throat and my abdomen. When I broke the surface, my vision was dim, and I treaded water, my mouth just barely exposed. My muscles were exhausted already. I felt all I could do was breathe and keep treading. I let my legs drop earlier than before, feeling for the bottom, and the water was over my head. I had to kick to the surface and push and push another foot or so. Here it was chest deep. I turned the body and pulled the head towards the surface, so its face was upward. The body seemed denser, and when the face surfaced it was a man. He resembled the woman—thin and pale, with short, almost black hair. His weight was like hers—dead, molding to whatever position it was pulled into—and though he seemed larger, I pulled him just the same, lying him down next to her.

There was a large dark patch of blood on the front of his shirt, near his heart. It was syrupy, like blackberry juice, and a haze of what looked like blood fibers floated just above his chest. I knelt and put my fingers to his neck. Soft and cool, no pulse. I listened for breath, then listened at his heart. I sat back on my heels. The woman's color had changed, a blue tint around her eyes. I put my hands to the man's chest and pushed. His mouth gurgled. A cloud of blood was in the water next to his head, hazy, settling onto the rock. I pushed again. Another haze.

I leaned back, dripping. Small waves slapped my lower back. The air smelled like old water, a standing pool of green algae and fish. I closed my eyes and took a deep breath. The world seemed murky, as if I were underwater. I opened my eyes and looked at their faces. They were in their late thirties, maybe, and could have been brother and sister, though his cheekbones were more prominent, his jaw thicker and wider. Maybe they were husband and wife. He had a gold watch on his wrist. *They're dead*, I thought, over and over and over.

The muscles in both my arms were shivering. On the shore were the boulders and my pack. Probably little more than fifty yards, but it seemed like an impossible distance. I stood, my muscles shivering weakly with my weight. I would go back to shore and decide what to do.

During the steady crawl back to my gear, I paced my breathing like I was running long distance in track again. When I made the shore, I slid onto the mud and flopped onto my back. The shadows had moved, and all but my feet were in shadow then, the breeze cooling the water on my body. I felt done, incapable of moving, and I lay there breathing, looking at the blue sky.

After a time, I looked out to the plane. It hadn't moved, though a part of me almost expected it to disappear. It seemed very small. I squinted, but I couldn't make out the bodies.

"Jesus," I said. "What am I going to do?" It was strange to hear my own voice.

I was twelve miles from the fire road I had taken in. No radio. I was exhausted.

I lay there for what seemed like an hour, until I no longer felt the sun on my feet. The shadows had darkened the water of one side of the lake. I decided I would get the bodies back to shore. It seemed wrong to leave them out there. But the bodies hadn't wanted to come up on their own—they seemed to want to sink towards the bottom. I couldn't see myself doing a one-arm crawl and hauling them back at the same time. So I thought for a moment, devising a log float, to somehow push a log or two out there and lay them both on top.

At the edge of the tree line was a dry cedar log about fifteen feet long. I pushed through the high grass, avoiding scattered patches of devil's club. The log was bleached from the sun and partially rotted on one end. I knelt down and lifted the rotted end. It was too heavy to carry all at once, so I moved one end at a time. I worked it through the grass, flinging one end into the water. Waves pulsed out in even rings until they neared the plane where the breeze caught the water and made it choppy.

I spotted another log in heavy brush, but I got scratched up by devil's club pretty good, blood smearing my bare thighs. A third log was farther back in the pines where the dense growth of trees had killed the brush off and covered the ground with pine needles. It was lighter. I dragged it to the rocky shore and flopped it in the water. My body was shaking, so I took a breather, resting my hands on my sides. I began to worry about the swim out to the middle

When I had rested, I got the nylon rope out of my backpack, cut it in half, lashed the two logs together as best I could at each end, and then cast the whole float out in the water. The logs were buoyed well by the water, and I waded in beside them. I leaned my stomach on one end so my legs dangled in the water. The logs went down, but my chest was still at water level. I started kicking.

Before long I could see them again. They appeared to be sleeping in the water. Their skin was much paler. It spooked me, almost sending me back. It was very hard to go near them. I slipped off one side and let my legs stretch down until my feet settled onto the rock. It took some effort to slow the float, which wanted to keep going towards the other side of the lake—I didn't blame it—and I had to pull hard to get it back.

When I grabbed the man's arm to pull him towards me, his body was very stiff, and it seemed to be caught on something. I knelt and lifted him like I would an armload of firewood, curling both arms around his torso. He was fairly light until I began lifting him out of the water where he took on a sudden weight. I noticed the smell then, it came in a waft, feces, but something else, something danker that settled into my bones, like the odor of someone deathly who is sweating out disease. I heaved him hard. He almost rolled off the other side, but I jerked him back and ended up settling him chest down on the logs, his face nestled in the crevice between them. I noticed a dent in the back of his neck, just below his hairline; there wasn't blood, but the skin was cracked, showing raw muscle beneath the skin.

It was horrifying work, nothing I can really describe. There is something extremely unsettling about touching death like that, the smell and the stillness. But I did it. I did what I thought needed to be done. I pulled the woman over and hoisted her onto the other end, so that her feet were near his head. She was face up. There was a dent near her temple similar to the one on the back of the man's head. Her mouth was open slightly, as if she were about to say something. I tried not to look, but I couldn't help it. She was so delicate. She must have been beautiful. She was, still, in a way.

I got behind the logs and kicked them to shore. As I kicked, I saw both of their faces, pale and unmoving, in my mind's vision. So I thought of splashing at the beach when I was a child, kicking along behind an inner-tube my father had been given by a neighbor who owned a tractor. I thought of people laughing, crowding the beach. I thought of canoeing at church camp at Cullaby Lake. I almost forgot what I was doing.

I hit the beach, and then had to drag the bodies onto the sand. I finished and leaned against the rock with my backpack. I did everything I could to look away from the bodies. I looked at the trees, which on any other day would have soothed me, made me feel at home.

A robin landed on the man's stomach and began picking at a button on his shirt. It lifted the button in its beak, straining against the weight of the shirt, then dropped it, cocking its head for a new perspective. I ran over and shooed it away, but as soon as I sat back down, the bird returned. Pick, pick. I threw a few pebbles, but the bird just hopped down his leg, pecking at grits of sand on his knee. There was nothing to cover them with but my tent and thin sleeping bag, but I couldn't sleep exposed, not around a lake with all its mosquitoes. So I would have to leave them out. And since it was too late to head back, it would probably be overnight as well.

Out on the lake, birds were whipping along the surface, spiraling and chattering. The plane was still unmoving. Watching it, I tried to imagine what it had been like flying in it; it seemed so sleek and strong. The trees must have flashed by in a blur. Were they going too fast to see what was coming? At that time, I had never flown in a plane, and so the man and woman's last moments were all a deep mystery to me.

I decided to set up my tent. I pitched the tent between the two boulders where I had sat down after I had first seen the lake. The ground was flat and looked as if it had been camped on before. I took my time, pounding each stake slowly with a rock, setting the rope lengths perfectly. I brushed rocks away from the entrance, humming to myself songs that reminded me of dances and friends laughing. I tried to drag out time, to break every movement into its parts and make it use time.

Then I crawled over to one of the boulders and sat back, trying to figure out what had just happened. It didn't make sense. People don't just fall out of the sky like that and die. But they do. I just saw it. And my friend Derek had driven his truck into Hell's Canyon the summer before. Is this what it was like for him? Stillness and a serene face, as if death was a gift from God. And a horror for those who must find them and go on living. I had no idea at the time how often these images would play again in my mind—the white plane half-submerged in the calm water, the two bodies lying side-by-side. I was numb with cold of all kinds.

When the sun dipped below the mountain to set on the Pacific, the shadows covered the whole lake. The chirping of birds was gone. The woods became silent. I looked around, feeling very alone. Nothing moved.

Then I saw something on the water. A wall of white was moving across the lake from the far side. It was low, a thin stretching haze. Within minutes I could see that it was a mass of large flying bugs, pecking the water, spinning and diving. They looked like large mosquitoes. There were thousands, maybe tens of thousands.

I headed quickly for the tent, sensing that more bugs of other kinds were about to emerge like armies. I lay back against my small, limp camping pillow. My body seemed to be vibrating, a humming sensation to the tips of my fingers. I lay there until the crickets began chirping steadily and the dim light outside was nearly gone. The large flying bugs from the lake fluttered slowly along the tent wall, sometimes bumping into it and then buzzing away. Exhaustion made my mind spin. Sometimes when I closed my eyes it would feel as if I was flying, falling, and I would open my eyes suddenly. It was painful to stay awake, but I kept fading into that free fall, and the faces of the man and woman kept looming in my mind's vision. It was as if I knew them, as if we had a long history together. They seemed so alive—a sleeping relative.

They were outside in the dark, their spirits in them and not in them.

I was almost asleep when I first heard the howling. The sound was faint, far away, but it held for a long time and then went quiet. Then there was another howl off in a different direction, equally as distant, and the first one yowled in answer.

I sat up, my heart thumping. *Dogs or coyotes,* I was saying to myself, *Probably coyotes.* Everything was quiet for a good ten minutes or more while I listened. It took me a while to calm down. I lay back and closed my eyes.

It wasn't long before I heard a noise, soft, almost like breathing. Then more distinct breathing, and then silence for a long time. My body keened. I mentally located the knife—in the tent, in my pack, near my pant leg. I slowly moved my hand towards it. They couldn't be wolves. They had to be coyotes. Normally I wouldn't be worried about coyotes, but just three months before, my buddy Toby had told me when we had seen a coyote at the beach, *Coyotes are scared animals, flighty, and if they're in a pack they might attack anything.* I braced myself.

The breathing turned into panting, more than one animal. There was a growl, and a low, vicious snarl. A yap. They were definitely coyotes or big dogs, more than two. The aggressive sounds somehow gave me courage, adrenaline like a soldier readying himself for a confrontation. I sat up and yelled, a long, loud burst, my head tilted back. My lungs resonated with my voice, and when I was done, there was silence. I reached for the tent zipper and cried out more, incoherent sounds to scare the animals, loud and angry. I grabbed my knife and rolled out of the tent. Dizzy from pushing so much air out of my lungs, I sat there, looking around in the darkness, not seeing anything, incredibly scared. Then I could see the pale forms of the bodies, and three shadows nearby. They were coyotes, their heads held low. When I focused on them, they shrank back from the bodies and trotted a few steps towards the tree line. I stood up, and they all jumped back like I had kicked at them.

They turned to watch me. A twig popped near the tree line. Two more were standing together, their gray pelts making them look like ghosts. It was too dark. I couldn't tell if there were any more. One of the three nearest the bodies took a few tentative steps. I clapped my hands, and they all jumped. They didn't run; they just watched me.

Then the three made their way back to the bodies, slowly, as if I weren't there. I ran at them, yelling. They bolted back about twenty feet, and then stopped all at once. The two on the tree line moved out onto the smooth ground, slinking around lone shoots of devil's club, and stopped near the others. Off in the trees, a hundred yards or more, another coyote howled. The five in front of me became restless then, panting hard and pacing. Two of them trotted towards me and stopped. They were getting used to me. I stood near the bodies, which gave off a smell, rank but not strong; they were becoming a part of this forest, and the coyotes wanted them. I had to do something, but I didn't know what. I had no gun, and I couldn't run around all night chasing them.

I decided to build a fire. I had matches in my pocket, and there was plenty of wood around. I grabbed a few dried branches that were lying nearby and threw them in a pile. The man and woman were near the water, so I put the wood between the trees and the bodies, to have the lake and the fire as barriers. The coyotes spread out and sniffed the ground. One of them tried to sneak in, real low to the ground. It was extremely clever at this, and I didn't see it, but after a moment I heard it, snarling and tearing at the man's shoulder, trying to get a prize quickly. I yelled and raced after it, and then ran back to the wood. Before the hike I had stuffed strips of shredded newspaper into a plastic zip lock bag and put it in my back pocket; I pulled it out and wadded the paper under a few small branches, and then lit a match and put it to the paper. The flame grew quickly, lighting up my body and the bleached ground. I lay small twigs into the flame, and they bristled orange and popped. Everything was dry from the long steady sun of the past week. The coyotes watched the fire, the flames reflecting in their eyes; they were as faint as everything else in the woods, but their eyes were piercing, little embers. I stood and ran towards them, trying to push them back to give the fire more time to grow. The branches caught, and the flames cast a light on the tree trunks at the edge of the forest, giving the area a feeling of enclosure, as if it were a large room. Soon another howl off in the trees broke the illusion, and I was again surrounded by an unending forest.

The coyotes kept inching in, and I would throw rocks and dirt clods at them. I wanted to throw burning sticks, but it would catch the whole mountain ablaze. Their focus was incredible, and I knew they weren't going away. It was a matter of time. They had tested me out and found I didn't have a gun, and that's all the knowledge they needed. They knew I couldn't stay here forever.

I held it off as best I could, but soon tears filled my eyes, blurring the fire and everything it cast light upon. The intensity was overwhelming me, and it felt unreal, a terrible dream. I was protecting two people who were no longer alive, who I had salvaged from a half-sunken plane that had wrecked not a hundred yards from where I was seated, from hungry animals whose sole purpose this night was to eat this man and woman, and no one was there to help me. I felt incredibly far away from everything I had ever known. A pressure inside me wanted to burst, to let it go, to let the coyotes eat what they found, and I could hide away from them in a pit in the forest or out on the rock island in the lake. But there was something else inside me, almost like a voice, insistent and powerful like the voice of God, that said no no no no.

And then I heard a low growl, at my fingertips. I glanced down, and a coyote was staring at me, baring its teeth. A second coyote had attacked the man's shoulder again. I kicked at the coyote near me and hit it in the snout; it yipped and raced away. I jumped after the other one and chased it a few steps, then picked up a stick and threw at it; the stick hit its back, and it bolted for the tree line. But the other three remained where they were, aloof and watchful.

I stopped. I knew I couldn't keep it up. There were too many, and they were too hungry. What about the ones I had heard howling earlier? I stood there breathing, thinking. I looked at the fire, and the gray shadows lurking close by. I looked at my tent, wishing I were inside sleeping and none of this had happened. Take me back twelve hours, and make it different. Give this man and woman back to whomever loved them.

Quickly I thought of what I could do then. An image of them sealed in my tent flashed in my mind. So I yelled and chased a coyote, and then went straight to my tent and pulled the stakes from the ground. I collapsed it and dragged it over to the fire. The coyotes stood back, wary. I pulled the sleeping bag out, along with my backpack. I unzipped the sleeping bag and laid it next to the woman, opening it wide for her. Her face was pale and serene, her eyes closed, as if sleeping. I pushed my hands beneath her, feeling her cold weight, and rolled her onto the sleeping bag face down. She was a slight woman, and she fit inside completely. I zipped the bag closed. I then dragged the tent around so the opening was nearest the man's head. I stood over him and grabbed him under the armpits, heaving his head into the opening of the tent. When I set him down, I noticed his shoulder. The shirt was torn away, and it showed white flesh around a gaping hole of red glistening muscle. It didn't bleed at all. I hoisted him further, and once his waist was in, I was able to slide him inside by pushing on his feet. I zipped the tent closed.

By the look of his shoulder I knew that I had to get them out of reach; otherwise the coyotes would just tear through the tent and sleeping bag like wrappers. I took the rope I had used to lash the logs together and wrapped it around the sleeping bag where the woman's ankles were, and then I dragged the bag to the nearest tree, a Douglas fir. I flung the rope over a branch that was twelve or fifteen feet up and caught the other end to hoist her up. At the time I weighed nearly two-hundred pounds, built up from lifting weights after track season, and though my arms shook I had no problem getting her up in the air. She hung behind the mask of the bag, swaying slowly. I wrapped the end of the rope three or four times around the tree trunk beneath a branch so the rope wouldn't slip.

When I turned back, one of the large coyotes was at the tent, sniffing and pawing frantically; it didn't know what to do with it. I yelled and ran towards it. I was exhausted, getting delirious, and my breath hardly slowed even when I knelt by the tent to get the man and tent ready to be hoisted. My muscles were cramped, and I had to hoist him up and then go a dozen miles when the sun rose. I wasn't sure if I could make it. Slowly I wrapped the rope around the tent-cloth at his ankles like I had hers, and then followed the same routine of hoisting him up the branch. He was heavier, and when I pulled sometimes I was lifted off the ground. I braced my feet against the tree truck and heaved. I did the rest mechanically, in a blur, and when he was up, the loose folds of the tent enveloped the woman in the sleeping bag. I went to the fire and collapsed, my arms burning like I had lain my muscles on coals.

I slept.

As the sky began to light, two coyotes emerged from the forest. I had awakened shortly before, my arms and legs trembling from overexertion, and I lay there staring at the stars in the sky. The fire was still burning, the coals hissing. The coyotes came out from the tree line as silent as spirits, their noses lowered to the ground. They stopped and stood sideways, watching me. I stood and clapped my hands, and they crouched, ready to bolt, but after a few seconds they straightened up, and we stood watching each other. They were waiting patiently, and we both knew they weren't going anywhere.

It was time to go.

I kicked the fire apart, spreading charred logs and smoking coals. The flames were still burning on a few pieces of wood, and I stomped them with my soles. I went to my pack and got the small pot I would have used to boil water, and I filled it up a few times at the lake and poured it on the glowing coals. They sizzled and popped. The coyotes watched.

I grabbed all of my things and put them in my pack. There was a thin drift of smoke coming from the charred remains of the fire, but I was confident it had died. I looked up at the tent hanging from the tree, its shape solid and formed like one massive body. It didn't seem real—there must have been something else wrapped in there, tents within tents that filled it with weight.

I turned and without hesitation began jogging along the trail that led out of camp. I quickly settled into a rhythm and concentrated on my breath and on the solid feel of my feet pounding the soft earth of the trail. Miles lay ahead. I pushed on, getting scratched by wiry tree limbs and patches of devil's club, my feet thumping the ground and jarring my breath. I began to feel confident I could make it in good time.

Less than a hundred yards out, I heard noises behind me. Twigs popping, a branch cracking. Silence except my breathing, and then another branch would pop. This is when things changed. I kept running, glancing back every few feet, seeing nothing and pushing on, but it wouldn't let up. When there weren't noises, I *felt* something behind me. There was breathing just like my own. I sensed a presence behind trees ahead of me, and I ran harder, passing the trees quickly and glancing back to see nothing. I felt things watching me, about to grab me, certainly, something. And then it was looming, rising above the woods behind me like a massive lifeless bird. Like the moon on a clear night, it followed me.

THE SECRET OF RAIN

G. Davies Jandrey with Rosemary Solarez

Voy a cantar un corrido escuchen muy bien mis compas
Para la reina del sur traficante muy famosa
Nacida allá en Sinaloa, la Tía Teresa Mendoza...
Teresa la Mexicana, del otro lado del mar
Una mujer muy valiente, que no la van a olvidar
                    —Teodoro Bello Jamies, "La Reina del Sur"

China was lying on her bed, golden belly protruding slightly between hip hugging Spandex and cropped top. As she listened to Radio Fiesta, she was contemplating the strange twists and turns fate, or God, or whatever, imposes. It was the capricious nature of these impositions that bothered her, though China wouldn't use the word capricious, had never even heard the word. She would simply say that la vida es una chingada.

Conceived during one of Tucson's kick-ass summer storms that knock out electricity and leave la gente to huddle in the warm dark while water the color and consistency of chocolate milk laps at the foundation, she was named Lluvia, though nobody called her that but her sister, Vela, and her father. Since sixth grade, everybody that mattered called her La China, for her slant eyes and golden skin.

Bored and vaguely pissed, she readjusted the pillow. Los Tigres del Norte were singing La Reina del Sur, a corrido about una mujer con muchos huevos who ran drugs all over the world. Usually the song energized her, but this afternoon, she wasn't even motivated enough to call one of her home-girls so they could go to the mall, at least. Since her novio, if that's what Billy was, left town, China had lost her ambition. She missed Billy, missed his sweet, jokable ways. She also missed her sister, Vela, who ran away from home last month to escape their father's rules. For now, Vela was cleaning rooms at a Ramada Inn in La Mesa, but pretty soon, she'd find a real job, one worthy of her, perhaps something like a dentist's receptionist. But China wasn't allowed to even mention Vela in her father's presence, much less discuss job prospects, pues, though sometimes when he wasn't home, she'd call Vela's cell and they'd talk for hours. If her papá noticed the charge on the phone bill, he never said nada.

And she missed her mother, or at least the idea of her mother. China had been only four when her mother's Ford Escort was run over by a monster truck with outsized wheels. According to Vela, they had to use the Jaws of Life to extract her from the wreckage, but in her mother's case they'd been the Jaws of Death.

She'd been one of those white Mexicans, her mother, with hair the color of autumn leaves, green eyes and a dusting of freckles across her nose and shoulders. Delicate and beautiful, she'd been the exact opposite of her father who was a tall Cubano from Miami with lustrous dark skin and a deep, resonant voice.

When he first moved to Tucson to begin training for airport security, he thought it would be temporary, but then he met her mother at a party and it had been love at first sight and for reals, or so Vela tells it.

Suddenly, China had such a longing for her mother. She felt as if her chest had been opened, and instead of a heart, there was a stone that bled. Only a mother would have the words to explain such a feeling.

The only photo of her mother was in a silver frame on the shrine in the corner of her father's bedroom. China needed to look into her mother's eyes, needed to behold the lips that still might open to whisper the words that could alter her life. She rolled off the bed. On the way to her father's room, she passed the kitchen where she grabbed an apple from a basket on the counter.

China absently gnawed on the apple, as she stood before the shrine. Illuminated only by small votive candles—there were always seven—and the weak, sulfur light that passed through the drawn shades, the photo stood before a statue of La Virgin de Guadalupe. China picked it up, stroking the wings of the doves that lit on each corner of the frame as she gazed at her mother's face. The lips held a faint smile, and the eyes seemed to caress China's face. Her mother had loved her very much. Many times, Vela had told her so.

She wiped a slick of apple drool from her chin and then kissed her mother's picture. Carefully replaced it exactly as she had found it. Her father didn't like her to touch the shrine and it's mysterious articles of devotion. In addition to the seven candles, there were seven blue plastic carnations in a white vase, seven polished stones, smooth and dark as her father's skin, a glass with a bouquet of watercress, pale roots feathering the green stems. All was arrayed on a tablecloth of white crochet, beautiful and, at the moment, serene.

It was getting late. Soon her father would be home and she needed to start dinner. China wandered back into the kitchen, still dissatisfied with life in general and her own in particular. Some days she wanted to run away like Vela, but that would leave her father alone. He was one crazy nigger, especially when it came to boys, but she couldn't hurt him like that. No, for better or for worse, she loved her father. Often he told her how much she reminded him of her mother, so China knew he loved her too. That's why, no matter how crazy he might get, pues, with his voodoo shit and duendes—he kept chickens out back and there was a box turtle named Orfeo in a pen that he'd bring in the house every so often to chase out los espíritus malos—she'd never tell another soul, not even Billy, that it was her father who killed Alfonso Longoria, the one everybody called El Joker.

It all came down not long after Billy left town. China and her homies, Li'l Chica, Roja Loca and La Gordita had been kicking it at Los Betos when El Joker drove up in the old Buick he thought was so fine he even polished the rust. Chuy was riding shotgun and Kiko, looking sorry, was in the bitch seat. El Joker jerked his chin at her and smiled his big yellow smile.

In China's mind, El Joker was at the heart of her pain. Because of him, Billy had left town, left her. Did Joker actually think he could put the moves on her? Ni modo, she thought, turning her back.

"I don't want nothing to do with that pinche mule-face cabrón," she said to her home girls.

Joker laid rubber pulling into a parking spot. Before getting out of the car, he untied the sharply pressed blue bracero scarf that he wore around his head, Comanche style. This he hung from the rear view mirror, then smoothed back his black, well-oiled hair with his palms. Flanked by his homies, Joker ambled over, legs splayed as if to make room for a pair of enormous huevos between them.

"Here he comes," Gorditia whispered.

China rolled her eyes and twisted her plump lips, exposing the deep dimple at the side of her mouth. When she felt the hot weight of his hand on her shoulder, she shrugged it off, saying to no one in particular, "Do you smell something feo? Something kinda like a steaming pile of dog shit?"

Her home girls, especially La Gordita, really thought that was funny. They laughed like crazy, slapping each other on the backs. China turned then, took El Joker in from the top of his seal-slick head to the bottom of the oversized jeans that covered his shoes and said, "Oh. It's only Joker." Again a roar of approval from the home girls. China had a hard time keeping her mouth straight.

"Who you dissing, bitch?" he said, grabbing China by the arm.

China held him with her slant eyes. "Nadie," she said, digging her lavender acrylic nails into his wrist. "Cus, you ain't nobody, pendejo."

That's when he hit her, a quick jab to the mouth.

She fought the urge to bring her hand to her lip. "Is that all you got, Joker?" She said to his back, as he swaggered to his car, a study in indifference.

That was only the second time in her life anybody had dared hit her in the face. The first was when she got jumped into Westside, but that was with her permission, more or less, so it was okay. This time it was definitely not okay. "Damn," she whispered, as tears threatened to shame her in front of her friends. "I'm going to kill his sorry ass."

When she got home she'd put ice on her mouth but it hadn't done much to dull the pain or lessen the humiliation. Now she winced as she applied another coat of black cherry to her lips. But even black cherry couldn't hide the swelling and the angry split. Man, she thought examining her lip in the mirror. How am I going to explain this? Part of her wanted her father to know nothing about her life outside the house they shared. Part of her wanted to tell him everything so he could take care of it for her, just as he had always taken care of her, matter of factly, without an excess of emotion.

He didn't notice it right away. Just came in the house, dropped onto the couch with no more than a glance in her direction. "Bring your papá a glass of iced tea," he said, clicking on the evening news.

When China set the glass on the coffee table, he asked about school. "You stay out of trouble?" When she didn't respond immediately, his eyes snapped from the television screen to her face, where he expected to see the answer.

Before she could turn away, he grabbed her tightly by the wrist. "Sit down, mija," he said quietly, putting the television on mute. "I thought I told you not to get into any more fights. Thought I said, one more fight and I would take your cell away, ground your little yellow ass for the rest of the year. Did you think I was joking, mija?"

"I wasn't in a fight."

"¿Entonces, que le pasó a tu boca?" He said, reaching out to touch her bottom lip.

"Nada," she lied, jerking her head away. "I just… bumped it on…a door."

"On a door? Either you're telling your papá a lie, Lluvia, or you've become very clumsy. Since I've never known you to be clumsy, you better bring me that cell phone you love so much that it seems like it's growing out your ear."

"It wasn't like that," China said. The tears she'd been trying not to cry, suddenly slipped from her eyes in ones and twos at first, like the start of a summer rain. Soon there was a flood of tears, and she could not speak. Her father sat quietly at her side, waiting out the storm.

Several minutes passed before the clenching in her throat eased enough for her to tell him how it had happened. China opened her heart to her father then, as she hadn't since leaving childhood behind. She told him how her friend, Cuco, had been killed, and how Joker had beaten Billy up, the one with the twisted spine, pobrecito, and how everything that was making her life chingada was Joker's fault.

"No usas palabras tan groseras, mija," was her father's only response to this outpour, so China told him how Joker had laid his hand on her shoulder as if he owned her. Of course, she edited her response to this advance, saying only that she had told him not to touch her.

"Y por eso, Papá, he hit me in the mouth," she said, watching her father's skin grow a shade darker as she waited for him to speak.

For a long time he merely sipped his tea while gazing at the muted television. At last he said, "You bring me...let me think." He sat there another long minute, lips pursed, patting his fingertips together. "Bring me a piece of his clothing—a cap, a handkerchief. Any little thing will do."

"What are you going to do?" She asked, picturing the blue bandana hanging from Joker's review mirror.

Her father shrugged. "You are the blood that runs through my veins, mija, entonces… I'm going to make him regret."

The four girls met in the bathroom at the appointed time. La Gordita wanted to comb her hair first, but China grabbed her hand and pulled her into the hallway. Since it was only midway into third period, the halls were empty. Quietly, they descended via the northwest staircase of the second floor. It was farther from the exit to the parking lot, but they were less likely to run into the hall monitors who usually hung out in the southeast stairwell, gossiping and complaining instead of canvassing the second and third floors. The detour necessitated that they pass the big window in front of the counselors' office. They did this one at a time, each girl striding along purposefully, a slip of white paper held aloft to simulate a hall pass. Once outside, they scanned the parking lot for the faded Buick. It was not there.

"Now what?" Li'l Chica wanted to know.

China shrugged, tonguing the split in her bottom lip. "Damn."

"Why don't you just touch his arm and say you're sorry," Roja Loca suggested. "You don't have to mean it, pues. Then he'd let you have anything you want, the fucking engine from his fucking car even."

"Say I'm sorry? Nunca, girl. Let me think."

La Gordita took her compact from her purse. Smiling into the reflection, she pulled a coil of stiffly moussed hair from behind her ear and let it dangle along side her round face. After a moment, she slipped it behind her ear again and closed her compact. "Hurry up and make up your mind, well. I've got to get back to class before El Pelón sees me gone."

"So go, bitch. No one's holding you back."

"Don't get all hard, China," La Gordita said, refusing to take offense. "It's just that if I get another cut...My Dad will kill me if I get suspended one more time. Besides, I still don't get why you want to steal Joker's stupid bandana. What kind of revenge is that? If it was me, I'd just key his car and be done with it."

"I'm going to his house," China said with finality.

"Shit," Li'l Chica whispered. "Now?"

"¿Cómo no? He's probably home right now, just sitting around getting high with his compas."

"You're crazier than I am," Roja Loca said, arching one slim red brow. "I'm going back to class."

"Me too," Li'l Chica said.

Only La Gordita hesitated. "If I get another cut..."

"Go on, pues," China said, clearly disgusted. "I'll do it by my own damn self." She regretted the words as soon as they were out of her mouth. The idea of going to Joker's house alone made her stomach roil. Then she thought of La Reina del Sur. La Reina didn't need nobody but La Reina, and La China didn't need nobody but La China. Gordita, Chica or Roja, pues, they had their own fucked-up lives to live, qué no?

Though it was only April, the sun was hot, and by the time China arrived on Joker's block, perspiration was making her scalp itch. She stood in the shade of a mesquite to cool off while she studied his house. Though she'd driven by it once or twice, she'd never really noticed what a dump it was. The torn screen door and weeds poking through the chain link fence gave it a lonely, hopeless feeling. Why didn't somebody fix the place up—a little paint, a new screen door—she wondered. At least Joker, that lazy cabrón, could pull a few weeds.

The old Buick was parked in the shade of the house, the blue bandana hanging from the rearview as usual. China was about to make her move when the front door opened and a woman with a face to match the house came out the front door clutching a large black purse. China stepped deeper into the shade.

"Apúrate, mijo," the woman called, turning back towards the dark opening. "We're going to be late for your sister's doctor's appointment." After a moment, Joker stood in the doorway carrying what at first appeared to be a heap of clothes. When he adjusted the load, China realized that the heap had arms and legs and a head larger than one would expect from so small a bundle. The child was smiling broadly, and she screeched unintelligibly, but with obvious delight, as Joker bounced her playfully in his arms. Joker was smiling too, a smile with light in it. China had never seen such a smile on his face before. The woman got into the back seat of the car, and Joker laid the child across her lap as if she were some delicate and valued cargo, a dozen long stemmed roses perhaps.

From her hiding place beneath the mesquite, China watched until the car was out of sight.

On the way home, she couldn't escape the image of a bundle with arms, legs and a head, and how tenderly Joker had carried it to the car. And the mom, pues. She looked like her sorry life had beaten a path across her face.

How does that happen to people, she wondered, and vowed it would never happen to her. From now on, she'd only smoke dope on special occasions. And she would never get pregnant until she was old, twenty-five or even thirty, when she could afford a good house. Maybe she'd even start doing her homework. After all, she wouldn't be young forever. She had to start preparing for real life, pues, whatever her real life might turn out to be.

Lo que pasa es lo que Dios desea, a voice whispered in her ear. Part of China believed that God had a hand in all things. The other part, La Reina del Sur part, figured you get what you go after. All a person needed to do was figure out what she truly wanted then go for it.

They never caught her, La Reina del Sur. One day she just disappeared. China liked to think of her in some tropical place, mangos and plátanos free for the taking hanging from the trees, where she would live the life of una reina de verdad, dispensing food, clothing and medicine to the poor. She would have started an orphanage and built everybody a new house, because for La Reina, drug running had never been about money. No, it was about survival against all odds, it was about fighting injustice, it was for the love of life and adventure.

Once home, China stood before her own house, really seeing it as others might. In the yard, the oleander bushes were covered with red and pink flowers; her mother's irises bloomed along the walkway. Her father had repainted the house just last fall, pale pink on the walls and bright blue around the windows and on the door. Here, it seemed, a hopeful family lived.

By the time China walked through the front door, all thoughts of revenge were gone. But what would she say to her father? Although Joker had no right to hit her, she had misled her father, lied actually, about her part in it. China went into her bedroom and stood before a closet so crammed with clothing that she had trouble choosing. Finally, she selected a blouse at random and tore off a button.

Is this all you could get, a button?" he asked, an edge of impatience in his voice.

"But you said any little thing would work okay."

"Did I? Then this will have to do, pues." Getting up from the couch, he added, "Don't you have some homework to do?"

"Not tonight," she lied, and followed him into his bedroom where he dropped the button on the crochet-covered table before the statue of Virgen de Guadalupe.

"Go to your room, mija, and do your homework," her father directed quietly.

"You can't ask La Virgincita for revenge, Papá. She won't do it."

He simply shrugged. "Before she was known as La Virgincita, mija, she was Yemayá, so it depends on who's doing the asking and how. Ándale, pues. I'll call you when it's time for dinner."

Reluctantly, China left him contemplating the photo of her mother. Not ten minutes after she closed her bedroom door, a single strangled squawk lifted the fine hairs on the back of her neck and along her arms.

It grew dark and she grew hungry but China knew better than to leave her room before her father called. When he did, she smelled the stewing chicken and her appetite left her.

"Heat up the beans and rice, Lluvia, and set the table. This stew is almost ready."

"Why did you kill her? There's chicken in the freezer."

"She was old. Hasn't laid an egg in months, pues."

When China still hesistated, he added, "Las orejas no pasan la cabeza." It was a phrase she heard often and hated. The ears never get ahead of the head. What the hell did that mean anyways. Rolling her eyes, she did as she was told.

While her father took his usual nap during the ten o'clock news, China crept back into the bedroom to see for herself what her father had been up to. Everything seemed to be in its place, the picture of her mother, the Virgincita, the blue plastic flowers. But as she turned to go, she saw in the flickering candlelight that the once beautiful, smooth stones were now covered with the tarry blood of the old hen.

For awhile, China waited for some disaster to befall Joker or herself, since it had been her button. But weeks passed and nothing out of the ordinary occurred. Once in awhile, China would think of Joker's mother and her own promise to change her ways, but mostly she ignored such thoughts. Figuring there was still plenty of time to grow up, homework assignments were left untouched, and she looked forward to each weekend when she and her friends would score a couple of leños and get high.

Then one morning before class, China was in the girl's restroom applying another layer of midnight blue mascara, when La Gordita came running in, eyes as round as her face. "Did you hear what happened to Joker?" She said, nearly panting.

"No! ¿Qué pasó?" China asked, the mascara wand already trembling in her hand.

"Está muerto."

"¡Muerto! ¿Cómo?"

"They say his car hit a telephone pole. They say he was doing ninety, al menos. They say he was tripping or drunk or something."

China let these words sink in for a moment. "Drunk?"

"That's what they say."

All day she had tried to convince herself that Joker's death was not a direct result her father's voodoo shit. After all, Joker had been drunk. Whose fault was that? Still, her father always did what he said he would do. If he said he'd make Joker regret hitting her, then he would do everything in his power to make that happen. Like a hen that refused to leave her clutch of eggs, China sat on her bed, brooding over her clutch of guilt. ¿Por qué yo? She asked the air. ¿Por qué no? The air answered.

When the front door opened, she hurried into the living room to tell her father the news, hoping he would assure her that his little brujería would have caused nothing more than a flat tire, say, or at most a broken arm.

"Papá…" she started to say, but fell silent when she saw him standing in the doorway sniffing the air suspiciously. "¿Papá, qué pasá?"

"You don't smell it?"

China sniffed. There was something. It wasn't a smell exactly, but rather a density to the air, a feeling of closeness as if she were standing inside her closet, rather than her living room. She shrugged.

"Bring Orfeo," he said. China felt her the flesh beneath her skin ripple.

China and her father followed the turtle from room to room as it crept along the baseboards. Though their house was small, it was dark before Orfeo finally came to rest with his head in the last corner of China's bedroom. Her father took a deep breath. "That's better," he said, leaning over to retrieve the turtle.

China sniffed, noting a subtle, but definite difference in the quality of the air, as if a breeze were blowing through the open windows, except that there was no breeze and the windows were closed. "Is he gone?" she asked.

"He's gone," her father said, stroking the leathery folds along the turtle's neck.

"El Joker?"

He shrugged. "Some lost spirit."

"There was a car accident. He's dead."

Again he shrugged. "People have accidents all the time, pues." He put the turtle down and stood, slowing stretching his spine until he reached his full height. "Let me tell you something, mija. When I was fifteen, I came over to this country with my uncle, un santero muy famoso en Cuba. We were piled into a rickety old boat with a bunch of jotos, criminales, locos. The boat might have sank, but it didn't; I might have been shipped back to Cuba, but I wasn't; I might not have met your mother, but I did; she might have lived, but she died. There are many things that happen in this life, and what's the explanation? The one thing I know for certain is that the only thing that stays the same is that nothing stays the same. Even you. You used to be so much like your mother, but as you grow you become more and more like yourself."

China wondered if this meant as she grew up, he would love her less and less. But then he opened his arms and drew her to his chest. "Life is like a great big bowl of menudo, mija. You dip in your spoon. Sometimes you get tripa, sometimes not. But always, if you keep spooning you'll eventually get some tripa."

"But I hate tripa."

He released her then and smiled. "I know, mijita. Así es la vida."

As she got ready for bed that night, it occurred to China that in her short life, she'd eaten a lot of tripa. She'd endured loss and had been a first-hand witness to tragedy and injustice, for reals. Each loss, each tragedy and every injustice, had created a wound to her heart. But wounds, even those that are self-inflicted, heal, qué no? And though China hardly noticed it, as she brushed her hair in front of the mirror, from each healing, she gathered strength like the summer monsoon gathered moisture. Some day, she was certain, she would disperse her strength to others, like rain over the desert.

But as she gazed at her reflection, she knew only that Joker was dead. This fact brought no satisfaction. If she could take back the ugly things she said to him, travel backwards in time to change the future, she would. For now, she could imagine a time in the past when Joker was less of a pinche pendejo and more of a little boy with a mother who loved him. And she could project to a time in the future when Joker, had he lived, would be a man with a mother and the sister to take care of. In time he might have had a wife and kids of his own. ¿Cómo no? Nobody stays a pinche pendejo forever. But now because of her actions, he'd never change into the man he could have been. It was a secret burden she'd always bear, one even her father couldn't help her carry.

Still, and beyond all reason, China expected that the future would be an improvement on the past. ¿Quién sabe? Maybe Billy would return, his spine miraculously straight, or if not his spine, then his outlook would straighten, as hers had when she realized that every life, no matter how ugly or cruel, had some value to someone, somewheres. ¿Qué no?

THE LADY WITH THE DEAD DOG

Katy Whittingham

And it may be that in this continuity, this utter indifference to the life and death of each of us lies hidden the pledge of our eternal salvation, of the continuous movement of life on earth, of the continuous movement toward perfection.

— Anton Chekhov, 1899

There was nothing dramatic about the way the woman scooped up the small tangled mound of brown and black fur from the pavement of his driveway. Adam had prepared for an emotionally intense scene. He sent his seven year-old son, Eric, directly into the house without making him shake out his cleats, despite whiny protests and hard to answer questions. He quietly assured him that, "yes, the little dog is really dead" and "yes, kind of like the way Grandma Alice is dead but different too."

Adam then relayed the basic facts of what had happened to the dog's owner, his new neighbor, because he felt he owed her an explanation, but he was sure she saw most of it for herself from her front lawn only a few feet away. She had pulled herself up from a mound of dirt where she had appeared to have been planting dahlias and was relatively quick to the scene.

Even if she had not seen it all for herself, just looking at the aftermath made it pretty obvious; the woman's terrier had somehow found itself in Adam's driveway and, without seeing the dog, he had run over it with his Volkswagen. Adam had not been going very fast, and it was a little car after all, but it was also a very little dog. If it had been a retriever or even a hound, maybe it would have had a chance. "A good size beagle might have just needed some patching up," Adam thought without feeling.

Adam had not had the chance to meet this young lady, previous to killing her dog, since she had only moved in a few days before, so he first addressed her as "Miss" because she looked to be no older than a sorority girl at the local state college. When he caught a glimpse of the large, emerald cut diamond on her ring finger as it divided rays of afternoon sunlight, he realized he might have made the wrong assumption. The diamond was surrounded by two thin gold bands. Her pale, creaseless hands looked even younger than her face. "Poor girl; married too young," he thought, but when he looked more closely at her face as she squinted down at the remains of her dog, he saw what he might have mistaken for youth was really a simple kind of beauty that he had always admired but had become unaccustomed to.

Adam prided himself most on his ability to connect with people, even in tough situations, so he would have normally reached out and patted the woman's back. He would have found something very appropriate and consoling to say, something sounding sincere, although in actuality entirely manufactured. There was an aura about this woman, however, that prevented the perfect execution of his normal protocol. She was so assured in her movements. Adam had noticed that even in her travels from her yard to his driveway, she had moved at a quick enough pace, appropriate for the situation, yet also seemed to glide over as if in one of the neighborhood kid's giant bubbles. Very Glinda the Good Witch like, he thought.

Continuing with his usual movie character associations, the woman with the dead dog reminded Adam of Winona Ryder; not the real actress and not *Girl Interrupted* Winona, but more like the character she played in *Edward Scissorhands*, whatever her name was. She was petite like that and her dark hair was styled in the same kind of way. He felt a fondness toward the woman despite his newfound nervousness, and although he could not pinpoint the real reason then, it may not have been so much that she reminded him of a film character, but something he saw in her when he allowed himself to quickly glance into her dark, round eyes. Someone more perceptive might have characterized it as innocence, innocence usually reserved only for children like Eric. The comparison between the woman and his son might have meant something more profound to this more perceptive person, but Adam just felt warm and a little dizzy.

"I'm sorry. I just didn't see it," Adam finally managed to continue.

"Tuttle," the woman said. "His name was Tuttle." If her tone had been sharper, Adam might have thought she meant to achieve something by telling him this personal information. After working in client relations at an advertising agency for almost twenty years, he would have been able to pick up on her attempt to make him feel guilty. He would have been able to pick up any range of anger; the most passive sort was actually his specialty. Strangely, he could not detect a hint of bitterness or even sadness in the woman's voice. Thus, Adam had extreme difficulty navigating though this interaction with another person where no immediate motives could be detected.

The woman pulled out a pack of American Spirits from a pocket in her gardening apron. She put one cigarette in her mouth like she was going to smoke it, but instead she held it tight between her lips and crossed her arms over her chest. She continued on like this, all the while looking at her dog. Adam didn't have a light, so he was not able to offer her one, and she didn't offer him a cigarette.

After what felt to him like another extended silence, although merely moments, Adam forced himself to regain a hold on situation. He offered to take care of the dog's remains, knowing this would be a delicate and nearly impossible task to perform in front of its owner if she decided to stay. There was no nice way to peal a dead dog off your driveway, and what would she want him to do with it when he did? He had a weak stomach when it came to blood. He had once thought that he would have been an excellent doctor with his people skills and attention to detail, better in those regards than all of Eric's doctors combined. But Adam was just kidding himself when taking into consideration the actual physical work a doctor must do. He could not watch his wife Pam give Eric an insulin shot. Even when she tried to force him to learn "in case of emergency," he had refused. Now, even Eric knew how to administer the shot himself, if he needed to.

Adam thought about Eric for the first time, consciously at least, since he sent him into the house. He pictured him crying over this woman's dog: Turtle, Tobey, whatever the dog's name is... or was. So odd, Adam thought. He found it difficult to accept that Eric was the type of boy who was brave enough to give himself a shot if he had to, but emotionally ill equipped to deal with the death of a dog he never knew. This was just another confirmation he was his mother's child.

Of course Pam would not have approved of Eric being in the house for so long by himself. "What were you thinking?" she would ask him as she often did, never really wanting an answer from him. This would only be the case if she found out Eric had been left, and in the midst of a fit over the dead dog, Eric might just tell her.

Adam was roused from his thoughts by the woman thanking him for his kind offer. To Adam's relief, she told him she would take care of the remains herself. The woman excused herself and crossed into her yard and into a large aluminum shed. Again her movements were a mixture of purpose, grace, and magic. The shed she retreated into had just been put up the day before by a man who Adam now knew must be the woman's husband.

"The husband," Adam thought in sudden realization. How was the man who put up the shed going to react to the death of his wife's dog? Maybe he would come over and confront him, fight him, sue him. He didn't know this man, and just because the woman appeared to hold no grudge, the husband could be another story.

Adam had never even seen the woman's husband, but Pam had. She saw him from their kitchen window putting together that very shed. The man had sprawled pre-cut pieces and parts of what looked like a complete do-it-yourself kit and was walking around with an open instruction booklet, examining each piece and arranging them into a series of piles. "He's very muscular," Pam told Adam, "maybe even into weight lifting; he's that big." Adam was not jealous of these comments because he knew that didn't match his wife's type, or at least what he perceived his wife's type to be. "You should have seen how quickly he put that thing up," she commented.

Adam promptly told his wife that in his experience "things of quality are not meant to be put up quickly." He didn't like that his neighbor had put up such a trashy looking shed. "It doesn't match the decorum of the neighborhood," he told her. In all honestly, he was amazed that Pam, his own wife and a woman who came from money, was either unable or unwilling to make the distinction between a shed that could be sitting for sale in front of the enormous Save-and-Shop out on Route 30 and the type of solid, well crafted structures that were expected in their part of town. He went on to provide a list of reasons why the shed was a poor choice, but Pam was no longer really listening to him. She had the radio on trying to catch the weather and was cutting yellow peppers for the quesadillas she was making for supper.

"I don't see what the big deal is," Pam said when there was a momentary lapse in Adam's listing. "Don't people have the right to put up anything they want in their own yard? It's not like we live in a gated community."

Adam was very excited with himself that he had saved the best part for last. Pam was always acting smarter than him, more laid back, more reasonable, but he had correctly anticipated her response to his criticism of the shed, and she had fallen into his trap. "That's just it," he said trying for a matter of fact tone, yet sounding smug instead. "The shed is three quarters of a foot on Dickerson's property. I consulted the original contractor's map that I ordered last year. I consulted it twice!"

This information did not have the effect he desired, and without missing a beat, Pam asked him if he had actually gone over, "trespassing no less," to measure the amount their new neighbors' shed was over their other neighbor's property line. "If you did, I feel very embarrassed for you," she said. "Besides," she added, "let Dick worry if the shed is on his property."

Adam was furious and stormed into his home office. Once again Pam was asking a question that required no answer. It was irritating especially when he was trying to prove a point. It didn't matter that she was the one who was actually right. Of course, it didn't directly affect him, but he couldn't go to Dick Dickerson for help. He wouldn't care that the shed was on his property. He had bigger problems. He had the lifelong affliction of being named Dick Dickerson for starters, and Dr. Richard Dickerson's wife had left him for her Pilates' instructor only the summer before.

Now she lived in Costa Rica and didn't even have a proper address to send divorce papers to. Dick was also being sued by a woman he performed surgery on who said he left her with uneven and sensation-less breasts. This wasn't the first time either. Even if Adam was able to make Dick understand that he was being taken advantage of by the crafty, yet tacky, new neighbors, he wouldn't actually do anything about it.

As far as Adam knew, the only thing he did, when he wasn't in court or in bed weeping, was drink sour apple martinis and watch his absent wife's complete collection of *Friends* episodes on DVD. Dick's wife had been told sometime in the late 90s that she looked like the character of Rachel and had become mildly obsessed with the idea. To be fair, she did bare a slight resemblance, if perfect television Rachel gained twenty pounds, spent twenty years in the sun, and had twenty nips and tucks under her belt.

Instead of wasting his time with Dick, Adam planned to talk directly to the new neighbors about the unfortunate situation with the shed, out of courtesy for all parties involved. He would bring over a Freihofer's coffeecake and divert casual, neighborly banter into serious talk about the shed. If they were decent people they would take it down immediately and honor Dick's property rights. In his current state, they wouldn't likely have a chance to talk with Dick at length and wouldn't need to know that he didn't care or even know his rights were being violated. Maybe the husband wouldn't bother putting the shed up again at all, or maybe, under Adam's suggestion, he would move it to the backyard facing a wooded area, so at least passing cars would not see it.

Adam had delayed this planned interaction with the new neighbors because he had a strong suspicion that they were not decent people after all or why would they have put up the shed in the first place? Just because something made sense to him, didn't mean that these classless newcomers would follow his line of thinking.

Pam had, more often in recent years, chastised Adam for his lack of tact. However, while waiting in his own driveway, standing over the neighbor's dead dog and not doing anything to help the woman knocking around in the same shed he had been brooding about, even Adam was aware enough to know that it was, not only a very poor to time to bring up the three quarters of a foot, but there would likely never be a good time in the foreseeable future. He began to feel so uncomfortable that he thought he might get sick and stepped back in a motion to flee toward his house, but within seconds the woman was back, and he was stuck in his tracks.

She still had the cigarette in her mouth. A metal toolbox was dangling from her Snow White hands. Resting on top of the box was a magazine, a paint scraper, and a pair of gardening gloves freshly coated with soil. She looked up briefly as Adam changed his stance to face back to the scene with his hands on his hips, and then she went right to work. He was amazed, almost horrified, at the precision in which the woman scrapped the dog's body off the driveway, propped it onto a copy of *Glamour,* and slid it into the empty toolbox. When she latched the lid, she put the box on the ground, took off her gardening gloves, and offered Adam her hand. "Sarah," she said.

Adam looked at the porcelain hand, then at the closed box on the ground, then at that exquisite hand again, then at the cigarette, and then at the perfectly folded gardening gloves resting on top of the box. Had he even seen her put them there? He finally reached out his hand in front of him, but she had to move in closer to shake it. Her hand was warm from being inside of the glove. "Adam Hart," he said with great effort under his breath and barely audible.

"Ah, Adam," she said. Then, "Adam, you have a son?" It was as if she was asking and telling him at the same time. Coming back to his senses, Adam wondered if it was all women who insisted on asking questions they seemed to already know the answer to. He nodded and reluctantly let go of her hand.

Three days after the incident, Adam found himself peering into the new neighbors' sitting room window from his yard, trying to appear inconspicuous, while adjusting his sprinkler system. They had not yet put up blinds or curtains, which he found a little odd, but he was happy to find there was little to obstruct his view. The woman was not currently in the sitting room, but it looked like she had been. He could see a coffee mug, although he imagined she drank only tea, on the table and a book, spine up and spread. The television was on and a local public access correspondent appeared on the screen, but he assumed that she probably had the volume off while she was reading. Adam's own mother, when she was alive, used to keep the television on, but turned down, just to give herself "a little company" after he and his older brother left to start lives of their own. The woman, this Sarah, seemed to be alone a great deal of the time too.

Adam still had not even seen her husband. He saw his truck there late in the evenings, but it would be gone again by early morning. He was no longer afraid of the husband's reaction to the death of the dog, as he had received no calls and no visits. This freedom allowed him to think more about Sarah out of the context of her dead dog, and he had been thinking about her pretty continually.

Although he had strained to see the print and images on the book's cover, he couldn't make out anything distinguishing without his distance glasses. If he just knew the title, he could pick up a copy at the bookstore he passed on his way to work, read it, and then manipulate a conversation in which he recommended the book to her. She would be shocked and tell him she was reading the same book. Wouldn't that be something?

Pam had been after Adam to adjust their sprinkler's spray for weeks, but was particularly adamant when she "re-reminded" him, her word, about it that morning. "It doesn't cover the entire lawn and shoots across the sidewalk," she complained. "People have to walk into the road to avoid it." He had first thought to be humorous by responding that it was less expensive than a security system, but he didn't share this response aloud because lately his kind humor was not humor that Pam seemed to appreciate.

"Just wait until Mr. Ferriera hobbles by with his cane and slips on the wet pavement," she continued. "Then we will have a lawsuit, like Dick's, on our hands to add to all of our problems." When she said "our problems," Adam understood what she really meant was an all encompassing collection of issues that were caused by him and dealt with by her. "People will say," she went on, "'He sure doesn't brake for small animals, so I guess further crippling the old and feeble is not much of a stretch.'" She laughed after she said this, whole heartedly and without discretion, before going back to something other than talking to him. He was surprised that she could be so flippant about the dog considering how upset she was over its death, but it seemed it was now okay, for her at least, to make light of it. It was not surprising to him, however, how apparent it had become that Pam didn't care whether Adam still appreciated *her* kind of humor.

The woman continued to be on Adam's mind during the days that followed, but he hadn't again had the opportunity to speak with her. He had so many questions and only his own imagined answers. Over time, he had decided that the woman with the dead dog looked more like Mia Farrow than Winona Ryder, but, of course, a younger version of Farrow and with darker hair. Sarah wasn't beautiful by catalog standards. Those kind of women Adam saw everyday in the ad biz, but her features struck him, caught him off guard, moved him in a way he was not entirely comfortable with.

He had asked himself whether he wanted to have sex with this woman, and he honestly didn't know. It bothered him that he began now to think consciously of Eric when he thought of her and what his real intentions were. Again, instead of trying to understand this connection, he started to resent the distraction.

One particularly troublesome memory continued to play back for him. It was the last time Adam took Eric to the park before school started back. Eric had wanted to be pushed on the swings. Adam told him he was too old to be pushed; he was going to be in second grade, and that he should learn, as boys half his age already had, to pump his legs, to get himself going. Adam had tried to teach him this many times before, but Eric would just sit limp on the swing, slowly swaying his legs in circular motion, not even really trying. As he always did, Adam told Eric he would provide a few pushes to get him started. As he pushed he yelled, "Now, pump, pump!"

Not only did Eric not pump his legs as directed, but once again, as soon as he reached some real height, he dragged his feet in the dirt to slow himself down. On this particular day, Adam was unwilling to put up with the familiar routine. He jerked the chains of the swing to bring Eric to a complete stop. He told him they were leaving that instant, and that there would be no monkey bars and no Burger Hut afterward. Even without the stares from some young, hippy parents by the merry-go-round, Adam knew he was overreacting, but Eric, head down, was already following him to the car, so it was too late to modify his behavior.

As his lousy luck would have it, when Adam drove them home, they got stuck at the traffic light right in front of Burger Hut. It was a long light, and Adam wasn't very angry anymore. It appeared that someone had had a birthday party, and the kids, younger than Eric, were filing out with goodie bags and balloons. An overweight girl with freckled skin let go of a purple balloon and watched it sail up over the Price Mart building. It was sunny, and Adam couldn't tell if the girl was crying or delighted. If Eric had asked, Adam would have stopped as they had planned, but he didn't, and when the light changed, he drove them home.

Eric didn't even tell Pam what happened when they got back as Adam had expected he would. She asked how the park was, and they both said fine. She probably was suspicious, but she didn't push the issue. Adam had to give her credit in that regard; she usually didn't try to interfere in his relationship with Eric despite her growing resentment. She was a good mother and did what was best for their son.

This may have been why Adam had never seriously considered cheating on Pam before. He had his fair share of opportunity, and in his usual list format he could have weighed the pros and cons, mainly the pros and cons for himself, of course. But, it just wasn't something he thought about taking action on.

At times, he didn't really want Pam anymore, but he also didn't really want anyone else either. There were times when he could see why a woman would be desirable, but there were times when Pam seemed okay too. His wife may have been frustrated by him and condescending to him, but others didn't catch on. Men they knew envied him for marrying a woman like Pam with beauty, intelligence, and charm. After eleven years of marriage, he may no longer have appreciated these qualities, but having others appreciate her in this way had been enough.

He hadn't seen anything wrong with this justification. At least, he was still there, and, in his experience, it was completely natural for people to fall out of love. Like when his father left his mother with two young children to go off with his much younger Pamela or Mrs. Dickerson leaving poor, pathetic Dick with nothing but some DVDS to remember her by. Love was an unexplainable thing and not something that was meant to last.

Unlike his own father or Dick's wife, Adam would not allow himself to be bullied by this inevitability. No matter how he felt or what happened, if anything, between him and the neighbor woman, Adam would not leave Pam. There was Eric to consider, and he didn't know what he would do if he couldn't see him on a day to day basis.

Eric had been diagnosed with diabetes when he was only three years old, and Pam had, and continued to, handle the situation much better than Adam. Eric was sensitive, yet, physically, an incredibly resilient child. His mother was also responsible for both of these qualities. Eric was never going to be the sports' star that Adam had dreamed of, and because of their differences, no one would call him "his father's son," but something slowly began to take the place of his old expectations for him, and Adam needed that boy more everyday.

Two weeks after the dog's demise, Pam was preparing to take Eric for a long weekend at her mother's in Albany. "So whatever happened with the lady and the dead dog thing?" she asked as she prepared a snack bag of carrots and celery for Eric to take on their road trip.

"What do you mean?" Adam asked, trying to sound coy. He purposely didn't look up from his paper, so she would not see his eyes.

"Well, you killed a family pet. I just wondered if there were any consequences that followed for you, or if you just went on with your life as usual, unbothered and unaffected," she said. She seemed to be trying for sarcasm, but just sounded sad.

"It's not a family: just a woman and a man, and he is gone half the time, and I didn't mean to do it. It's not like it was a crime, and don't forget the dog was on my, our property," he said.

"Oh, I forgot about your preoccupation with property," she snapped. And when he didn't respond she added as an afterthought, "And, you know, or maybe you don't because you don't think of things like this, but maybe that dog was everything to this woman. Maybe because she has no children and her husband is working all of the time. Maybe the dog was her only… thing."

Adam shrugged, and Pam shook her head disapprovingly. "Did you even get her name? I want to go see her when I get back. I should have gone over before, but frankly I was embarrassed."

"No!" Adam shouted.

"What?" Pam said and turned around to face him. She looked straight into his eyes forcing him to at last lift to meet her glare.

"I mean, no, I didn't get her name," he said trying to recover.

"Of course, you didn't," she said as she snatched the plastic baggie from the counter and went about preparing to leave.

An hour and a half after his wife and son's departure, Adam was busy trying to hide an empty bottle of Merlot under a week's worth of newspapers in the recycling bin on the back porch. The wine was a gift from Pam's sister Leslie after her annual spring trip to France. It was old and expensive, but the only alcohol in the house. Neither Pam nor Adam was a big drinker. Pam had an occasional glass of bubbly on special occasions or when amongst her blueblood family of lushes, but that was about it. The missing wine might have gone unnoticed, but Leslie would be in the city the next week for a business meeting. If she stopped by on her way out, Pam would get the gifted wine out for the grape fiend to slurp up.

As Adam had been drinking, he had also been thinking. Thinking, of course, of the woman. It was Friday. On Fridays, Adam had noted, the husband's truck came home even later than usual. Maybe Friday was a big day in whatever business he was in. Maybe he was having an affair on her. No matter really, he thought as he began to come around to the idea that regardless, maybe it was now a good time for him to go check in on her. This idea became more and more appealing and doable as he drank. He felt really confident and quite well overall. He made a mental note that he should drink more often.

Before very long, Adam found himself on the front porch of the woman's house. He stared at the brass door bell. It was cold outside, but he felt flushed, in a good way. "The bell or nothing," he thought as he finally lifted his heavy hand up to the fixture and watched as his waving index finger pressed the tiny circle in the middle. For such a little action, it produced the loudest and longest lasting ringing sound imaginable. Having been shocked by this intense sound, when the woman swung open the door, Adam didn't expect it.

"Sarah," he said trying to cover up that he was stumbling backwards the way a drunk person does when their body starts to betray their best intentions of appearing sober.

She was wearing a gray silk pantsuit. Her hair, although short, was pulled back from her forehead with a headband. This look made her look older, not old, just older.

"Adam, come in," she said. She was apparently not that surprised by his visit.

He wasn't going to make up excuses when there wasn't a need for any. He felt his drunkenness more now that he was in the presence of another person, and he had to be careful not to talk too much.

"I hope I'm not disturbing you at dinner time. Is your husband at home?" he asked. The woman told him that he was not disturbing her, and also, what he already knew, that her husband was not at home. She told him that she was having a glass of sherry, and asked if he would like some. Despite his newly acquired appreciation for alcohol, he maintained the slightest bit of good judgment and said no thank you.

They sat down on the couch. It was a loveseat really, so they were closer than strangers would be in most situations, but there were no other seats to be had, which she apologized for and told him some of their belongings had been delayed in the move. Her breath smelled very sweet. Adam didn't know if sherry was some kind of brandy or a port, whatever that was. He had only seen it on dessert menus when they were out to eat at fancy places with his in-laws.

There were black and white photographs all over the walls. The pictures were mostly of a man who Adam concluded must be the husband. He was more handsome than Adam had anticipated, but black and white always made people look better than they did in real life. Judging by the photographs the husband looked to be a sportsman of sorts and also some other choice things Adam quickly characterized: a jerk, a snob, a first class asshole. Adam's assessment may not have been fair, but his advertising expertise allowed him to trust his impression of the images and the face value they provided.

The woman observed Adam observing her work. "I'm a photographer," she said taking a cigarette out and putting it in her mouth unlit. "My husband thinks all the photos are overkill. He's only letting me keep them up until he has time to repaint the walls," she murmured with the cigarette still clasped between her lips.

"I like them," Adam managed but could see why a room full of pictures, especially almost all of him, might be creepy. It could have been the wine, but they seemed alive. There were just so many of them, all staring, all expecting.

"Do you need a light?" Adam asked pointing to the cigarette.

She seemed absorbed in the photographs herself and his question came off as an interruption. "Oh, no. Trying to quit," she said without further explanation.

Adam focused in on one photograph of the husband with a captain's hat on steering a boat with his elbow. His other arm was raised in salutatory greeting. What an absolute tool, Adam thought enjoying the mounting criticism he was building against the man until he noticed a detail he missed at first glance.

There was a small creature on the man's lap with its fur blown wildly back by the wind to reveal two eyes the color, size, and shape of lumps of coal. Could it be the little dead dog? A disturbing pattern started to emerge as Adam began to frantically scan all of the photographs on the wall. The little urchan was everywhere: in a tropical scene under a palm tree, in front of a Christmas tree, in a shopping cart, in the husband's truck bed, in a bike basket, on a sleigh in the snow, next to a fish hanging from a line, at a barbecue, with a bone, by a fire, at the beach, with a stick, at the park, on a picnic.

"Your dog," Adam managed, feeling compelled by its presence and possibly a small amount of guilt brought about more from the wine than any real reflection. "You must miss him."

"He was Charlie's dog. I actually hated the rat," she said. "He doesn't want to try for anymore children. He thought bringing Tuttle home would appease my motherly needs; it didn't."

Adam's confusion must have shown on his face because the woman quickly continued. "I had three miscarriages, then the last one was stillborn at eight months."

"Oh, I'm sorry," Adam said.

The woman didn't seem to hear him or just took for granted that is what any normal person would say in response. "You are so lucky to have a son," she said. "You are lucky to have a family and have purpose. My husband is gone all of the time as you might have noticed. We have drifted apart over our losses and are not the same people; maybe not even people that should be together anymore if we ever were. He only married me because I was pregnant, the first time. An accident. Who knew we would end up here? I used to have a passion for all kinds of things, including my work. Now it's hard to even have a reason to get out of bed in the morning. I'm thirty-five, and my life might as well be over. But, oh God, listen to me. I'm so embarrassed to put this all on you! You just asked about the dog. Yes, Charlie misses the dog very much, bordering on way too much, to be honest. I guess I have had too much time by myself lately, too much time to think, and I have forgotten how to properly talk to other people. I'm so sorry."

There was silence and Adam shifted on the cushion closer to the armrest and away from her. He held in his breath like he did when he was young and heard his parents fighting. This woman who was such a mystery only moments before had managed to reveal a life story in a short collection of sentences. A sad story; one Adam hadn't anticipated and didn't know if he wanted to be a part of. He thought he might throw up or explode.

"You shouldn't feel that way," Adam said as he let out a breath.

"Why not?" the woman questioned.

He waited thinking this was one of those women kind of questions that didn't need a response, but the woman continued to have an expectant look on her face.

"Umm, I guess I meant children aren't everything. It seems like you travel a lot by the pictures. Do a lot of activities. You can't do that as much when you have kids. We, my wife and I, we don't do anything much anymore, not by ourselves anyway, and my son, he has a lot of problems. Health problems. He has diabetes. His mother babies him a lot. He's really different, or I mean, we, my son and I, Eric and I, aren't anything alike."

"But you love him?" she asked.

"Well, of course, I love him," Adam said. He was now wishing not to be at the woman's house at all. He felt sorry for her and all of her problems, but he had no words that could help her or even support his previous reasoning. He felt strange to have a son, something she wanted so desperately and tried so hard for, and he had done nothing in his life to deserve Eric. Being a father was just something that happened for him.

"Wait here just a minute," the woman said and walked into the other room and out of sight. Adam wondered how he could make a clean break. He fumbled in his pocket for his cell phone to make it sound like he was getting a call, but he had left it at the house.

When she returned she sat even closer to Adam. She leaned in, and he thought she was going to kiss him. He could smell the sweetness again. He tipped his head back on his neck and closed his eyes. He decided that he wouldn't initiate anything, but he wouldn't fight her advances either. He was nothing now, but exhausted, and he had come this far for better or worse.

With his eyes still closed, he felt a warm, wet, almost coarse thing pry open his lips. It took a moment for him to process the strange sensation before he opened his eyes. Sarah, the focus of his fantasies for the past few weeks, was vigourously scrubbing the inside of his mouth with a damp dish rag. There was nothing less fantastic and more real than a dish rag.

Adam pushed away the cloth, got up with stiff legs, and went for the door. "You just had some purplish stains on your teeth," she said. "I was trying to clean you up, so I could take your picture. That's what I do. I take pictures."

"Your shed," Adam murmured and continued to flee.

"What?" the woman asked after him. Then, "wait." She sounded desperate like she needed something from him, but Adam had managed to get the door open and was half way to his garage and safety.

The light was on in the front room of his home. He was almost sure he had shut all of the lights off before he made the ill fated decision to get to know the lady next door. He couldn't get the garage door open, but hadn't remembered locking the front one, so he started across the yard.

As he approached the stone steps, he saw Pam standing in the door. She was illuminated by the porch light and little bugs swarmed all around. She looked like an apparition until she spoke.

"We saw you next door. Through their window. Eric and I both saw you. You looked like you were kissing the lady with the dead dog. Adam, were you kissing her?" she asked.

"No, I wasn't. I swear. Why are you home? Is Eric okay? Did he have an episode?"

Pam crossed her arms. "The thruway is closed. There was an accident, a fatal accident. We decided to come back for the night and leave in the morning. Why were you kissing that woman, Adam?" she asked again as if he had not yet responded to her question. Although she wanted to appear calm, she seemed hurt and scared. She seemed confused and shaken, and Adam felt more love for her than he had in a very long time.

"I didn't kiss her! I went to talk about the shed. She's a photographer. I had stains on my teeth from drinking wine," he started to ramble.

"Drinking? Adam, you know what, on second thought, don't even try to explain," Pam returned. "You have really outdone yourself here. I have come to expect some downright shitty behavior from you, but I never expected this. I'm going to try to put Eric to bed; he's very upset right now. Just leave us alone, please."

Adam began again, but she put her hand up and turned her back on him. The screen door slammed behind her. He watched from outside as she took a waiting Eric's hand and began to ascend the stairs.

He wanted to call after his little family. He wanted to tell them that no matter how bad the scene looked, it wasn't his fault, that the woman tricked him, that she had problems like everyone else, that he wasn't thinking clearly before, but now… Now.

Instead he sat on the steps, feeling very sorry, mostly for himself. "And," he said finally looking down at the ground with no one left to argue with, "it wasn't even her dog."

NAMES ON MY TONGUE

Rebeca Antoine

The last time I saw my mother, she had Aunt Vivian on the brain. My mother and I were sitting side by side at the slot machines at the Indian casino when she turned and looked at me.

"Last night I dreamt of Vivian again." She turned away from me then and slipped another quarter into the machine. That's the way she likes to do it. One quarter at a time.

"What was she doing?" I asked. My mother often offered dreams for interpretation.

"We were just girls. Sitting behind the old oak tree, looking out at the cotton field, smoking one of Poppa's pipes." She pulled down the slot machine's arm.

"They have buttons for that now," I said. I always reminded her of the button.

"I like the arm," she said. "Feels like I have more control."

"There's no difference." I put a bunch of quarters in and pushed the button. Five quarters gathered in the machine's gullet. I smiled, winked at her, then asked, "But in your dream, you were young and blissful?"

She nodded. "You look so much like her." She ran her finger down my cheek. "Especially when you were younger. So much like her." My mother got a wistful, faraway look in her eye, and I hoped she would not tell it again. "We had such good times together."

I know the story. My aunt Vivian moved up North years before my mother did. Vivian was fifteen and came up to New Haven with my aunt Ginny, who was twenty at the time. Ginny had a particular affection for alcohol and men with conked hair and shiny cars. The two of them worked in white people's houses. Vivian was a nanny to a doctor's children and went to school, while Ginny was the maid for a bachelor lawyer and got to sleep in her own home at night. The doctor Vivian worked for used to come to her room at night and mess with her. I've always admired Southerners uses of euphemisms. "Messed with" sounds so much easier to take than "rape." After a while, Vivian got used to the doctor; she figured that white men liked to mess with black girls. That was the way her own grandmother was conceived. Vivian stayed one whole weekend with the children because the Missus was out of town visiting her people. The doctor let his friends have at Vivian as well, and one night six men raped her. This she thought was too much, and she told Ginny, who in turn told their mother. Vivian never went back to the doctor's house, just left all her things, nice dresses and all. Grandma Penny came up and got her, but Vivian was never the same. She could barely ever sleep after that. My mother used to say that Vivian had bad dreams and always thought someone was after her. Turned out that she was pregnant, and when she found out, Vivian couldn't sleep at all and was always trying to hurt herself. Grandma Penny knew a woman in the next county who could get rid of the baby and so they drove three hours to the woman's house. Aunt Vivian was just starting to eat normally again when my mother found her face down in the creek behind their house. My mother always ended that story saying, "Vivi never did learn how to swim."

But my mother did not tell me that day. Now I wish she had so I could have heard it just once more from her. She tells it better than I do; she has a certain flair about her words, a cadence that camouflages the tragedy of it. Instead, she just turned back to her slot machine, fed it another quarter, and pulled down the arm. She came out ten dollars ahead that day. That was three weeks ago, and I didn't know my mother was dying. Not in the way that we're all dying, life seeping out of us day by day, but dying in the way that something faulty inside consumes you.

I never met my aunt Vivian. She died a lifetime before I was ever born. To me, she is forever a girl smiling up from a grainy black and white picture. The girl in my mother's dreams. And she is my namesake.

"Repeat after me, Vivian," the doctor says. "My name is Vivian Rogers."

The doctor seems not to understand that if I could do such a thing, I would not be sitting before him dressed in paper.

I open my mouth, but only a low, guttural sound comes out. I pick up my notebook and write, *I can't.*

Jean, my husband, is in the room as well. It seems lately that he has seen me more inside of hospitals than out. At least this time I don't need a D&C. In the two years we've been married, I have had four miscarriages. I just kept trying again, like something would happen. Like suddenly I would no longer have an inhospitable uterus. Despite these recent misfortunes, Jean still manages a soft, empathetic look when he sees me this way. His head is slightly tilted as he shakes it, always maintaining eye contact with me. I offer him a smile, and he mirrors my weak gesture.

"Look," he says. "Vivian says she can't talk. Aren't you supposed to figure out why?"

The doctor turns around and begins speaking to Jean. Now it is the two of them, talking about me as if I am not here, as if I do not exist. I have faded noiselessly into the background. I close my eyes and listen to them. Jean is French, and despite his years in America, he holds onto a thick accent. Words sound so much better coming from him. My name sounds like music, broken, staccatoed, with a flourish at the end.

"I told you last time," the doctor is saying, "I didn't find anything physically wrong with her." He is trying to whisper, but I think my hearing is better since my speech is gone.

"You said some time," Jean says, "but it's been weeks now, and I'm worried."

I open my eyes and tap my pen loudly on my notebook, and the men look at me again, both with soft, empathetic looks, and I wonder if they've practiced those looks over time, that these are the looks found to bring the most comfort to damaged women.

The doctor sits in front of me again. He is convinced that my muteness is psychosomatic.

I found my mother's body lying on her living room floor, just a few feet from her phone. I imagined that she had fallen there on her way to answer my weekly call to confirm our slots date. That was our mother-daughter time. Sitting at slot machines pretending not to listen to one another. When I didn't hear from her that night, I worried, drove over to her house and there she was. I took care of the arrangements, we buried her next to my father, and when the first handful of dirt landed on the coffin, I opened my mouth to ask my husband for his handkerchief, and I couldn't say a word.

When I am at work, people pretend nothing is wrong. I realize that talking is overrated. I do everything by e-mail; at staff meetings I go unnoticed. My assistant takes messages. Most things work themselves out without my interference. It is when I get home that the trouble begins. Jean constantly tries to prompt me to speak, as if he could just wear down my will and fully formed words would magically appear in my mouth.

So there's nothing wrong with you, Vivian," Jean says over dinner one evening. He has taken me out to a nice restaurant where they place several types of wineglasses on the table, then remove the ones that are inappropriate for the wine you order. I have brought my notebook and pen so that we might not spend the entire evening in silence, so to speak.

It's something, though.

"So, what shall we do?" he says, and punctuates his question with a sigh. He has been sighing more often lately. I believe my silence frustrates him because it makes me no longer a willing partner in his games. With Jean, it's always talking. Talking about things we'll do, things we'll be. Jean has the habit of asking me questions that he knows I cannot really answer. He'll look up from the Travel section of the Sunday *Times* and say "Why haven't we been to Cairo?" as if we'd ever actually spoken about going to Cairo and perhaps decided against it. Then we go back and forth, intermittently, all day on the pros and cons of going to Cairo.

"Is it just me you don't want to talk to or is it everyone?" he asks, sipping from his ballooned wineglass.

It's not my choice.

Nevertheless, we spend most of the evening gazing over each other's shoulders at other couples who are laughing, smiling, and playfully touching each other's noses. Jean seems to find comfort in his sighing. I find it strange, the stagnation our relationship suffers when we cannot play these games, when I have nothing to offer my husband but my mere presence. When he looks at me, it's as if I'm far away, just an image, two-dimensional.

My mother left me her photographs. There are a number of pictures of my parents and my brothers and me. But there are also photographs from my mother's childhood, the photographs Grandma Penny left when she died. I am sitting on the bed, pictures spread before me, trying to choose which ones will be framed, which ones will be digitally reborn, and which ones will simply return to the velvet lined box my mother used to keep on the top shelf of her closet. Jean lies down next to me and runs his fingers along the scars on my thigh. He kisses a spot of reformed skin and pulls me into a firm hug.

"I think I fell in love with your scars," he says.

I reach for my pen and paper and scribble, *???*

"When I first saw these scars, I thought that you must be a risk taker." He gives me a little squeeze, and I pull away from him.

Clumsy. That's all.

"I don't believe you've ever been just clumsy." He fingers a dark spot above my knee, about three inches long. "Tell me, how did this happen? Every scar has a story."

He's right, maybe. Up and down each of my legs is a multitude of scars, and every one just might have a story. Not all of them good ones, I know. Jean rests his fingers on the spot again; his eyes plead with me to tell him something.

I remember the pain I felt before the skin grew back. I remember the blood.

The last week of every June, my brothers and I stayed at Aunt Trudy's up in Windham. She had two girls around my age and a boy the same age as my oldest brother. On that day, I'd been upstairs with the girls and they had been trying on clothes. They wouldn't let me try on any of their dresses because they said that maybe some of my black would rub off on them. They were all light-skinned beauties, and their mother wouldn't let them out in the sun. The girls called me Hershey's Kiss because I was dark like chocolate, and they called my oldest brother Hershey's Special Dark because he was even darker than the rest of us. That day I sat on the bed, watching them preen in the mirror until they pushed me out of the room. I ran out into the yard and followed the boys up the tree. But I lost my footing and fell right onto the boulder that sat at the tree's root; a sharp, jagged piece of rock scraped deep into my thigh. I probably should have gone to the emergency room, gotten stitches or something, but Aunt Trudy sprayed it with some antiseptic and told me to keep it covered with Band-Aids. I never spent time at Aunt Trudy's after that.

Jean is still looking at me, waiting. "I can tell you're remembering. Aren't you going to tell me?"

I kiss his forehead and quickly scrawl, *I fell.* There is only so much that I can write, and I find myself forced to return terse replies.

"But how?" he asks. "How did you fall?"

Doesn't matter.

Jean sits up, kisses my cheek. "Maybe some other time, then."

He leaves the room, and I am alone, faded photographs in my palms. The pictures remind me of the stories my mother used to tell, and the stories keep going around and around in my mind. They are a history of my mother's family, my family, our lives. Jean doesn't know these stories; I haven't had occasion to tell them. He knows that I love red wine, and I am not such a good listener most of the time. He knows my family as the working-class New Englanders we remade ourselves to be, people whose prized possession is a Weber grill that is pulled out systematically on Memorial Day, the Fourth of July, and Labor Day, people who vacation on the Cape in the off season. This is who we became, and it all seemed so easy.

We were sitting at the slot machines when I first told my mother that Jean and I were engaged. She told me the story about her cousin Mansy, who thought she would marry up by not marrying black and spent years living with a man from Ireland who ended up killing her when she was pregnant with their second child.

"He killed her but good," she said.

"I don't think I'm too good for anybody," I said.

"I wasn't talking about you."

"And Jean's not Irish."

"Didn't say he was," my mother said, pulling down her machine's arm.

My mother had a sad story for every occasion. I guess that's what happens when you live long enough, or your family's large enough.

My great aunt Tookie smiles up at me from a faded photograph now limp with age. She stands beside a man who holds a saxophone, and I wonder how they met, what they were doing that day, whether they were lovers. On the back of Aunt Tookie's picture, someone has written "Tookie with Arthur Ruddy."

I pick up my pad and write, *Tookie*. I compare the handwriting on the back with my own, noting where the gentle slopes of my cursive match that on the photograph. The handwriting is decidedly feminine, and I wonder whom it belongs to. My writing is identical to my mother's. I write the name again, *Tookie*.

Tookie was a spinster. She was always the pretty one, high yellow and good hair. She probably could have passed like some of her sisters did, but Tookie was too proud for all that. Too proud to always worry about being found out, to worry about what color her children might turn up. But white men sometimes don't care about having children; they're happy with pretty wives and money and vacations in Paris. Tookie could have been a doctor's wife. In 1921, Tookie packed up her hats and moved to New York. She was nineteen, should have been married and pregnant by then. Should have been married to Rue Kingsly, who lived about five miles down the road. He was a nice boy with golden skin and a few acres his family owned outright. Tookie took a shine to Rue, but two weeks before she got on that train to New York City, Rue's daddy found him hung from a tree on their property. Sheriff said it must have been suicide, that Rue must have been upset over a lady friend or whatnot. Tookie cried a little and packed up her hats saying that she wasn't going to have any children just so the white men could kill them with nothing she could do about it. Tookie danced in clubs in Harlem, drank whiskey like a man, smoked cigarettes, and never went to church. She said it wasn't worth her Sundays for a God that did nothing for her. Tookie didn't say, but she never did get over Rue, and she never married or had children. One man whose name escapes me courted Tookie for a while and wanted to take her away from that life, but she never could settle. Tookie always used to say "Love well, or not at all."

Jean reaches over me and pulls the picture from my hand. "Earth to Vivi," he says. He reminds me that since my voice left me, I have the tendency to let my jaw go slack, and I stare off into the distance with my mouth hanging open.

He holds the photograph up to his face, then flips it over to read the back. "What kind of name is Tookie?" he asks, inspecting the faded writing.

I flip to the next page in my notebook. *Her name was Anna Beth,* I write.

"They just called her Tookie?"

I nod my head.

"Why?"

Why not?

Jean concedes at this and leaves me once again in silence with my mother's photographs. I watch him as he leaves the room. He walks slowly, stopping to pick up a pen from the dresser as though that is what he came to the room for in the first place. He stops again at the door, takes a lingering look back and smiles. He reminds me of the last episode of a sitcom, where the characters always seem to be moving from where they live. This always signals the end; we apparently cannot follow them outside of the world of that single space. They stop, turn, and look back on what was before they embrace what will be. This thought amuses me slightly, and I smile. Jean thinks I'm smiling back at him, and his smile grows wider before he saunters down the hallway.

I don't know the answer to Jean's question, why they called Aunt Tookie by that name. But it seems that everyone had another name back then. There was the name they were given at birth and the other that they earned. Grandma Penny's real name was Lacy, but when she was three years old, she almost choked to death on a penny. They used to call my mother Funny because she never liked to be near boys; they thought she'd grow up to be a lesbian. I used to be called Bunny because I liked to jump up and down. Nobody calls me Bunny anymore.

I have an appointment with a new doctor to discuss my options. Much to Jean's dismay, I have been putting this off. I wonder maybe if this is the source of his sighing, not my lack of vocal communication. My new doctor is a woman. She is five feet tall at the most, and the chair in her office has clearly been made for a much larger person. It is brown and leather and sturdy. She sinks into it, and she looks to me like a child playing dress-up. Jean sits beside me holding my hand, patient and assiduous; he wrinkles his forehead pensively as the doctor speaks.

"The HSG your previous doctor did came up normal, but when we performed the hysteroscopy it showed that you have some scar tissue on your uterus."

My stomach sinks even though the doctor's voice is quick and light. She gives me the empathetic look, though I believe she is smiling too much. She is staring at me as I nod my head. I gather that she expects me to say something, but I have left my notebook in the car.

"My wife has laryngitis," Jean offers.

"Oh. For how long?" the doctor asks.

"A month now," Jean says.

"Have you seen a doctor?" she asks.

I nod.

"Well." She flips through my file and explains that the scar tissue is what makes my uterus a bad place for a baby to grow. She tells me how I would have been able to tell there was scarring and how cases as minor as mine can be easily missed, but can cause horrible damage to a pregnancy as we well know. Jean wants to know what we can do about it, how we can make my body safe again. "This could have happened after your first miscarriage," the doctor adds. "Possibly why they did the HSG in the first place."

Jean appears satisfied by this answer. That everything has been explained away. We have a new lease on life. He turns to me, smiling, his brow still furrowed. I nod thoughtfully, though I fear my smile to be as inappropriate as the doctor's. I immediately know where this scarring came from. I remember the pain instantaneously.

Jean tightens his grip on my hand as the doctor explains the surgery. She uses the words doctors usually use, like "simple procedure" and "routine." She spouts off risks and percentages and chances of conception post-surgery.

"This can be extraordinarily successful for you," she adds. "We can go in with a scope and repair the tissue."

"That simple?" Jean asks.

"Pretty much. Of course I can't promise everything will be perfect." The doctor smiles at me.

Jean holds my hand tighter and looks at me, smiling. "You see, Vivi. Simple."

I motion to the doctor for a paper and pencil. She looks befuddled for a moment, then hands me a pad of Post-it notes.

I have to think about it.

Jean's face falls farther than I have ever seen it fall before. He seems as confused as I am. I begin to ask myself if this is my penance for past deeds done. Perhaps I do not deserve to heal. I wonder if maybe I've liked the slow torture of it all. Perhaps everything has worked itself out for the best.

Late at night, Jean and I are lying in bed in the dark, turned away from each other, pretending to sleep.

"I think Barbara is a good name," he says.

I grunt my acknowledgement. The name is barely recognizable in his accent. He says it Bub-a-rah, with the emphasis on the final syllable, and I imagine that we'd call her Bubby.

Jean rolls onto his back and sighs loudly.

"When my father died," he says, "I was devastated."

I turn toward him and see the silhouette of his hands reaching for his face, and then I can hear his heavy breaths collecting in his palms.

"I was twelve years old," he says, "and I didn't know how to be a man yet. I had to learn myself. You're a grown woman now, Vivi. You can't just retreat."

I flip on the light on the nightstand and grab my notebook, knowing that he expects an answer. I write slowly, rip out the page, and hand it to him. I watch him as he reads.

I have written, *It's the weight of it all.*

Jean crumples the piece of paper, sighs again, then tosses it towards the wastebasket, but the ball of paper lands to the left. I turn off the light, lie back down, and close my eyes. I feel Jean's arms wrap around me.

"What do you think about Barbara for a girl, huh?" he says and gives me a quick hug.

I grunt again. I wonder why Jean insists on keeping up this charade. He doesn't seem to understand that this is a game that I no longer want to play, that I do not want to talk about our children and the names we'll give them or the instruments they'll play. Everywhere I look, there are women, swollen, mocking me. I have failed to do the one thing my body is built for, and I feel as though I am a husk, as if I am closed up, cut off, as if something has crawled up inside me and grown over all that was there.

Jean rolls over again. "I love you no matter what," he says. When I don't offer him anything in return, he sighs. I hear his breaths slow as he drifts off to sleep.

I know that I am not blameless as the doctor implied; it is my fault, this scar.

My mother didn't tell me that she was sick. She told my oldest brother and his wife, but not me. Apparently she found out about the cancer while Jean and I were visiting his family in Paris. It was just after my first miscarriage, and my brother said that my mother didn't want to upset me in my own time of need. She opted not to get treatment. She spoke quite often about the natural course of things, that we should not mess with our lives, that God would take care of things in his own way. My mother died of a massive coronary; the cancer didn't have enough time to eat her whole.

I am sitting cross-legged on the bed surrounded by photographs. I feel as if I can hear them calling to me. To my left is Aunt Gracie, who died in childbirth after being beaten by her husband. To my right is Grandma Penny, who had fifteen children, twelve who lived past their first birthday. Before me is my mother, a woman who allowed her body to be eaten by cancer without a fight, only to be killed by something else. In the picture, she is pregnant with me; my brothers stand at her side. My father's finger is to the right of the frame. She's not smiling; instead, she looks as if she's saying something. Most likely she's yelling to my father to get his finger off the lens just like she always did. I am still making piles. The largest is of pictures to be fixed. They are cracked, some of them a little torn. Fragile. I want them to be new again so that others can see them after I take my own inevitable plunge into death. On the top of this pile sits Aunt Vivian, still smiling, her body not violated, her lungs not filled with water.

Jean enters the room and stops at the edge of the bed. He holds a bouquet of flowers in his hands, my favorites, Gerber daisies. Jean surveys the bed and hands me the flowers. I mouth a thank you, and he kisses my cheek.

"So when will this end?" he asks. "When will this little project of yours be done?"

I shrug, although I know that I am almost finished. I have surveyed the bits and pieces of my relatives lives. As far removed as I am from them, I realize that my life is not much different. We all swim in a river of loss. And now, every time I open my mouth, I am inexplicably tripping over these names on my tongue, the stories that I am obligated to share. I want to give them air and life so they do not fade away into some uninhabited void. There are lessons to be learned, I am sure of it.

"Damn it, Vivi," Jean begins. "Just talk to me." He pushes aside some pictures, and they float onto the floor beside the bed. He sits, quiet for a moment, then strokes my hair in the way he always does when I'm sick. "The doctor said we could get pregnant, that you could have this procedure and everything could be okay. Don't you want that? Don't you want to try?"

No matter what happens, everything will not be okay. The doctors can remove the evidence, but the memory will still be there.

"I don't care if you never say another word to me." He kisses me lightly on the lips. "But I need to know if you want to try to have a child or not. Just a yes. Or a no."

Yes or no. These seem like terms I no longer understand, that whatever answer I could give would be more than that. The answer would have to be more than that.

"Yes or no. Either way, I still wake up beside you tomorrow."

I look in his eyes, and I know that he loves me, that he wants us to be a family, that he is simply trying to traverse this silent chasm between us. It is time for me to open; the memories are there forever whether I speak them or not. I look down at the piles of photos that surround me; these are the remnants of lives already lived and deeds already done. I still have the chance to unmake one of the tragedies of my life.

"Okay," I whisper. "Let me tell you a story."

EGYPTIAN COTTON SHEETS

Gina Hanson

She was on fire again. Walking through a crowded city street, skin melting, the fierce firestorm creating small wind tunnels that blew through the hair of the women and children that quietly passed her by. She smiled at me. She always smiled at me. Only this time, the fire soon melted her lips downward into a frown. Her tears kept the fire from moving up her face and into her eyes. She crept closer, arms extended, charring the ground she walked on. I knew I couldn't touch her, so I didn't even try. I just watched her burn until the heat grew uncomfortable, and I woke up.

I kicked the sheets off of me. I took a moment to make sense of my surroundings. Since my thirteenth birthday, it had become a ritual that I spent the day's first few minutes recalling the previous night and the circumstances that had led to wherever I lay. This morning, the coolness of the sleeping bag on the floor of the windowless utility room reminded me that I was still in the Malibu house.

I was too claustrophobic to actually sleep inside a sleeping bag. So instead, I slept on top of it, blanketed only by a pair of light blue Egyptian cotton sheets. The sheets were soft and warm. They reminded me of my mother. Which explained the dream. During the hot summer months, whenever my mother appeared in my dreams, she was always on fire. It was nice seeing her in my dreams, even if the condition in which I saw her wasn't all that pleasant.

It was too dark to see the time on the small clock hanging on the back wall of my makeshift bedroom. But I knew it was close to daybreak. I always woke close to daybreak. We'd been in this Malibu house for almost a week now, and I hadn't missed a single sunrise. I stood up, felt around for a pair of shorts. I could smell fire, but I didn't pay any attention to it. I was often surrounded by the scent of fire after dreaming of my mother.

A giant game room sat just beyond my sleeping quarters. As I stepped onto the game room's cold marble floor, I saw Bugs playing a solo game of pool. "Mummy, my boy. You're up early," he said.

"I like to watch the sunrise."

The eight ball rolled awkwardly toward the corner of the pool table, stopping just short of its intended pocket. "You were making a lot of noise in there," Bugs said.

I tapped the ball into the pocket with my index finger. "I must have been dreaming."

Bugs tossed his cue stick down onto the table. "Was she hot?" He winked as he smiled.

"I guess." I'd never really liked Bugs's smile. His teeth were deceptively straight, and his top lip formed a fleshy point just above his front teeth. It was odd.

Bugs plopped down onto an antique couch that looked sorely out of place with all the modern game room furniture surrounding it. He rubbed his hand along the furniture's fabric, making designs on its surface.

"Weird looking couch," I said.

He lay back and kicked his feet up. "It's called a récamier. It's French."

"I never pegged you for a furniture kind of guy."

"My grandmother used to have one...a *récamier*." He mocked a French accent. "She got it in France."

I looked out the window. "You going to be around for a while?" I asked.

"Where else do I have to go?"

"I'll cook breakfast when I get back."

"Sounds good, but do me a favor..." Bugs sprung from the couch and picked up a rack for a new game. "Don't make so much food. I hate seeing all that shit go to waste."

Outside, the glow of the eastern sky betrayed the summer heat with its icy blue color. Waves were quietly rolling in, careful not to wake the residents asleep in their houses on the sand. Small birds chased waves into the ocean only to retreat when the waves turned against them. The sand was cold but refreshing. I sat in my usual spot, a relatively uneventful area that afforded me a picturesque view of the sun as it inched above the South Bay cities.

I dug my bare feet deep into the sand. I could feel the sand get cooler as my toes made their way to the layer of sand still wet from last night's high tide. There was no one on the beach yet. That would change in an hour or so, as soon as Malibu residents woke up to walk their dogs before heading out to their high-powered jobs as actors, lawyers, studio execs. I knew I would sit here until I saw the woman with the Weimaraner. Partly because the dog was so beautiful and partly because the woman reminded me of my mother, I felt the day had a better chance of being agreeable once a cheery "Good Morning" escaped the Weimaraner Lady's mouth.

A lone dolphin moved in and out of the water, his dorsal fin slicing through the ocean's surface. The scene reminded me of a children's story my mother used to read to me. It was a story of a young dolphin who was separated from his mother and traveled for months looking for her before he met up with a seal and a walrus. A family of misfits they were. The dolphin never did reunite with his mother. My mother had said it was *inshaalha,* the way God wanted it. I had said God was unforgivably cruel.

I only remembered bits of my mother's language. Egyptian words came to me intermittently and when I least expected them. Like the first night I was here in Malibu and I saw a dying fish on the shore. *Samak,* I thought to myself, that *samak* is dying. I couldn't remember the word for dying which was disappointing because it was the last thing I ever heard my mother say. One would think you would always be able to remember your mother's final words.

The woman with the Weimaraner emerged from around the craggy rock formation about a mile down the beach. Her wide brimmed hat bounced with each footstep. She wore what she always wore—a cotton skirt and cotton blouse— just like the clothes my mother wore. My mother used to say that back in Egypt, cotton made the hot summers more bearable. I didn't know if that was true or not because I had never been to Egypt, but I trusted my mother. She had no reason to lie about something as simple as that.

"Another beautiful morning, isn't it?" the lady with the Weimaraner said.

"Yes. Yes it is." I said. I pet her dog as he tried to lick my face.

"You know, I've seen you out here every morning since you moved in," she said. "I think it's only right we introduce ourselves."

I stood and wiped the sand from my behind, careful to not get any on her dog. I extended my hand. "My name is Naar, but everyone calls me Mummy."

The lady smiled as she shook my hand. "Now why would they call you Mummy?"

"Naar's too odd, I guess."

"Odd? I think it's beautiful."

"*Agmal,*" I said softly.

"Excuse me?"

"Nothing." I clapped my hands together to rid them of sand. "It's just that my mother used to call me *agmal Naar*. Agmal means beautiful."

"Really? What is that? Middle-Eastern?" The lady grabbed the stick from her dog's mouth and threw it down the beach.

"It's Egyptian," I said. "Hence the nickname Mummy."

The woman turned and looked at me, shaking her head up and down slowly, like she was contemplating me. "What are the odds? My son lived in Egypt for six years. He taught English at a university in Cairo." The Weimaraner ran bouncing back with the stick. "It's strange; I'd never suspect you were Egyptian. You're so pale."

"Not all Egyptians are dark."

"So I see. I'm Martha, by the way, and this here is Raymond."

"Nice to meet you, Raymond," I said, taking the stick from his mouth and tossing it down the shoreline. "And nice to meet you too, ma'am."

"Please, darling, don't call me ma'am. Makes me feel so old." Martha's smile was warm. I wanted to hug her, but something about her was too frail. "How long ago did you move in?" she asked.

"I'm only visiting. Couple more days then it's back home."

"Oh? Where's home?"

"North. Seattle."

"Well then, no wonder you're out here on the beach every morning. Must be delightful to see the sun rise."

I smirked. "It is."

The Weimaraner barked. "Alright, Mr. Mummy, I believe Raymond is wanting to continue on. It sure was nice to meet you."

"Likewise," I said.

I watched for a little while as Martha and Raymond walked down the beach, Martha adjusting her hat every so often to keep the sun off her neck. As she adjusted her hat, she'd expose the cotton scarf wrapped around her head. It was odd. Wearing both a scarf and a hat.

Once Martha and Raymond were no longer visible, I turned and made my way up the sandy slope and into the Malibu house.

"This shit is fucking good, man," Bugs said, scrambled egg hanging off his lip. "You really should be a chef or something. How'd you learn to cook like this?"

"They're eggs," I said. I rinsed off my plate with the restaurant-style pullout chrome faucet over the kitchen's extra large stainless steel sink. We had a faucet just like this in the restaurant my parents owned. My mother loved that faucet. Always said she would get one for the house, but she never did.

Bugs ran his index finger across the plate and then stuck it in his mouth to get every last morsel off his plate. "What you got planned for the day?"

I carried the frying pan with the remaining eggs over to him. "You want some more? You can have some more."

"Naw. I really shouldn't. I don't want to eat all these people's food, you know."

I set the pan back on the stove. "We're squatting in their house, Bugs. I hardly think they're going to care about a few eggs gone missing."

"People are strange, Mummy. You'd be surprised what angers people." He stood and carried his plate over to the sink. "You didn't answer me about what you're doing today."

"Hadn't given it much thought."

"Think I'm going to check out the whole movie-library-room-thing. It's the one room I haven't got to yet."

Bugs and I had been squatting in this house for seven days now. When Bugs was at the post office a few weeks ago, he had overheard the owner of the house stopping mail delivery for three weeks. A few days later, Bugs was scoping out the place and spotted the owner's husband putting a spare key under a rock. It isn't everyday that homeless teens get to stay in a Malibu mansion, but I guess it was, as my mother would say, *inshaalha*. And I guess we were also just a little *masud*—lucky.

"I got the paper this morning." I said as I rinsed Bugs's plate. "Why do you think they didn't stop the paper delivery?"

"Why should they? These kinds of people don't care about saving a little money on things like newspapers."

I handed the plate to him to put into the dishwasher. "And you aren't at all worried about that note I found in the mailbox?" I asked.

"I think you misread it."

"How many ways can someone read, 'Teddy, please bring in the mail?' It's pretty obvious they're expecting someone to come by here."

"You're paranoid, man." Bugs poured dishwashing liquid into the compartment and closed the dishwasher door. "I told you I saw the lady stopping mail delivery. No mail to bring in, my friend." He pushed several buttons on the dishwasher and the machine shimmied to life. "I was up pretty late. I think I'm gonna lay down for a while." Bugs grabbed a soda and walked out of the room.

"*Lie*. You fucking moron," I said quietly once he was gone. "You're going to *lie* down. Get it right."

The day's newspaper was not filled with anything new. Same old stories, with different names, different dates. Someone once told me about a poet who claimed history was like a widening spiral. If that poet had been alive to see today's paper, he'd probably think the future was also spiraling—spiraling around the proverbial drain.

Last week, I read in the paper that my father was up for parole. The *L.A. Times* reported that no one from my mother's family was present at the parole board hearing.

I would have shown up if I had known, but I wasn't even expecting his parole for another six years. One of the witnesses at the park that day, informed the court that there was a young boy with the victim when the crime took place and asked if anyone knew where the boy—who had to be about seventeen now—was. It was reassuring that no one knew my whereabouts. Meant that my father didn't either. But I guess it didn't really matter anyway. If my father was indeed paroled, I was leaving California. I wasn't going to stick around and wait for him to find me.

I moved out onto the second-story deck, sat on a covered patio swing, and watched the waves grow larger as the high tide moved in. I thought of my mother and how she used to tell me stories about her and my grandmother sitting and watching the waters of the Nile rise and fall. She used to say that when the waters were low, you could find all kinds of lost treasures. One time, her mother found a solid gold headpiece, and they were sure it had once belonged to an ancient pharaoh. They gave it to my father's family when my parents met. My mother said that my father's mother later had it melted down into a gold cube as a wedding gift for my mother. I don't remember ever seeing it, though. I wish I could have asked someone where it went.

I was bored. I hadn't been bored in years, and now, here, in this enormous house with a million things to do in it, I was bored. I went to go wake up Bugs so we could watch some movies.

She was on fire once again, only this time, she was wearing a beautiful gold headpiece that was melting, bathing her face in molten gold. I sat on the curb watching her move toward me, stopping just feet from me before smiling and wiping the tears from her eyes. I could feel the warmth of the fire decrease as pieces of her flesh blew away in smoldering embers.

Agmal Naar, she whispered. *My beautiful boy.*

I awoke to a sliver of sunlight coming from somewhere within my windowless utility room. I was about to miss sunrise. I wrapped myself in my sheet and headed out to the shore.

I only had seconds to spare before the sun made its debut above the distant Edison Company smoke stacks. The ocean was a lake, hardly a wave, hardly a ripple.

Martha and Raymond appeared from around the craggy rock. They were early. Martha walked fast, and Raymond trotted alongside her. No stick throwing today. No toys. Just a straightforward walk.

"Another beautiful day, isn't it, Naar?" Martha asked as she walked into earshot.

"Yes it is, Martha," I said. Raymond continued past me without stopping.

"You'll have to excuse Raymond for being rude, we're in a bit of a hurry," Martha explained. "My son—the English teacher—is stopping by today. We haven't seen him in quite a long time. He gets so busy. Raymond was his dog, and so you can imagine how excited Raymond is knowing his Daddy is coming home."

"Smart dog."

"Just like his father." Martha stopped for a moment, removed her hat, and tucked a lone strand of hair up under the cotton scarf she was wearing below her hat. She looked almost bald under that scarf, but I was sure it was just my imagination. "Well, I really shouldn't stop for too long. I've got so much to do to get ready for my lunch date with Jeffrey."

"Of course," I said, nodding and smiling. "Enjoy your visit."

"Thank you, Naar, I will. Will you be here tomorrow? You're leaving soon, aren't you?"

"Yeah, but I should be here tomorrow."

"Very well, then." She moved past me and on down the beach. "Don't you leave without saying goodbye," she said over her shoulder.

I gathered up the bottom of the sheet and stood to go inside. Martha had seemed unmoved by the fact I was wrapped in a sheet. Perhaps it was not a strange sight here in Malibu. I plodded through the sand to the house's first-floor landing. I unwrapped myself and shook out the sand from the sheet.

A thick black spot filled the middle of the sheet. Tar. I took the sheet into the laundry room to try to remove it. I couldn't remember how to get tar out of fabric. When I was a kid, my parents and I spent the day at the beach and my mother had gotten tar on the white cotton sarape my father had bought her on a trip to the Mexican Riviera. My mother was devastated. She thought she was going to have to throw it away, but Mrs. Chan, our neighbor, owned a dry cleaning business and she knew how to remove the tar. I wish I could remember what Mrs. Chan had advised her to do.

Bugs came into the laundry room with the clothes he was wearing the previous night. "You using the washer?" he asked.

"No, go ahead."

"I fucking puked all over myself last night. Didn't think I drank all that much, but apparently I did." Bugs laughed. "Who knew I was such a lightweight these days?" He shoved his clothes into the washer. "Hey, found some documentaries on the pyramids, if you're interested."

I picked at the tar on the sheet. "You know how to get tar off something?"

"You got tar on their sheets? What the fuck you do that for?"

"I didn't do it on purpose."

"Use some baby oil. There's some in one of the cabinets in the entry way." Bugs closed the washing machine and switched it on. "Make sure you get all that tar out of that sheet and then do me a favor, and don't take anything from the house outside. It's not your stuff to do with whatever you'd like."

Bugs walked out of the laundry room. "Meet you upstairs in a few hours to watch those documentaries," he shouted from down the hall.

When I was seven, my mother took me to see an Egyptian archeologist speak at UCLA. His name was Dr. Albert Gruning. He was an old friend of my mother's. I don't remember much from what he said in that talk, but I remember a lot of the pictures. I remember a close-up of the Sphinx in which Dr. Gruning pointed out the birds' nests that filled many of the holes in the Sphinx's face. It was such a funny place for a bird's nest that I laughed out loud, causing my mother to pinch my leg. The more I tried to stop laughing, the harder my mother's pinch got. After a few moments, I was in an equal mixture of laughter and pain, which sent my mother into a fury. She yanked me up out of my chair by my arm and pulled me outside the auditorium. She yelled at me about how much of a disgraceful little boy I was. "He's a bona fide Egyptologist, Naar. You disrespect our ancestors and our people with your bad behavior."

I sat on the beach in my usual spot, passing the time until movie-watching with Bugs later. The wind had picked up, but so many birds were just sitting around. There were a million seagulls perched on some of the rock formations just off the shore. I wondered why seagulls didn't dig holes into the rocks and make their nests there. I wondered where their nests even were. There weren't very many trees around here.

My bird watching was interrupted by a cold lick on the face. "Raymond," I said. "What are you doing out here, buddy?"

"Hi, I'm Jeffrey Cohen. I'm Raymond's pop."

"Hey," I said extending my hand.

"You must be Naar," Jeffrey said. "My mother said I might see you sitting out here."

"Where is Martha?" I asked.

"She's lying down. She hasn't been feeling all that good lately, you know, with the chemo and all."

"Chemo? I didn't know."

"She didn't tell you? Well, don't tell her I did...I'll never hear the end of it." A cocker spaniel and a poodle appeared by Jeffrey's side. "Hello, little fellas," he said as he knelt down to pet them. "Always greet the dogs with genuine enthusiasm," he said quietly to me. "It's a chick magnet." He stood back up and smiled at the young woman who owned the dogs who was headed our way.

Jeffrey looked a little out of place here on the beach. His suit trousers and dress shirt made it look like his beach outing was unplanned. He had on some nice dress shoes, the sight of which caused me to squirm, thinking of how much sand he must have accumulated in them so far.

"Hey, before I forget," Jeffrey said, his heavily hair-sprayed hair starting to flap in the wind. "My mother wanted me to give this to you." He pulled a gold barrette from his pocket. "She said you might like it or want to give it to your mother or something."

I took the barrette. It was covered in hieroglyphics and ornate etchings. It looked expensive. "I really shouldn't," I said, offering the barrette back to him.

"Keep it. She doesn't need it." Jeffrey scratched Raymond's head. "My mother says you're Egyptian."

"That's right."

"You don't look Egyptian."

"No?"

"No. You don't look Egyptian to me at all."

"How does an Egyptian look?"

"Not like you. Full-blooded Egyptian?"

"Yep."

"Where's your family from?"

"Right off the Nile."

"Wow. That really narrows it down."

"I don't know actually," I said. "I've been here since I was five."

"I used to work in Egypt. I taught English in Al Qahirah."

"You're mother said you taught in Cairo." I wondered if this guy was going to tell me his whole life story. I didn't like him. He was starting to give me the creeps. I stood to go inside, get away from him.

"Wait." Jeffrey threw Raymond's ball down the shore and then waved to an old gentleman jogging our way. "My mother's too polite to ask, but I, well, I'm just too curious, I guess." He pointed a thumb at the Malibu house. "Just how do you know the Simmons?"

"The Simmons?"

He pointed to the house. "The Simmons. The owners of the house you're staying in."

"Oh, them. I don't know them. I'm staying here with a friend of mine. He's a friend of theirs." Raymond returned with the ball. I ruffled his head and gave an awkward wave goodbye to Jeffrey. "Nice to meet you." I turned and walked toward the house.

"Does this friend of the Simmons' know you're not really Egyptian?"

I stopped. I kept my eyes on the dog at my feet and smiled, unsure of what to say.

"You're not, are you?" Jeffrey added. "Egyptian?"

I turned to face him.

"What's your real name, kiddo? And don't tell me it's Naar. Egyptians don't name their kids, 'fire.' So what is it? John? Mike? Finnigan?" A solid chunk of Jeffrey's hair flapped furiously up and down as a small wind tunnel swirled around his head.

"It was nice meeting you, Jeffrey." I said. I turned away from him. "Tell your mother I hope she's feeling better."

"She's knows about your little deception too, you know. I bring her home that barrette, a get well gift, and she says

'You should give it to the boy,' but I say 'Why are you encouraging his delusional behavior?' You know what she says? She says, 'He's a good kid, Jeffrey; he's had a tough life.'" Jeffrey scoffed and shook his head. "I just looked at her. Couldn't believe it. I earned a Ph.D. at UCLA . . . I guess she thinks that wasn't tough at all, just wine and roses."

Raymond sat at my heels looking at me with sympathy. I scratched him under his chin. "Sorry to hear about your Ph.D. I bet that was real tough." I turned and walked back to the house.

"You do know that I'm going straight home to call the cops and report a bunch of squatters, don't you?"

"Whatever." I walked up the sand to the house, my breath rapid. I tried to convince myself to breathe in slowly, but the air burned and it took all I had just to take in the shallowest of breaths.

In the house, Bugs stood at a first floor window, looking out over where I had been talking to Jeffrey. "Who's the guy with shellac flap?"

"A neighbor," I said. I hesitated. "He says he's going to call the cops on us."

"Fuck him." Bugs chugged the last of whatever he was drinking. "Fucking rich snobs. Think they own everything around here. This is my fucking house." He smiled at me. "I found it. As far as I'm concerned, it's mine."

"Sorry, Bugs."

"Forget it. Let's go watch those documentaries."

She isn't on fire. She isn't hurt. She isn't sad. She isn't any of the things that would make her recognizable to me. It is the afternoon of my thirteenth birthday. I am sitting with her in the park, eating the *kishk* and *koshaf* that she has prepared special for the day.

I've bought you a special treat, she says softly, but you mustn't show your father. She gives me a small package wrapped in brown paper. She has drawn hieroglyphics all over the wrapping. I recognize some of the words: 'son' and 'love.'

Inside the package is a six DVD set of my favorite documentary on Egypt. My mother lights the candles on the small birthday cake she's baked for me. *It's not much,* she says.

A loud voice booms from behind us. *I thought you had ended this, Jane.* My father's unexpected presence causes me to jump. *You promised me you weren't encouraging his insanity any longer, Jane... you promised me!*

Sweetheart... it's nothing... it's just harmless imagination... honest. The fear in my mother's eyes ignites my father's rage.

He thinks he's fucking Egyptian, Jane. It's not harmless imagination. It's insanity. Our son is a god-forsaken nut job... I've got a nut case for a kid. My father's face is enflamed with rage. *You buy him this shit...* he picks up the DVDs and throws them at my mother... *you think it's cute. You take him to those ridiculous Egyptian lessons. You turn our restaurant into a goddamn King Tut exhibit. Why do you encourage it? What are you going to do when he comes home one day, and suddenly decides he's going to be Irish? Buy him a fucking leprechaun and start calling him Seamus?*

Honey, my mother pleads, *you're making a scene. People are looking—*

Eight years we've been having this battle... eight fucking years, Jane!

As my mother stands up, I am no longer beside her. I am no longer within arm's reach as my father slaps my mother forcing her to step close enough to my birthday cake that the lit candles catch her white cotton dress on fire. I am no longer close enough to my father to feel him holding me by the arms, screaming at me, eyes filled with hatred. I am no longer close enough to hear my mother's screams or feel my father's hot breath as he shouts at me. I am floating above my burning mother, above my raging father. Floating above the people in the park who are on their cell phones calling the police but who have no intention of coming near the crazy man ranting at his son. I'm above the people coming out onto the porches of the houses that surround the park. I'm no longer close enough to plead with them to do something. I'm even farther away now. I am no longer able to see my mother when she finally stops moving.

I woke up in the family room where Bugs and I had been watching the Egyptian documentaries. I could smell fire. *I can still smell her,* I thought.

The waves outside were crashing against the house's pilings. I looked out the window, but it was too dark to see anything. I could hear the crazed voice of the wind as it screamed at me inside my shelter. The stench of fire was strong.

Bugs came into the room and plopped on the sofa. "You were out like a light, man." He picked up the remote. "You missed like three-fourths of the documentary." He hit play on the home theatre system.

"Maybe we could finish it later," I said.

"Better finish it now. There's not going to be a later, I'm afraid." He kicked his feet up on the ottoman and rested his arm behind his head. "The fire's moving fast. They'll evacuate us soon."

"Fire? What fire?"

"The hill. It's on fire. Always catches on fire during the Santa Anas."

"Fuck, dude," I said. "If they evacuate, they're gonna come knocking door-to-door. What'll we do then, huh?"

"Don't worry about it." He grabbed a fistful of popcorn from the bowl at his side and shoved it into his mouth, several kernels crashing to his lap. "This is a great part, man," he motioned to the television, popcorn fragments spraying out of his mouth. He chewed quickly then swallowed. "You won't believe why the Sphinx has all those holes in its head. Birds! Fucking Birds. Can you believe that shit?"

"Bugs, we got to go. Seriously. I don't want to spend the night in jail."

"I said 'don't worry about it.'" He stared at me. He was serious. After a few moments he spoke. "Listen. I'm going to tell you something. You tell anyone else, and I will... I promise I will beat the living fucking breath out of you."

"Who would I tell?"

He hesitated. "I live here. I mean this is my parents' house. I grew up here. I didn't find no spare key under a rock, I have a key. I come here every time the asshole shit-fucks of mine leave town." He tossed a couple popcorn kernels in his mouth. "Now you know, so shut the fuck up and let me handle this."

I sat for a few minutes unsure of what to do. Bugs had been lying to me. It's not that I was all that surprised, people lie, but now I starting to feel a little guilty about some lies of my own. "I'm not Egyptian," I finally said.

"I know."

"I'm Irish."

"Figures."

"My real name's Finn."

Bugs sat up and washed his popcorn down with a swig of beer. "I'm Theodore Eldridge, the third." He dusted his hand off on his pants and extended it to me. "Nice to finally meet you, my friend."

The doorbell rang.

"That, my dear Irish buddy, is our cue. Grab up your stuff and let's get the fuck out of here."

One of the upsides of being homeless is that all of your belongings fit into one bag and can be packed rather quickly. I met Bugs at the door where he was talking to a short firefighter with a much too thick mustache. "This is my buddy, Mummy." Bugs points to the firefighter. "This is an old friend of my parents'. Name's Nelson." Nelson held his hand out to me.

"Nice to meet you, Mummy. You two better get going before too long," the firefighter said. "I think Malibu Road is already closed. You may have to walk out. You got somewhere to go?"

"We've got a million places we can go... ain't that right, Mummy?"

We slipped past the flashing lights of the many police cars and fire trucks that filled the street in front of Bugs's house. "Where are we headed?" I asked.

"Pacific Palisades," Bugs answered. "Seems my aunt and her new husband are in Europe with my parents. It's not the Ritz, but it'll do."

"Hey, Bugs?"

"Yeah?"

"Why'd you leave home anyway? If I lived in a place like that, I'd never leave."

"Nothing is ever what it appears, my friend."

"Then why go back?"

"I don't know. I hate feeling like an orphan, I guess."

The news helicopters flew over us as the fire lit up the night sky. Bugs whistled *Walk like an Egyptian*. I knew he was mocking me, but in Bugs's world, that meant he forgave me, too.

We continued to walk. We didn't speak. We passed a city library that looked a little too rundown for this area. I knew I'd return to it in the morning to find some books about Ireland. I tried to remember exactly how far it was to Pacific Palisades. I was tired, and I longed for a good night's sleep.

FAMILIAR SPACE

Maureen Pilkington

Gray and Shauna Pope stood outside their old apartment door wiggling their key in the lock, trying to get it open just the way they used to. "Here, let me," Gray said gently nudging his wife to the side. "I've got the touch." Click. He pushed the door open and heard the familiar squeak in the hinges that sounded like hee-haw-hee. They hadn't been there in six months, since before the baby was born. Shauna's father left the apartment to her in his will. They used to live there full time; now it was a vacation spot.

"Gray—everything's the exact same." Shauna walked into the stuffiness and stood in front of the six-foot oil painting with her hands at her sides in a little girl stance. The painting hung on the first wall; you could see it when the front door was open. It was a man, standing, with a bird in his palm, and a fish out of water at his feet. His shorts poofed out in the thigh; he wore maroon stockings and velvet shoes that curled up in the toe, his hair in a pageboy cut. "There he is, Gray. Our Monk Man hasn't changed one bit." Satisfied, Shauna headed into the kitchen.

"He's not a monk—but tell him to shut his reverent eyes in about fifteen minutes," Gray said, snooping around, breathing in the old excitement. "He's the medieval type—bathed once a month. Probably liked his women that way, too," he added for himself.

"He is a monk. He just shed his robe. No more twelve rules to live by. He's got his own rules."

"I don't want to hear his rules right now." Gray was used to this—his wife, her fictional add-ons. An odd strain ran in her family. He was finally learning to shrug off this part of her.

The first thing Gray did was stand in the bedroom doorway, checking out the familiar space under the bed partially covered by a shag rug, the one he carried up twenty-one flights in a roll that felt as heavy as his future. They had one of those high country beds, the kind you need a little two-step to get up on—even though it really didn't fit in size or style, in their bedroom. Shauna had wanted a completely new look so she wouldn't be reminded of the way it was when her father lived there.

Gray took the dust mop from the supply closet and pushed it under the bed, near the woodwork and around the rug. "Yep," he yelled out to his wife, giving the mop a shake, "everything is A-OK."

Gray walked into the bathroom and started running the water in the sink at full force, then the bathtub, which came out watery brown before quickly turning into pure, Grade A, New York City water. The best. He flushed the rusty bowl, once to put the water in it, then flushed one, two, three times, the water flow anxious and responsive once again.

"Oh my God, Gray, why now?" Shauna yelled out from the kitchen.

It was funny how without their baby Audra around, Shauna turned into her old baby self, with that munchkin voice, the one that needed Gray for *everything*. A smell was coming from the refrigerator and why did Gray have to deal with that now?

"Please, Gray, we can't have this smell while we're here. You know," she said, looking down at herself as if she was envisioning later, too. "Please," she said, clipping her nose with her fingers. Bravely, she looked for the offender.

Shauna *was* brave, about so many unfortunate circumstances in her fortunate life—the suicide of her muckity-muck father, a mother who drank increasingly and lost interest in her, an older brother who cut himself off from her, after their father's death. Although to look at her you'd never suspect she'd been cheated out of the basics. Her facial expression was always hopeful.

The perpetrator in the fridge was obviously the green, lumpy, previously orange block of cheese. It was the only type of cheese Shauna ever cooked with—American. Gray got the industrial garbage bag from the hall closet, swaddled his hands in the dishtowels and removed the cheese, throwing it into the bag, quickly securing it with extra long twist-ties. He ran the bag, holding it out in front of him, directly to the garbage room down the hall. This was something he would have enjoyed as a kid. He saw himself playing an FBI agent, black windbreaker billowing out a bit as he ran down the hall of an Upper East Side apartment building wearing a serious, putrid-cheese expression on his face. Trim and medium, he was light on his feet, but, he admitted, a little too good-looking for undercover.

When Gray returned, Shauna, now in Playtex gloves, was spraying Lysol with the kitchen window open. He jogged around the apartment, a few steps backward and a few steps forward, checking behind things, pulling books off the shelf and letting them fall on the floor—still in agent form—and called out to his wife, "Found it!" His hand fingered the bag behind all those issues of *Business Week* where Shauna's father was listed "Best CEO of the Year" for several years, the gold book marks sticking out of the tops. The articles highlighted his philanthropic generosity, accompanied by photos of him with inner city children and board members of the older New York charities. As Gray's fingers walked over the magazines he was also tapping his father-in-law's head thinking, *Hey asshole, you had everything to live for.*

He waved the sandwich-sized Ziploc—not even a quarter-filled with pot, about two joints' worth. "We'll make do," he said while sticking his nose in the bag, sniffing for freshness, then knocked the six-month-old magazines off the cocktail table. Now Shauna was dipping the sponge in the bucket of Mr. Clean.

Gray made a decision that would affect them for the rest of their married lives as Shauna infused the kitchen with a mountainy fresh smell. He decided this is what they would use this place for—to keep themselves intact. The kid (he realized Audra was too young to call a kid but pretty soon she'd have that long wavy hair, drifting around the way her mother did) would never see the inside of this place.

Gray picked up *Parents Magazine* and opened to a random page, dumping the pot over a photo of a blue-eyed, cue-ball, double-chinned infant. He was surprised they even had this magazine, but the mailing label said Lenox Hill Hospital, where Shauna worked before Audra was born. He started to sift the seeds out, letting them fall in the seam of the magazine, covering the baby's drool with the usable leaves as he tilted it up next to the article, "Is Too Much Fantasy A No-No?"

He sat there on the leather couch—the place had a completely different look from their new, old house in Larchmont with the wrap-around porch—and let the view do to him what it always did. He was relieved about so many things today, one that he had his wife all to himself, without Audra sucking on her every minute. Two, it was simply a day off from the floor. Shauna was always afraid he would turn dirty and volatile being a trader downtown. He had almost turned dirty when his boss's girlfriend came on to him the other night, it would have been easy. And, volatile, well, he had his moments.

They couldn't see the water that encircled Manhattan

from their living room window—it wasn't that kind of place—but the surrounding apartment buildings made a strong jagged fortress, their windows as yellow as flaming stars against black nights in a switchboard pattern. While Shauna fawned over the Monk Man, Gray had this painting—his blinked with life. He never felt claustrophobic here the way he did in the suburbs, shying away from guys his age that, he felt, were parochial, playing poker in the basements of golf clubs, their cigars—not one Cohiba among them—were emblems of what they thought was style. Here the buildings were a beautiful distance from Gray and Shauna's apartment—there seemed to be fields and fields of open space outside the windows of the twenty-first floor, a long fluent ride to the next co-op, according to his mind's rail system.

Gray could point their standing astral telescope into any one of those windows and dip into a kitchen, or a bedroom. The windows in the stairwells were good tidbits also. He wasn't looking for sex, not really. It was like flipping through every satellite channel only the sound was on mute: a Confederate Flag substituting as a curtain (that was his center marker), or the roommates that were rebuilding the Twin Towers out of beer cans on the table in their kitchenette. The woman with the balcony who never slept—and he would be back to check on her that night. Once, when skimming, he believed he saw two priests.

When he finished rolling, Shauna was standing very still by the kitchen window, in one of her trances. She had dewy ethereal looks, as if she walked on a vapor fresh from a myth. She must have been thinking of her father and Gray didn't intrude. In one of Shauna's rare, open moments, she told him that as a little girl she would sit by his bed when he was unable to get up—during the on-again-off-again depression—hold his hand, sneak a puff of his cigarette, and tell him Monk Man stories. Sometimes, she would hide under his bed, and stay there until he fell asleep.

How many years ago did all that happen? Gray was beginning to wonder if Shauna was hiding something. The way he saw it the poor Irish bastard was sick—while his wife was in the kitchen, he walked down the hallway from this very same apartment, up the stairwell and onto the flat roof. Gray found himself imagining the scene, the focused and humble look he must have had on his face much like Shauna's. When they moved in after the wedding, Gray scraped the paint off every wall, hoping to get rid of any residue of mental instability his father-in-law may have left in the air.

Gray watched his wife from where he sat in the living room. He missed that close proximity in their house. The longest strands of her hair in the back reached the pockets of her jeans. The first time he met her at a party in a loft downtown, she reminded him of a woman with a flower crown, hiding in a mossy glen. The see-through skin. He had to lure her out of the woods and into a conversation. Now, Gray wondered if she was simply having baby withdrawals. If so, he was doomed.

He was admiring his work, holding up two even joints so his wife could see. Not the freshest, but the smell would destroy any trace of cheese.

"Hello hello are you there?" Gray asked. Granted, his wife was a head-in-the-clouds type—an English lit major—but there was plenty going on. He just couldn't figure it out. Shauna claimed she couldn't understand him, especially when he partied all night with his friends, sometimes over at the bar in The St. Regis, and didn't call to say he was in no condition.

"Oh, Gray, I don't believe it," she said at the window. "He's still here."

Gray knew exactly whom his wife was talking about. The arm, the hand, the cigarette, whatever. Shauna called him, The Smoker. Their other neighbors on the floor were old women who never seemed to die off, probably because of rent control.

"His wife can't take it," she said. "The wife is an ex-smoker, and the smell is intoxicating to her. But he doesn't have the willpower to quit, of course. He is actually pretty thoughtful—he hangs his hand out the window, so as not to tempt her. Later, she smells his fingers."

Gray knew his wife smoked an occasional cigarette on the sly. He also knew she would attach a story to the arm. "Oh, did you decide he's married? Fuckin' weirdo probably lives alone. Maybe all the guy needs is a night out with the boys." Gray was good at providing temporary solutions.

"He's not so weird. Do you see the way he dresses? Perfectly starched white shirts, rolled neatly and evenly to the elbow."

"The way his *arm* dresses?"

"He has some wardrobe, I can tell."

Shauna stood there and watched the cigarette between two thick fingers; the smoke rose and coiled in a noose. She appeared mesmerized as if she were watching a genie's bottle. "See—not between the tips, but between the fingers near the knuckles. Macho type. And, look at that watch."

"A match—I need a match." Gray was digging around. "Guess I could yell over to that fucker," he muttered.

"You know what, Gray? He's going to smell our stash after we light it," Shauna said with her Playtexed hand on her hip. "Our smoke is going to go out our kitchen window and directly into his living room and up his nose."

"Believe me, the cheese will get him first." He was looking under the couch. "Maybe we don't like that shit coming over into our window. Second-hand smoke and all that. If you know where his apartment is, we should get the cheese out of the garbage and put it outside his door. A little something for our neighbor."

"I do know. 21X."

"There are no X's."

"I don't know why I even bother to talk to you, Gray. You never believe a thing I say."

"Let's take a walk down the hall—for proof." I want all of this over in about three minutes so we can start doing what we came here to do."

The phone rang.

"Shit," said Gray. "Don't answer. Has to be a telemarketer anyway."

"You know damn well who it is—Mrs. McCarthy."

"You gave her this number?" They left their cell phones home in compliance with the vacation weekend rule.

"What's wrong with you?"

"The old bag knows the origin of every fart, burp and ounce of spit-up. That's what she's calling about now. She gets off on that shit—makes her life meaningful."

"Hello, hi." Shauna peeled off her plastic glove with her teeth. Gray could see her thinking in a bubble over her head: *maybe Audra was lying on her back—to prevent SIDS— but choked on her spit-up.*

Mrs. McCarthy wanted to know where the rectal thermometer was, in case she needed it during the night. She always did a run-down of supplies.

Gray lit the joint.

Gray and Shauna were high and dry-mouthed, and went under the bed in their old spot. There must have been two-and-a-half feet under there, plenty of room to flap against each other like two fish caught in a net. Gray was used to Shauna's milky scent now. It was as if fresh skin had just started to turn so her smell was a little off. Gray's face was mashed between his wife's legs when the phone rang again.

"The phooone—oh my God the phone, Gray. Oh, God, something happened to Audra. I knew it. I knew this would happen. This is what we get for being selfish."

Shauna turned herself over, practically twisting Gray's neck, until she shimmied on her stomach and elbows out from under the bed and onto the parquet floors. "I can't deal with another surprise," she said on all fours.

Gray wanted to believe that Shauna was still under the bed with him, so he sent Shauna Number Two out to answer the phone. Gray and Shauna watched Shauna Two get to her feet and run out of the room in lanky strides. Gray thanked the original Shauna for not being so fucking responsible like Number Two, for putting him first in her life the way she should, for her devotion, and he began to kiss her.

The phone rang and rang.

Gray heard panic in his wife.

"Mrs. McCarthy? Mrs. McCarthy? Hello, hello, is Audra OK?"

If you would like to make a phone call, please hang up and dial again. Use the area code first.

Gray listened to his wife slam down the phone. "I can't take this. I can't." She pressed Star 69 to make sure it wasn't Mrs. McCarthy.

"I'd come out there and get you, but I'm paralyzed from the neck down. Your scissor legs. I told you not to answer—it would be nothing." Gray didn't get a response, but he knew exactly what Shauna was doing, visiting her Monk Man, lighting a candle, her face glowing like a fairy. How often he caught her staring at the painting that belonged to her father.

Gray still lay under the bed with the comforting smell of their mixture. For a moment he drifted, too, and imagined Mrs. McCarthy holding Audra on her shoulder in a diaper, trying to get her to burp. It's too cold for a diaper, it's fucking November. She didn't stop patting her back. Gray couldn't stand the patting, couldn't stand the old bitch's spotted face, because the baby was limp and ashen.

"Gray, can you come in here?"

His fears were confirmed. Everything was different now. He was warned by his friends who had them, and warned by his friends who didn't have them. Babies changed your life, they changed your wife. Your own mind could never relax. Because of the baby, things would never be the same. It went without saying.

"Gray—can't you come in here?"

"No—can't you come in here and can't we do what we came here to do?" What they would always do here, Gray reminded himself, mapping things out for them because it was not in his wife's blood to plan.

The apartment had become a very expensive mailbox since the baby was born; Shauna inherited it, but they still had to pay the maintenance every month, on top of the mortgage for the modest house, with charm, they just bought in Larchmont. They never seemed to get the opportunity, or the energy, to use this place.

Gray realized they were slipping, turning into those Larchmont parents, the ones attached to running strollers and congregated outside Bradley's on Sunday mornings with their giant coffees, discussing elementary school academia. Soon to come: Volvo wagon, a little back fat, loss of libido (for everything except golf and weekends in Stowe), play-dates, pushing your pre-K kids—now—toward the Ivies. Chicken nuggets. The only thing Gray felt he could contribute to his community, if he was included, was his theory that the women there had no breasts.

"Gray—"

The other depressing thing he thought of was that neither one of them was as high as they were ten minutes ago. He crawled out from under the bed, grabbed the joint on the bureau, heard a strand of pearls drop and roll across the floor like marbles, and headed into the living room. Gray saw his wife sitting in some kind of yoga position, the candle on the floor in front of her bare folded legs. She lifted the candle and he stuck the joint in the flame. He dragged on the joint and handed it to Shauna. They exchanged it over and over again until they were in a space where there was no baby.

Gray and Shauna made love and now he was practically examining her, kissing her under the arm with eyes open, pressing his nose there as if the pressure would make her pop out. This is where he might find her. He could never pinpoint her, exactly, and he was afraid that this is how she kept him loyal, by keeping him tangled up, never giving him enough information.

The phone rang and it was as funny as a joke. Their legs were too tired to stand so they started crawling around on their knees and this gave the night a new dimension.

"Gray, I feel syrupy—oh—there's that ring ring ring again, sounds just like a telephone."

Gray rested on his laurels, seeing his wife finally giving up the new mother act, having a good time. It was possible. They would always come here and be this way.

"Persistent caller—maybe it's The Smoker. He's at the window and sees your iridescent ass," he said.

Gray made it to his feet, walking as lightly as the first man on the moon, and stepped over to the telescope. This would distract his wife from the sound of the phone. He stuck his eye on the lens and started skimming.

The phone rang and rang.

"I bet if we put this over here we can get into The Smoker's living room."

The ringing began to lure his wife out of her high and she looked to Gray as if she were sleepwalking towards the sound. The joy of watching her a moment ago was already bittersweet. She was on a mission now, her pure white hand already raised in front of her, moving faster. When she got there and put her hand on the phone it stopped ringing.

"Good. It shushed. Must have been a telemarketer."

Gray was wondering how it could have been a telemarketer in the middle of the night.

Shauna stood there staring at the phone. "Well, if it *is* Mrs. McCarthy, and it's a problem, she'll call right back—if I know *her*."

They stayed in the same positions until enough time had passed.

"I'm going out there," she said in a song. "I'm going to find that apartment just to prove to you there is a 21X. I'm so sick of you and your know-it-all ways."

"Going out like that?"

He watched her body walk out of the room and into the bedroom. When she returned she was wearing a sheer nightgown. She picked up the burning votive in front of her painting and cupped her hand around it as she walked passed him.

Gray admired his wife's face over the candle's flame, starry-eyed and provocative. She seemed to float over the floor. Had she morphed into a spirit? Sufficiently stoned now, it didn't occur to him to stop her from drifting through the hallway in that transparent nightgown.

She pulled the front door open. The sound of the hinges reminded Gray of soft-spoken angels trying to squeak out a warning. She walked out of the apartment and through the hallway.

Gray carried the leggy telescope back to the living room. He made neat piles on the cocktail table, putting all the magazines together—*Psychology Today, Fortune, East Sider, Parents, Vogue*—and brushed off the dust. He left the dead roses in the vase because dried, they were standing as straight as they did last spring.

Gray was startled by the sound of the phone ringing again. He felt relieved his wife was in the hall so she wouldn't have to be sentenced to this again. Sloppily, he pushed the couch away from the wall and yanked the wire out of the socket. That's all it took. He should have done it before. Or, silenced the ringer. Now all he could hear was the faint sound of a siren from the street.

He vowed to take advantage of every moment tucked away, here, in their own clubhouse. One last spin with the telescope, a housewarming gift that was meant for finding the Little Dipper in Larchmont. He'd promised himself earlier that he would try to find the woman who never slept. How nice it would be to see her again. Would she be dressed? Eating ice cream out of a bowl? Still high, he looked down into the lens. He searched the windows across the way, but he couldn't seem to get the focus out of his own living room. He concentrated, thinking of nothing else at that moment. Gray, with the skills of an amateur pilot flying his first night solo, couldn't find his horizon, couldn't navigate, and couldn't make a landing.

He turned his lens clockwise and counterclockwise still looking for the woman—but instead, he found an image. The necks of two swans. One was so white and delicate, the other thick and shades darker. The image continued to blur because it was imbedded in smoke. His legs weakened as he realized he wasn't looking at the building across the way, but the building in the back, through their kitchen, and the swans were the arms of Shauna and The Smoker, their cigarettes like two beaks yapping at each other.

What were they talking about? The Smoker would be getting off on Shauna's breasts, her visible pink nipples, her starry ways. He tried to see his wife's expression through the window. The tilt of her head. He could already picture her waltzing back into the apartment, smug, without an explanation, taking her yoga position in front of her painting.

Gray raised his head from the lens. He was dizzy and nauseated; maybe he needed to eat something, but there was no food in the place. He lay down on the floor but the position did not stop his head from spinning. He closed his eyes trying to figure out where he was. On a cold platform near the ceiling? His body felt too heavy to stay up much longer.

The sound of the phone ringing vibrated in the center of his brain. He thought of the old cliché and how true it was— so loud it could wake the dead. Gray broke into a sweat, thinking of all the possibilities. Aware of the floor now, he began to crawl towards the phone, towards the powdery scent of their baby's head, but he fell on his back in great relief, remembering how he'd pulled the plug out.

He stretched out on the rug, still without clothes, meeting the placid eyes of the fish at Monk Man's feet. He envisioned Shauna as a little girl, sitting on the side of her father's bed, telling tales, relaying advice from the man in the painting. Gray remembered now what Shauna told her father and how he wished he could have been there to stop her. She told him Monk Man followed his craving, the darkness over his face. It freed him from the rules. Gray could see her skillfully taking the cigarette from his unsteady hand, putting it to her lips, then back between his fingers, without her father ever realizing what she had done.

DOING IT OVER

Toby Tucker Hecht

The room was crowded by the time Jane arrived. She stepped over laptop cases and water bottles and sat down in the last empty seat. She should have gotten to the lecture earlier, but she was having a wave of morning sickness from her pregnancy that was in its thirteenth week, and she'd been rummaging around the office trying to find some dry crackers. It was her second baby, but the process had not gotten easier with experience.

The room was hot and she was beginning to feel claustrophobic. She feared another surge of nausea—locked in this jam of scientists. Thinking about the possibility made it worse. She popped a cracker into her mouth and tried to concentrate on the fresh notepad in front of her; she wrote down the date and title of the talk.

The lights dimmed slightly and an audio-visual technician appeared and adjusted the portable microphone around the speaker's neck. At that moment, Jane felt a hand on her shoulder and soft breath on her ear. "Janey? It's really you. Isn't it?"

Jane's face tightened and tingled. She hadn't been called Janey since high school, over twenty-five years ago, and the faint New England accent in these few words brought back a flood of memories of the one boy who almost destroyed her life. She hesitated a moment, considered pretending not to hear, and then turned.

"Zachary!" She recognized him immediately, although he'd aged into manhood and eyeglasses. "It's great to see you," she said.

The lights went down and a hush fell over the small auditorium. The first slide came onto the screen and the woman—the cancer epidemiologist Jane had been eager to hear—began to speak. Jane stared at the screen and realized that the smile she'd prepared to greet Zachary was still fixed in place. She relaxed her face and tried to focus on the lecture. In a short while, a map of Europe and Africa was displayed, with various colors depicting the frequency of genes in populations across countries. Jane had missed the connection between the speaker's words and the chart. Her mind was several decades and four hundred miles away remembering the obsession—because that's what the doctor had called it when she was finally taken for help—with the boy, now a man, sitting behind her.

She had stopped sleeping and eating. By wasting down to nothing, she imagined she might become nearly invisible, all the better to shadow Zachary's every move: with whom he was talking and what was being said; what he ate for lunch and who sat next to him; what he did when he wasn't in school and who kept him company. She joined the drama club because he was in it, even though she had no interest in performing. She wanted to crawl into his skin. Fuse with him into a single being. And yet, despite her erratic behavior, no one knew about the shadowy corner of her life, her unexposed feelings. She didn't understand them herself, really. This was nothing like the lighthearted crushes most of the girls her age had on boys. This was ferocious pain. Yet, in her most lucid moments, she couldn't say what it was about Zachary exactly that caused the manic attraction.

She knew only that wanting to be with him made her feel alive.

She hadn't confided in her girlfriends; she'd let most of her friendships slip away through neglect, pretending everything was perfectly fine with those who remained. She was careful never to utter Zachary's name, to link him to her in any way. She never spoke to her parents about the demons orchestrating her actions; they noticed nothing wrong until just before graduation. And Zachary—he was oblivious. As far as she could tell, he knew her only as the cheerful good sport he kidded around with in drama club and who sat in front of him in their advanced biology class. And now, twenty-five years later, she was sitting in front of him again.

Jane found herself smiling. The speaker had told a joke and the room had exploded in laughter. What could possibly be funny about cancer epidemiology? She looked up at the projection screen and found no clue. Her notepad had only a few stray phrases—nothing of any consequence. The lecture was half over and she had been daydreaming for most of it.

The decision about her tenure would be coming up in less than a year. As an assistant member of the research institute, she had done everything by the book: published scientific papers in high-impact journals, obtained government and foundation grants, collaborated with big-name laboratories, and mentored several promising young scientists. But lately, she felt something slipping. Maybe it was her pregnancy. She'd be reading a scientific article or even a newspaper story and twenty minutes later, she'd find herself on the same paragraph with absolutely no comprehension of what she'd just read. But she wanted the baby, badly. She was forty-two and although she was healthy and still fit, she knew there was no more time to wait. Her husband Marty came from a large family and wanted more children. And her daughter Daphne was already eight.

She didn't have to turn around to know what Zachary was doing behind her. He was taking notes with a fountain pen; she could hear the scratching on his pad. It occurred to her that he must be in her field of study. But how was that possible? She knew everyone in her area, at least by reputation. And what was he doing in her institute? She had to find out somehow. The room was brutally hot and the woman's voice was droning. If only the lecture would come to an end.

She couldn't talk to Zachary today; she looked like hell. It wasn't obvious that she was pregnant, but already her waistline had thickened as though she had let herself go; and a few blemishes appeared in patches on her chin and forehead. At home, she'd tried to cover the blotches with makeup, but it looked cakey and the color was off. She ran her tongue around her top teeth; there was a remnant of cracker stuck to her gum line. Zachary must have been sickened by her appearance when she smiled at him.

The lecture was finally over. Jane had to go up to greet the speaker and ask her something intelligent or make a comment about the talk. She sidled through the crowd and stood, waiting until the group standing around the podium dispersed.

"Thank you for a most enlightening seminar," Jane said. She hated that phony professional voice. She hoped the speaker wouldn't ask her what it was she found enlightening.

"Jane! How good of you to come," she said. The woman shook Jane's hand with two-fisted vigor. "I've read your papers and they've contributed quite a bit to my own research, as you've just seen. I'll be in town for several days. Perhaps we could get together to discuss what you've been doing lately." She handed Jane a business card.

Jane hoped that the seminar would be available as a videocast so that she could replay it later when she'd calmed down enough to pay attention. She turned to leave. Zachary was standing in the back of the room.

"Finally, I have you all to myself," he said. "Let's go get coffee." Jane had a meeting with one of her technicians, but she heard herself saying, "That sounds great." He gazed at her as though she were some sort of long-lost object. He ran his hand down her arm and held onto her wrist.

Jane could feel the heat rising into her face. She extracted her hand and as she did she noticed he was wearing a wedding ring.

They sat down facing each other in the cafeteria.

"Wow," he said. "I can't believe it. So many years. But as soon as I saw you they all melted away."

The charisma. It was still there.

"What brings you to the Institute?" she said.

"After ten years, I finally got a sabbatical from my medical practice at a hospital in New York," he said. "I thought this would be a good place to learn some genetics, so I'm hanging around Dr. Gruen's lab while my wife works her butt off as a White House Fellow."

Jane wanted want to hear about his wife, and didn't. She pictured a beautiful, brainy woman with boundless energy hobnobbing with the President. She wondered if she knew her, if she was someone from high school. Probably not. Zachary didn't have a girlfriend back then—except that girl he took to the prom.

"…and taking care of our almost eight year old daughter, Vanessa."

Jane missed most of what Zachary had said, but she now knew something that bound them together.

"I have an eight year old daughter, too. We'll have to get them together while you're here." Jane paused and then said, "I'm expecting again in April. But you probably noticed that."

"I think pregnant women are gorgeous," he said.

Marty was busy helping Daphne with her math homework when Jane arrived home. The kitchen table was set for dinner and a pot of lentil soup simmered on the stove. Marty was an architect and, since his company encouraged telecommuting, he did much of his work from their house in the attic he transformed into a drafting studio. It was a godsend for her that Marty enjoyed domestic chores. Her own interest and skills in that department were nonexistent.

"Hi, honey," Jane said. "How was school today? What did you do?"

"Oh Mommy, look…I got a ninety-five on my vocabulary test. The only word I didn't know was *bazaar*. I thought it meant *weird*."

Jane laughed and hugged her daughter. "No that's *bizarre*. It sounds pretty similar. But ninety-five is almost perfect."

"I don't remember such hard words when I was in third grade," Marty said. "I don't think it's even English, is it?"

"Speaking of bizarre," Jane said to Marty, "I ran into an old high school friend today at the Institute."

"Really! Someone I've heard of?"

"Just a guy I knew once. He and his wife moved here recently and they have a daughter Daphne's age."

"Nice. What do you think about inviting them for dinner?"

"Oh, I don't know. It's been such a long time. I really don't know him anymore and I've never met his wife."

"Well, unless there's something *bizarre* about them, I can't see why not."

The dishes were washed and Daphne was asleep. Jane heard Marty walking around in their bedroom upstairs. She wanted to make love. Not because she was relaxed and feeling secure, but because of some demanding force— something strong and greedy. This pregnancy was strange. One minute she felt weepy and sick to her stomach, and the next she raged with pheromones.

She slid into bed beside Marty. The room was chilly and she snuggled up to him, her breasts pressed into his back.

When he didn't respond right away, she slid her hand down his leg and began to caress him.

"You're obviously not tired," he said, drowsily.

"I want you," she said.

But while they were making love, her bedroom vanished and she was on a blanket, lying naked with Zachary in the overgrown field near her old high school, a place kids used to go to make out, imagining him first above her, then pulling her over to straddle him—taking no time at all to build the exquisite sensations that finally slaked her hunger.

"I've got to remember to cook lentil soup more often," Marty said, and drifted off to sleep.

The next morning, flashing thoughts from the previous day, one wrangling with another, interrupted her work, making it impossible to get anything done. Why in the world did she mention Zachary to Marty? She tried to dissect her motive, but all she came up with was recklessness and stupidity. She should call the epidemiologist and get together with her to go over experimental results, but she couldn't make herself pick up the phone. It was as though she'd entered an elevator, pushed the wrong button, and had come out on a lower, unfamiliar floor, where the layout of her life was the same, but with the characters and the raw, primitive emotions of an earlier time. Zachary was once again creeping under her skin, possessing her. She had to shake him off. Everything was just the way she wanted it—her husband, her child, a new baby, her career—the whole wrapped package. She was not going to be taken over by a sort of living dybbuk, to discover if she could go back and do it over. She would focus on her work. She would stay clear of Zachary.

When she got home from the lab that evening, Marty said, "Surprise! We're having guests this Saturday. Your friend and his wife are coming for dinner and they're bringing their daughter to meet Daphne."

Jane stood in the doorway, staring at him. "How did that happen?" she asked.

"He called earlier this evening and introduced himself as your old friend from high school. So I told him you'd mentioned him yesterday, and one thing led to another. Very pleasant guy."

"I wonder how he got our phone number."

"Did I do something wrong?"

"Of course not. I just wondered." She kissed him on the cheek and set the table.

When the doorbell rang on Saturday, Daphne was the one who ran to open the door. She had asked her mother several times that day about what Vanessa liked to do, if she had any pets, and if she liked the color pink. Jane explained to her daughter that she really didn't know these people; she'd been friends with Vanessa's dad more than twenty-five years ago.

"Twenty-five is a big number for years," Daphne said.

But the moment Zachary and his family entered the house, Daphne whisked Vanessa to the playroom where they could be heard having fun with the dollhouse Marty constructed, a model of a real house in a suburb north of town.

The adults sat in the living room and made pleasant conversation in an attempt to get to know one another. Zachary's wife, Cassandra, was younger, in her thirties. She wore a suit, as though she were going to work. Her cell phone, which was attached to her belt, rang soon after they'd sat down, and she left the room to take the call.

"Cassie works for the President's Chief of Staff," Zachary said. "She has to be on call 24/7. It's a great opportunity for her, but the interruptions to our lives are driving me crazy. And most of the year is yet to come."

Marty got up to see about the main course still in the oven, leaving Jane and Zachary alone.

"You look wonderful, Janey," Zachary said. "I remember you being pretty, but now you're simply stunning."

Jane blushed and felt a quiver of excitement zap through her. Hardly anyone ever commented on her appearance, except for Marty who occasionally said, "You look nice" when she dressed up. *Nice* was her husband's favorite word. Finally, Marty returned and announced that dinner was ready.

The girls joined them at the table and insisted on sitting next to each other. They were involved in a discussion about jigsaw puzzles. Cassie returned with her phone re-clipped to her belt.

"Nothing important," she said. "I would hate to miss what looks like a fantastic dinner. I hardly get to eat with Zach and Vanessa any more. My usual evening meal is microwaved instant oatmeal. And I haven't seen anyone socially outside of work since my year in Washington began. So this is a real treat."

Jane brought in the salad bowl and sat down in the only unoccupied chair, the one next to Zachary. She couldn't swear to it, but she thought somewhere between the last bite of romaine and getting up to clear the plates, she felt the slightest pressure of Zachary's hand on the side of her left thigh. The table wasn't large and the chairs were close together, so it could have been simply an adjustment of the napkin on his lap.

The crazy door, the one that she managed to keep closed for so long, was opening a crack and behind it was the beckoning abyss that could pull her down as it did years ago. She looked across the table at Marty, who smiled at her. He was such a gracious man: never an unkind word about anyone. And he loved her unequivocally. Why wasn't she obsessed with him?

When they were dating in graduate school, Jane found comfort in the fact that Marty didn't provoke the same strange emotions in her that she had spent such a long time purging. They shared the same values. He was solid and mature, and offered her a normal life. A *nice* life. That was what she wanted for the long haul. He was not exciting. But excitement did not necessarily equal love. Commitment and trust did.

And yet she was aching for Zachary to touch her again under the table. She extended her leg slightly in his direction, but he was talking to Marty about the house they were subletting for the year and was using both his hands to describe the size of some architectural detail. She looked at Cassandra and wondered if she felt passion for her husband. Cassandra appeared cool and business-like. It was hard to know what went on between two people.

Marty's chicken was delicious and the frozen dessert that Jane whipped up went over so well that Zachary asked for seconds. "I can't remember the last time I had *anything* so satisfying. It's positively addictive." He licked his lips slowly and then smiled at her as though this was an in-joke.

Jane caught Daphne glancing at Zachary and then at her.

"You must have been very good friends in high school," she said.

Marty turned to his daughter and said, "Mommy and Vanessa's dad were in some of the same science classes."

As Zachary and his wife and daughter were about to leave, Vanessa said, "Mommy, can Daphne come to my birthday party?"

"Well, of course," her mother said. "It's two weeks from today. We'll send you an invitation, Daphne, with all the information on it."

The two girls hugged each other and then the family left.

I really like them," Marty said while they were cleaning up. "Very unpretentious, even though Cassandra has a big-time job. And the girls were in love with each other." Jane was amazed that Marty hadn't noticed the tension between her and Zachary. Or had he? It was possible that he was testing her with these comments. She said nothing.

Marty left the room and came back with his appointment book. "By the way," he said, "can you take Daphne to the party? I'm tied up in an all-day contract meeting that Saturday. I might not even be home for dinner."

"No problem," Jane said. She wondered if this was one of those parties where the parents dropped off the children and then came back later to pick them up. She really didn't want to spend time again with Zachary and Cassandra, though she'd be grateful to have a day with Daphne. There were so many times when Marty had to play the roles of both parents because of her lab experiments, and Jane feared being shut out. She wanted to be on solid footing with her daughter before the new baby arrived. She would plan something special—maybe a movie and pizza after the party.

But by Monday, Jane was walking around in a net of dread. A knot of anxiety pressed into her stomach every time she even thought about Zachary and that was almost non-stop. She couldn't go on interacting with that family, even if the girls liked each other. For all the years that had gone by, she had been only in remission, not cured.

She really needed to talk to her mother—the one person other than her old psychotherapist who would understand. But her mother had died six year ago, leaving her to deal with this alone. Marty had no idea, and she couldn't tell him her secret. That was the one problem with Marty: he didn't deal well with human complexity, particularly the dark side of behavior. He expected everyone to have a sunny disposition, or at least cope with their problems *sub rosa*, as though life were a blueprint allowing for little deviation.

She tried using a relaxation technique she had been taught; she pictured herself a desiccated sponge and then imagined pouring water on it, allowing it to soften and expand into its normal shape.

And yet, her memory—hibernating for so long—awakened and reached out with a ruthless grab. The senior prom. In many ways it was the end, but also the beginning. If she could think about it objectively, she might be able to find the path out of the morass, again. She'd convinced herself that Zachary would invite her. How could he not? They had spent so much time together. But even in her most deluded moments she recognized the truth: that most of what she believed was in her imagination. It was five days before the event and still nothing.

And then she heard from a classmate that Zachary had asked a girl who lived in his neighborhood, but who went to a private high school. It was as though she were told she had a terminal disease. She could not stop crying. All through the night, her mother tried to find out what the problem was, but all she said finally was that she didn't have a date for the prom. Her mother held her in her arms and said, "I know someone who would be glad to take you," as if going was itself the goal. And that's how she got stuck with Boyd Lemmon, the son of one of her mother's bridge club friends, as a prom date.

Prom night would be endless: a dance at the biggest hotel in town and then an after-prom party back at the high school finishing off with breakfast sponsored by the PTA. Jane's mother had taken her to an expensive boutique and bought her a pale pink gown with tiny beads on the skirt. The dress was childish: sweet and unsophisticated, but Jane didn't care what she wore. The only reason she consented to go with Boyd was to spy on Zachary. Once she saw the girl Zachary was with and convinced herself that she was nothing to him, she would somehow ditch Boyd and go home.

It was a particularly warm night in May. Although some of the prom attendees stayed inside the decorated ballroom waiting for the deejay to set up his equipment, others spilled out onto the hotel terrace and lawn. Most were coupled up, but a few, mainly girls, arrived in groups, hanging out and talking among themselves. Jane was glad she at least had Boyd to escort her. He wasn't bad looking, but he had almost no personality. He didn't say anything to her from the time they left her house until they arrived at the hotel. Then he said, "I don't know anyone here." Jane understood that included her, and he was as uncomfortable as she was about the evening.

The lilac bushes along the edges of the terrace were heavy with perfumed blossoms. Boyd had gone inside to get a soft drink, while she stood silently watching her classmates arrive. No one spoke to her. Finally, she spotted them: Zachary and the girl. Despite the heat, Jane felt a coldness wrapping around her heart. Not only was the girl beautiful, with long, shiny black hair and a model's posture, but she was wearing the most provocative dress Jane had ever seen on a girl her age. It was a tight-fitting strapless gown in shimmering peacock satin, exposing the tops of her breasts. When they walked through the small crowd of people on the terrace, everyone—male and female alike—stared. One boy whistled. The girl turned and flashed a brilliant smile.

"The music's playing. Do you want to go inside and dance?" Boyd said when he returned.

Jane stared at Zachary and his date as they entered the hotel. Then she turned to Boyd and said, "I don't dance, but I want to watch."

Inside, she searched the dimly lit ballroom until she found them. They were dancing to a slow song of longing. The girl's bare arms circled Zachary's neck and she rested her head on his shoulder. Zachary pulled her close, caressing the small of her back, kissing her hair.

Jane blinked over and over, trying to clear the watery film that was preventing her from seeing. She felt blood pounding in her ears and had a terrifying sensation that she was deep under the sea, needing to breathe, but unable to find the way up to the surface. She saw the red light of the exit sign and began to run. Boyd called to her, but she kept on—out to the terrace and over the gentle mounds of lawn, propelled by the fire of fury, in the waning light. She could barely see where she was running. The nauseating stink of the lilacs smothered her. When she got to the street, she couldn't decide where to go next. A car, filled with students, rounded the curve. The headlight beams bobbed up and down. Jane took a breath and pitched herself into the illumination. A horrible screeching noise and then howling and screaming overtook her consciousness. She lay on the ground, vomiting. The car had swerved and missed her. A girl who had been in her English class was crying, "Someone call her parents!" And someone did.

Jane was sure there was more to that evening than her memory could hold. But what she remembered clearly was the aftermath—the long stretch of therapy sessions during which she was made to understand it was within her power to decide how she wanted to live her life from then on.

Between the dinner and Vanessa's party, Jane devoted herself to her work. She finished writing a paper for publication and worked with a graduate student on a plan for his thesis. She sat in committee meetings, volunteered for projects, and got in touch with a colleague at a different institution to begin a new collaboration. At home, she spent time playing with Daphne, taking walks, and talking with Marty about a short vacation together before the baby came. She slept and ate well, and stopped having morning sickness. On the Saturday of the birthday party, she thought she felt the baby move. It was thrilling.

She dropped Daphne off at Vanessa's house and went to a nearby public library to read for the two hour wait. Cassandra had asked her to come in, but Jane said she had work to do and would be back when the party was over.

She made herself comfortable in a reading carrel and began reviewing an article that a journal editor had asked her to evaluate. But after a while she grew restless and wandered over to the childrearing books in the nonfiction stacks. As she passed through the psychology section, she noticed a volume on relationship addiction. It was jutting out, as though someone had recently removed it from its place and then quickly returned it. She pushed it back in alignment with the others on the shelf. Without examining it, she knew she could have written that book. She'd been deep in a hole and had willed herself out. And she would stay out because the risks and the consequences would be even more disastrous than they were when she was a teenager. Everything now was just a test of her resolve.

When she got to the party, the driveway was busy with parents buckling their children into booster car seats and leaving. She was a few minutes late. She parked on the street and walked across to the house. Before she had a chance to ring the bell, Zachary opened the door and smiled at her.

"How did it go?" she asked.

"Fine, I guess, but Cassie had to leave in the middle," he said. "So I was in charge of games and serving the ice cream and cake." A bit of chocolate icing smeared his sleeve. He looked beyond Jane to the last car pulling out and then back to her.

"Come in. Come in. Daphne and Vanessa are in the basement playing with her new toys. I could use some company."

"Well, I should really…"

He interrupted her. "The girls get along so well. Let them play together for a while. Sit down, Janey. Make yourself at home."

He went into the kitchen, got a beer for himself and a sparkling water for her, and showed her into the living room. Jane wondered if he might have had one or two drinks beforehand because his voice was a little singsong, although she could also imagine that being around a group of eight year old girls for a couple of hours might do that to you.

She sat on the sofa and he sat next to her with his arm draped across the back.

"You look happy, Janey. Are you?" he asked.

"Yes, you could say that. My only worry now is about tenure." She spoke for a while about lab politics, but Zachary seemed bored.

"And your architect husband, is he all you dreamed of?" he asked.

"Zachary, what an odd question."

"Not at all. When old friends get together, isn't that what's usually asked?" He got up and returned with another beer.

"The kids fell asleep on mats downstairs. Let's let them nap while we talk." He resumed his position on the sofa. "You're lucky to be having another child. I wish we were. Cassie didn't even want the one we had. Can you believe it? Vanessa was an accident before we were married. I swore to her that I would take most of the responsibilities if she would have the baby and marry me. I thought in time she would get used to the idea of a family. She does love Vanessa, in her own way, but her career comes first."

He stared at his hands, clutching the beer bottle.

"I shouldn't say this," he said after a long silence, "but back in high school, I had this mad crush on you."

Jane stared at him. She felt lightheaded and was afraid the dreaded nausea would return.

"You know that's not true. Wouldn't I have known?"

"No, it was a secret. I used to fantasize about you all the time."

"Stop it. You're making this up." Jane took a deep breath and continued. "You used to have a girlfriend, the one you took to the prom."

He put down the bottle and reached across the back of the sofa and touched her shoulder.

"You know, I can't even remember her name. Funny… considering."

"Considering?"

"I was an eighteen year old boy and horny as hell. All I could think about was scoring. That girl had been around the block a few times and she liked me. I didn't want to go away to college without experience."

"And did you…score?" Jane felt as though she were on a boat in rocky seas.

"God, yes! In Thompson's field—remember, the one by the school? We missed the PTA breakfast."

"And you don't remember her name." Jane got up from the sofa. "I should get Daphne and go."

She walked down the hallway and saw a door that looked like it might lead to the basement. Zachary was behind her. He grabbed her shoulders and pinned her to the wall. His mouth was inches from hers. She could feel his hardness pressing into her.

"You always had a thing for me, Janey. Don't think I don't know it. We have a chance now, to go back, to do it over."

A predator. She could see that. And yet, all she had to do was reach down, unbutton his jeans, and lift up her skirt. The years of yearning would be over. It was *the* moment—now or never again.

She put her hands on his shoulders, looked into his fiery eyes, and gently pushed him away. She still wanted him; oh yes, dear God, she did. Maybe more than ever. But now it wasn't enough.

"I never cared for you that way," she said. "I'm sorry you thought otherwise. I was just being friendly."

They stared at each other. Her words gave her power. This was the payback for all those years. She could not drop her gaze.

Then she heard footsteps and a door opening. A small figure appeared in the hallway. Daphne had sleepy eyes, but a great toothy grin spread across her face when she saw Jane.

"Ready, honey?" Jane said.

"Are we still going to the movies?" she asked.

"It's a date."

They left the house and walked to the car. Daphne was bubbling over with chatter. Jane wondered if Zachary was standing in the doorway, watching them. She wanted to turn around, but she didn't.

WOUNDEDNESS

Nick Ostdick

It's those damn cicadas chirping away, turned up loud in the tall roadside grass and echoing off into the star-filled sky. They keep at it, keep yakking, whether I'm home or out for a walk like tonight. I'm heading into town to see a movie, hoofing it from my apartment on the very outskirts to the old movie house on the main drag, a real busted up kind of place with a faded ready-to-crumble facade and a bulb-less marquee with letters that never seem to stick; sometimes if the wind is right, you can look down on the sidewalk and find all the letters and piece together the titles of the films, moving the plastic squares with your foot, creating your own words, your own stories. It's a dump, always has been, even when I was young and came here to try and get laid. They're jumping good tonight though, the cicadas, sticking to my pant legs in between strides and then bounding off with each of my steps. It's not that I don't like them, in fact I find their small choir to be quite consoling on a sticky summer evening like this, the air pricked with stale moisture as if God's wringing out a gym sock. It's that they're massive in these parts, about as long as your index finger and fat, and they blend with tree bark and sometimes, if the year is right and you look closely enough, you can see entire tree trunks slowly moving, shuffling up and down, blanketed in the damn things.

Andy and I used to beat them off each other after a day's worth of playing in the field across from my house. We'd take turns swiping a stick down the length of each other's leg or arm, clearing them away. In the summertime, Andy would die. He said he was preparing himself, not to die necessarily, but for the life of an army man. Most often I'd be the one to do it, the one to deliver the fatal blow, humoring him just so we could ride our Schwins into town to see Andy's older brother at the auto shop where he would sneak us cigarettes, so then we could chase girls and look cool, our eyes thick with smoke. Andy was a late bloomer, never really that concerned with girls, and we were too old to play solider by then, but it was as if Andy's imagination was stuck in a loop. I kept up with it because of loyalty, because of years of prior friendship and aside from this it was easy hanging with him, even though I would pray for no one I knew to drive by and see us, especially a girl, especially one of the movie-house girls who let you grope them. God was on my side back then. He was listening. We were never spotted.

"Kill me," Andy would holler across the field, a good hundred yards off, a maple branch held longways at his chest as a rifle, smooth stones from the pond as grenades drooping his pockets. "Kill me already." We'd have spent the hot afternoon crawling on our bellies through cattails, our shadows long in the dirt, searching out snipers and securing hills and taking bridges. We'd have been at this all day, since sunup burned off the fog, and all through the heat, sweat rolling off our cheeks.

"Let's see a flick," I'd shout back. "Take in some A/C."

Catching a flick meant chatting up the movie-house girls. We both knew that. That's half the reason I'd make the mile walk into town, down the hill and into the valley, through dirt farm roads and onto Main Street. Girls like

Chrissy Jones or Valerie DeMarko would let you sit next to them in the theater and as soon as the lights went down and the sound funneled up, you could just reach over and touch them and they wouldn't tell you to stop. It had to be dark, that was the only rule. You just did it, just held your hand against their breasts like you could, like you should, and by the middle of whatever B movie was playing, you'd have your hand snaked under her dress and between her legs. Except there was this one time when Bobbi Flick, all chopped black hair and faded blue jeans and barely enough to grab onto, slapped my hand away as the coming attractions flashed by. She wasn't a usual movie-house girl, in fact I had never seen her there before. She wasn't friends with Chrissy or Valerie. She was just sitting near them, near me, and I didn't take no for an answer and snatched her breast in my hand so hard she squealed as if something had bitten her. She never stopped me again. She let me go all the way with her a few weeks later, and I took her to prom. After our boy came along and we had to get hitched, she kissed with more teeth than tongue.

"C'mon," Andy would grumble. "Do it, then we'll go."

"Fine," I'd say, and raise my baseball bat bazooka onto my shoulder and fire, and Andy would make as if the shell landed right near him, throwing himself up into the air and then down on his side, writhing, crying out loud and shrill. I'd rush over to him. He'd be lying still, holding his breath, not blinking, spit glistening against his chin, bits of grass sticking in his brown crewcut. His commitment was king. He wanted everything to be real. His face was like one of my mother's porcelain dolls: steady, dark eyes and awkwardly parted lips. Most of the time I just let him play it out, just lie there until some amount of time passed that he deemed appropriate, but once I nudged him in the the side with my foot.

"Get up," I said.

He didn't move.

"Hey weirdo," I said, giving him another tap. "Get up."

"Stop," he shouted, eyelids shooting open. "I'm dead. Show some respect."

Years later when I took a job at the feed store in town, Andy would call me once in a while from the desert on the army's dime. He went in right after high school, making good on his childhood. He was a private first-class and drove tanks and had been over there for nearly two years stationed at the foot of a small mountain range that sliced right through the heart of the action. He'd ask after Bobbi and our son and I'd dodge those questions because why unburden your marital issues on someone who lives in a place where bullets buzz like flies in the air. Besides, there wasn't much to tell. Sometimes Bobbi got lippy with me and I'd take care of that. Sometimes she'd be a pain in the ass, nagging. Sometimes we'd fight, scream, cuss. Sometimes, after we put our boy down for the night, we'd sit out on the porch with a bottle of whiskey and watch the stars pop into view and she'd sit on my lap with her head against my chest and I'd palm her kneecap, holding my hand over her bare skin, and we wouldn't clutter everything up with a lot of talk. We'd just be there, together, quiet and calm, like how I thought normal couples did. Like we were actually in love, or at least something terribly close. Once she lifted her head from my chest and whispered, "Your heart doesn't sound nearly as angry as you act," and I hefted a good laugh, replying, "Or maybe it sounds too angry for you to take," wondering why she had to speak, why she felt the need to ruin everything.

So I'd tell Andy we were fine and our boy was fine, getting big, starting to take after his old man, and then I'd make him tell me about what it was like over there. His duties. The weather. The terrain. The women he'd go around with.

"No smooth beavers here," he'd say. "That's for sure."

"Panty-fros?" I'd ask.

"Oh man, a country without razors."

"You keep 'em in line?"

"They know who's saving their asses. They're grateful."

We'd talk about home. He'd want to know the gossip: who was pregnant and who was dying, who left town and who came back.

"When this hitch is up," he said once, "I'm coming back for a while. I miss it."

"Dumbest thing I heard all day," I said. "Nobody misses it here."

The line went fuzzy. His voice was diminished in a sea of static. It felt like he was yelling just to get the words in clear: "You've never left. You can't understand."

Then there was the night Bobbi split. We'd gotten into it, her and I, and it got a bit rougher than usual, her lip-munching and my temper. I'd only ever hit one other girl in my life, I swear, and that was my cousin Ruth when she fished a dead frog from a pond during a family reunion one year and tossed it at me, nailing me right in the forehead. I didn't hit her hard then, just a little slap across the face, mostly fingers, very little palm. It was a frog-slap, the one I gave Bobbi, nothing too serious, when she called me a name I can't remember now. But one night after I fell asleep on the couch she snatched the station wagon and our son and took off beneath a real blue moon as if it was lighting her way out. Andy called a few hours after Bobbi'd gone, woke me up from a good boozy sleep, the house cool and airy, moonlight breaking in through open windows. There was this great tremble in his voice, a shake I could feel through the line.

"I can't believe you haven't got the time difference down yet," I said, my throat in my mouth.

"I know damn well what time it is," he said. "Just figured I'd call anyway."

We talked for a good hour and ended up reminiscing about the games we played as kids. About the empty field across from my house. The burrs that stuck your pants and pricked when you pulled them off. I kept him on the line longer than even he wanted, staving off a suddenly quiet apartment, the lack of sound menacing, as if it was going to swallow me up during the night. I reminded him how he'd fake woundedness, how he took it so damn seriously, how foolish it all was, just to make myself feel better.

"You'd pretend to die," I said. "That's twisted."

"I remember," he said, his voice pinched. "I just hope I didn't waste all my lives."

"Some cats got more than nine," I said.

He chuckled. "Here's hoping."

There was a pause. I could hear muffled voices on his end. I'm sure he could hear nothing on mine.

"So Bobbi left," I said.

"When she coming back?"

"No, no, she left. Like left left."

"For good?"

"I think so."

"You surprised?" he asked.

"Thanks," I said quickly.

"Sorry. You OK?"

I didn't say anything. A heavy quiet settled between us. Looking back I couldn't have been surprised, but right then, hot rubber from Bobbi's tires still burned into the street, the scent still holding in the air, I was shocked. And angry. And alone. And I didn't need to hear it from him, especially on the phone, thousands of miles away. Fuck him. I let the line crackle. I wrapped the cord around my finger a few times.

"You there?" he said. "Hello?"

A few pops of static and then the call went dead. I don't know what happened. I don't know if he hung up or if we were cut off, but that was the last time I heard from him. He stopped calling, stopped writing. We never got things right between us. I started going back to that movie theater after that, hiking into town by the side of the main road, the stars blinking on. I hadn't been there in years, since before our son was born. When the theater lights went down, I breathed deep and drank in the soft glow, and in the darkness I pressed the heels of my boots hard into the sticky floors, the urge to grab and hold filling me from the bottom up.

These days I have trouble sleeping. It's the heat. It's thick. Summer comes through bright and hot, and at night the moon smolders like a piece of charcoal. I'm sure the dream doesn't help either and sometimes I wonder where Bobbi's got to. I think of her often, I do, but once and a while when I grab a snooze, sometimes I dream of Andy. I dream we're young again and playing in the windblown field and he's standing a good distance away, arms held out, hollering "Kill me," and I'm chuckling at him and trying to coax him into a movie, and then the field goes dark and fiery and the land is pockmarked with jagged bomb-craters and we're in the middle of a vast expanse of desert like the surface of Mars, so I raise a Louisville Slugger onto my shoulder and tell him I'm not kidding this time, and Andy just stands there still begging for it, so I make rocket noises with my mouth as I fire and Andy is hit, pumped so full of hot metal he explodes, a brilliant flash and then nothing but a wisp of smoke curling upwards, choking my lungs as I breathe him in. That's when I wake, cold and damp and sucking on my bottom lip. I have a drink, a smoke, blow it out through a cracked window near my bed, and remind myself that's not how it actually happened, that it wasn't my fault, that an IED is how he went.

But after I calm myself, maybe sit out on the front porch and close my eyes, the scent of fresh dew resting heavy in the air and the crackling sounds of night filling in the quiet, I know that if I could talk to him he'd probably have no regrets, and I then find myself thinking about Bobbi. Like tonight, shuffling along, the glow of town resting just on the horizon, checking my watch with certainty that I'll miss the coming attractions, maybe even the first few minutes of whatever film is playing. Because I'm sure she has regrets; I know I do. And I'm sure she never looks back. I'm sure she doesn't tell our boy about me and probably won't, even if he asks. I'm sure she'll just tell him I'm a bad man, someone God gave up on, hoping to dispatch his curiosity quickly and with authority—I wouldn't be able to argue either, at least with the part about God. I'm sure she's got some new beau, a real gentle, kind motherfucker, although sometimes when I picture him, the guy she's taken up with, I imagine he has my blue eyes, and that that's the feature Bobbi is most struck by, perhaps even the whole reason she loves him, even though she can't quite put a finger as to why. And I'm sure the wink of the pretty young girl who will take my ticket will bring a stab of happiness into my chest as, for a moment, I won't feel so lonely, like a fool who knots the present with the past, confusing the two, losing touch. And I'm sure later in the night when someone asks me how I'm doing just in passing, just to be polite, maybe a bartender at Sam's Tavern or the pimply kid working the drive-thru at Hardy's, I'll say, "I'm just fine," and for a second I'm sure I'll believe it.

THE RULES OF DIFFUSION

Derek Tellier

Why'd You Take Off?

It was January, dark. City-light surrounded the Minneapolis skyline like a dim atmosphere. On the shore of Lake Minnetonka, sailboats rested in marina-hoists; million dollar homes hid in the trees. On the lake's frozen surface, two pick-ups sat near an icehouse—a portable shanty for fishing. Garrett and I heard the hum of their space heater, fifty yards away where we were standing with our hands on our hips, staring at his Dodge Avenger. Its back tires had fallen through the ice.

I shoved my hands against the front of the car and told Garrett to give me a hand. We pushed. Nothing. I stomped on the ice. It felt pretty solid. "Garrett," I said. "Start it."

The car wouldn't start. He got out and gave me this Samantha-will-divorce-me-and-you're-on-probation-for-DWI look. We were both wasted.

"We'll lift it," I said.

"They got a truck over there." He pointed. "Let's ask for a tow."

Garrett shook his head and frowned. We kneeled. There couldn't have been a centimeter between the back bumper and the ice, but we got our fingers wedged under and

struggled our asses off. The ice started cracking, so I bailed.
I looked back. Garrett was still trying.

I ran back and shoved him away. As we slid to safety,
we heard ice give and water lap at the car's guts. Garrett's
Dodge floated for a second before sinking. You could hear
water gush into all of its crevices.

Someone came out of the icehouse: "Hey!"

We ran off.

"I'm calling the police!" they yelled.

"Samantha'll divorce me," Garrett said.

"We'll say it was stolen."

"It won't fucking matter!"

Can You Say Ankle Monitor?

It was there, transmitting my whereabouts to the police,
bulging at the foot of my pants, as I stared at our blank TV.

It was there, in bed, when my wife, Twiggy, would run
her soft leg against mine, and I would turn away because
Samantha had left Garrett.

It was there, when I almost tire-ironed it, when I was
stuck in traffic on the commute after being fired. Someone
had found my police report online and showed it to my boss.

It was there even when it was gone. On job applications,
where it says: *Have you ever been convicted of a felony or a gross
misdemeanor?*

It was there, even when it wasn't, wrapped around
my ankle, under our spare blankets, as I slept on the air-
mattress, out in the garage. Twiggy's orders.

And yes, it was there, as I sipped Old Crow and Mountain
Dew, e-mailing my resume to Intech of LuVerne. Iowa.

Intech of LuVerne?

By the end of the twentieth century, so many farmers and
small business owners had gone under that rage and

crystal meth threatened to become Iowa's main commodities. Democrats dominated the legislature, so the solution was simple, "let's provide," and thus, Intech, a cable, telephone and internet services provider that received a state grant if they set up shop in LuVerne. At the time, three thousand people lived in the town and twenty thousand lived within an hour's commute; but, Intech stormed into north central Iowa so fast they couldn't find as many qualified tekkies as they needed. They checked my criminal record and weren't mortified, which is understandable, I only have one DWI and a violated probation.

Intech started first, second and third shifts and caused a blitz of gentrification. Two new gas stations, a Best Western and a Wal-Mart came to town. Not just any 'ol Wal-Mart either, The Wal-Mart Of All Wal-Marts, complete with a grocery store and an auto-service center. However, all these amenities were located on LuVerne's affluent South Side.

If you enter town from the north, like Twiggy and I did for the first time, you'll go past a cat litter plant, an implement that's been closed for Christ knows how long, and a drag strip with no grandstand. And just when you start thinking, *If I drove through here during a funeral procession, the hearse would probably break down,* you go down a hill and you're staring up at a giant cow's ass. Yes, a giant cow's ass. Years ago, Hardees set the record for people served in one hour via the drive-through. Their prize: a statue of a giant cow, which they placed ass-to-the-road.

When I interviewed at Intech, Twiggy rode along. We stopped at Hardees to get an order of curly fries. They were closed. A Post-it note read: *Manager Out Of Town.* As we were leaving, I apparently nudged the nose of the car too far into the road. A guy on a motorcycle—it was forty degrees and windy—swerved into the other lane like it was a matter of life and death. He flipped me off and yelled, "Fuck you!"

Those were the first words said to us.

How Did You Survive?

Rock 107 The Power Loon: Brenda Gandell in the mornings. I listened every day, in my car, in my office. She'd belch and fart, better than most men, and she'd throw out more sexual innuendos than Aerosmith, funny as hell. But it was the kind of funny where you wondered if there might be some truth lurking behind it. I never cared to find out until I saw her broadcasting one Saturday from The Bar & Grill. She was a little on the chunky side, not fat, but voluptuous. Bleach-blonde hair flowed down to her breasts. The Bar & Grill had hired her to promote their flag football tournament and their new fried goose nuggets. She did an on-air interview with The Great Goose Nugget Chef, smiling as though they were getting married, shifting back and forth and tossing her hair off her shoulders as if she had rehearsed.

Twiggy waited tables at The Bar & Grill and had convinced me to shuttle drunks back and forth between the bar and the football field. Between trips, I sat in a booth and drank coffee while trying to check my e-mail, but as soon as I would log on, I would get a call from my boss. "Just reboot," I'd say. "Iris, it isn't a big deal. I promise." I had to be patient. She had an ankle bracelet card she could play if any more-desirable applicants applied.

And of course, I had to keep checking the college football game on the big screen. I love watching football. It totally screws with my head.

Psst, Why's It Screw With Your Head?

I've always felt like the best of life is passing me by, and nothing I've done to remedy this has worked, i.e. joy riding on a frozen lake. In high school, I played football, did some speech—always part of a supporting cast. When I went to college, I went to be the motherfucker-of-all-men, a champion with hyperbolic milestones I could flash on a scoreboard: evidence of my victories. I discovered a quest and embarked, possessed no tools but continued. I walked-on at strong safety for the Minnesota State Mavericks.

Assistant Coach Jamison, and he insisted on being called that, was twenty-seven when I was a freshmen. He used to sit in the training room and give words of encouragement. "Lived in an apartment nicknamed 'The Apollo,'" he'd say. "It was always showtime. Girls dancing on tables, you name it."

We won four games in three years. No one came to the team's parties.

The players hated my guts. I was an idiot walk-on, the psycho special teams guy, thumping myself on the helmet before I ran down and over-pursued the ball carrier. Assistant Coach Jamison told me to chill out, and it wasn't just in regards to football. "Jason man, you're trying way too hard. Have some fun."

My senior year—Bam! Scholarship opportunity. Spent the summer at home, worked out three times a day, went to bed early, rose at the butt-crack of dawn, ran, more so for the mental endurance than for the physical. I figured if there were sophomores-gone-pro in the NFL, the least I could do was put the Maverick defense on my back. That summer, Damien Townsend, strong safety for the Minnesota Golden Gophers, beat up his girlfriend, got suspended and transferred to Minnesota State. He beat me out as the starter. I broke my leg after four games and lost my spot on special teams. We finished 3-8.

Whoa, Get Back To That Brenda Chick Why Don't You?

Brenda shut off her broadcasting equipment and sat down with a guy I'd shuttled. His tan was incredible, total construction worker. His hairline came down like a wolfman's; in back, his hair hung low enough to blow in the wind when he rode his Harley.

Brenda laughed and waved, and she was "on the air" even when she wasn't. I wanted to be that person. If nothing else, I wanted to be around her, someone living in the moment. My office responsibilities, for the time being, had been taken care of. What did I have to lose? Twiggy and I had no friends. We were trying to start fresh. Before moving to LuVerne, she had dreadlocked her hair like a warrior princess: "The Iowans we encounter might be hostile," she had said, giving me a hug. "I'm going to be excited," she added. I could tell she was lying. She had funked-out her hair to hold on to who she was, to let LuVerne know that she was Twiggy, like it or not. And judging by the glances, LuVerne liked her just fine. A couple of braids hung along her face. She wore a Vikings jersey knotted at the stomach, had painted her nails purple, was hustling to refill beers. If we could make friends, this place could be home. I saw Brenda waving a cigarette. Harley Hair smiled. I got up.

"I'm Jason," I said to them.

"Hi," said Brenda. Her and Harley Hair looked at me like, who in the hell are you?

"I've been meaning to e-mail a joke to your show, but since you're here... How come rednecks like to do it doggy-style?"

"Why?"

"So they can both watch NASCAR."

Brenda put her hand over her face and laughed. She said it was true. Harley Hair shook his head. "I'm telling that at work," he said, thrusting forward his hand. "I'm Steve Gandell, you need a beer?"

"I gotta van more drunks to the field."

"Nope. Nope. Nope," he said. "I'm buying you a beer."

Brenda dug through her purse and said she'd go get me one. Steve waited for her to reach a safe distance. "We should have let that cutie in the Vikings jersey bring it."

"That's my wife," I said, pulling up a chair.

Steve raised his eyebrows. "Damn, nice job."

I wanted to tell him the same thing, but my phone rang. "No, Iris. I promise. Just re-boot the system. Nothing bad will happen." Steve smiled and rolled his eyes. I hung up.

"You do computer nerdology for Intech?" he asked. I admitted that I did. He said, "People were sure griping about that place, but jeez. Look at this bar. A year ago, you think they were having a football tournament?"

Brenda came back and handed me a beer. Her hair smelled of apple conditioner, soft and blonde, so different than Twiggy's. "Have any more jokes?" she asked.

"No, but if you tell me what's up with the Hardees cow, I'll think of one."

"That's from the drive-through competition," she laughed. "I was there broadcasting. It was terrible."

"Do they need to place it ass-to-the-road? It was the first thing we saw in this town."

Steve pointed out Twiggy. "That's his wife," he said.

Brenda raised her eyebrows. She gave me a once-over. "What's her name?"

"Twiggy."

"Twiggy?" they both said. These Gandells were laughers.

"Her name's Michelle, but yeah, call her Twiggy."

Brenda put her fingers to her mouth and whistled. "Twiggy!"

She came over. There was small talk, but all I could think about was getting sloshed with Brenda and Steve, sitting there all afternoon and saying to hell with my responsibilities. I wanted to yuck it up, keep an eye on the football scores, and then... Yup, Iris called.

When I was done driving, Brenda snatched me out of my booth and herded me over to the table where Steve and their friends were devouring goose nuggets. Twiggy came over and watched me smother a nugget in ranch sauce. I had eaten gas station chicken that was more flavorful, but I pretended the nuggets were great. Steve revealed secrets:

the shocking inside story of his tan and Brenda's bleach-blonde hair—they water-ski. In the summer, Saturday was Adult Day. They piled in friends, drank, sped out to remote sandbars and grilled. Sundays were for kids, their boys who were five and three. The five year old could already get up on one ski. "Next summer," Brenda said, "you guys'll have to come with us. It's great!"

The bar closed, and the Gandells had Twiggy and I over for omelets. Not two weeks later, we were on a plane to Jamaica to swap partners.

Were There Any Kind of Rules?

The bellboy offered us some weed. Brenda said, "I think we should be sober for this. It's our first time."

On the shuttle, I was checking my voice mail. "Could you please not check that?" she said. "We're on vacation now."

She said we'd shower, eat at the resort's finest restaurant, spend forty-five minutes with our spouses, switch, meet back outside and then adjourn to the piano bar. At the restaurant, she kept right on going. Tomorrow, we'd snorkel. The next: "I want to get absolutely shitty at Jimmy Buffet's Margaritaville."

Twiggy and I returned to our room, opened the patio door, and I must say, the view really was stunning. The sun was going down, casting orange and pink light across the Caribbean. Barefoot lovers strolled up the beach. Some sat in oceanside gazebos and held each other. One couple bargained with a vendor who had paddled up in a kayak loaded with hemp necklaces and woodcarvings of Bob Marley. A bonfire burned out on the island of Kokomo. Steel drums played in the distance. There was beauty everywhere and all I could do was think of Brenda: *Could you please not check that? We're on vacation now.*

I snapped a picture of Twiggy pouring a shot of rum. She tossed it back and grimaced, got a picture of that too.

"We're supposed to stay sober," I said, kicking off my shoes and lying down. The sheets were cold from the air conditioning.

"Brenda's just nervous."

"Are you?"

She nodded, set her drink on the nightstand and put her arms around me. We kissed, took off each other's clothes. Why I didn't carry her out to the beach and let the waves roll up on us, I'll never know. I should have at least thanked her. She didn't want to swap, even though she had said that she did. She was only along because I was hopeless, charming as hell, but hopeless. She probably figured if I could swap partners, I'd consider myself the motherfucker-of-all-men and move on with my life. I think she thought I was the best she could do—if she embarked on this adventure I'd be indebted; she could then turn me into the better someone she needed. It was almost surreal. She ran her nails up my back, cupped my head and nudged my face into her neck. She led me down, between her breasts. Her nails tickled the top of my head.

I went to slip it in, but she said no. "Save it for Brenda."

Out on the sidewalk, Steve stared at a peacock. It strutted through our section of bungalows. "Well," I said, "what do you think?"

Steve shrugged and raised his eyebrows. I nodded.

Brenda wore a black nightie and sat waiting for me on the edge of the bed. Her legs were crossed. *Could you please not check that? We're on vacation now.* She got up, took off my shirt, undid my belt, pushed me down on the floor and pulled my pants off. I was lying there in my socks and boxers watching her shut off my cell phone and throw it in a chair. She found some reggae on the radio and started tossing her blonde hair around and rubbing a bottle of rum down her neck. Chunky or not, she was sexy as a model. She dropped her nightie and crawled on top of me.

She smacked the back of my head and pulled my lips toward hers. Our mouths were together for less than a millisecond. I turned her over, kissed my way down her neck to her nipples. They were covered in apple lotion. I couldn't help it. I licked and bit down. She dug her nails into my back. I sat up. Then, she started sucking my tits, and I have to admit, it felt pretty fucking good. She made her way down, yanked my dick through the hole of my boxers and gave me head that way. She hopped on. I was in my socks and boxers, thrusting to poke her head through the ceiling, and...

We rolled over. I hung in. She didn't seem upset. She pressed against my ass. I stopped.

"That's why I wanted you and Michelle to do it first." Brenda put her panties on, sat crossed-legged in a chair and poured a drink. She had great curves, nice and soft, nothing out of proportion, except maybe her breasts, which were out of proportion in a good way.

I stretched out on the floor and felt like a failure. Steve was primed and probably long-hauling Twiggy. Brenda belched, let it rumble and smiled. "You think we'll ever think of ourselves as grown ups?" she said.

"Probably not."

"I used to think I would when I had kids."

"Me too." I saw Brenda's confusion. "Twiggy can't have kids."

"You'd be great parents."

I have no idea what she was basing that on; Twiggy and I would have been terrible parents. I sat up. "I'm sorry about this," I said. "We fly all the way to Jamaica and this is what you get." I wiggled my toe inside my sock.

"The expectations are impossible," she said. "I was a bitch earlier. It's weird. Having gone through with this, I feel crappy."

"Thanks."

Brenda slapped her knee, threw her head back and scrunched her face into laughter, but no laughter came out. "I didn't mean that," she said. "I feel guilty. There's no reason to. We're all consenting… Whoa, I almost called us adults."

"What's it take to get in that mindset," I asked, "cancer? Is there a certain amount of money that makes you start thinking you're an adult?" I got up.

"Youth is practically worshipped," she said. "What's our problem? Why are we ashamed of acting young?"

"We're not young. We're immature."

"You're a clown."

"Just relax." I walked behind her, told her to shut her eyes and started massaging her temples. She asked me what I was doing. "Shhh," I said.

Lightly, I ran my fingers in circles on her forehead until she dozed off.

The air's salty crisp smell. Night lamps illuminated the vines and the thatched roofs. Steve and Twiggy stood on the walkway with their arms crossed and their heads tilted. We listened to the waves, the echoes of the steel drums, the air conditioners. I put my arm around Twiggy and kissed her hair. Steve hugged Brenda. He asked how it was. Brenda looked at me. I took a deep breath, and why I said this, I have no fucking idea, but I said that we couldn't go through with it.

"Oh bullshit," Steve said. Brenda looked him in the eyes and said that we couldn't. She was keen. At first, I thought she was going along with my joke, but then I started wondering if what we had done could actually be called sex. It hadn't lasted very long. Maybe Brenda wasn't counting it.

Twiggy spun around. "We just couldn't go through with it," I told her. "We hung out."

"Fucking incredible," Steve said. "We couldn't do it either."

Twiggy nestled in behind me, rested her chin on my shoulder. She hugged me as tightly as she could, wrapped her arms around my waist and lifted me off balance. I looked over at Brenda. She wanted me to keep my mouth shut, I could tell. Her eyes were popping out of her skull. I let Twiggy shuffle me around. She was excited. In Jamaica, they have these little newts that run around on the buildings at night. We watched them. There were a few moments of weirdness, but then we all agreed we should probably adjourn to the piano bar.

Brenda caught me at the men's room door, put her hand on my chest. "That answer was perfect," she said. "If they didn't do it, we can't let them know that we did."

"Did we actually do it?"

"Shut up. It wasn't that bad."

When Brenda returned to the table, Steve was talking about how relieved he was that no one had done it. Brenda chimed in, "Why did you two want to swap? You seem great together."

I knew this was coming. The subject had come up twelve thousand times. Brenda had insisted, though, that it would be fun to tell such things at the piano bar. Fine, but was she serious? Was this a ploy to make it look like we hadn't had sex? She leaned over the table. I scrunched up my brow to think, and out of the corner of my eye, I could see her breasts. She knew it. She wanted me to see. She laughed and wiggled her shoulders. Steve sat beside her, still in shock. I said that we wanted to swap to keep things fresh. Living in Iowa wasn't going to work if we had to live like Iowans, no offense. It was more of a matter of not growing up, not going to the bathroom with the door open like a couple of old married people. Steve laughed: guilty.

Brenda was intent on showing me her tits. She leaned over the table so far I could practically smell the apples. The sex hadn't been good. The only thing was, she must have enjoyed being the dominant figure. I looked at Steve. He sat there with a shit eating grin, puffing on a smoke. Soft light reflected on his tan skin, that triangle of hair combed forward like a wolfman's. He must nail Brenda's socks off, probably nailed Twiggy's off too. He was awfully damned adamant about his relief.

The piano player began playing The Police's "I'll Be Watching You." I pointed at the guy in disgust.

"Jason hates The Police." Twiggy laughed and rolled her eyes. "He had to wear an ankle monitor for house arrest." She reached over and squeezed my knee. "He has a thing with people keeping track of him. He's the motherfucker-of-all-men."

Steve laughed and raised his drink. "To the motherfucker-of-all-men," he said. "Let's change Brenda's schedule and go to Jimmy Buffet's tomorrow, get absolutely shitty, and then go snorkeling the next day." We all toasted and agreed. Brenda shifted back in her seat and cancelled my view of her tits. She didn't say one word about the schedule change or the swapping or anything.

To celebrate our return, Twiggy ordered portabella mushrooms from Wal-Mart and got kalamata olives delivered via U.P.S. She wanted to feed the Gandells something crazy. She cut off all of her warrior-princess hair and was more or less going with a buzz-cut. She looked cute, but boyishly so. Her nails were still purple. Around the house, she'd wear army pants that sagged half-way down her hips. Her thong would show. Her t-shirt would end at her mid-riff. These clothes were normal, and I usually enjoy that kind of scenery, but with her boyish hair, it was weird.

Steve and Brenda brought over a case of Bud Light. I went out to the garage refrigerator for an ice bucket. Brenda came out with the beer. She took my hand, led me to a corner, grabbed my cock and pulled my head to her mouth. We kissed. She turned away, smiling. That was our little secret. We ate, got drunk and played Taboo.

Who Got Honked The Most?

Garrett—you remember Garrett, the guy who got divorced because his car sank—had been living in an apartment. He had been renting a storage unit for all of his tools, and then one day, he called and said he was getting rid of them. He was sick of renting the storage space. Why he was sick of it, I don't know. I wasn't really listening. I liked the guy, but he was there when I violated my probation. It wasn't his fault, but just hearing his voice made me feel crappy. It was like he had stirred up a big tornado and shit me out in Iowa. I put him on speaker phone so Twiggy could chime in and I wouldn't have to. He offered us his tools, for free. I didn't want them, but Twiggy started salivating. Tools became her new thing.

She made me go with her to the Home Depot grand opening to pick out a new leaf blower. I didn't want one. When our yard needed raking, I would just rake it—raking was good exercise—but Twiggy said we could also use a leaf blower to clean our gutters. When our gutters needed cleaning, I would just take a bucket up on the roof and scoop out the gunk—cleaning gutters wasn't bad exercise either—but Twiggy finally said, "If you can athlete all these things done, then why don't you?"

Later, when I was out in the garage mixing oil and gas for the new leaf blower, I started wondering if that was the space I had been relegated to, the garage. For many men, the garage was a refuge. I had never seen it as anything other than a storage space, but Twiggy's dad spent every free moment in his. He'd fire up his leaf blower once a week and blow out his garage whether it needed it or not. I think that was Twiggy's idea of a mature man. She figured if she could get some tools in my hands then I'd grow up. It didn't matter that Garrett had an entire storage unit full of tools and he was as immature as I was. I started getting pissed off. Had Twiggy ever considered the possibility that her father spent his time in his garage to escape from her and her mother? I kicked the leaf blower out of the way and marched inside.

Twiggy slept in a chair with a blanket over her. The leaf blower instructions were spread out on her chest.

I went to the Bar & Grill to make a waitress love me. I was going to leave the country and play football in Europe. If there had been ice, I would have driven on it and fallen right through. I felt like a woman, oppressed by family and home. It was ridiculous. My phone rang. "Iris, god damn it!"

Nothing seemed more important than becoming Steve. He had two boys. He worked construction. I seriously doubt that he had any issues with his tools. Steve lived wildly and still had morals—water-skiing, partying at Jimmy Buffet's, choosing not to mess around on his wife, even when it was okay. I should have grilled the man a steak. It would have been an honor.

Brenda had been foolish to swap him out. She'd been inspired by some swingers she'd met at a biker rally, but still, what kind of crap was going through her and Steve's heads when they decided that swapping was a good idea?

I swear, the lies people tell are amazing. I had told a police officer that Garrett's car had been stolen when it had really fallen through the ice. It was his only hope with Samantha who divorced him anyway. In Jamaica, in lieu of my poor performance, I had lied to protect myself. If I could crack the first joke, I could diffuse the situation. I could make it sound like I wasn't as embarrassed as I was. Brenda's reasons for playing along with my lie were probably similar. Lying was her only...

Maybe Steve wasn't the hero I thought he was. Maybe he had been unfaithful and Brenda wanted to swap to diffuse *her* situation, to relieve some of *her* embarrassment. It fit. Steve had to prove his commitment, and thus, he couldn't sleep with Twiggy, even though it was permissible.

I was the motherfucker-of-all-detectives, racing to Steve and Brenda's, drinking and driving, wanting to tell Brenda what I knew. I wanted to sit with her on the couch and watch the kids play, but when I got there, Steve was in my spot. I couldn't pull in. My scenarios were all false. I wasn't going to try and mess these two up. They were just living their lives, the best they knew how.

EXQUISITE RESTRAINT

Nicki Gill

It was a Saturday. They had just returned from the ultrasound, where they'd seen their child on the monitor, startlingly human shaped, its jaw working as it sucked its thumb. A tiny stranger.

They'd been given a copy of the scan, and Dante put it on as soon as they got home. Jonesy made sandwiches, and brought them to the couch, so they could eat together and watch. Absently, she took her husband's hand and laid it on her belly. "We're your people, little one," she told the screen. He drummed his fingers on her stomach.

After a few minutes, she turned to him, some notion of the baby's nasal heredity half-formed in her mind, and was struck by his look of cartoonish transfixion, straining forward in his seat, sandwich poised halfway to his open mouth, whole in his hand. "Feast your eyes," she wanted to say, "on our child in formation!" Instead, she laughed out loud. The sound seemed to rouse him. He stood abruptly, took a savage bite of the sandwich, and turned to her. There was resolution in the way he chewed. He strode across the room and turned off the television.

"Hey!" she said.

"I'm addicted to porn," he said, his mouth still full of food. He told her from all the way across the room, disposing of the words, flinging them away in a burning rush. After they left his mouth, he sighed. He still held the sandwich, awkwardly, like when he held her purse. She had the idea it was an incongruous prop.

"Hang on. What?"

"I am addicted to pornography."

She hadn't had a clue. Porn wasn't something they had watched together. He had never even hinted that it was something he would like; but then, it wasn't exactly considered a legitimate part of the marital repertoire for youth pastors like himself.

Although the idea was not intrinsically appealing, she probably would have watched it if he'd asked. The whole thing seemed a bit ridiculous, funny rather than erotic, with those women like caricatures. But everyone knew that men were more straightforward, like grade one maths; one plus one equals two. Seeing such child like simplicity manifest in her husband made her gentle towards him, protective. She patted the couch beside her.

Jonesy crossed the room to her, but refused a seat.

"I think that's fairly normal, hon," she said, and tried to take his hand. He began to pace, so she asked, "Do you have something we could watch together?"

"No baby!" She was shocked at his vehemence. "I would never do that to you."

"But I might want you to," she said, and winked.

Now he sat and faced her front on. "Dante. You don't understand what I'm telling you. I don't just watch porn. I look at it every day. It's a problem. It's all up in my head. I had to have the Internet disconnected at work."

"At work!" A scenario came to her. Her husband, pantsless in his office at the church, member in hand, grimacing at the moment of climax. Reverend Stevenson, bursting into the room and quickly struck silent by the view, ill-equipped in his kindness, cringing at the obtrusiveness of the floorboards creaking under his weight, grappling with the question of how best to go about exiting the room, to back out slowly, or turn and flee? She recognized this was not how it would happen. He would be more furtive, wouldn't stand half-naked amongst the furniture like that. He'd keep it under the desk. That's what she'd do.

"Why are you smiling?" he asked. "It's not funny."

"I'm not smiling. I'm smirking."

"You'd lose a regular office job for less."

"Jonesy, my love, it could be much worse than that, you know." Sometimes, he was alone with one or the other of the youth group kids. Advice in his office, a ride home after church—scenes, weighted for her now with fearful implications, like water-gorged clothes on a man overboard. "You have the care of adolescents. Untrue things might be imputed."

"It's bad," he said. "But that's what I mean. I'm not in control."

"Does anyone know?"

He shook his head. "I don't think so."

She let out her breath. "Okay. Good. Disaster averted."

"For now," he said. He dropped down onto the couch beside her and took her hands in his. She looked into his face—he let her do this, she could tell—and saw a shadow there. Inside her something stirred for him, not butterflies in her stomach but a baby rolling, left to right, top over tail. "Oh, my darling," she said. And then she thought of his closed office door, of the laptop he'd bought her. Of the mornings she'd woken that he'd never come to bed, and she'd found him, asleep on the sofa in his home study. Disparate threads, drawn together.

"You've been hiding this from me."

"Yes."

"For how long?"

"Always."

He's right, she thought. This isn't funny at all.

L ater that day, Dante went into the garden, pushing her swollen feet into her gardening clogs, and picking up her gloves on the way out the laundry door, even though there wasn't much she could do at this stage of proceedings. She'd ordered a load of mulch from the gardening store the week before, had trailed the delivery boy as he wheeled it down the path beside the house, and dumped it where she told him, in the back corner near the fence.

"What do you need that for?" Jonesy asked that night, when he got home from work.

"For the garden," she said.

"That's a lot of dirt."

Now, in the garden, she saw his face again, as he'd looked on the couch with his hands in hers. Personified regret, all open and unpacked. There was real grief there, she'd seen it, and it moved her. But otherwise, she felt a strange emotional remove from what he'd told her. She wondered, did that make her heartless? Maybe she'd be angry later.

The mound had stood untouched since its delivery. All the while she'd struggled to keep herself from it.

They would have to address it, she knew that much. What she didn't know was how to hold him accountable for a whole deep channel of his life that he felt he had to hide. It was like he'd sprouted a new leg, or—no, she thought, not sprouted a new one, but had it all along, tucked into his pants, and somehow she'd failed to notice. What are you meant to do with that?

She understood that active secrets were demanding of their keeper. They required orchestration. She wondered what her husband's secrecy had cost him, whether he'd grown vigilant to the sound of her footsteps, if his heart hit his ribs when she spoke outside his study door.

Now, standing above the mound, she glanced back over her shoulder, even though she knew she was alone. She removed her gloves.

It was very good soil. It made her ravenously hungry.

For the past several weeks, Dante wanted to eat dirt. The craving was strong and physical, like thirst, distracting as the need for the day's first cigarette when she'd been quitting. Daily, she had to stop herself from going into the garden and cramming her mouth with handfuls of the stuff.

She hadn't mentioned it to Jonesy.

Her tastes were strangely particular. She retched at the thought of mud in her mouth, of dust, sucking the moisture from her palate. It was soil she wanted, moist soil, rich and crumbling. When it first started, she trolled the supermarket for a substitute. Dry semolina was the best she could find, grasping in its color and texture some vague echo of the flowerbed. When Jonesy was at church she cooked and ate it by the bowlful. The box she wrapped in a green plastic bag, and kept hidden behind a sack of potatoes in the pantry.

It was nothing, something to do with lack of iron in the blood. She couldn't say exactly why she hadn't told him, but it didn't matter because she'd never do it, would never open up her mouth and fill it from the great mound before her, flower food she'd ordered like a pizza and taken from an awkward teenaged boy in cargo shorts, for folded notes pressed in his earth-dry hand.

The next day, she found herself standing with bare feet on the carpet outside his study door.

She lifted a hand to knock, then changed her mind and let it drop.

Careful to balance her weight, she bent awkwardly, pressing her ear into the door. What was she listening for? She didn't know. She heard nothing, other than the sound of the house, the faintest echo of the world through the door-wood.

With exaggerated slowness, she closed her fist around the knob. Her chest was a drum-roll. She threw the door open, and it flew around its hinges, hitting the rubber door-stop and rebounding with an impotent thud. She paused a second or two, letting the extravagance of the gesture settle, then walked in, striving for casual. Jonesy sat at his desk, cocking an eyebrow above the computer screen.

"What was that?" he said.

She smiled and shrugged, feeling sheepish. "Oh, I don't know," she said, and leaned a shoulder against the wall, appraising him, in a pose that might be coy if not for the enormous boulder throwing her off weight. "Looking at something dirty?" she asked, glancing meaningfully at the computer. She couldn't see the screen.

"Just working on a sermon."

"That's a shame," she said. She went around behind the desk and rested her hands on his shoulders. "Sorry to make light." She leaned her bump against his back, stared absently at the text on his screen. The hunger, which had trailed her all morning, was beginning to gain momentum. She imagined swallowing a mouthful of loam, drawing it down into herself to nourish something good.

"Jonesy. Do you think I'm going to love this baby?"

"Of course you're going to love it." She took a step back, giving him room to swivel his chair around to face her. "You tell me all the time how much you love it already. You loved it when it was just a heartbeat on a screen."

"But it's just an idea. Sometimes I wonder whether it might be easier to love an idea of something than the thing itself, than an actual child in the world."

He was silent for a moment, wearing his thinking face. Then he took her hips in both his hands and kissed her belly. "She's going to love you Marmaduke, don't worry."

"I loved you before I knew you," she said.

"Rubbish. What? Love at first sight?"

"No, that's not what I mean. I mean once we'd started dating, those first weeks and months. It was like you hit me at resonant frequency. The things you said. The blueness of your eyes. It was enough. The real action took place when we were apart. Alone in my bed, that's where it happened. Late at night, after you'd dropped me home."

"And now you know me? Is it harder?"

"Yes. But it's too late. Damage done."

"There you go, then. No need to worry."

"Hmm." She wandered over to the couch across the room, and lay down. He turned his attention back to the computer and began picking at the keys. She studied his face, intent on the screen. "What are you looking at?" she asked.

"Dante. I told you. Sermon?"

"I thought our sex life was good," she said.

Between the time they met, at nineteen, and the day they married, their lust was fuelled by years of frantic but ultimately unsatisfactory dry humping. Then, two months before the wedding, she had gone on the pill, and her libido had vanished, leaving her dry and defective. It seemed to happen in the space of a day. She wondered whether the problem was chemical or psychological. She had been angry, as though she'd been cheated of something.

They couldn't do it on their wedding night, had tried and tried but couldn't get it in. In the morning she lay in his arms and sobbed gently. In the end they deflowered each other incrementally. On the second night of the honeymoon, they got her drunk on champagne, and managed to break her hymen. She'd screamed in pain, thrown him off and run to the bathroom with blood between her legs. It was not until the third night that they managed to work him inside her, slowly and painfully. They just lay there with it inside, not moving around, silent so the elderly owners of the bed and breakfast in the next room wouldn't hear them.

"We're doing it, baby," she whispered, and he smiled, and kissed her.

"We're doing it," he whispered back. They were twenty-two.

His patience had been revelatory. It was only once things got better that he told her how difficult it had been, to feel she didn't want him.

"What do you look at?" she asked now.

"What do you mean?"

"What is it you like? I want you to show me. I need to know what you like."

"I like you," he said, and she rolled her eyes. And that was all he'd tell her.

A day later, while he was at work, she wandered back into his office, not knowing exactly what she wanted. She shut the door, closed the curtains, and sat down at his desk. The computer screen was black. When she shifted the mouse, a document appeared, the sermon he'd been working on the day before. She hit an icon at the bottom of the screen, and a browser subsumed the sermon, the two windows layered like a cake.

She let the arrow hover over the History menu for one heartbeat, two, and clicked on the third. "View All History," she said aloud.

The previous day's record showed a modest list of hits. News, sport, weather. Boring, and the day before—the day of his confession—was the same. But when she clicked the link for three days earlier, the day before the ultrasound, before he told her what he'd told her, a page-long catalog of sites visited sprang onto the screen. She worked through them methodically, one after another. Some were what she expected, naked women, enormous breasts, uniform vaginas, couples having sex. These she understood. But there were others.

There was one site in particular, that he'd come back to again and again, that was difficult to reconcile, a kind of specialty site. The first clip showed a woman, naked on her knees, closed in a standing ring of anonymous, masturbating men, their faces covered by stocking masks. They didn't touch her, but pressed up close around her with their legs spread, shoving themselves in her face. The stance of one, hairless, with thick thighs, made her think of Jonesy using the toilet, the way he leaned back at the waist with his hips thrust forward, rocking slightly on the balls of his feet. This man grabbed the woman's face with one hand, pushed his thumb and forefinger into her mouth and prized her jaw open, folding her lips back over her gums. Dante thought her smile seemed desperate around his fingers, and then he came, and the other men started coming, over her face and in her mouth and down her back and in her hair. They had impeccable timing.

Many of the pictures and clips were variations on the same theme. It wasn't the acts themself, although she found them distasteful. It was that they seemed so far removed from the man she knew, not just in bed, but in the world. She spent hours trolling the site for some refraction of him. She found nothing, and wondered that this was even possible. When she tried to remember what had passed between them on the day he viewed these images, she came up bare.

Then, out of the midst of fatigue, she felt something, a single, responsive pulse in the seat of her pants. She seized on this, focussing on the clip on the screen, on the woman's hips and breasts, on the arch of her back as she lay on the floor, and the thighs and buttocks of the men. She used her hands, reaching around under her belly, badly wanting to understand, to see these things as he saw them, to feel as he felt. But it was no good. Her body would not respond.

Later that day, when the craving came, she ate semolina, with eyes closed, willing satisfaction. She ate past the point of fullness, ate until she was sick in the sink, awkward, leaning forward, aiming over the top of her belly. Heaving, she clasped the taps for balance.

Afterwards, as she caught her breath, she appraised the box of semolina, supremely innocuous on the counter by the stove. She knew that cravings in a pregnant woman were just as banal, a simple sign of what her body needed. But what was happening felt like something more than basic physiology. Scrubbing out the sink, she tried to pin it down. If she had to name it, she'd call it madness, or something close, but that might be too strong, too loaded a designation. All she knew was that it made her act in ways she couldn't explain, split her reason and her will, as though they were two separate entities acting discretely inside her, rather than parts of the same whole. She turned on the cold-water tap and let it run as she stared out the window at the heap of dirt by the fence, which was shooting now, here and there, with green.

It was illogical, to want something so badly that clearly was not to be consumed. That might actually do harm, full of bacteria and who knew what else. She understood this, unequivocally, even as the cravings took her over. And yet. She had taken her credit card from her wallet, and read the numbers over the phone to the garden-shop-man, all for the pleasure and torment of proximity. True, reason allowed her mostly to modify her behaviour; to sit at the kitchen table in the mornings, rather than running into the garden, to eat the toast and drink the tea Jonesy placed in front of her, instead of burying her face in the mulch pile. But reason didn't bear on what she wanted, and in these moments, she was not herself. She wanted it like sex. She thought of nothing else.

That night, she left the semolina out, on the bench by the stove, tentatively hoping that he'd notice it there, that he'd say something. She promised herself that they would talk if he did. She would tell him about the dirt, and that she'd been on his computer. Maybe then he'd be able to share with her about the substance of his struggles, instead of ducking and weaving, shy of any meaningful divulgence beyond his basic confession of addiction.

Later, when he was home from work, he stood at the counter in the kitchen, and uncorked a bottle of wine. Dante watched, intent, as he poured, splayed fingers anchoring the glass just inches from the box of semolina, the juicy suck and dribble of merlot through the bottle's neck magnified to Hitchcockian clock proportions. He took a long sip, replacing the glass once more on the bench beside the box, and it was then that he noticed it. He took it up and read the text on the back, seeming to consider it with the weight of decision. Dante held her breath. Come on! she wanted to shout. Come on, baby! But he put it down, disappeared into the pantry, and emerged with a packet of spaghetti. "My night to cook," he said, and went about pulling ingredients from the fridge.

As they ate, she sat with her back to the stove, and felt the box behind her, a questioning presence in the room. But he said nothing, and with each forkful of food her frustration grew. Clearing the dishes away after the meal she could abide it no longer, and sent the box tipping with a sweeping backhand. The grains spilled out across the counter and over the edge onto the lino, a pasta waterfall.

"You're the one who brought it up," she said.

"Huh?" Jonesy went to the pantry for the dishpan and broom.

"Oh, nothing, Mr. Bubbles."

He blanched. "You can hardly compare it to—" He crouched to the floor and began to sweep up. "I mean, Mr. Bubbles is a freaking paedophile, Dante."

She clapped a hand to her mouth to stifle a giggle. "Sorry, low blow."

"Anyway, I told you, I've stopped that." he said. "I mean, not that I was ever…you know what I mean." He stood, and emptied the contents of the dishpan into the bin. The lid slammed shut.

"Just like that? And suddenly certain things are no longer of interest?"

He sighed, started running water into the kitchen sink, pulling on rubber gloves and dumping plates and glasses into the suds. "I don't know. How do I put this?" His eyes took on the distant look of sight turned inward. "I've killed the guilty act." He spoke slowly, carefully. "But yes. I'm still working on the guilty mind." He snapped out of himself, met her eyes. "I'm sorry." And he was. She could tell.

"Your guilty mind. I'd love a peek at that, a good poke around. Before you expunge it completely. I've lived with it so long. I'd like to get to know it a little bit."

From the look on his face, she might as well have knifed him. She wanted to throw up her hands. Continued cruelty was impossible when he was wounded. She could only manage it in thrusts, in jabs, and then she'd be compelled to comfort him, to make him know she had his back. He blinked at her. "What if I let you see mine?" She spoke quietly now, serious.

"Let me see what? Your guilty mind?"

She nodded.

"Dante. I don't understand what you're saying. Stop being so bloody oblique."

He stood, waiting, and she gathered herself, girding her loins for her little proclamation, on the grounds of which she'd let him sift her soil through his appraising fingers. But she faltered. And then he started to speak, and she had lost her nerve, each word from his mouth stretching safe space between the raft of her confession and the shore. Later, she told herself. Later. Relief was tinged with regret. And then his words themselves took shape in her mind, how long after he'd said them? Seconds? Milliseconds?

"I've cut it out of my life. What more do you want me to do?" That was what he'd said.

"You've cut it out?" She hesitated. "But - you know that that's the smallest thing here, right? What you do with your eyes, with your hands. That's the smallest part of it."

His chin dropped onto his chest and his hands went to his hips, and she thought of football, of a player exhausted at the end of a game. He shook his head and smiled. The smile was bitter, and she knew that she'd lost him, at least for the time being. "Right then. I'm going for a run," he said, and left the room.

Standing in the kitchen, with his footsteps on the stairs above her, she tilted her chin at the roof. "Okay then," she shouted. "I think I'll take a turn in the garden."

Later, she turned toward him, sleeping beside her. She knew that he was injured, that damage had been done by whatever had gone on all these years, and badly wanted to enter this sore place in his life, and ease it. But she could never be a balm to him. Not while she was so ashamed of her urges, so troubled by her own inexplicability as she had been tonight. She inched toward him on the bed. She'd have liked to burrow into him, to mould her limbs to his limbs and her head to the crook of his neck, but she didn't want to wake him. Instead, she touched his foot, silky and cool, with her own.

She closed her eyes, and pictured the child being knit together inside her. There was cartilage and bone, drawn out of herself, there were toe and fingerprints on fingertips and toes. A whole new brain, another person's source, where before was only space between her organs. "You are fearfully and wonderfully made." As she fell asleep, the words rested over and around her. They seemed to fill her, she felt as though she breathed them, in for the baby, and out for herself. In for the baby, and out for herself.

She felt the craving the morning of the day of her labor. Stronger than usual, it led her out into a morning shower, into the garden in bare feet. The unmown lawn was sodden, and soaked the hem of her green kimono. She went to the mound. It had sprouted all over with pretty weeds and grass. She got down on her hands and knees.

Not eating took an exquisite restraint.

Once the baby came, the hunger went away. To Dante, this was natural. She felt that she'd been all poured out, that the labor and her new son left her nothing to crave with.

A t three months, the baby needed her touch to sleep. She put him down in the mid-afternoon, and hoped for sleep herself. They had wheeled his cot into their bedroom, and set it next to her side of the bed, so she could reach him without getting up. His eyes were on hers.

The crisis had passed without further conversation. In the first months of her motherhood, there were more immediate needs, more pressing questions of survival. In this way, what had happened lost its central focus, faded into the background, one tree of many in the landscape of their lives. Thus, she'd surprised herself the night before when she'd told him, with her son on her breast, that she'd been on his computer months before, that she knew what he looked at, that she knew what he wanted. She hadn't planned it. But Jonesy brought the hungry baby to her, and sat down beside her, and something imperceptible dislodged a pocket of air. The words bubbled up. She simply opened her mouth to let them escape.

Now, she lay on her side, and gave the child her hand through the bars. He rolled onto his back, and held a finger in each fist. She knew her baby intimately, every inch of him. She knew the grain and growth of his hair, the tiny, circled cowlick over his right ear, the way he smiled with top and bottom gums, that his fingernails were sharp like razors, and could cut her skin. She knew that his blue eyes were just the same as hers, down to the almost imperceptible absence of symmetry, a slight irregularity of shape. She knew his smell, which was also hers, manufactured in her body. It seeped out of her, marked her clothes, so she smelled him everywhere, even when they were apart. She knew that he was guileless, that he told her what he needed, could easily identify from the tone and intensity of his cries whether he was hungry, or tired, or wanted to play.

He had a particular look that she called The Camus, a sad face that seemed to come from nowhere. They would be cuddling, or she would hold him out in front of her, and he would be happy and laughing, kicking his legs. Then suddenly his face would be washed in sadness, his lips turned down at the edges like a codfish. And he would wail. This cry was different than his other cries, which seemed entirely practical. It was purer, like despair. It had no object that she could see. Somehow it seemed to her as though he was seized by something profound, like he was staring into some baby abyss.

"I am a sticky beak. It's like I sifted through your rubbish or something." Speaking the words the night before, her heart beat slow and unalarmed, and her voice reached her ears infinitesimally delayed, as though she called to herself from a distance, all the way from the end of the garden. What she'd felt was blasé.

"You saw?" he had asked.

"Yes."

He was silent. She awaited his response. The baby detached himself from her nipple, and looked up, searching for her face. She leaned in over him, and he smiled into her eyes, milk drunk and rapturous. "Yes, my little darling," she said. His balled hand reached out and touched her cheek.

"Damn it, Dante."

"It was a violation. I apologize. Have some more," she said, and eased the boy back onto her breast.

"I don't care about that!"

"Then what?"

"It's just. Now your head is full of those things too. I didn't want you to even have to think of them. Didn't want them taking up the mind space."

"You were protecting me?" She was incredulous. He shrugged, as much to say it was true, and his face turned sheepish, hoping, she supposed, that this beneficence would smooth the way between them.

"Wow. That's retarded. I mean, thanks. But you sell me short, you know that? We're meant to be partners, Jonesy."

They fell into silence. Eventually, she spoke. "Can I ask? Why did you even tell me? If you didn't want to go into it with me?"

"I thought it might help me stop."

"Has it?"

He dropped his head back against the top of the couch, and closed his eyes.

"They were just words, you know. Not a spell. So, you're addicted to porn. What does that even mean?"

Again, he was silent. Again, she waited. "Those images," she said finally, and his head snapped up. He looked vigilant, ready for flight, but soon he seemed to still himself, and met her eyes. And he just looked tired. "What is it about them?"

"I don't know," he said, and frowned, and she saw him three months earlier, working to unknot the fine gold chain he'd brought to her in hospital, which had tumbled into tangles in its box. He had strained, holding it close to his eyes. "I don't know," he said again. "It's something I don't understand."

In his cot, the baby was asleep with his legs in the air. Holding her breath, she gently disentangled her fingers. He'd been a part of her body. Now he was separate, a whole new person. He could be anybody. She might try to conjure his character from herself or from her husband, but he could grow up to be anyone, a good man or bad. Even a serial killer. She wouldn't know.

Dante rolled onto her husband's side of the bed, and buried her face in his pillow. She could smell him, and breathed deeply. She wanted to fill her lungs with him. She got up and went to his closet, flicking through the hangers of jeans and shirts, before grabbing the t-shirt he'd slept in out from underneath his pillow, and pulling it over her head.

Taking the baby monitor from her bedside table, she went to his study. She shut herself inside, lay down on his couch, and closed her eyes. But the t-shirt wouldn't let her sleep. "I Survived Queenstown White-Water," it proclaimed, and he'd bought it after they'd done just that, on their honeymoon five years before, the day after the night before, when they'd finally, at long-last, managed to have sex for the very first time. Details of the day came to her. She recalled that the elderly gent who ran the place made them lunch, muesli bars and sandwiches cut in quarters, packed in plastic for the road. That she wore diamond earrings, a gift from her mother for the wedding, wore them with the wetsuit, underneath the helmet. That on the river, he sat in the prow, and she behind him. That the sun shone, direct overhead, and on long calm stretches there were stars in the water. That she trailed her hand outside the raft, and the river felt clean on her fingers, as though she breathed through them, pine or eucalyptus.

They learned that a woman had drowned on the largest rapid, two weeks earlier, when her raft flipped. They said she was caught in a hole. Hearing this, and seeing the bucking and the violence of the foam on the rocks and the waterfall just down stream, many of their raft-mates got out to walk the rapid. But it was a matter of pride for her that they did not. The thought of him hurt was unbearable to her, but she herself felt fearless and strong, like her bones wouldn't break on the rocks beneath the surface, as though her lungs were impervious to water. Even knowing the error of these impressions, she was careless of herself, keen to put them to the test.

One image came to her particularly strong. Jonesy, half standing at the prow, leaning into the towering rapid, burying an oar horizontally into the water-wall. There was a sense in the moment that they might shoot straight up it and into the air, like a geiser. But the wave began to crest above them. And then she was under water.

For how long was she under? When she breached the surface there were heads around her with gasping mouths, bobbing over jackets, and maybe one of them was Jonesy, but then they were dispersed, swept away like twigs on the water, and the raft crashed on top of her and thrust her down again, into shocking dark and the cold.

She was alone there, tumbling in the water, left to right, top over tail, aware that somewhere he was tumbling too, powerless to help her, just as she was him. For her this was something profound, coming as it did not a week after all their holy promises, their covenant to cleave one to the other, for all of their days. Coming hours—only hours! after they had finally been joined, their bodies lock and key to their life together. Maybe she believed until that moment that they couldn't be divided, even by the forces of nature. But she should have known. Till death parts us. It was right there in the vows.

Did she think these things, there, under the water, as her air ran out, and her jacket buoyed her up and pressed her head into the raft floor, and she clawed above her to free herself? She can't have. Not as such.

Eventually, the rescue boat picked her up. She lay panting on its floor. "Have you seen my husband?" she asked the driver. Her legs shook, and her voice was weak. "Have you seen my husband?" she asked a man who was pulled in after her, his wetsuit torn and bloody at the knee. Finally, she sighted him smiling and waving for her, amongst a group of refugees on the bank. "That was fun!" he said, as they took their places in the raft again, preparing for relaunch. He reached out behind him and squeezed her calf, caressed it with his thumb. Back on the water, she raised her hands to her ears and found an earring gone.

Lying on the couch in his study, she pondered all these things. She stored them up in her heart.

Later, she hung out the washing on the line. The baby was inside, happy in his cot. She brought the monitor, which she propped in the grass, and was delighted by his wordless chatter.

The sun shone. It soaked her skin. She admired the lilies growing along the fence, went to pick a couple for a vase. Remembering her irrational hunger on the morning she went into labor, she crouched down to inspect the mound. She tried to remember what the craving felt like, but she couldn't. It was hard to comprehend that she ever felt it at all.

ALBERT'S WAR

Abi Wyatt

Albert Eustace has locked up his shop and is sneaking like a thief through the house. He tiptoes along the gloomy passage, past the stairs and the sitting room door, then through the chill of the slate-tiled kitchen and into the scullery beyond. He listens for a moment before lifting the latch and closing the door behind him. Wincing at its metallic click, he pauses, listens again.

Tall and round-shouldered, with salt and pepper hair, he wears a pair of grey flannel trousers. His sleeveless pullover is hand-knitted to a complex Fair Isle design. Albert Eustace is fifty-four. He is Wilton's only grocer. It is late in the summer of 1942. Everyone is weary of the war.

Once outside in the early evening sunshine, Albert fills his lungs. He will dead-head the Michaelmas daisies and tidy between the rows. Though Cristobel is nowhere to be seen he is mindful that she might be watching. If she is, what harm could she possibly find in a short spell in the garden lifting carrots for the dinner table and watering the young tomatoes?

Slowly, row by patient row, Albert makes his way down the garden, passing from one well-tended crop to the next one and the next. At last, via the carrots and parsnips, he arrives at the strawberry patch which occupies a sunny yet sheltered position some five or six yards from his shed. With one last glance at the curtained windows, Albert makes a dive for safety where he presses his cheek against the unplaned wood and listens to the pounding of his heart.

From behind the blackout in the spare back bedroom, Cristobel keeps a lookout. Her grey-green eyes are narrow slits and her thin lips are pursed. As the shed door closes, she turns away from the window and re-ties the strings of her apron. Whatever she may make of her husband's antics, there are chores that demand her attention. There are new potatoes and a mess of runner beans in the sink in the scullery downstairs.

Cristobel is a homely woman with little to commend her as a beauty. In the eyes of the ladies of Willingham, she was never a woman of account. Since the introduction of rationing, however, she has attracted the envy of many and, it must be admitted, she has eaten better than most. Today, for example, is Wednesday and the middle of the week but Cristobel is making a real cottage pie. The minced beef that now simmers in a pan of rich gravy arrived fresh very early this morning. It was weighed and wrapped by the butcher's own hand and came innocent of any charge. Admittedly, it came in the wake of Albert's gift of three pounds of sugar— the butcher's son had taken a bride and a wedding calls for cake—but there was nothing underhanded in that. It was an act of neighbourly kindness. It was natural enough to help one's friends in any way one could.

The onions, of course, were a different matter; they came from Albert's garden. Onions are a staple crop: he always grows as many as he can. There's nothing like an onion or two for making the most of your meat ration. Bacon and onion in a nice suet pud, a supper fit for a king. And you had to hand it to Albert, he never was a shirker. Most days, after he had closed up the shop, he would spend a good two hours in the garden, often not stopping even for a quick cup of tea.

The soil was very good, of course, but you still have to put in the effort so it was down to him that they always had their share of fresh fruit and veg. There was generally something left over, too, just that little bit extra, something they could sell in the shop or use to make a trade. Gooseberries were popular—and blackcurrants and rhubarb—which made a lovely crumble. It was difficult to come by the sugar, of course, but Albert had his ways and means.

Albert had never been what you'd call a handsome man; he was a good provider, though, and clever with his hands. He was quiet, too, perhaps even dull. Some would say he was timid. He was fond of walks in the countryside and radio comedy shows. What is more, although he did smoke a pipe or two, he hardly ever bothered with alcohol. Even at Christmas, he wouldn't have more than a couple of bottles of stout. Perhaps a single glass of port as a nightcap at bedtime but that was more medicinal; he said it helped him to sleep.

All of which made it more of a shame when you thought about the other business. If it wasn't for that, you would have to admit that, all things considered, Cristobel had done very well.

Albert is down on his hands and knees and perspiring heavily. He is rooting through the confusion of the equipment that is stored under the potting bench. On the floor around him are the many items he has already dragged out of position. The thing that he wants is the cardboard box lodged tight in the corner at the back. There are old flower pots and watering cans, kneelers and worn out gardening gloves, balls of green garden twine, and half-empty bottles of paraquat. Amongst the propagators, slug pellets and unplanted bulbs, there are seed trays and pesticides; fertilisers and compost spill from torn sacks and bags.

In the midst of all this, Albert has arranged himself so that both his size eleven feet are firmly braced against the bottom of the closed shed door. In this position, it is scarcely possible that he can be caught off guard since, unless he consents to get out of the way, no one will be able to enter. The only window is badly placed to afford a view inside.

Eventually, after prolonged rummaging and yet more shifting, the cardboard box is visible and its exit is clear. There is a dragging sound as, in fits and starts, it lurches over the concrete. It is heavy enough to make it hard to move and he cannot get a good, firm grip.

Once the box is in front of him, Albert takes out his pen-knife and slices through the parcel tape with a single swift movement of the blade. He cuts along the central line where the uppermost flaps join together, lifts the flaps apart and slides in a trembling hand. When it emerges, it brings with it a single slim package, about the size, more or less, of a foolscap envelope. Albert studies it and grunts his satisfaction; he slips it between the pages of *The Gardeners' Weekly News*.

Now he is almost done: he has only to find among the litter a roll of brown parcel tape from which he must cut three strips. He positions these along the line he has cut, so re-sealing the aperture, and heaves the box and its precious contents back under the bench. Finally, he restacks the pots, the seed trays, the compost; everything he has taken out is returned to its place. Now you would be hard pressed to tell if there was a box in the corner. Albert whistles tunelessly as he opens the shed door.

Albert and Cristobel are eating their meal in not quite companionable silence. Cristobel wears her second best day frock; Albert dines in his shirtsleeves. He has, however, washed his face and scrubbed under his nails. Cristobel has warmed a little olive oil and rubbed it into her legs. One of the best things about the summer months is the fact that you can get a nice tan. In winter, she uses gravy browning, but Albert isn't keen. *Better on my potatoes*, he says, *than plastered all over your thighs.*

"I saw that Vera Ellis this morning."

Cristobel is smiling. She is picking daintily at her runner beans, taking one tiny forkful at a time.

"She was all done up like a dog's dinner: high heels, lipstick, everything. Lord knows where she thought she was going, done up to the nines like that."

Albert nods his head in recognition of the fact that his wife has spoken but he does not answer and he does not look up. Instead, he spears another potato and pops it into his mouth, chewing slowly, thoughtfully. He has all the time in the world.

"Tasty," he says, "slightly earthy, perhaps, but still very tasty."

He spears a second potato and chews all over again.

"I pretended not to notice," Cristobel says, unflinching, undeterred. "Course, it was plain as a pike staff that she wanted me to ask."

"Ask what?" says Albert, his eyes on his meal. "I didn't think you liked her."

"I *don't* like her. That's the point."

Cristobel is impatient.

"She wanted me to ask her where she was going so she could spin me some yarn. It'll be another one of her fancy men, you mark my words. No respectable woman has the coupons to dress up like that. Shameful is what it is. There *is* a war on, you know."

"Yes, dear," says Albert meekly, and his head ducks into his shoulders. "But I think you will find she was going to see her sister. Some kind of trouble, I think. She mentioned it just the other day. She popped in the shop for a quarter of tea and four ounces of lard. She was planning to do some baking, I think, a nice jam-tart, something to take with her on the train.

I tried to sell her a pot of your jam but she doesn't care for blackberry. Anyway, apparently, she has plenty of her own."

"That," says Cristobel, smoothing out her skirt, "is hardly a matter for surprise. No doubt the jam also came from one of her so-called friends."

The word *friends* is preceded by a pause that gives it an unpleasant emphasis, just as the *also* implies some previous, unspecified gift or gifts.

"Yes, dear," says Albert. "I'm sure you're right. Shall I do the washing up? You sit down and put your feet up. I'll make us a nice cup of tea."

Though Cristobel sits in the easy chair she could hardly be less at ease. She listens to the clang and clatter of pots and vipers nest in her heart. Is it jealousy or is it envy? And does it really matter, after all? Is it the shame of rejection she fears or her husband's hungry presence in her bed? Cristobel pushes this thought away and with it the image of her rival. Dreamily, she runs her fingers along the length of her leg. She caresses the long curve of its calf and lingers in the hollow of the ankle. "My legs," she says softly, "are better than hers. They are so much better than hers."

In the cool and narrow safety of the kitchen, Albert stacks the crockery. Cristobel can think whatever she likes, he doesn't really care. Vera Ellis is nothing to him now, just another painted trollop. In the short term, though, she might be of use—as a scarlet herring, so to speak. Albert smiles at his little jest and moistens his lips. He wipes down the draining board and hangs the damp tea towels in front of the range to dry. Then, when the kettle steams and sings, he warms the earthenware teapot. Tomorrow, he thinks, is another day: the matchless excitement of the chase.

There you are, my dear," says Albert. He offers her the tea cup.

Seething, Cristobel smiles her thanks and takes the cup from his hand. What is the nature of bargain she has struck and did she ever truly understand it?

"Cristobel, Cristobel," she asks herself, "what is it you have done?"

A lbert, though, is far, far away and lost in his vision of the future. He is thinking of Belinda, the pink and dimpled wife of the butcher's only son. He is imagining her sloe-coloured eyes and the plump curve of her haunches, the fragrance of her chestnut pony tail, sweet as a warm day in May.

Three times this week she has called in the shop and things are progressing very nicely. He has promised her two pairs of nylons, the first that will ever touch her skin.

SIREN

Michael Bigham

The town's fire siren wailed, long, lonely, but almost comforting. Susan sat awake with her back pressed against the headboard. She nudged Darwin. "Time to get up," she said.

"Fire?" he asked still half-asleep.

"Curfew, 10 o'clock," she said. "Time for kids to be home and for you and I to go to work."

"We have time," he said opening his eyes.

"Get up," she said. "Ray will have a cow if you're late again."

"He'll get over it," Darwin said.

"Clothes," she said.

"Leave your husband," he said, continuing the conversation they had started before he had fallen asleep. "Move in with me." Susan didn't answer, but busied herself putting on her clothes. Bra, panties, nylons, half-slip, the pink waitress uniform came last. She and Darwin both worked at the Del-Ray Cafe. Darwin, the cook, was ten years younger than she. When he started there, he had flirted with her, joked about her yellow VW calling it the "Love Bug." She'd ignored his advances until she discovered her husband's deception.

"I could drive you," he said. "We could go in together."

"No," she said heading to the door. "We couldn't."

Susan drove onto Main Street. It was deserted save for a flashing yellow traffic light and a red and chrome Buick idling up ahead. She turned into an alley by the hardware store, killed her headlights and watched the street through her rearview mirror. The Buick belonged to John Neidermier, manager of the local grocery and insomniac. Susan and her husband, Baxter, sometimes played pinocle and drank gin with John and his wife, Marlene, on Sunday nights. The muscles in Susan's neck relaxed after Neidermier's taillights disappeared. Then, she drove by the Texaco station—the attendant asleep in his chair under florescent lights—by the park with ancient diseased elms, and by the courthouse with its granite block clock tower and in its bowels, a police station.

She turned her car into the parking lot for Steele's Department Store, pulled around back and set the parking brake. She listened for a moment for the hum of tires on pavement or the rumble of an engine. Warren, one of the town's police officers, patrolled the central part of town on the graveyard shift, and although they were friends, she had no desire to see him now. The night was quiet except for a song sparrow whistling under the eaves of the store.

Susan opened the dumpster at the store's loading dock and looked inside. Perfect.

Squashed cardboard boxes filled the bin and no animals had settled there for warmth. She propped open the lid of the dumpster with a scrap of lumber, took a sheet of newspaper from the back seat, twisted it into a baton and lit a match. She held the paper until the flames climbed to her fingers, then tossed it into the dumpster. The fire caught the cardboard inside. As she left, she could see smoke curling up behind the department store.

The fire siren wailed again just after Susan started her shift at the Del-Ray. It was Baxter's duty night. About now, he would be stumbling around half-awake, then he would jump into his turnout suit swearing like a Marine, open the overhead doors, fire up the town's antique pumper rig, and swing it onto Main Street. The town's volunteer firemen would meet him at the fire.

In the Del-Ray, Warren, the cop, sat at the counter eating a cheeseburger and fries and Susan made sure to keep his coffee cup full. He used to talk and joke with her in his shy way, even courted her for a year or so. They went to the Lake Shore roadhouse on their nights off and danced the two-step until closing. In the spring, they'd ride his motorcycle up through the gold-toned sandstone to the Painted Hills by John Day. Her father thought more of Warren than she did. A man you can trust he said. Susan imagined that he might ask her to marry him, but when Baxter arrived in town, thoughts of Warren as a suitor faded. He had silently pouted when she and Baxter became engaged. She didn't know how to handle it, so she just let him go on the way he was. Now, when he came into the cafe, he spent most of his time writing reports, head down, paperwork spread across the counter.

Susan turned to the order window. "I think I lost something in the walk-in cooler," Darwin said and leaned his head through the window. "Want to help me find it?"

"The only thing you lost is your brains," she said, but with a smile. "Ray will have your little fanny in traction if you don't clean out the back room." A fire truck whizzed by the window, lights flashing. Baxter would be driving. He always drove.

"It's quiet, plenty of time. Come over in the morning."

"Can't." She kept her hands busy filling salt and pepper shakers. "Baxter will be home."

"You could still come over. Tell him you had to cover the morning shift."

"I could," she said, thinking about it.

The bell over the front door dinged and John Neidermier walked in, his shoulders and belly filling the doorframe, taller than Baxter and a bit older. He sat at the far end of the counter, putting an empty stool between himself and Warren, and took off his light jacket. His white shirt was open to the neck with the sleeves rolled up, showing a tattoo on his forearm: a dagger and a snake, the words "Semper Fi" in blue on hairy flesh. He and Warren nodded, then Warren returned to his paperwork.

Baxter had told her that Neidermier had been in VietNam, but he didn't talk about it much. Susan always felt awkward around him, never wanting to say something that offended him, worrying for no good reason that he might explode. Sometimes he and Baxter would sit out in the backyard, smoking cigars, drinking beer, both seemingly content in an unhurried silence. When they talked it was in spurts: routers and sanders, shotguns and pickups, hunting dogs and small town politics. Susan chewed on the mystery of their friendship, but couldn't figure it out.

Susan greeted Neidermier, poured a cup of decaf from the pot with the orange top and took his order: chicken-fried steak, eggs and gravy. The usual, but she never assumed with him. She put in the order. "I lost my contact," Darwin said. "Come back and help me look for it." Susan didn't smile when she pointed to the order slip.

When she picked up the chicken steak, Neidermier was looking out the window and smoking a cigarette, his mouth drawn into a thin line. Susan put the plate in front of him and he placed his still-burning cigarette in the ashtray.

"Did Marlene get the kitchen painted?" Susan asked. Neidermier said that she still had the trim and the cabinets left. He looked down at his plate and asked how she and Baxter were.

Warren glanced up, curious.

"We're fine," she said thinking it was an odd question. "How about you and Marlene?" Warren had told her that Neidermier and Marlene sometimes got liquored up, did a few hard rounds on Saturday night and woke up Sunday morning bruised and hung over.

"Great, just great." He looked into her eyes before she turned away.

Susan wondered if Neidermier knew about Darwin. Would he say something in front of Warren—or worse to Baxter? To Warren, he said, "My son, little John, joined the Air Force yesterday. The Air Force," he said as if aggrieved. His son was a tall, angular quiet kid who came into the cafe after school. Quiet like he'd been beat down too much and the stutter didn't help.

"Sometimes the military is good for kids." Warren put down his pencil. He had trimmed back his mustache to a thin line. He looked older now, more confident than two years ago.

"You were in the Coast Guard," Neidermier said.

"Navy, you know that," Warren said. An old argument and the pair traded a few jabs, Navy and Marines, swabs and jarheads. Good-natured on the surface, but hostility flowed beneath the words.

"So the going into the military isn't good?" Susan poured Warren another cup of coffee.

"You have hopes for your kids," Neidermier said. "I wanted him to take over the store."

"There's still time," Susan said. The fire truck rumbled past, quiet now, back to the firehouse.

"Sure there is." As Neidermier speared an egg, yellow yoke ran across the plate. The bell over the door rang again, three long haul truckers walked in and Susan excused herself with a sense of relief.

"Come to my place," Darwin said at the end of their shift.

"I can't" she said. "Baxter."

"Always Baxter. When then?"

"Friday. We'll talk Friday."

Susan and Baxter lived in a two-story house on Juniper Hill, a place with a view two miles from town. Susan bought the house years before she married Baxter. She had wanted a home as long as she could remember, so when her mother died and left her a little inheritance, that and her hoarded tip money was enough for a down payment. In the mornings, she sat and drank coffee and looked out her dining room window, watching the line of pickups and old beaters moving up Main Street. The people in them, mostly friends or customers, headed for the day shift in the pair of lumber mills that flanked the road at this end of town.

Susan passed the oak tree that anchored her property. A stub of a rope dangled from a ten foot high branch. When she bought the place, a frayed truck tire hung from it. She found she liked the tire, the feeling it gave the place character, and left it there. Three days after Baxter moved in, he cut down the tire while she was working and stored it in the rafters of the garage. Organizing, cleaning up what didn't belong. "Be practical," he said. She was being too sentimental, a woman's basic fault. It was their first fight and she hated him for a week after that, maybe two.

A barking dog greeted Susan as she drove up the gravel driveway. Two dogs lived with them: hers a sweet-tempered Australian Shepherd named Esther, and Baxter's dog, Duke, an arrogant neutered chow mix with a twisted tail. She worried that the dogs might fight, but they never did.

Baxter sat at the kitchen table when she entered. He'd cranked the heat up too high again, and wore a sleeveless T-shirt and cotton pants. She stooped down to kiss his cheek, just grazing the surface to avoid the bristly gray whiskers. . "You're up early this morning," she said. She walked to the stove. "More coffee?"

He waved his hand. "Dumpster fire last night," he said. "Damnedest thing, the third fire in a month."

"For gosh sakes," she said.

They sat at the dining room table and drank their coffee. Baxter told her that the damage to the dumpster would be covered by insurance, but Herb Miller had tossed out his back and had gone to the hospital in Bend for evaluation. Baxter would drive over to check up on him later this afternoon. "A shame," Susan said. She felt sorry for Herb, she never intended for anyone to get hurt. Baxter said they had a firebug on their hands. Susan fixed him pancakes and eggs while he pulled out his reading glasses and read the paper.

"I'm going back down to Las Vegas for another conference in May," Baxter said.

"The tunnel conference?" Susan slid his pancakes onto a plate. "So soon?" It had only been two months since the last one. Maybe he was getting a checkup.

"Confined space rescue," he said. Susan could never keep the technical jargon straight. No need, Baxter told her, she should leave that to the experts. He ate his eggs with his attention on he sports page. Without looking up, he said, "The Blazers won again."

"That's nice," she said. "What do you think we should get for Brenda Sue's shower?" Baxter's grown daughter was pregnant. He'd be a grandfather soon.

"Something useful, maybe we could set up a college savings plan."

"Steele's has a beautiful bassinet, pink." She considered another cup of coffee, but decided against it. Sleep would be hard enough to come by.

"A pink bassinet? That's useful?" He offered her a cigarette.

"I quit," she said.

"Good for you," he said.

"I want a baby," she said.

"Maybe a diaper service." He snuck a peek at the paper.

"If it's a girl, we could name her Alice."

"We're trying, be patient," he said with a serious tone.

"It's hard." She took his plate to the sink and rinsed it off. "Waiting, wondering."

"I know," he said. "Be patient." She wondered how he could lie so easily.

Susan took her time in the shower, letting the hot water run over her shoulders and back, cleaning away the grease of the diner, the lingering smell of Darwin and her guilt. At the cafe, when she threaded her way through the tables with the coffeepot and her cowgirl body, just past thirty-three, the men—truck drivers, ranchers and loggers—watched her with sidelong glances, joked with her over ham and eggs, tipped too much in the hopes of a smile. Since she married Baxter, she'd let her platinum blond hair fade back to its natural soft brown. She liked it more that way; less pretense, more honest.

She'd met Baxter one snowy January, soon after he moved to town to take over the Fire Chief's job. He had spent twenty-five years in Southern California, fighting big city fires. Now, semi-retired at the sage of 47, he organized volunteers, shopkeepers and mill jocks, taught them how to eat smoke and feel important. He slept at the station every third night, answering the phones, sounding the town siren when there was a fire. On his days off, he fished, hunted birds and read Zane Gray westerns.

After starting the new job, Baxter dropped into the Del Ray most mornings, always ordering the same thing, a man of habit, eggs over medium and a short stack. The first thing she noticed was his voice. He talked to the regulars low and earnest about fishing holes and hunting mule deer, then he seemed to notice Susan all at once. When he talked to her his voice shifted even deeper, became even smoother. He seemed so solid and honest. When he proposed, she told him she wanted kids. No problem, he said. Me, too. But after they were married, he insisted on managing the details, the checkbook and the bills. She found herself resenting that.

She had prided herself on managing the little things in her life.

Susan put on her flannel pajamas and pulled back the comforter. The door slammed. Baxter was gone for the day. He never stayed in the house when she was sleeping. Las Vegas again. She screamed and the dogs set up a howl.

Baxter's pickup smelled like stale cigarette smoke and pine tree air freshener. Susan had come home well past 1 a.m. and Baxter was already asleep, exhausted from the first tunnel class in Las Vegas. She'd forgotten to buy a pack of cigarettes on the way home and she needed a smoke. The Texaco station was ten minutes away, but a cold Oregon rain pelted down. Baxter kept a spare pack or two in his pickup, Camel lights. She preferred menthols, but it was late and she was tired.

She rummaged through the jockey box and found a full pack. As she stuffed everything back, an envelope from a Las Vegas out-patient clinic caught her eye. It contained a receipt for Baxter's vasectomy.

All night, Susan sat in her chair, smoked cigarettes, lighting one off another and listened to sad country songs on the radio. Baxter must have spent that long weekend in a Vegas hotel room with an ice bag on his groin. After he had returned home, he withdrew into work and fishing and Susan had worried that he had hooked up with some red-headed woman in the casino bar. Now she wished he had. She thought about confronting him, but growing up she'd learned confrontation didn't solve anything. Look at how her mother had tolerated her father's drinking. Susan wasn't sure if that was the right way, but she didn't know any other.

After her discovery, Susan let her feelings simmer for a week, then on impulse, she spun Darwin's head around and said yes when he suggested they adjourn to the cooler to toss the salad. He almost hesitated then, but she was pleased he had gone through with it. This past week, she'd felt subtle changes in her body, an unfamiliar heaviness, a missed period. She figured she was pregnant, but didn't know how to tell Baxter. A voice kept telling her it was none of his business.

Darwin and Susan embraced beneath a mercury vapor lamp in the Del-Ray parking lot. The parking lot was empty save for Ray's car, Susan's VW and Darwin's dented, primer gray and black pick up.

Susan pulled back. "I'm not feeling well."

"You're sick." Darwin's face looked green in the lamplight.

She folded her arms across her chest. "Maybe the flu."

"I got you a present." He leaned into the truck and reached under the seat.

"Our anniversary, two months together." He handed her a package, red and white paper creased at odd angles, too much scotch tape and a store bought bow.

"Oh," she said and "Oh," again. She opened the package with diligence, folding the paper and saving the bow. "Soap."

"Gardenia scented."

"How sweet." Something my mother would have loved, she thought. I don't want to cry.

Headlights turned onto the street and a police cruiser with a down-turned spotlight pulled toward them.

"Come by, just for a while," Darwin said in a low voice.

"Fine," Susan murmured. It was their anniversary and all.

Warren rolled down the window. "Ah, it's you. Hi Susan. Everything okay?"

"No problem here, Officer." Darwin stuck his hands in his pockets.

"Just a routine check," Warren said.

"Thanks, I'm fine." Susan pulled her cardigan sweater tight around her. "We'll be leaving soon," she said.

"If you have a minute," Warren said, "I'd like to talk with you. It won't take long."

Darwin tensed, but Susan whispered, "Later." Warren invited her to the front seat of the police car. She felt claustrophobic, sandwiched between the door on one side and the shotgun, mobile computer and radio rack on the other. Behind her was a scratched Plexiglas screen that divided front seat from back. They watched as Darwin drove away.

"It's none of my business," Warren said.

"Probably not," Susan said.

"But I'm worried about you."

"How so?" Susan heard the barely audible chatter of the police radio flowing beneath their words.

"You have a husband. Darwin isn't right for you."

"How do you know that?" She shifted her weight against the door trying to find more room.

"I have eyes, people talk. It's a small town."

"I didn't mean to hurt you," Susan said.

"You're hurting your husband, not me." Warren wouldn't look at her.

"I can't explain what's going on. Sometimes, I'm not sure myself."

"You don't owe me any explanation," he said. Susan asked him why the sermon then. He didn't answer for a long time, then shrugged and said he still cared for her, not that he wanted to intrude on her personal life.

She wanted to say that he never told her about his feelings. Instead she said, "But you are." She regretted the words as soon as they were spoken.

Susan left and as she drove to Darwin's apartment, the scent of gardenia overwhelmed the little car. She couldn't tell Warren the reasons she married Baxter, they sounded too trivial. Baxter would be a good provider for her children, stable, dependable. He was important here, he wouldn't want to leave town for a better job and he wouldn't get beat up by some sloppy drunk logger in a bar fight or shot on a lonely county highway by some stranger he stopped for speeding. She tossed the soap out of her window behind the Texaco station.

One red and one white satin sheet," Susan said. "Curious."

Darwin pulled back the comforter. "The clerk called them strawberries and cream." He lived in a half-furnished, pine-paneled studio apartment in the basement of a Victorian home.

"I thought you may have bought them out of some catalog," Susan said. Darwin laughed and unbuttoned his shirt. Susan walked over to the only table in the apartment, a small Goodwill dinette. "I'd like a drink first," she said.

"All I've got is wine."

"That's fine." Susan sat down in a plastic patio chair and put her feet up on the table.

"Make yourself comfortable." Darwin opened the wine.

"I am."

"When are you going to leave Baxter," Darwin asked handing her a tumbler of wine.

"Strawberries and cream. I like that." She sipped the wine, too sweet, but she didn't say anything.

"I said..."

"I heard you." She downed the wine in two quick gulps. "I'm pregnant."

Darwin plopped into the other chair. "Is it mine?"

"Baxter had a vasectomy a while back." Her stomach burned. Stupid, drinking that wine.

"Have you told him?" Darwin stood and paced the small room.

"Not yet."

"Not yet," he repeated. "What are you going to do?"

"I don't know. What do you want me to do?"

"I hadn't counted on have a kid... so soon. I kinda figured I'd go up to Alaska next summer and do some salmon fishing. Commercial salmon fishing," he added as if she might not think it was important enough. "I need time to think about this. You know?"

"I know," Susan said.

"Still want to go to bed?" Darwin looked pale and tense.

"Sure," she said. It might just be their last time.

B lues and pinks barely shaded the eastern horizon. Susan circled block after block, like a cabby searching for a fare. Darwin slept in his bed. Warren's cruiser was parked at the courthouse. Coffeebreak, she thought. Someone sat inside the Texaco, framed in fluorescent, talking to the attendant. They laughed and Susan wondered if it was about her.

She passed Neidermier's market for the third time, then pulled around back with her headlights off. Darkness shrouded the loading dock; the light had burned out. She navigated by memory and intuition down the gravel alley, past the blocky incinerator and dim outline of stacked freight pallets. As she got out of her car, she smelled sawdust and old diesel oil. Her hand shook as she lit a cigarette, the first in a week. Just one won't hurt, she reasoned. The sky was clear and a million stars receded before the dawn. People say that stars move in slow circles in the sky, but to Susan they all seemed to be looking the other way.

Susan snubbed out her cigarette, then went to her VW and took several sheets of newsprint from the trunk. The pallets would go up nicely. She crumpled the newsprint into balls and stuffed them into the pallets. She took a book of matches from her sweater pocket and lit one. Suddenly, the loading dock light snapped on and the overhead door clanged up. Neidermier jumped down next to her.

"I knew I'd catch someone out here someday," he said. "I didn't believe it would be you."

Susan turned to run, but he grabbed her hair and twisted it, pushing her to her knees. She felt the anger in his hands and smelled the whiskey on his breath. She knew she deserved his rage but said, "Don't hurt me."

He looked at her like a strange new animal he was seeing for the first time and released her hair. "I told myself, I've got to stop hurting people." His lips twitched in a failed attempt at a smile. "I'll let the cops handle you."

Susan twisted her shoulders trying to find a comfortable position on the hard plastic back seat of the police cruiser. The handcuffs grated against her wrist bones. How many bad, dirty, diseased people had sat back here? Outside the cruiser, Neidermier gestured and Warren shook his head. They both looked pissed. In the end, they parted without shaking hands.

Warren opened the door and slid inside. "This wasn't the first time, was it?" he said, his voice fuzzy through the Plexiglas.

"I didn't set the other fires," A weak lie. She didn't know what else to say.

"You got caught in the act, Sue," he said. "Call it cop curiosity, but why?" She wanted to tell him all of it, the vasectomy, the affair, the anger that had kindled inside her like dried grass in the blaze. But he wouldn't understand, she thought. Maybe she didn't understand all of it herself.

"I don't know," she said finally. They passed the courthouse and turned up Main. "Where are we going?" she asked.

"To see your husband." Neidermier owed Warren a favor. Warren had cut him some slack on one of their Saturday night go-arounds. Neidermier had broken Marlene's nose, but she didn't want to press charges and Warren had smoothed things over. Small town politics, now the two were even. Susan realized that Baxter would now owe Warren. The Chief of Police was approaching retirement. The City Council had come to respect Baxter's opinion. For the first time, Susan felt tears squeezing out the corners of her eyes.

They pulled into Susan's driveway, Neidermier had called Baxter to meet them there. No need to air their dirty underwear in public. They sat and waited in the car, neither speaking until Baxter arrived. Warren removed the handcuffs and the men settled at the dinette waiting for Susan to perk coffee. Warren explained the morning's events, quickly, succinctly without emotion.

"What are we going to do about it?" Baxter asked.

"What do you think?" Warren said.

"I think we could reach an agreement that's mutually beneficial for everyone involved." Baxter lit a cigarette. Susan poured the men coffee from a ceramic pot with blue and white flowers on it, then leaned back against the stove.

Warren scooted his chair back half a foot. "What concerns me is what happens to Susan."

"Of course," Baxter said, "we need to think of Susan's welfare above all."

"Arson is a felony in this state," Warren said.

"Just dumpster fires, no real harm done. No need for this to become public," Baxter said.

Warren glanced over at Susan, then shook his head as if he wasn't sure that would work.

"We'd all benefit," Baxter said smiling. "You included."

"We're taking a risk if this gets out." Warren's lips were tight as if he were taking about a disgusting secret.

"I'll take care of everything," Baxter said. "Don't worry."

Susan rubbed her wrists, still sore from the handcuffs. "What about Herb?" she asked. "He hurt his back."

"Herb's fine," Baxter said without looking at her. "He enjoyed the time off."

"I'm not fine," Susan said.

"There's a good shrink up in Portland," Warren said. "The department uses him for hiring."

"She can go up there to visit her sister," Baxter said.

"I don't have a sister," Susan said.

"We'll think of something," Baxter said.

"I'm pregnant," Susan said.

Baxter stammered. "You're distraught. You need some rest. A nap would help." His face turned as white as the enamel on her stove.

"I've already been in bed. Darwin's," she said. "Not more than two hours ago."

"We'll call that psychiatrist for an appointment," Baxter said.

"I know about the vasectomy, you bastard," Susan shouted.

"This is where I came in," Warren said heading for the door.

"Do we have a deal?" Baxter said.

Warren opened the door. "No more fires and make sure Susan gets some help." Without waiting for a reply, he shut the door and left them alone.

Baxter stared at the floor, not speaking.

"I want a divorce." Susan paced to the windows and back.

"Because of your lover? I don't care about him."

She picked up the coffee pot and slammed it down on the table cracking it. "Because you lied. You betrayed me"

"Do you want to marry him, this boy?" he asked.

"No," she said. She realized that. She'd have to tell Darwin, but he wouldn't mind.

"We both could use a drink," he said.

"Get out!" she shouted.

"Sure, sure." He held up his hands. "I have to go back to work, but we'll hash this out this afternoon."

She turned her head away. "Go on, go back to your firehouse." Part of her hoped he would stay, but he didn't. "Take Duke with you," she said as he was leaving. He stopped as if he was going to say something, but then just whistled for the chow and the two of them left.

Siren

Susan sat at the dining room window drinking coffee and watching the traffic move up Main Street. When the mill whistle sounded she began gathering up Baxter's clothes, fishing gear and guns. She carried them out to where her drive way met the road and deposited them on the gravel. The task took her several trips and by the time she finished, the sun was high in the sky and warm on her back. Too warm to start another fire. Instead she headed for the garage to get her ladder. She figured she could rehang the truck tire on the oak, then head downtown. She hoped Steele's hadn't sold that pink bassinet.

SHE THREW HEAT

John Azrak

She threw heat and he caught it behind the chain-link backstop, the whip of her windmill delivery sending an electric current down his spine. The days she was pitching he drifted through his classes in a pre-game reverie: the manicured grass on the campus's remote diamond, the chorus line of purple-striped uniforms, the virgin mound she would grace, the auburn ponytail swinging across her square shoulders like a metronome.

He knew what he had to do to get noticed: keep his head in the game, stay focused, believe in himself and his intimations of fate.

She picked him out, after a mid-season win, from his customary seat in the sparse stands.

They dated. She threw a three-hit shutout in the Division II playoffs. He ran out to home plate, threw himself into the celebratory scrum of female bodies and emerged with the imprint of a glove on his forehead. She laughed. He grabbed her hand and they danced up the third base line. She said he was crazy. He said in love. They poured beer into their beer, their hearts full of each other.

They married after college.

They taught high school in suburban school districts. She was the charismatic phys ed teacher who earned a reputation in the athletic department as a coach's coach. Her student athletes wanted to be like her. He toiled, without fanfare, beneath endless stacks of essays. He escaped some nights writing narrative poems hinged on sports metaphors ("Walk-off Homerun," "Hitting for the Cycle,"and the like). They had two kids, two years apart, bought a house between their school districts. Their boys starred for their high school lacrosse and soccer teams, made their way into their father's verse. He daydreamed about attending their college games. He'd root for them with the same fervor he'd courted his wife, grateful for a life that had come full circle.

Their younger boy left for college, also out of state. His wife became Athletic Director of her school district. Supervising the coaches kept her in the field late hours, all seasons. She vowed not to lose the shape she'd kept since college. She joined a gym that sapped her free time. He got hooked on sports' talk radio; ghost-like callers filled empty rooms. Joe from Bayside and Manny from the Bronx became dependable company. He began wearing headphones to bed, lonely voices seeping into his dreams.

He missed his wife. He told her so, but said he didn't begrudge her the life she was creating for herself. He was impressed, her biggest fan. As ever, he said with a half smile. She lowered her eyes. No worries, he added, no harm, no foul. I've met a woman, she said, and looked up. She didn't know how not to hurt him. He screwed up his brow. From my yoga class, she said, her face burning up. He froze in place. With everything on the line, he went down looking.

INK ON SKIN

Alex Baldwin

E rnie Trippett zigzags on his orange Huffy along the streets from gutter to gutter, an eleven year old marble encased in a pinball machine. He makes arcade noises when his front wheel hits one side and diagonals back to the other. *Bing. Cheedleedop. Zwoonk. Fashwing.*

The ride to the Frisbee golf course lasts longer this way, and makes the trailer park that everyone calls Firth, Idaho seem bigger. The homes are no larger than campers—and if they had wheels—would find the fastest way to I-15, leaving Ernie and the other five hundred inhabitants behind with their mouths open and eyes fixed on the fleeing caravan of pale blues, greens, and yellows shrinking into the setting sun.

At a stop sign, he pulls a pen from his pocket, writes "Pinned Ball" on his right arm, and pedals along smiling, proud of his sense of humor.

On a shelf above his bed, Ernie keeps his books in order of thickness: Whitman's *Leaves of Grass*, Milton's *Paradise Lost*, Shakespeare's *Sonnets*, and Collins's *Sailing Alone Around the Room*.

Stila Trippett loves pickles.

Twice, she almost died eating zesty dills. The first time happened at the Frosty Gator, celebrating her engagement to Chet Montgomery, her high school sweetheart. She ordered a salad for the spicy pickle spear that always came balanced on the porcelain edge of the dinner plate—escaping the thick puddle of dressing by the width of a romaine leaf. Her first bite too big, her swallow too fast. Their waiter, Walter Michael Stein, squeezed the chunk out of her throat.

Chet laughed. "The tip's still gonna be the same, hero." When Walter cleaned their table a folded note flipped down onto the vacant booth seat: "Be happy I'm not sueing." He tossed the worthless tip into Stila's leftover sea of Thousand Island and took the plate to the kitchen sinks, thinking about Chet's misspelled word.

The second time happened when Stila's second fiancé, Walter Michael Stein, punched her in the face during a fourth of July barbeque. The hit knocked her out in mid swallow. Ketchup, fat free mayonnaise, hamburger bun, and two zesty dill chips lodged in her throat with nowhere to go. Earlier that morning, Walter drove the hour round trip to the Wal-Mart in Idaho Falls to surprise her with the jar of pickles.

Ernie calls these tales his bitter pickles. All he knows is that he is Stila's only begotten son, and either Chet the Cheap or Walter the Whacker is his father. Stila and he share a pale blue home where she has let him crayon *Walter* under the two fist sized holes on the back of her bedroom door, and with a Sharpie, lets him write Chet next to each new hole in his clothes.

"Mom, my favorite socks are chetting pretty bad in the heels."

"Alright. Remember where you put that Sharpie, Ernest?"

Every Saturday Ernie plays Frolf with Chet and Walter. The course is an empty field except three spruce trees surrounding the last hole.

Every Saturday the same script. Chet and Walter spend the first six holes catching up. *What you reading? Paradise Lost? Sounds like porn. Whitman? Oh sure, I love his stories with the runaway boy going down the Mississippi. Or was it the Missouri?* The middle six holes, their fatherly advice. *Always listen to your mother. She loves you. Make yourself useful, bud. Don't be wasting your time. Especially with girls. You messing with girls yet? Well, use protection when you do.* The last six holes are arguments. *What do you mean three under? No, you bogied Eleven. Like hell, I'm bringing scorecards next week. Three under, my ass.*

But this morning, Stila slammed his door and everything fell off his shelf and landed on the outer space blanket draping his bed.

Ernie looked at the books spread across the solar system — worlds Ernie wished he could live on, worlds better than his own. Pulling a pen from his pocket, Ernie wrote on his right arm "What Orbits My Sun?" Stila's stomp, stomp, stomp came down the hallway/kitchen/living room. The doorknob twisted high and loud and the door swung open.

"I thought we passed this lying phase, Ernie?"

"Mom, I swear I wasn't swearing in class yesterday."

"Then why did Mrs. Bowen call me just now? Is she the liar?"

He's let her down; he knew it.

He wasn't the simple boy of a simple mommy in a simple town. Ernie Trippett was a raconteur. Ernie knew the word raconteur, and knew Stila didn't.

She talked about Firth's fickle weather, whole stories about hail storms in July. She gave such enthusiasm to *guess who came into the store today* and began laughing while saying *you won't believe what she said,* as if acting out the moment again, as if knowing her story needed the pomp. An actor in Small Stage, USA. She'd ask Ernie about his day, what he was thinking, but he knew she wanted the giggles of recess; the notes weaved through desk legs as the teacher wrote math problems on the board. He couldn't discuss the effect of Milton's blindness in Paradise Lost with her, so he'd say *not much* or *nothing really* and hope she'd understand.

"Bastard." This surprised Ernie. Not the word. He had Stila's face, Chet's brown eyes and big ears, and Walter's curly hair and crooked teeth. Ernie Trippett, bastard of ambiguity. What surprised Ernie was that he got in trouble for saying damn. But he lived for such opportunities of storytelling. He compared the thrill to what skydiving must feel like, only having to put the parachute together in the free fall.

"What?" Stila's tense posture guilted into a slouch.

"Yeah, Mom, bastard. Conner asked me why I didn't have a dad. I told him I'm a bastard. Is that swearing, Mom? Am I a cuss word? Am I your cuss word? The expletive in your life?"

Stila helped put the books back on the shelf, apologizing between each hug. *No, of course not. Sorry, sweetie. Oh, I love you. You're my life.*

She popped in an Icebreaker to cover her pickle breakfast and gave Ernie a kiss goodbye on the cheek. Ernie rode a block, pulled his pen out, wrote "Pickles and Mints" on his right arm, and began zigzagging down the street.

FIVE BUCKS

Gary V. Powell

I was looking at porn the morning my girlfriend's five-year old son announced he couldn't rouse my daughter from sleep. I thought it was a joke and expected to be back at my desk in no time, so I left the porn open while I followed Ryan upstairs. Except this was no joke. Kara lay sprawled across the bed, a ceramic paring knife resting on the sheets, superficial cuts to her wrists. Bu the real culprit was the two weeks' worth of prescription drugs my ex-wife had sent along for Kara's visit. The pills, designed to combat bi-polar disorder and obsessive-compulsive behavior were missing to the last soldier.

I tried all the usual stuff—shaking her like a sheet in the wind, dragging her limp body around the room—but she showed no response. Her breathing was shallow, and she was cool to the touch.

Ryan brought his mom to the door just as I was beginning to grasp that this was a situation I couldn't fix by myself. Still in her pajamas, Maddy said that an emergency crew was on the way. She didn't seem all that surprised this was happening.

Then, while I waited for the medics to arrive, she whisked Ryan off to the neighbors. By the time the medics arrived,

I was making trivial bargains with a God I'd long stopped believing in, thinking that nineteen was too damned young to die, and wondering why I hadn't hidden those prescription drugs like I'd hidden the liquor. I should have monitored Kara's consumption like I'd monitored her activities since her arrival the day after Christmas. It was no secret she was a mess and couldn't be trusted around drugs or alcohol.

The medics were wrapping up their shift, and had probably seen more than their share of overdose and trauma victims that night. One of them, a young lady not that much older than Kara, took my information while two burly guys checked my daughter's vitals, brought in a gurney, and got an IV going. I followed them to their vehicle, and was told I could ride shotgun. The young lady popped a stick of gum in her mouth and took the wheel. The two guys continued to work on Kara in the back.

Some of the neighbors stood in their front yards watching our little drama unfold—after all, not too many years earlier Kara had babysat their kids. The thing was, the neighbors didn't look any more surprised than Maddy, sad and somewhat smug actually, as if they'd known something like this was just a matter of time, as if that knowledge was their little secret, and I was just now getting in on it.

The young lady flipped on the siren and pulled away from the curb. I asked her what she thought. I was still in my t-shirt and boxers.

"You know what," she said, "you seem like the kind of guy who's tried his best. Your daughter owns this, not you."

"You think so?"

She smacked her gum. "I'm just saying that's how it looks."

Maddy discovered the porn when, shortly after I accompanied Kara to the hospital, she closed my laptop. "Thank God, Ryan didn't see it," she said over the phone.

It wasn't that big of a deal, just a naked girl with a site. My former college roommate, Jack, had forwarded the link. It wasn't like I went looking for that kind of thing. Jack sent the link, and I followed it out of curiosity.

Maddy cut my claims of innocence short. "We'll talk about it later. You've got enough on your plate right now."

A high-school physics teacher, she processed life with a cool logic. Her ex-husband, a university professor, had cheated on her, taking advantage of his undergraduate students while she'd been pregnant with Ryan. Once she figured out what was going on she was in the wind before the day was out.

"I'm still in my boxer shorts," I said. "I haven't eaten anything. Christ, I haven't even had a cup of coffee."

"I'll be there as soon as I drop Ryan at pre-school."

"You're not going to work?"

"I won't let you go through this alone."

Maddy had been there for me when Kara had run away from home and come to live with us four years earlier. She'd stood beside me during those scary nights when Kara partied it up and ignored our phone calls. She'd even tried to be a friend to Kara, knowing she couldn't be a mother, her hands already full with her own young son. Maddy really did love me, even if I was an under-employed lawyer who looked at internet porn.

"Thanks, babe," I said. "You're the best. I mean it. The absolute best."

"Yeah, well. Anyway, I found a suicide note in the trash."

That was a new twist. In the past, we'd found cuts on Kara's wrists. We'd been witness to binge drinking, near overdoses with drugs that weren't sold in pharmacies, and other reckless behavior, but never a note. All along, her therapists had told us she wasn't trying to kill herself, just seeking attention. She definitely had our attention, now.

"So, the note. What does it say?"

"I'll bring it along. How is she?"

"Listed in critical condition, but a doctor told me she's stable."

"You want me to call the probation officer?"

I'd forgotten about that. Most recently, Kara had been living with her mother and undergoing rehab in Des Moines. She'd come to Indianapolis because she owed her probation officer a visit.

"That would help," I said. "I don't have his number."

"I'll call your office, too. Let them know you won't be in."

"I don't know what I'd do without you."

"I'll be there within the hour."

Kara remained unconscious, but by noon was stable enough to be moved from ER to a regular hospital room. There was nothing to do but wait while the drugs she'd taken ran their course. The nurse, a woman in her mid-forties with tired eyes, told me that being young and strong worked to Kara's advantage.

Throughout the afternoon, Maddy and I watched daytime TV and took turns reading Kara's handwritten suicide note. She'd been on a tear since her freshman year of high school. In just the last nine months, she'd been dismissed from two colleges and convicted of buying an eight-ball of cocaine from an undercover cop. She'd never shown an ounce of remorse, except in her note. Apparently, she'd written it while ingesting the prescription drugs. After beginning with a robust confession and an apology, Kara's logic soon dissipated into a rambling explanation of her actions over the last few years, referencing her various disorders and asking forgiveness from loved ones. Eventually the words trailed off the page in a loopy scrawl.

"That girl she used to work with," I said.

Maddy nodded. "One of the few I trusted."

The girl, Robin, was a single mother with a three-year old. She and Kara had worked together at a pizza joint, and we'd hoped she might be a good influence. But according to the note, when I'd allowed Robin and her kid to stop by after dinner the night before, she and Kara had done a few lines at the bottom of our driveway. After the initial rush, the world must have closed in on my daughter. She'd felt the hard slap of genuine guilt for snorting Robin's blow. She'd felt unworthy of life in the wake of six weeks of sobriety.

Maddy gave me a bleak smile. "Maybe, it's a good thing she's able to see how much she's hurt people."

"It's not a good thing if she doesn't live."

"It's a breakthrough. You have to see it like that."

I laid the note on the table next to Kara's bed. "We should save this for her therapist, assuming she makes it."

Maddy scratched her chin. "Have you called Jean?"

Jean, my ex-wife.

I stood outside the hospital in a cold drizzle. Before calling Jean, I fired off a message to Jack, telling him to stop sending links to websites with naked women. Next, I deleted pics from my iPhone, only fifteen or twenty, downloaded from earlier e-mails he'd sent. There were more downloaded pics and even a few video clips on my laptop at home, and I wondered if Maddy had found those, too. I promised myself to delete it all as soon as I got a chance, as if deleting it could rewind things to the point where I'd never downloaded it to begin with.

The girl Jack had linked me to most recently, Brandi, claimed she used subscription fees from her site to cover tuition at a prestigious east-coast university. It could have been true, but more than likely the site was run by the Russian Mafia. She was pretty enough, this Brandi, with full lips and incredibly blue eyes. For fifteen dollars a month, subscribers could watch her dally with her boyfriend, pleasure herself in his absence, and go about her daily routine in various states of undress. A few pics were available for free. The one I'd left open on my computer screen showed her leaning over a chair, legs apart, backside thrust into the air.

After messaging Jack and cleansing my iPhone, I forced myself to call my ex. Even after all this time, Jean still considered Maddy, who was fifteen years younger than me, as nothing more than the physical evidence of a mid-life crisis. So far as I could tell, it never crossed her mind that by the time I met Maddy our marriage was already over. Jean couldn't imagine me falling in love with another woman.

"You should have taken her meds away," Jean said.

"Yeah, and maybe you should have Fed-exed them to me, instead of sending them with Kara."

"I told you I was sending them with her. I told you to watch her."

"I don't know. She seemed pretty together. She said she thought rehab was working this time. She said she could relate to her therapist and that the meds were helping."

"You can't believe a word she says."

"I didn't see this coming."

Jean sighed. "We never do."

"Anyway, I'll stay in touch."

"I could drive over."

"There's no reason for that. The doctors are optimistic. I'll send her back as soon as I can."

"Is this ever going to end?"

"I don't know, Jean. I don't know."

Maddy went home at dinner time to be with Ryan. I stayed at the hospital until eleven that night. By then, I was exhausted and the nurse assured me there was nothing more I could do anyway. Kara had made minor progress throughout the evening, coming out of her comatose condition more than once to mumble a few unintelligible words. I took a cab home, not wanting to bother Maddy for a ride. She met me at the door.

I gave her the update while she slapped together a ham sandwich. I would have liked a beer, but the alcohol remained hidden in the attic.

"It sounds like she's going to pull through." Maddy slid the sandwich across the counter. "She may not be so lucky next time."

Jesus, next time. "How's Ryan taking this?"

"He thinks she couldn't wake up, and asked if it could happen to him."

"What'd you say?"

"That it only happens to girls."

Kara had wanted nothing to do with Ryan when she'd first come to live with us. He was a baby, and he smelled bad. Then, within a month, she was feeding him his bottle and changing his diaper. They bonded like Ben and Jerry, and for a while we tried to convince ourselves that their bond might be enough to save Kara from herself.

"Any news from school today?"

"More budget cuts. More teachers laid off."

Except they wouldn't lay off a physics teacher, at least not one as good as Maddy. Her class size would increase, her resources would dwindle, but she wouldn't be laid off. I pulled a strand of hair from her face and leaned across the counter to kiss her. She turned away, took my plate, and rinsed it off.

"You want anything else?" she asked.

I sorted through the mail—credit card bills and catalogues for expensive merchandise the marketers thought we could afford.

"Maybe some cherry pie. Get yourself a slice, too," I said. "Let's watch TV. I need to unwind."

She returned to the refrigerator, brought out the store-bought pie, and served me a slice. "No, it's late. I'm going to bed."

I caught her hand. "Thanks, Maddy. Thanks for everything."

She was pretty and slender, dark Irish with the most beautiful brown eyes I'd ever seen. Her usual pragmatism could take a turn, though. She could withdraw, become cool and distant as the burnt-out stars she taught her students about. I took solace in the fact that she didn't reserve that side solely for me. Ryan, Kara, and Maddy's sisters also got their share. We'd talked marriage off and on, but I'd always backed away, saying I wasn't ready. It had been a while since she'd brought the marriage thing up.

"No problem," she said. "It comes with the territory."

"Anyway, I just wanted you to know I appreciate it. Goodnight, Maddy."

"Goodnight, Ray."

I waited until she was settled in bed before deleting the porn from my laptop. The pic of Brandi and her perfect ass no longer graced the screen. Maddy had saved it to file, which meant she'd most-likely stumbled onto my other pics and videos. I felt a pang of embarrassment, but it wasn't like I was the only guy who looked at a little porn. And it wasn't like I subscribed—there was no way I'd give the Russian Mafia my credit card information. I just looked now and then, and downloaded free stuff, nothing all that kinky, just run-of-the mill porn.

Next, I checked phone messages and e-mail from work. My gig was wealth transfer planning, wills and trusts, tax minimization. Business had slacked off with the recession, and there was nothing that couldn't wait a few days. I sent a note to my partners, sharing the bloody details of Kara's latest adventure. It wasn't like they didn't have errant teenagers, ex-wives, and claims of ethics violations of their own. Like Maddy said, it came with the territory.

Finally, I settled into my easy chair and flipped on the TV. I was nearly out when Ryan came downstairs, dragging his tattered red blanket behind him. On NatGeo Wild, full-grown male lions ate their babies, two headed black mambas menaced the jungle, and fire ants threatened the border.

Ryan crawled into my lap without a word and laid his head on my shoulder. Undersized for his age, he looked more like his dad than Maddy. After those fire ants devoured an unfortunate old woman who'd fallen from her horse onto their nest, he asked if Kara was going to be all right. I assured him she'd be fine and switched off the TV. He snuggled closer and began sucking his thumb. We both fell asleep. About two in the morning, I carried Ryan to bed and tucked him in.

On the wall were photos of the two of us from a recent camping trip. On the floor, a half-finished model of the USS Enterprise we'd been working on for weeks.

I might have been a shyster lawyer who made his living helping rich clients take advantage of tax loopholes most people never heard of; I might have been the kind of guy who left his wife for a younger woman and raised a daughter who tried to kill herself, but I was the only man this little boy called Daddy.

When we arrived at the hospital the next morning, Kara was sitting up, chatting away with the nurse, a different one from the night before. She still had an IV in her arm, and heavy leather straps held her to the bed. Sponge Bob Squarepants blared on the TV.

"It's Daddy and Maddy," she announced. "Daddy and Maddy, this is Trish."

The nurse, Trish, and I nodded at each other.

"So, you're feeling better?" I asked. I didn't know what to make of it, but that was the way things always were with Kara.

She beamed. "Oh, yeah, I'm fine. You should've seen how much I ate for breakfast."

I crossed over to the bed and hugged her. "My God, Kara, you scared us to death."

"I'm all right," she said. "I just needed to sleep it off. I want to go home. I want to play with Ryan."

She'd gained a few pounds since high school, and could have used better hygiene, but none of that mattered. She was alive, alive and talking and laughing and sounding almost normal.

Trish made her way to the door and motioned for me to follow. On the way past, Maddy rolled her eyes. She pulled up a chair next to Kara, the two of them talking, while the nurse and I stood in the hall.

"That's quite a recovery," I said.

"She's still high from the anti-depressants. There's a risk of liver damage."

"Is that serious?"

"Serious enough. Plus, a psychiatrist is coming by later on. Dr. Welch. He's recommending additional medication to level her out. He'll tell you what happens next."

"Next?"

"He's recommending involuntary commitment to the psychiatric ward."

"You mean she can't come home?"

"You could go to court, try to stop it."

"The psychiatric ward?"

"It's downtown. What you're seeing now isn't real. It won't be pretty when she hits bottom."

"Does she know?"

"Not yet."

"How long will they keep her?"

"Ten days. It's standard procedure with suicides."

Kara's zany cackle carried into the hall. She pointed at something on the TV. Maddy stared out the window.

Images of *One Flew over the Cuckoo's Nest* flashed in my head.

Even as the day wore on and Kara's mania subsided, she maintained she was fine, the whole thing a mistake. She wanted to go home and get about her business. Dr. Welch told her she needed further treatment. I called my partner, Manske, who specialized in domestic matters. We could fight Kara's commitment, probably get a judge to issue a stay. I conferred with Maddy and Jean, before deciding against it. The truth was, Maddy and I didn't want Kara back in our house in her current condition, and Jean was in no position to argue.

Mid-afternoon, while Kara dozed, Maddy discovered the remains of her suicide note, torn to shreds in the bottom of a trash can. If for one fleeting moment, Kara had owned her actions, she wasn't owning them now.

Late that evening, long after Maddy had gone home, I signed papers. A little while later, two young cops arrived. Kara fought them, screaming and kicking, when they removed the straps that held her in bed, and cuffed her hands behind her. I followed the squad car uptown to County.

Upstairs, I was given a password that granted entrance into the psychiatric ward. Even with the password, I had to go through two sets of locked doors. *Cuckoo's Nest* wasn't far off the mark. At one end of a large common room, populated with sofas, chairs, tables, and a couple of TVs, was a nurse's station. In hallways leading away from the common room were individually-assigned rooms. By this hour, most of the inmates were asleep. Those that weren't—a skinny, highly-inked young man and a middle-aged woman with a shaven head—zoned out in front of one of the TVs, wordlessly watching Leno.

They had Kara at the nurse's station. On each side of her, two large, black men sat with hands folded in front of them. She had a red spot on her forehead, which I later learned was the result of a scuffle with the orderlies. Under threat of a straight-jacket, she remained animated, but under control.

She explained she was already in rehab, that she was making progress with her current therapist and needed to get back to Des Moines. The nurse told Kara she'd be with them until she stabilized.

"Fuck you," Kara said when the inevitability of her situation settled on her. "And fuck you, too," she said to me.

"Kara, please. Give these people a chance."

The orderlies led her away, screaming and kicking again. They were assholes, the doctors and nurses douche-bags. I was a cocksucker.

The nurse kept her head down until the moment passed. When she looked up, she said, "Mr. Carter, you should get some rest."

The house was dark except for the light from the screen on my open laptop. I checked on Ryan and found him asleep on the floor of his room, surrounded by toys. I lifted him into bed and pulled his covers up to his chin before heading down the hall. The door to our bedroom was closed, and I knew Maddy was asleep, too. We'd texted each other off and on throughout the evening, and there really wasn't much left to say. With Kara in the psychiatric ward, she couldn't hurt herself or the rest of us for a while.

I made myself a ham sandwich and sat down in front of my computer screen. I didn't get far. Maddy had gone through my e-mail and found some deleted correspondence from a few weeks earlier. It had started with a Facebook message from a woman I didn't know—Jessica Someone. She'd seen my profile and thought I looked "intriguing." Now, the only reason I even kept a Facebook account was because Kara was on Facebook and I wanted to keep track of her life in Des Moines. But here was this young woman who wanted to "friend" me. Me, a fifty-something white male with graying hair and an expanding waistline.

As stupid as I knew it to be, between shopping for Christmas presents online and paying bills, I confirmed Jessica as a friend. I could have ignored her, but it seemed so harsh. Then, late one evening, on a whim, while Maddy graded papers in the next room, I e-mailed Jessica, asking if she'd like to chat sometime. She got right back to me. Oh yeah, she wanted to chat. I responded with a time when I wouldn't be in meetings the next day, even though I suspected a scam. Surely, she'd ask for money once the chat turned dirty.

But that was the end of it. I swear to God, we never chatted. My meetings ran late and I missed our rendezvous. She "de-friended" me and I never heard from her again.

Next to my laptop, Maddy had left a hand-written message of her own. She wanted to know how things were going with Jessica and me.

For the next ten evenings, after grinding it out at work all day, I drove downtown to visit my daughter at County. Kara spent the first two days in the psych ward sulking. The third day she got into a catfight—hair pulling, biting and scratching—with another patient. Days four and five, she retreated to her room. Every evening, she complained about her plight, begged me to get her out of the nut house. Day six, she met another young woman she liked, a willowy blonde girl who told me she'd tried to kill herself thirty-three times. Days seven through ten, Kara went back to complaining. The doctors sucked, therapy sucked, life sucked. Being the responsible party, I sucked most majorly.

During this time, Maddy and I rarely spoke. She kept the bedroom door closed, and I slept on the sofa.

The day they let Kara out, I brought her home and cooked one of her favorite dinners—crab cakes with saffron rice—while Kara and Ryan played a board game. Maddy watched the news, and we all pretended everything was fine.

That night, I couldn't sleep. I checked on Kara every hour, making sure she wasn't doing something stupid. The next morning, I took her to see her probation officer. He had the pharmacology report from the hospital. Sure enough, the cocaine Kara had snorted with Robin showed up, and the PO could have revoked her probation and sent her to jail. She shrugged and told him to do what he had to do. Me, I prostrated myself on his office floor and begged for another chance. Kara would re-enter rehab, re-start her twelve-step program, and have the support of friends and family. I laid it on thick. The idea of Kara sitting in jail was more than I could handle. I'd donated *pro bono* legal services to the poor black and Hispanic kids who ended up there because no one cared enough to go their bail, so I had a pretty good idea of how bad it could get.

In the end, the probation officer relented. They didn't have room for Kara in jail anyway.

Afterwards, I drove her to the airport, and we flew to Des Moines. I waited around until Jean arrived to take her off my hands. While we waited, I drank a beer and bought Kara a Coke and cheese-fries. I asked if there was anything she needed from me.

She pondered it, using her fries to mop up the cheese. After a while, she said, "Yeah, you could pay me the five bucks you owe me."

"Five bucks?"

"Yeah. That first night I came to town, you said you'd give me five bucks if I helped Ryan pick up his room."

It could have been true. I didn't remember, but I couldn't dispute it.

"Well, you never paid me, and I helped him clean up."

"That's it. Five bucks?"

She finished her fries and Coke. "You owe me."

I fished out my wallet and dropped a twenty on the table. A little while later, Jean arrived, and I turned Kara over to her.

I made it home in time for dinner.

Except there wasn't any dinner in the real sense. With me out of town, Maddy and Ryan had opted for take-out pizza, leaving me a couple of greasy slices on the counter.

After eating, I worked on the *Enterprise* with Ryan for a while before putting him to bed. When I came downstairs, Maddy was grading more papers and watching a TV show about Yellowstone. The entire region was a caldera. When it blew, other natural disasters like the Malaysian tsunami and Katrina would pale by comparison. It could happen anytime changing life as we knew it.

I pulled up a footstool and sat down. "Do you mind if we turn this off?" I asked.

"Do whatever you want."

"Can we talk?"

She set her papers aside. "You get Kara off?"

I related the story about the five bucks. Maddy chewed on her pen and said, "Sounds about right."

"I want to talk about us."

"There's nothing to say."

I gave it a beat. "I'm thinking we need to clear the air."

"Look, Ryan and I are leaving next week. The only reason I stayed this long was because I wanted to see this through with Kara. I figure I owe you that much. After all, I'm the home-wrecker that ruined your marriage and fucked up your daughter."

"You know better than that."

"Maybe, maybe not."

I took her hand and explained that I had no interest in other women. The downloaded pics and videos were sent to me by that asshole, Jack. I never asked for them.

She sat back in her chair. "So, why does he think you'd be interested in stuff like that? And why's it taken this long for you to tell him to stop?"

"He has a list of people. It's everyone he knows from school. He likes to pretend we're still nineteen."

"Just boys being boys?"

"I guess. I told him to take me off his list. I should have done it before."

"So, what about this Jessica?"

I'd rehearsed my story a hundred times on those trips to County and back.

"So, you're completely innocent?"

"I did something stupid, but I'd never cheat on you."

"You cheated on Jean."

"That was different."

She looked me straight in the in eye. "I fucked Manske," she said, her voice barely audible.

It hit me harder than an audit letter from the IRS. "What? Manske?"

"A few years ago. He was handling my divorce, and you and I were just starting out."

"Manske?"

"I was pretty vulnerable. We hadn't made any commitments."

I went into the kitchen, took a couple of beers from the refrigerator, and returned with them. "I always thought it was love at first sight with us."

She took a sip from her bottle and wiped her mouth. "You know better than that. There's no such thing as love at first sight. Anyway, I need to know if you can you handle it? Manske and me?"

I took my own sip. "Maddy. I don't want you to go. I don't want you to take Ryan away."

"And I don't want my son hanging around a man who looks at porn and cheats on his mom."

"Maddy, I swear to God..."

She put a finger to my lips. "So, can you handle me and Manske, or not?"

I might have been a dumb lawyer who clung to old friends longer than he should have, who had his own vulnerabilities, especially with old age breathing down his neck. I might have been living with a woman who had slept with one of my partners, but I wasn't so dumb I didn't know the answer to that question.

"Let's get married, Maddy. We can do it right away. Anytime you want."

She took another sip of beer. "Let me think about it."

CHECK-OUT

Michael Giorgio

A s the keycard slides into the slot, you know this is where you are meant to be. You have as much right to be in this room as they do, you figure. After all, the credit card paying for it is half-yours, and the reservation does say Mr. and Mrs. Your other, so-called better, half made the reservation for two. Unfortunately, you aren't one of the two intended to enjoy the king-size bed, the oversized bath, the drape-shrouded privacy. You're supposed to be at work.

Oblivious.

How stupid do they think you are? Didn't they think you'd see the bankcard statements with various local hotel charges? Didn't they think you could check the internet reservation system to see what rooms were reserved with money from your joint checking account? Didn't they care?

They should have cared.

Prying open the air conditioning unit, you chuckle. The internet is a wonderful thing, you think. Not only did you learn exactly what hotel they'd come to, but you learned all about inhaled poisons. Your eyes practically popped out of your head when you read the dangers of refrigeration and air conditioner coolants. Odorless inhaled gasses. Can be deadly. The words whoosh around in your brain as you alter the internal workings of the AC. The room is warm. Too warm for a hot summer's evening tryst. The air would be turned on soon after their arrival.

You picture them in bed, fully-clothed because you can't bring yourself to think of them any other way. As they inhale their slow deaths, their lips burn a cheery cherry red. Their eyes sear with pain. The coughing collapses them, keeps them from reaching fresh air. Keeps them from living.

You replace the AC cover and move into the bathroom. You know from following them into their room after prior rutting encounters that they always share a bottle of wine, using the provided plastic cups to have a pre-, or perhaps post-, coital drink. And you have another plan, just in case they leave the air conditioner alone.

Fishing in your bag of tricks, you find the needle. You were amazed how easy it was to steal from a diabetic coworker. How easy, too, it was to find a tasteless, odorless, colorless poison. There was that internet again, providing you with a wealth of information on unfaithful spousal elimination, cloaked under cover of helpful first aid hints and poison control sites. You learned what household products will cleanse your life of your cheating partner.

As you fill the syringe, you remember the old bug trap commercial. The one with the little baited traps that resembled cockroach resorts. Pests check in but they don't check out, the company claimed. Injecting enough liquid through the protective cellophane covering the hotel's plastic cups to coat their insides with a deadly lovers' potion, a pun pops into your mind and you laugh. In this trysters' resort, the rutters check in, and they do check out. Permanently check out, to join the pesty cockroaches in hell.

The last item in your old pharmacy bag is a little sack of powder. A skin-absorbed anecdote to the poison of infidelity. You hold up the baggie, marveling at how something that seems so innocent can be so deadly. The white dust looks like something sprinkled on a newborn's behind to eradicate a rash. Only what this powder eradicates is more irritating than a simple rash. You are eliminating a disease from your very soul, a festering rot that eats away at you from the inside out.

You check your watch, realize that your 'quick break to take care of a few personal things' has stretched to an uncomfortable length and you need to get back to work. Quickly, you strip the bed, throwing the comforter, blanket, and top sheet into a heap of gaudy flowers and beige velour. You open the baggie, sprinkling powder on the bare bed. A blizzard of lethal snow falls from a vengeful sky.

The storm over, you remake the bed, striving for the perfect look that hotel maids achieve effortlessly. Satisfied, you slip out of the room. In two hours, the lovers will arrive, debauchery on their minds. In three, you'll be free of your sham of a marriage.

Scot-free.

Back at work, you sit in your car, sweating despite the artic blast from the dashboard. Will it work? It has to. Will they figure out what you did? No, they don't know that you know. You're safe. If you're found out, imprisoned, even executed, what have you lost? Nothing worth saving.

Nothing.

Filled with this triumphant realization, you shut off the car engine and return to your job. Your absence isn't mentioned, probably hasn't even been noticed in the hectic workplace whirlwind. You aren't important enough to be missed, a fact that normally grates on you but for which you are grateful today. The realization that the same could be said of your marital position hits you, and you think maybe it's time to look for a new employment situation as well.

The afternoon is a new blaze of questions. Will the hotel clerk remember you, or will she just remember that one half of a couple checked in before the other? That's common, isn't it? When will you be notified? How? At work? Or will you have to wait until you get to home and hearth?

At day's end, you head outside, back to the car that delivered you to salvation. Reaching your parking spot, you see balloons have appeared in your backseat.

Your spouse sits in the driver's seat.

A surprise, you're told. A romantic night for two. A bottle of wine waits to be chilled in an ice bucket in a hotel room. The hotel room. Your mind whirls desperately, searching for escape, a way to reverse what you've done. But why bother? At least this way, you aren't checking out alone.

As the keycard slides into the slot, you know this is where you are meant to be.

HEARTS AND MINDS

Glenn Cassidy

The families spread out on blankets like an early Labor Day picnic, or they stand at the rail and point at husbands and fathers on the aircraft carrier. Even though Jason can't pick him out, he knows Danny is somewhere in the formation of sailors in dress whites on the flight deck. When a woman standing on the lawn glances back at Jason's truck and then up at the ship, Jason turns the visor down to block the late August sun and place his face in shadow. He doesn't want to leave yet; he wants Danny to know that he's there watching over him. Danny should at least be allowed that little bit that other sailors take for granted. Reaching behind the seat, he feels the two magnetic signs that advertise his nursery, and is reassured his vehicle is just another anonymous black pickup.

Could that woman be one of the wives of Danny's mates in the mechanic crew? Jason never goes to cookouts or any other kinds of family gatherings with Danny's crewmates, but there are those times when he and Danny bump into someone unexpectedly at the supermarket or the veterinarian. At last the woman goes back to waving at her husband and Jason slouches over the wheel, taking a swig from his bottled water.

No one knows how long it will be before Danny comes back. There will be at least several months before the war with Saddam might start, and his ship will be gone until some time after the war is over. It took so long for Danny to slowly inch his closet door open, with Jason gently nudging. It took a year and half for Danny to feel comfortable enough to move in with him. And just like that, the war is taking him away.

They met at a nightclub in Norfolk. It never ceases to amaze Jason how many military men dare enter a club so close to base. Any given night he could spot a dozen or more sailors hanging out in the shadows, mostly solo, the braver ones in small groups, every one with a baseball cap pulled low over his forehead to hide his haircut and overshadow his face. When they dance they slip in along the back wall. They avoid the lights on the patio; if they do venture outside they sit on the edges of the planters under the crape myrtles, backs to the lights. For all the effort at anonymity, the military bearing gives the men away. They cling to the shadows, but they don't cower there. They stand confidently in defense of a strategic pullback, not in retreat.

Danny was different. He looked like he'd never been to a gay bar before, and it turned out it was only his second time. He looked like a caricature in his raver boy disguise— big baggy shorts, oversized jersey, wooden beads around his neck, and the obligatory baseball cap with the bill practically touching the tip of his nose. Jason just barely glimpsed his eyes peeking out from under the cap, and a little later he could sense Danny's presence behind him as he danced. Danny tailed him to the bar and shadowed him in a grand circuit around the club, only backing off when Jason went out for fresh air on the patio. Danny wouldn't brave the light, and Jason could see him poke his head out of the shadows from the doorway every once in a while. It was a childish kind of flirting, but for lack of anything better to do Jason enjoyed teasing him. When Danny wasn't looking, Jason slipped back into the bar by another door. After just a couple of minutes Danny had latched onto his scent and was tailing him again.

Jason had never considered talking to any of the sailor boys—no military life, no military closet for him. But when Danny finally roused the courage to talk to him, offering up a bottle of water after last call, Jason accepted.

"I hope you're stealthier than that when stalking an enemy," Jason said.

"It depends on whether I want him to know I'm stalking him." Danny touched the cold bottle against the back of Jason's sweaty neck and Jason was captured.

Staring absently beyond the aircraft carrier into the ship channel, Jason scrapes at the label on the water bottle, the same brand Danny offered him that night at the club. He raises his bottle in a toast and the woman looks his way again. What is so interesting about his truck? He throws the engine in gear and turns around, grabbing one last glimpse of the boat in his mirror while withdrawing back to work.

Jason is working on another sleepless night after Danny's departure, playing thermostat roulette without finding the winning temperature to award a full night's rest. Until just a few months ago he slept alone most of the time. Now nothing feels right without Danny there. He puts the thermostat back to the frigid setting that Danny likes and retrieves the comforter off "Danny's bed" in the guestroom.

"Danny's room" is part of the elaborate charade they maintain on the navy's behalf. It's all made up like Danny lives in it, with all his clothes and personal belongings stashed in its closets and drawers. Danny's buddies have been over to watch football a few times, and Danny made a point of showing them his own room with the single twin bed and his uniforms hanging in the open closet.

When Jason returns with the extra comforter, the dog's spot on the rug at the foot of the bed is empty. He peeks around the corner and Regina's green eyes peer up at him from the hardwood floor on Danny's side of the bed. "You miss him, too?" He squats down to scratch the top of her head. He can tell when Danny's let her up on the bed because the black-on-black quilt looks more like a white shag carpet from her shedding. Jason gives into her longing eyes, tosses the extra comforter aside, and calls her up on the bed. Lying on his side, his front cold and his back sweating where it butts up against the dog, at last he manages uninterrupted sleep.

The week after Labor Day Jason is cutting the lawn, riding the mower in ever shrinking circles toward the center of the front yard, oblivious to everything but the line of cut grass and the fragrance of tropical ginger whenever he passes near the flower bed. When he finally raises his eyes to the world beyond the lawn, there's that woman again, the one who was watching him the day Danny's ship sailed. She's parked across the street, talking on her phone. When she looks at him he turns his head away and drives the mower around the corner to watch her from behind the Japanese cedar in the side yard. She knows his truck and now she knows his house. He waits out of sight for more than five minutes while she keeps talking and taking notes then finally drives away.

That night he dreams about her, finding her in the bathroom when he steps out of the shower, and he watches for her spying on him wherever he goes. He peeks through the blinds periodically while watching TV and scopes the street whenever doing any yard work. After two weeks without seeing her, the paranoia dies down and he realizes she was the only distraction keeping him from worrying about Danny.

The talking heads on the cable news channels keep his jaw in a perpetual clench. He rarely paid attention to international news before, but now he keeps up on developments in the impending war and the failing diplomacy. The reporters cover it like it's some idle sports gossip. *Is there any way the Yankees can lose the pennant with all the troops they've got lined up in the Persian Gulf? That sophomore basketball phenom is going to jump to the pros, no matter how much France protests at the Security Council.*

Jason rolls on the ground on a sunny October afternoon, playing tug-of-war with Regina in the pile of leaves he's just raked. Leaves are tangled in the short blond curls on his head and scratching under his shirt. He sighs on his back half-buried in the pile, but the dog is still full of energy and begging for *fetch*. Lying on the ground, he throws the ball to the far corner of the yard, and she's back in an instant, paws planted firmly on his chest, tennis ball dripping over his face.

"You would never leave me, would you? Would you?" He says it in a squeaky voice and she tilts her head from side to side, floppy ears raised, keen for a word from their common language, like *out, stay,* or *come.*

The dog drops the ball on his sternum and stares, ready to grab at it and play tug-of-war as soon as Jason's hand moves toward it. He looks past her, up through the canopy of the giant maple whose leaves the two of them have just scattered again. It's a gorgeous autumn day, and with every puff of breeze a few more siren-red leaves shake loose and spiral to the ground.

His chest vibrates as a trio of navy jets passes low overhead, and he checks his watch. It's time for that roundtable on CNN with members of the House and Senate intelligence committees. All the experts think war is inevitable, even the ones who give half-hearted arguments for why it isn't. Each month the troop count rises: thirty thousand, forty thousand, fifty thousand US soldiers around the Persian Gulf. It kills Jason to watch it and in the two months since Danny left he can't turn it off.

He shakes the leaves from his shirt and hair, then leads Regina into the house.

The one benefit of Danny's absence should be that Jason could let his guard down and not worry about hiding their relationship, other than camouflaging their email or telephone conversations. But now he's been running into that woman all over town it seems: at a stoplight, in the parking lot at Wal-Mart, hammering a *For Sale* sign into a yard a few blocks from his house. He's sure she's one of the navy wives. Fortunately he hasn't had to speak to her any of the times he's seen her. But now she's cornered him thumping a cantaloupe at the supermarket.

"You're Danny's roommate, aren't you?"

"Landlord," Jason corrects.

"Landlord." She nods her head. "I don't know if you remember me, but you and Danny ran into me once—right here in fact." She points at the tomatoes, where they had a discussion about the differences between the yellow ones and the red ones. "I'm Rolene, Charlie's wife—he's on Danny's ship."

Jason knows Charlie, all right. He works on the flight deck in Danny's crew, maintaining jet engines. They work together every waking moment when they're on the ship and they bunk together. They're best buddies and Charlie is exactly the person that Danny would talk to about his sex life, about his spouse, about the romantic weekend in the mountains, if only Danny wouldn't get kicked out of the navy for telling him.

"You work at Campbell's Nursery?" she asks, reading the logo on his polo shirt.

He nods.

"Do you do lawn service, too?"

If she's spying on him, she has bad intelligence.

"I saw you tending a yard over on Tanager Drive, a while ago."

"I live there."

"Oh." She gives him the Junior League Eyebrow Raise, reserved for people who either reach above or sink below their social station. When she looks at his cart, Jason gently places the cantaloupe in it. He sets it down over the price tag on the porterhouse and nudges the bags of Halloween candy to hide two six-packs of imported beer.

When a cheesy electronic rendition of *You Light Up My Life* screeches from her purse, Jason sidles over to the lettuce bins. She digs a pad out of her purse and while she takes notes about some real estate deal, Jason slips away to the next aisle.

An hour later, after throwing the steak in the fridge and eating a takeout burrito in the car, Jason sits in the public library reading *The Advocate* and waiting for a chance to check email on one of the computers. He agreed to cancel his *Advocate* subscription before Danny moved in with him for fear of anybody finding it lying around or anybody spotting it in the mailbox, even though it comes wrapped in anonymous plastic, as though it's embarrassing like pornography.

He remembers the day in college when he first dropped *The Advocate* subscription card in the mail. He'd taken the card out of a magazine in the library and carried it around for a month. He opened the mailbox and held that card for what seemed like days, knowing he was officially declaring his gaydom to himself and to the world, with no going back. Canceling it was like donning those hooded gowns the Taliban women wear, the ones that cover every inch of you and wipe out your identity save for the eyes peering out of the shadows.

As Jason waits for a terminal he sees Danny's worst nightmare right there in *The Advocate*. A soldier was dishonorably discharged because some officer's wife saw a suspicious email address on a message that went out to a group. The army tracked down the person who used the account, read his email, and discharged him for homosexual conduct. They took away his veteran's benefits and access to VA medical care, and they're even demanding repayment of his college tuition money.

Danny agreed to email Jason from Iraq only on certain conditions, and reading it at the library is one of them. They argued about it for two weeks, right up to the day before Danny sailed.

"Don't you think you're being a little too paranoid?"

"Can't risk it." Danny didn't look up from pressing his dress whites in preparation for his departure.

"I don't think I can take six more years of secrecy and denial." There were only four months left in Danny's enlistment, and Jason wanted a commitment that there would be no re-enlistment. If Danny didn't make up his mind until he was out at sea, Jason feared he'd re-up.

Danny continued ironing, sticking the tip of the iron under the buttons of the shirt to press every last bit of fabric. He spent hours each week ironing and polishing and sewing, totally engrossed in details that would only be noticed at inspection.

"I can't risk my benefits with a dishonorable discharge."

"You won't have to risk a dishonorable discharge if you don't re-enlist."

Danny propped his body against the wall and sighed. "You wouldn't have liked me if you met me before I joined the navy."

Jason stood in front of him and leaned his forehead against Danny's. "You're not going to turn back into a nineteen-year-old screw-up if you leave the navy."

"I need to keep my education benefits and my VA benefits."

They stood silently, Jason's arms planted against the wall on either side of Danny. Jason could smell the steam iron resting in its cradle on the ironing board behind him.

"We have to be careful." As Danny spoke, his breath passed across Jason's face, and Jason tried not to think about how long it might be before they could be that close again.

Jason closed his eyes. "Whatever it takes to get you home for good."

Danny pushed Jason away and returned to his ironing. "Maximum security closet, I don't care how paranoid. If I can go to war, you can handle the closet."

Jason agreed not to read Danny's email at home. The military's official policy was "Don't ask, don't tell, don't pursue," but the navy tended to forget the last part of that. Jason opened a Yahoo account, *Mary23851*. Jason's sister works at the municipal library and she assured him his identity would be protected from military snooping. He has to sign in and show an ID to use a terminal, but the librarians protect privacy by throwing away the sign-up sheet at the end of the day and expunging any book titles from his account as soon as the books are checked back in. That isn't just to protect sailors. The Patriot Act allows the government to examine records about anybody's reading habits without a search warrant while libraries and bookstores aren't even allowed to tell the person they're under investigation. If the libraries keep no records, then they have nothing to share with the intelligence agents or the navy. Librarians are Jason's heroes.

He returns the *Advocate* to the shelf and picks up a gardening magazine. There are still two people ahead of him waiting for computer terminals.

Danny should be on his way home soon with his enlistment nearly over, but the navy has instituted a stop-loss. Nobody is allowed a discharge—not if you fulfilled your service, not even if they kick you out for homosexual conduct—while they need people for the war. They'll keep any bodies until they don't need them, and then discharge them afterwards. Danny's given them a full enlistment—four years—and the navy can change his contract just like that.

Danny writes all his mail to "Mary" so it won't be suspicious, and Jason only uses Mary's account at the library. Even when he works late and can't make it to the library for several days, as much as he might ache to hear something from Danny, he doesn't read the account from home. They're covered, so they hope.

Mary is the most common woman's name they could think of, so it would be hard to go through all the *Marys* in the area to prove Danny's lie. They've prepared a whole history for her—she's a nurse in the city hospital in Richmond, far enough away from the base that nobody from his ship would know somebody there. She works in the emergency room, so she works irregular hours and that's why she's never home on the rare occasions Danny is given a chance to call. They decided Jason would be her cousin, to cover Danny trying to reach her at Jason's house, and that's made the calls short the few times Danny has reached him. "Tell Mary that I love her and miss her. I'll call again soon."

After a half-hour it's finally Jason's turn at the computer. *Mary23851* has no new mail.

With his notes and measurements spread over the table at the sub shop, Jason is drawing a new client's yard on a sheet of graph paper. He just walked the property with her on a cold January day and he still has on the fingerless gloves he wore to take notes. It's his biggest job so far, with some grading and a backyard waterfront to plan. It makes him nervous, but it's just what he needs. He intended to expand into landscape design from the get-go but he never seemed to have the time. He didn't expect to turn thirty before landing his first serious design contract.

When he first opened the nursery he had to grow his inventory and build up relationships to supply all the landscape designers and contractors. By the time the nursery had reached a good size, along came Danny. Now he can't stand to be in the house alone, obsessing over CNN, parsing what the pundits are saying, digging for the wording that shows war could still be avoided. He's taking on all the work he can to avoid free time and get away from the war talk.

It's the middle of January and the anniversary of the start of the first Gulf War has just passed. Fox News is on the sandwich shop's TV, ranting like armchair quarterbacks cussing out a football coach for punting on fourth down. Saddam is trying to trick the United Nations again about his weapons of mass destruction, so it will get too late into the hot season to start an offensive: the war has to start soon! They sound like children threatening to go into tantrums if they have to wait until after dinner to eat their ice cream.

He's right in the middle of telling off the TV assholes under his breath when Rolene appears. His notes cover the table except for a tiny gap for his sandwich and his drink. Her lunch is in a take-out bag, and he doesn't make any effort to clear the table for her.

"You're Danny's friend." There's a hesitation before she chooses the word *friend*. "Jason?"

He nods. The talking heads have advanced to a discussion of the rules of engagement. The armed forces have to win the hearts and minds of the Iraqi people. It's not enough to throw off a government that all the heads say is hated by the Iraqis. The American soldiers have to avoid attacking or damaging mosques and hospitals and schools, even though it's already known that some are being used as ammo dumps or fortresses. The Pentagon is printing flyers to explain how Iraqi soldiers can surrender. Coalition troops will have to refrain from shooting until the Iraqis are given a chance to lay down their arms. The citizens of Baghdad will wave American flags when the third infantry marches into the city.

"It's gonna happen soon," Rolene says.

An ex-general criticizes the proposed rules of engagement for putting American soldiers unnecessarily at risk.

"It's about time one of those generals said something," says Rolene. "We're there risking our lives for them, fighting for *their* freedom, and then we're supposed to handicap ourselves?" She shakes her head. "We can't let them take pot shots at us before we shoot back."

"Sometimes all these experts sound like they're just pushing little plastic army men around in a sandbox," Jason says. He's been aching to share his frustration with someone who'd appreciate what it feels like to have a partner overseas. He says it with too much emotion, and he regrets it as soon as it passes his lips. It's another one of those stupid little things he has to be careful about, and the reason he just stays away from any of Danny's colleagues and their families. He sips his soda and stares at the perfect circle of a water ring left on the table by the dew from the drink cup.

"At least our—Charlie and Danny—won't have to deal with that on the ship."

He chews on his straw while pretending to watch the jingoistic rants on the TV. As much as he's grateful to share what it feels like to have your partner off waiting for a war, he just wishes she would go. As the silence drags on, the pressure grows to say something. He wants to say he just hopes the Iraqis don't point their missiles at any military targets, like Danny's ship, but she'd probably have something to say to that and stay awhile longer.

After studying the notes and drawings on the table, she looks like she's ready to say something, but she's interrupted by that annoying *You Light Up My Life* ring tone. She heads outside to take the call, with a quick "It was nice to see you again."

That night, as a snow storm is beginning, Jason answers the doorbell to find a reporter from the local news, the one who went to Iraq and interviewed local sailors on the ship in the Gulf and filmed all those spots where local sailors gave holiday greetings to family back home. A frigid gust lifts the corner of the throw rug by the door and threatens to blow it and Jason away.

"We're with Channel 9 News. We have a video of Danny Cortez from his ship for you."

Jason is taken off guard and blurts out "Mary's not here." He squeezes the doorknob until his fingers turn white. Did Rolene put the navy up to investigating him? "I'm sorry."

When he tries to push the door closed the reporter sticks his foot in the way. "He said to show the tape to Jason

Campbell." Jason stops pushing but slumps his full weight against the door so the reporter still can't get in or pull his foot out.

"I know why you're concerned," the reporter says. "I assure you, I'm on the level."

The reporter goes straight to the living room, notebook in hand, surveying the room. The cameraman follows, carrying two giant black cases and a backpack full of equipment. In short time electronic gear spills out all over the coffee table, the floor, and the sofa. The cameraman plugs a digital recorder into a jack on the TV. Jason starts to protest when the camera is hooked up, but then Danny appears on the TV screen.

"Hi Jase. I miss you a lot." Danny leans into the camera and speaks softly, like they're having a private conversation. He's suntanned and buff and looks like he's lost a few pounds. "You were right about that reporter from Channel 9. Don't worry, he says nobody else will ever see this."

He dodges a football whizzing past his head. "Assholes," he yells at somebody a good distance off-camera and throws the ball back. It's sunny and all you can see behind him are empty deck and blue sky. It has all the mood of a Carnival cruise ship rather than an aircraft carrier preparing for war.

"I'm doing great. It gets boring sometimes with all the waiting. I've been working out a lot." He flexes his arms as his dog tags swing in front of his bare chest . "Channel 9 is doing a story on gay sailors and their partners back home. I told them they could talk to you, if you're okay with that. They'll hide our faces and camouflage our voices."

He leans in close to the camera again. "I love you."

Danny calls Regina with an ear-piercing whistle and the dog barks at the screen. The guys off-camera whistle in imitation then yell for Danny to come back to the football game. "Well, I gotta go. I'll be home as soon as we kick Saddam's ass." He gives a fist pump and runs off, whistling back at his shipmates.

The cameraman turns off the video and turns on the camera lights. The reporter begins the interview like it's a casual conversation. "Your partner seems to really enjoy the navy."

"You don't know what we go through to protect his identity." His back is to the camera and he adjusts his baseball cap to block a glare from the camera lights. They're reflecting off the framed print of a garden at the University of Virginia designed by Thomas Jefferson. "I can't believe Danny's risking that for this interview."

"He said - " the reporter looks at his notes. "He said he's sacrificing his navy career for your relationship and he's coming home as soon as the navy lets him go?"

Jason nods.

The reporter flips a page and clicks his pen. "In his interview with me your partner said he wants people to know what that sacrifice is like. What's it like for you?"

The next time Jason sees Rolene, it's at work on a sunny day in March. Friends of his are having a commitment ceremony in a month and Jason is helping to choose potted plants to put around their patio for the reception.

"You sure you don't want us to pay for this?" one of the grooms asks.

"I'm just borrowing it from inventory for a couple of days. Consider it a wedding present, from me and Danny."

"You have to let us help you with yours."

"Yeah." Jason scans the list on his clipboard to make sure he's covered everything.

"You'll get your chance. They can't keep him forever."

Jason is kissing them goodbye when Rolene spots him from the camellia aisle.

"Are any of these fragrant?"

He tries to read her, but she isn't giving anything away. She had to see that.

"When I was a little girl my grandmother had this big red camellia as tall as her house. It was always in bloom at Christmas and smelled like a bouquet of roses."

He snaps the clip on the clipboard and slides his pen under the metal. "I think you want the ones that bloom around Christmas." They're standing in the japonica section, still blooming in mid-March and drawing the attention of everybody shopping the first warm day of spring. The fragrant sasanquas are another row over, all bloomed out and all alone. Jason points to the sasanquas and draws her eyes away from the affianced friends walking to their car.

"Mr. Campbell," an employee interrupts, handing him the phone. "Delivery problem." Jason steps away to take the call, but as soon as he hangs up Rolene is in his face again.

"I don't care about the color. I just want the most fragrant one you've got. Two, one for each side of the front door." She's looking at the Campbell's Nursery logo on Jason's shirt. "Does your family own the nursery?"

Jason hesitates.

"*You* own the nursery." She surveys the reach of the property. He can practically see LEDs flashing in her eyes as she estimates his annual turnover.

"You do design and installation too?"

He nods.

"Do you know that house down your street, at the corner of Woodthrush?

Jason drives past it every day. Its front yard has become a wasteland of dead shrubs, weeds, and bare sand where a lawn once grew. "I think so."

"It's the one with the front yard that looks like a slum."

He contains a nervous laugh. That's a landmark Danny uses when giving directions to their house: *turn left at the slum.*

Rolene pulls her date book out of her bag and hands Jason her card. "I'm about to list that house, and that front yard needs a makeover." She flips the pages back and forth. "I'd like to see what you could do for fifteen hundred dollars."

"Design, installation, and plants?"

She looks up from her date book. "Two thousand? I don't need Monticello, just a little curb appeal." She digs out her pen. "I'll meet you there Wednesday at four." She writes the entry in her book without looking up for confirmation.

"I'll see what I can come up with, but *little* is the operative word."

"It's just the front yard. Take the dead things out and put living things in." When her phone chirps—fortunately just a chirp and no song—she opens it to read a text message. "My babysitter. It's hard with Charlie gone."

The sun is eclipsed by a passing cumulus, literally dimming the conversation with an uncomfortable silence. It's over six months since Danny left, and spring bulbs are beginning to bloom. People expect the war could start any day now. After the cloud passes the sunlight returns but the silence persists.

Finally Jason leads her to the next aisle. "There's a camellia over here you might like."

That night Jason's interview for the gay sailors series airs on the late news. Even though they don't show his face, you can tell he's tearing up. The way the shoulders hunch, the way his head jerks to the side, the crack in his voice. "He wanted to make a career in the Navy, but how long can you stand being part of a group that doesn't want you?"

"Has your partner considered outing himself to get a discharge?"

You can see Jason's head straighten and his jaw clench. "They'll dishonorably discharge him and take away his benefits. Dishonorable, like he hasn't given over four good years to the navy."

When Jason pulls up at Rolene's new listing, two men are at work painting the fascias and window trim.

From their boombox an announcer reports that there are just two hours left in the ultimatum for Saddam to surrender or face invasion. Danny could be at war by the time Jason fixes dinner.

The yard's been a disaster for a couple of years, with skeletons of past glory still present in the half-dead boxwood too close to the house and too shaded by the spreading canopy of an oak tree. Jason winces every day he drives past, and he should be excited that its appearance is about to improve, but in two hours any remaining denial about the inevitability of the war will be over. He kicks up gravel and twigs from the bare spots in the lawn as he walks the front yard, plugging in plants in his mind while waiting for Rolene.

You just have to work with your environment. Maybe those boxwoods would work great as a foundation planting in a yard full of sun. They may have even been planted in this yard when it was sunny, before the trees shaded everything. But now they just don't belong, and they'll never be happy here. Better to rip them out and plant rhododendrons that could thrive in dappled shade and give some spring color to show off the house to potential buyers. And give up on trying to grow a lawn under that magnolia. Re-sod in the sunny areas, mulch in the shady spots. Learn to accept nature and don't force it.

When Rolene finally arrives she doesn't seem all that interested in hearing his suggestions. There's a pregnant woman in the passenger seat who stays behind in the car, probably another navy wife.

"We saw Danny at the videoconference Sunday." The same TV station that was running the gay partner stories arranged a conference on the base for the wives and families. "He and Charlie were in good spirits."

Unprepared for mention of Danny, the best he can do to hide his emotions is to turn away. Danny called him over the weekend, using the satellite phone from that reporter who's now back on Danny's ship. The call came at three in the morning and scared Jason and then scared Regina when Jason jumped out of bed. But Danny could talk frankly since he wasn't on a military phone. He was still frighteningly gung-ho, but he wanted to say one more *I love you,* just in case.

Now Jason just wants to get home, where he can let his feelings out and not have to hide them. He takes a step toward the middle of the yard, pointing up at the treetops. "You have some wonderful mature trees here. A high canopy and bright shade." When he starts to describe his plan for the yard Rolene cuts him off.

"Can you fix all this within the budget?"

Jason keeps his back to her while nodding agreement.

"Just do it then."

He tries again to give her an overview of his plan, but she just talks right over him.

"It sounds fine." She looks at her watch and says she has to go because the wives are getting together for a potluck to watch the news. "It's nice to be with—" She cuts herself off. "Just do whatever you think is right. I need it for an open house Sunday morning." She hasn't taken more than two steps away from her car since she got there, and she's in it and gone before Jason can say anything more.

The deadline has passed when the attack was supposed to begin. Cameras scan the skies over Baghdad and every sound or flash of light is urgently reported as the possible first strike. In the studio rent-a-generals talk about attacking from Turkey, from Kuwait, from Saudi Arabia. Attacks could fly over Israel from the Mediterranean, or fly in from carriers in the Gulf, where Danny is stationed. Jason has heard it so many times he could name all the air bases and bodies of water, all the major cities and strategic targets, and he could identify all the countries by their outlines on the map.

The analysts casually hypothesize about how long a war would last and how many American dead would be acceptable or likely. They've repeated it so many times, they're as matter-of-fact as a chef on a cooking show explaining lasagna. If you don't feel the pain of an absent face staring back at you from your nightstand, it's easy to forget they're talking about real live people, about human carnage and not marinara sauce.

It's nine and he still hasn't eaten. It seems every time he starts for the kitchen there's another false alarm about an imminent air raid. For three hours he hasn't moved except running to let the dog out, and she's barking now to come in. Sure enough, he hears the sirens, the explosions, and the shouting reporters while wiping the dog's muddy paws in the utility room.

But after twenty minutes the bombing is over, and he hangs on most of the night, waiting for more. Dinner is half a can of barbecue spiced peanuts and he wakes in the morning balled up on the sofa with peanuts spilled all over and the dog puking up peanuts by the back door. CNN is still waiting for the next attack on Baghdad.

Four days into the war, Jason leans against a doorway in Rolene's living room. Women and children are everywhere, a dozen or so of each, in the kitchen, on the deck, in the backyard. The local news is running unattended in the living room, but people periodically peek in from the kitchen or pause a moment to watch on their way to the bathroom.

Jason has hardly slept in the past four days, watching CNN all night at home and listening to it all day on a radio at the nursery. The Iraqi air force is destroyed, and no ships have been bombed. A couple of missiles have been launched at Saudi Arabia, but none have hit any American ships. Hopefully there aren't any more missiles in some hidden reserve.

It seems that most of the women are officers' wives, even though Rolene's husband is an enlisted man like Danny, in the same mechanic team on the flight deck. Given what Jason has learned from Danny, this kind of mixing is unusual. Rolene must have sold them houses or maybe knows them from around her development. It's giving Jason a new appreciation for the rarity of his own neighborhood, where there are no sailors as far as he can tell. He sees plenty of navy families at the nursery, but they tend to live in the other direction, toward the base. The enlisted men's families like to buy inexpensive and pretty boring stuff, annuals like marigolds and garishly red salvias—hopefully not planted together—and a lot of tomato plants. Most of them live in the lower rent areas—an enlisted man's paycheck doesn't go very far. The families seem to like duplexes with tiny yards, and they aren't out to landscape, just to produce a little summer joy.

Jason is watching the TV alone. The local affiliate is still reporting the war around the clock, interrupted only by commercials.

Rolene brings him a drink and introduces him to one of the wives. Rolene asked him over to plant her camellias and to give her ideas for sprucing up her backyard, then feigned forgetfulness when the guests started arriving. He's totally out of place and has been standing alone. "Anamary is an ER nurse at County General."

Jason coughs up a mouthful of strawberry daiquiri.

"Are you okay?" Rolene bangs her hand on his back.

Jason nods and exhales slowly while reviewing all the details about "Mary." Could he change her history? Have her work in obstetrics or oncology instead of the ER? Or has Danny already told them about her and they're testing him? At least the fictional Mary works at a different hospital from this Anamary.

"Jason owns Campbell's Nursery, and he's going to redo my backyard. His boarder works on the crew with my Charlie."

Anamary smiles politely, one fingernail slowly stroking the side of her drink. "He's your boarder?" She's the pregnant woman who sat in the car while he was meeting with Rolene at that house that's for sale.

"Danny does some installation work for me, too, to supplement his income," Jason blurts. "You know navy pay."

"My Charlie has one more year, and then he wants to work for a commercial airline," says Rolene. "They pay their mechanics a lot better, even after the cutbacks since nine-eleven."

"My Donald is a pilot," says Anamary. "Once he puts in ten years, he wants to be a commercial pilot." She turns to Rolene. "You are so right about pay at the airlines."

Jason rubs his hands around the frozen drink. It's not like Danny or Charlie would ever see anything like a pilot's salary.

"Has the deployment affected admissions at the hospital?" Rolene asks.

"Obstetrics is fixing to get real busy, but the ER is slow with the sailors gone." She laughs nervously. "Now, I don't mean to imply," she speaks very slowly, in a very genteel southern tongue that extends the ending y for about three syllables. After a pause she finishes the sentence, "that sailors are any more prone to accidents than anyone else. It's just that they're gone, and a lot of their children are staying with relatives out of town, so there are just a lot fewer people around."

Judging from the crowd on Rolene's deck, it does not appear that officers have sent their families away.

"It's a good thing it's slow," says Anamary. "I've had to cut back my hours some," patting her belly as she speaks. It's almost seven months since the ship sailed, and she looks about seven months pregnant.

Several minutes pass without anybody mentioning Mary, and Jason feels considerably more relaxed after downing his drink. He decides to do some intelligence gathering of his own. "How many nurses work in the ER?"

"Between all shifts?" He nods and she counts to herself. "About twenty."

"Do you do regular shifts, or do you get called in a lot, like if there's a bus crash or something?"

She laughs and shakes her head. "We don't page nurses. We page doctors when we need a specialist."

An ad for the series on gay sailors appears on the TV. A shadowy face is talking: "I can't talk to my partner on the phone, and I can't even talk to the family support group."

Anamary shakes her head. "I'd hate to think of a gay sharing a bunk with my Donald."

"I don't think your Donald would complain about a gay mechanic keeping his plane in good condition." Rolene looks at Jason after she says it, and Jason turns away. She might as well have said *like Jason's boyfriend Danny.*

After an extended uncomfortable silence, Anamary says, "There's a male nurse in my department that everyone thinks is gay."

A little while later, Rolene is coaxing Jason outside to play wiffle ball with the children. "You can't just stand here stressing out with the TV." She pushes him toward the door. "Come on, the kids could use a father figure for a little while."

The backyard is surrounded by stockade fencing that turns in to connect to the house just before the front yard. The only landscaping other than lawn consists of one young mulberry tree near the back corner and some unhappy azaleas with just a handful of buds in a low damp spot by one side of the deck. Bases for the ball game are marked with paper plates.

Rolene pitches the plastic ball and Jason helps her four-year-old daughter swing the bat. He stands behind her, with his arms around her, holding the bat with his hands over the girl's. It's a home run all the way back to the fence and he coaches her around the bases.

Next up is Anamary's four-year-old son. When Jason hands him the bat, the boy asks him to help him hit a home run, too.

Jason is showing him how to stand near the plate when Anamary calls from the deck. "Donny Junior, come on and get some ice cream." When Rolene looks up at her, Anamary asks, "Would you round up the rest of the children for dessert?"

Jason shares a knowing glance with Rolene and decides it's time to leave. A few minutes later, the children are enjoying an ice cream feast on the deck while Rolene is writing Jason a check for the camellias. There's a report on the TV that an American plane has crashed and the adults scramble for the living room.

Some of the wives hold hands and pray. When the reporter says the crash happened near Baghdad, the non-pilots' wives sigh with relief, then silence themselves as the pilots' wives crowd in closer to the television.

We have an eyewitness who believes the downed plane was a Navy F-18.

Anamary grabs at the nearest hand—Jason's—and holds it in a death grip. Rolene flips from the local CBS affiliate to CNN to NBC and back again. Some of the non-pilots' wives tend to the children on the deck while the rest stand in silence waiting on the TV. At last CNN reports the plane is an air force F-16 from Qatar. Anamary releases Jason's hand and Rolene pours another round of daiquiris. It doesn't take much convincing for Jason to stay for one more drink.

Two weeks later, Anamary shows up at Jason's nursery. He and his crew installed Rolene's new landscaping a week ago, thankfully with no surprise gathering of the wives, and he was thinking he'd finished running the navy wife gauntlet. He pretends not to notice Anamary as he goes about his business. She wanders about the nursery aimlessly, starting out in the annuals, which have only been on display for a few days. It's early April so he's only put out a few tables by the south side of the building where the sun-heated brick keeps the air a few degrees warmer at night and can help protect against any frost that might sneak up.

Anamary occasionally picks up a plant without bothering to look at the tags that tell how much sun and water it needs and how big it will grow. While Jason is arranging the perennials to make space for some new varieties, Anamary watches from the herb section. When he helps a customer in ornamental trees, she moves into shade-tolerant shrubs. He goes into the office to get some shelf tags and when he comes out Rolene is with Anamary. As soon as Rolene spots Jason she charges with Anamary in tow.

"One of your employees left this behind." Rolene holds up a baseball cap with the Campbell Nursery logo on it.

"You did a nice job on her yard," Anamary tells him, and he nods his head in acknowledgment.

"Nice job?" Rolene says. "She loves it. She's been over every afternoon this week for drinks and to admire the landscaping from my deck."

When Jason glances at Anamary's belly from the corner of his eye, Rolene adds, "Of course, she was only drinking tea."

Jason extends his hand to take the hat from Rolene and freezes mid-movement when she says, "Anamary would like you to landscape her yard, too."

"We're having a get-together at my house Sunday afternoon, and you're welcome to come." Anamary sounds like she's just as uncomfortable with that as he is.

He tries to improvise an excuse. "Sunday? This Sunday—"

"Come." Rolene places the cap in Jason's hand and wraps her hands around his. "We can have a little socializing along with business."

Rolene lets go of his hand only when he reaches for the printed invitation that Anamary is offering him.

Nobody peeks into the living room to check on CNN at Anamary's potluck. The TV isn't even on. Baghdad has fallen and the Iraqi army no longer has any weapons able to hit the ship. Activity on Danny's ship has even slowed down enough that Danny was able to make a call to Jason. It was on a military phone, so it was a brief call with a message for "Mary."

The only sound in the house other than the women chatting and the noises of children at play comes from the blender, churning out a continuous stream of daiquiris. The women trade theories and rumors about how soon their husbands will return. This is a game that Jason tries hard to avoid, expecting only disappointment if he gets his hopes up about seeing Danny anytime soon.

He's happy to join Rolene and two other wives for a game of wiffle ball with the children. It's a warm day in mid-April and all the children are in shorts. He helps two little girls who can barely swing a bat to get hits. As he chases them around the bases their arms flap with uncoordinated glee while Anamary observes from the deck, sipping virgin daiquiris and looking like she's about to deliver a beach ball any second.

When it's Anamary's son's turn to bat, Jason hesitates at first, then turns his back on Anamary and steps in behind the boy. It's uncomfortable, standing behind Donny Junior as far as he can while still reaching around him to help him hold the bat. They swing and miss the first pitch, and he can feel Anamary's eyes scorching the back of his neck. On the second pitch he stands closer to the boy in a more comfortable position and swings so hard he lifts Donny Junior off the ground with the follow-through, sending the ball to the weeds at the end of the yard. Instead of circling the bases Donny Junior runs toward the deck, shouting, "Mommy, I hit a home run." Jason has to fetch him to lead him around the bases.

After the game Jason is helping Rolene and another wife serve up brownies and milk for the children at the picnic table. He watches Anamary, holding her two-year-old daughter, try to get comfortable in a resin deck chair, while the other children are climbing onto the benches around the table. Anamary's son is practicing swinging his bat and just barely misses Jason's thigh as Jason bends over the table. When Jason looks at him, Donny Junior asks, "Can we play again after dessert?"

Jason sets the bat aside and lifts the boy onto a picnic bench while glancing at Anamary. "If your mother says it's okay." He sets brownies and milk where Donny Junior can reach them. "Make sure you drink your milk so you're strong enough to hit lots of homers."

After dessert and another game of wiffle ball, Anamary is waddling around the back yard working up landscaping ideas with Jason.

"Can you plant azaleas and hide the fence, like you did at Rolene's? Or maybe not azaleas. Rolene already has those, maybe something else?" She leans against a mature redbud that would make a good focal point for a planting in the corner.

"How about forsythias?"

"Oh, I love forsythias. But I like how Rolene's yard looks, all white against that dark fence."

"How about spirea? It looks sort of like a white forsythia, except it blooms a few weeks earlier." It's also tough enough to stand up to kids playing ball in the backyard. He's already talked her out of baby's breath and several other perennials that would be trampled to shreds by a soccer game.

"Earlier than azaleas, too?" She smiles when he nods approval.

"And to keep the blooms going, we can plant a dogwood in the corner and some white rhododendrons by the house, so you still have something in bloom while Rolene's azaleas are blooming."

Anamary's excitement keeps building as they circle the yard and fill in details for perennials and two more trees. In the far corner the dark fence ends and there are several feet of the back of a shed at the edge of the neighbor's property. Jason suggests red twig dogwood.

"That sounds exotic."

He explains it's actually more like a bush, with slender stems as tall as the shed that would stand out bright red against the whitewashed shed after losing their leaves in winter. "It looks especially dramatic standing up in the snow."

As he helps her climb up to the deck he suggests a Harry Lauder walking stick with its weird curlicue stems to go next to the stairs as a specimen piece, and a planter with daphne by the back door to give her some fragrance in February. When they reach the top step, there's a shriek from the living room.

On the TV, there's an image of a reporter in the studio with an audio feed from a reporter on an aircraft carrier via satellite phone.

The plane that was landing struck another plane on the deck that had landed just a moment before, setting off a huge fireball. The pilots were still on those planes and there were about a dozen people on the flight deck in the immediate area when the crash happened.

There's no group prayer this time and no one slipping away to check on the children. A few minutes later there's an update from the reporter with the satellite phone.

The navy has asked me not to provide details until the families are notified. I can tell you that two planes were completely destroyed in the fire and several crew members on the ground were carried away with severe burns. Choppers are preparing to evacuate the injured to a hospital in Qatar.

Anamary calls a cousin who's a producer with Channel 9 News, but he doesn't know any more than what has been reported on the air. He doesn't know who the pilots are, or whether the planes belong to the squadron of Anamary's husband or anybody else's husband. Even though the station can't broadcast detailed information, the cousin will call back to tell her personally whenever the reporter finds out who's been hurt.

Jason starts for the door. "I—I should go."

Rolene grabs his arm before he takes two steps and asks him to stay. He shakes her off, then Anamary speaks up. "My cousin will know before word ever gets to you otherwise."

No one in the room has moved since hearing the first details of the crash. They face the TV, but their focus is beyond. Some are quietly praying to themselves.

Anamary drops into a chair, clutching the phone like a life preserver. She motions for Jason to sit.

By now some of the children have wandered into the room and can sense something is wrong. When one child starts crying he sets off two others. Rolene goes out to the deck to keep the rest of the children occupied while checking the TV through the open door.

While Anamary holds her daughter, her son cries at her feet then latches onto Jason's legs as Jason stands in front of the television. Jason sits on the floor, and Donny Junior locks his arms around Jason's left biceps, his head resting on Jason's shoulder.

Jason closes his eyes. He clasps his hands around his shins and buries his head between his knees, Donny Junior still clinging to him. As the news runs on the television, he waits with the other wives for Anamary's cousin to call.

DRAGON-SLAYER

Ed Davis

be's hadn't changed much since Larry and I'd gone to Mound School right across the street. Except that his sour-faced old Lebanese dad was no longer behind the counter. It looked about like it did the first time I went into the beer joint on a dare to buy a Slim Jim and a Pepsi. It was after school one day in fifth grade, and Larry stood behind his dad, hanging his head. He was a year older and I barely knew who he was. But he flunked that year, putting him in my sixth grade class where we became best friends.

Now, twenty-six years later, I was hoping to see my old buddy, though I hadn't seen him once since graduation two decades ago. Twice a year or so, I'd come to see Mom, then leave town without seeing a single other soul, convincing myself (not without guilt) that I wouldn't have anything in common with anyone who'd stayed here. This was my first time back since her funeral two years ago. I didn't have anybody in Pittsburgh to go home to; it seemed like as good a time as any to renew old acquaintance.

It was still a long, narrow room with paint-chipped brick walls and vinyl and chrome stools bolted to the green linoleum floor. Willie Nelson crooned "You Were Always on My Mind," as I dropped into the booth beside the door, the only empty seat in the place.

"Getcha something?"

She had materialized from vapor to stand at my elbow. Curly raven hair framed her high crimson cheekbones and full lips. Her copper skin fairly glowed.

"A Corona?"

She put her hand on her hip, her eyes challenging. "Only American beer here."

"Bud Light?"

A mocking smile. "No light. Just real beer."

"How about a Colt .45?" It was the most macho beer I could think of. Her lips lifted over small, straight teeth.

As she sashayed behind the counter, I watched her swaying hips till she disappeared. In the mirror, one of the drinkers caught my eye and grinned at me before I looked away. Shivering, I glanced out the window. Snow had stopped for the time being. I could still make it home before midnight if I didn't stay long.

Thirty seconds later, she placed the can in front of me. "You a professor or what?"

And here I thought I was inconspicuous in jeans and flannel shirt. "Chemist for a mining firm in Pittsburgh. I'm on my way home. Been at a conference at Pipestem State Park."

She cocked her hip, stuck her belly out again, firm and round as a grapefruit. "Welcome to 'Wonderful, Wild West Virginia.'"

I raised the beer and toasted her. Her eyes followed my hand. "A good-looking man like you is not married?"

I smiled and shook my head. Aware of the drinkers' eyes watching me in the mirror behind the counter, I was suddenly enjoying myself for the first time since leaving the city Friday night after work—no, for a lot longer than that.

Ed Davis

"Why don't you sit down?" I gestured toward the other side of the booth. "And I'll tell you the sad story of my life."

"No, thanks." But she softened her refusal with a smile. "My name is Maria."

When she folded her arms across her chest, her belly bulged, firm and round as a grapefruit, and my heart fell. Now I knew what the healthy glow was about. Still I could pretend. Anything to stay a little longer and put off going home to an empty bed in my efficiency apartment. But before I could reply, a cold blast of air clobbered us, and the place erupted in shouting and cheering behind me. As applause subsided, voices rose. I knew what I'd see before I turned around: Larry the Dragon-Slayer, who'd always had my back since sixth grade, who'd beat up Jamey Chambers for saying my singing sucked in the junior high talent show. My singing *had* sucked, but you didn't say that to the band's drummer, Larry Hasser.

"Where'd you put 'im, Larry?"

"Dumpster."

The place exploded into howling laughter. Yet I felt an envelope of silence around me, radiating from Maria who still stood watching, as if on an island far away. Her hand on her belly became a talon, the long fingernails raking flesh beneath the thin material. It didn't take a genius to figure out whose baby Maria was carrying. In a moment he was standing above us. My old friend had aged well, only slightly fleshier in the jowl and waist. Blood trickled from the right side of his mouth. His eyes were on Maria, and I waited for him to grip my shoulder, rip the stranger from the booth and kick his sorry ass, too.

Feebly, I raised my glass. "To Sir Lawrence." I hoped he remembered how we'd loved *Lawrence of Arabia*.

Stepping closer, he peered at me. "Johnny?"

Maria uncrossed her arms, her mouth gaping. "Johnny Abshire?"

Nobody'd called me Johnny in a while, and it sounded good. She sat down across from me and took my right hand between both of her incredibly warm ones.

"Lawrence has talked so much about how good you played music together, how you sang like Mick Jagger and Elvis Presley. You must spend the night!"

When I looked back up at Larry, he was nodding and smiling.

The beer and talk flowed for the next two hours, Larry stopping by my table as often as he could to chat. Early on he'd told me his old man had died of a heart attack nearly ten years ago. After my third Colt, I'd stopped paying attention to the snow. Also, I'd grown considerably warmer. Only two men now lingered at the counter. Not for the first time I wondered why I'd avoided all contact with anyone from my past on my semi-yearly visits home, until, after Mom's death, they ceased altogether.

"Yeh," Larry was saying, sprawled on the seat across from me, "we made it through the first trimester, and we're happy as hogs at a trough."

"Congratulations. Kids are wonderful."

He wiped his mouth on his sleeve. "Got any?"

"A daughter, four."

"I'm hoping for a girl." He laughed. "Everybody that comes in here swears it'll be a boy, though."

I glanced toward the counter, where Maria stood like a queen, ignoring the last two drinkers. "I heard you kept playing in bands after high school."

He nodded. "Most of 'em sucked. All people around here want to hear is country or southern rock. *Damn.*"

We laughed. "Well, you obviously found other good reasons to stay here. I would've if I could've."

"You were too big a brain for that."

"Yeah, what a success story. I went to college and *still* didn't get out of the mines!"

"At least you're a chemist. You don't run a beer joint in Gardner, West Virginia."

"And I don't have a wife anymore, either."

His face sagged. "What happened?"

"We're separated. It'll be two months next week."

"But you've still got your daughter."

I shook my head again. "Erin won't let me see her right now. 'Too confusing,' she said. 'Not until we get some things straight.'"

He shook his head. "Man, is that even legal?"

"To tell you the truth, I don't even know."

"She'll come around. My old guitar player went through the same thing. Now it's all worked out." Larry grinned the tight grin he used to wear during drum solos when he beat the loving hell out of his used Slingerlands. "Any chance you'll get back together?"

"No." I was a little shocked; I'd never actually said it out loud before. Did I not want us to? Did I want that night in the kitchen to be the last time I made love to my daughter's mother?

Slouched in the booth, Larry was talking. "You make me glad I stayed here." His eyes widened. "No offense!"

I opened my hands. "None taken."

"It's just that I've got everything I want." He leaned back and patted his stomach as if he'd just eaten a great meal. "And it came right to me."

I imagined Maria lying naked on top of the covers in their bedroom, one hand on the mound of her belly she'd displayed to the men in Abe's all evening.

"To 'everything.'" I raised my beer even though it was, thank God, empty. "How did you and Maria get together?" When I glanced this time, she was glaring at the drinkers, willing them to leave.

"She came up from Florida two years ago, April. She's from this real tight-ass Cuban-American family. Her sister married this rich prick in Charleston who runs a fancy restaurant. After Lola sent for Maria to come up and work for them, brother-in-law Harry wanted to pay her slave wages as well as receive certain favors. So she caught a bus for Miami, had an hour layover and came in here for a drink, even though she said the place looked like Cockroach City."

He sat back, grinning like he'd won the lottery. "I had to marry her, though she raised holy hell before she'd finally do it. These jerks would've never left her alone, otherwise. I've had to beat some of them off her."

"Like tonight."

He cracked his knuckles and his hands looked scarred and callused. Over six feet by seventh grade, he'd been a good friend to have on my side. He'd been a great drummer, slamming snare and cymbals like a demon unleashed, but he'd missed gigs because of his Old World father Abraham, who used to beat him with a spatula. ("They say he beats his wife," Mom told me when I said Larry and I were friends, "but you can't always believe rumors.") Thinking of Abe made me shudder, the beers' warmth fading. Beyond the fogged glass, I couldn't tell if it were snowing or not. The radiator against the far wall had fought unsuccessfully for hours to keep the icy night outside, especially when someone left, like now. Maria's cold Cuban stare had finally convinced the last drinkers to call it a night.

As before, she appeared like smoke. "We close now, Lawrence."

"I'm talking to Johnny," Larry said flatly.

"*Basta!*" Both arms circled from her sides to include the room, the building, the town, maybe the whole state. "This is all shit."

"Shut the fuck—"

The wet rag he'd used to wipe the counter all night hit him in the face. Instantly on his feet, he threw the rag toward the counter. It hit the edge and fell onto one of the stools. Maria glared at him before picking it up. He calmly rose, walked slowly over to where she stood, and, in one motion, seized her right arm, jerked her onto the stool and raised his fist. Part of me lifted, though most of my weight, I'm ashamed to say, stayed glued to the vinyl. My face burned in the scorching cold air. The radiator hissed. Now Larry twisted her arm behind her while she struck his chest with her free hand.

"Lawrence... stop!"

I was on my feet but stood frozen to the floor. While I tried to will my legs to move, he released her, she locked both arms around his neck, pulled him toward her and they kissed. It lasted a long time. I tore my gaze away and looked outside. Through a cleared spot on the glass, I saw snow whirling around the flashing traffic light. My vision went black for a second, and behind my eyelids, I saw the yellow glow of the kitchen stove clock on Spring Street (the home of my soon-to-be ex-wife and daughter). Erin and I had made love on the floor in front of the stove the night before I left for good. If we'd waited to go upstairs, it wouldn't've happened. Cory had screamed from her room above our heads, having another bad dream.

"Johnny, you *are* staying, aren't you?"

I snapped back to reality. Maria showed me her beautiful teeth while Larry nuzzled her hair, staring straight at me. Gone was the dragon-slayer; back was the sixth-grader who refused to read aloud in class but spoke eloquently with his fists. My face was too frozen to return his smile, so I just nodded.

I couldn't sleep. The sofa was comfortable enough, but the unaccustomed amount of alcohol kept my mind humming. At first I couldn't get the picture of Maria out of my mind, the way she'd looked when she first appeared at my table, before I knew she was anybody's wife, before I knew what the healthy glow was about. And then I'd see Erin, her eyes turned away from me as she'd lain on the kitchen floor, before our daughter had cried out. It was the first time we'd made love in months. Then I recalled how

Maria had looked after she'd thrown the towel, her bottom lip thrust out. Defiance or... anticipation?

Then I heard the smallest thump—a dropped shoe, maybe—and opened my eyes wide, shot back to *that* night, the one I thought I'd forgotten, the one spent here in this very room, different, then, with Larry's record player and LPs stacked on the dresser, clothes all over the floor, posters of the Stones, Doors and Animals on the walls. That night we'd played at the youth center, which had been okay with old Abe, since it was local and there was no booze. Larry usually stayed overnight with me, but it was my first (and, as it turned out, the last) time staying with him, sleeping together in this very bed. I'd been dreaming, probably about gorgeous Karen Sykes dancing with her boyfriend Buddy Booth right in front of the stage while we ripped through *I'm a Girl Watcher*, when the high-pitched female voice woke me. I instantly glanced over at Larry, but he lay on his side facing the wall, unmoving.

After that first cry, the old man took over, his voice a bass rumble through the wall. I couldn't make out a single word, but I knew he was mad as hell at Larry's mom. When I glanced over at him, Larry lay still beneath the covers. *How could he be asleep!*

The woman's voice broke in for a second, but Abe quickly drowned her out, nearly screaming. I pulled the covers over my head (like now, I realized before pulling them back down) and squeezed my eyes closed. I wanted to be anywhere but here and could've kicked myself for letting my friend talk me into staying. The voices now rose together in a roar. I was about to shake Larry when it happened: a big thud, like the sound of a body hitting the floor. I lay paralyzed, not even breathing, heart pulsing like bass through bad speakers. The silence was worse, much worse, than the yelling had been. Every second increased my fear and guilt. Shouldn't we do something?

A minute, maybe two, passed before I finally sat up on my elbows, touched Larry and whispered his name. *Nothing.*

What could I do? I rolled over facing the opposite direction and waited—for what, I didn't know, exactly—more thuds, screaming, sirens, the sound of Larry's bedroom door creaking open. Was Abe sneaking in, brandishing a curved scimitar to kill the witnesses to his wife's murder? But though I waited in agony, mind-singing every lyric to every song I knew, not one more sound came from down the hall.

Finally when enough light shone between the curtains to let me know it was nearly daylight, I lifted my head from the pillow to hear Larry snoring. After slowly rising and dressing, I wrote a note saying I'd forgotten I'd agreed to help Billy Clark deliver Sunday *News-Sentinels.* Somehow I got outside without incident and caught up with Billy, who was so glad to see me, he gave me half his honey-bun and chocolate milk.

If Abe killed his wife that night, Larry never mentioned it, and I wasn't about to ask about what I'd heard. When Mrs. Hasser did die a few years later, the official diagnosis was heart failure. I'd always felt guilty I'd never told Mom what I'd heard, but it was the sixties, it was West Virginia. *They're foreigners*, Mom would've said. *Stay away from them.*

At last I could endure the ghosts no longer, rose, dressed, found the stairs and groped my way down. I had no paper route excuse, but I noticed I'd brought my coat.

At the bottom, I entered the small storeroom, totally black. Hands outstretched, I made it through and cut the corner, my eyes dazzled by the sudden shock of the blinking yellow traffic light reflected in the mirror behind the counter. Beyond the front window, illuminated by the momentary glow, quarter-sized flakes drifted. It was piling up; the turnpike might even be closed.

I stood staring, taken back to nearly three decades ago when, across the street at boarded-up Mound School, Larry and I had bonded, both of us bottom feeders from the first day. The very next year in junior high, we discovered rock and roll, which was almost enough. Again, I pondered why

I'd ignored my old friend for so long. I'd told myself it was just life; now I'd slept in that same bed, I knew better. I'd been too afraid to tell the truth.

Tiptoeing across the floor, I sat in the farthest booth so I could see my old brick alma mater, glad I'd brought my parka since I could feel the glass's chill. When I let it out, my breath steamed the window, obscuring my face. Our parents were dead and gone, the violence I'd witnessed ancient history. Facing Larry meant facing myself, a guy who walked away from fights. I majored in business in high school so I wouldn't have to compete with college prep kids, didn't even take the ACT until my math teacher forced me. Acing the tests meant college scholarships—my ticket out. It took me ten years beyond a bachelor's to discover I didn't have the instinct to fight, to *engage*. By that time I had a wife and daughter.

So lost in reverie was I that I didn't see or hear the approaching figure behind the counter until she was halfway to where I sat. Backlit by the mirror, Maria's form congealed from the shadows. She held her robe closed with her left hand, clutching a huge carving knife chest-high in the other. It was so much like a B-grade movie, I laughed.

As she walked around the counter's edge, I saw that the pink robe came to her bare knees, golden in the caution light's gleam. I wondered if she had anything on beneath it. For the thousandth time, I shivered.

"Oh. It's you, Johnny."

"Aren't you freezing?" I whispered.

"Don't you know Cubans have hot blood?"

She slid into the booth across from me and leaned her elbows on the table, resting her chin atop her tented fingers.

"I couldn't sleep," I said. "Too many Colts running around the pasture."

"You don't have to whisper. Beer knocks him out."

Her conspiratorial tone gave me a jolt up my spine.

"I know you love Larry very much," I said, the first thing that came to mind. She opened her eyes wider, placed her hands on the table.

"He's an asshole," she said, curling her lip, looking toward the counter where a cockroach scavenged in a pool of amber light.

"Everybody is, sometimes," I said.

"I don't want his baby."

"Then you'd better tell him before it's too late."

She shrugged, the robe slipping a little, revealing something silky on her shoulder. "One day he'll wake up and I'll be gone."

"It would kill him, you know."

Her eyes hung fire. "If I don't go, he will kill *me*. You saw him tonight. My God!"

Another night, I might've been willing to play. But not tonight. "I saw a game it takes two to play."

Her glare warmed me. "You saw but did not see," she hissed.

"Look, Maria, I didn't come here to—" We both heard footsteps on the stairs at the same time.

Within moments, Larry's huge, hulking silhouette appeared in the storeroom doorway. Before I saw his face, I saw his hand grasping the pistol. When he walked over to where we sat, gun held limply at his side, wearing only his jeans and cowboy boots, I didn't recognize him, his face sagged so badly. He'd become his father Abraham, old as dust.

"What the fuck is going on?" He said.

Maria looked straight at me. "Johnny and I are getting to know each other better."

"Cover up," he said flatly. "You'll catch your death." I waited for him to jerk her to her feet and backhand her. I didn't think I could sit idly by this time if he did.

"Stand up."

I glanced at Maria, but she was looking up at her husband. Following her gaze, I found him staring straight at me. "What?"

"Nobody messes with my wife. Nobody."

He raised the arm holding the gun until it pointed at the middle of my chest. The adrenaline surge left me breathless.

"Stand up, Johnny."

I stood up, wondering if my knees might buckle. I imagined him wiping blood from his split knuckles as he put his arm around me the day he'd beaten up Jamey Chambers for me. I'd felt just as ashamed then as I did now. Rising heavily, I faced him. He stood several inches taller and sixty pounds heavier than I and held the pistol pointing at my stomach. I thought of how his arm felt around me that day in junior high. Maybe even worse than his and Maria's pitying eyes on me now.

"*Idiot.* What are you doing?"

Half-standing, Maria groped toward the gun, but before she reached it, Larry back-handed her with his left hand, and with a sharp cry, she fell back into the booth. I hit him with everything I had. His head snapped back, and I feared for a second he might crash through the window, but he caught himself. We both stood panting, watching each other. My fingers ached, and I couldn't close my hand. Grinning, he touched his jaw.

"Not bad, Johnny, not bad."

While I waited for him to hit me back—or shoot me—I felt my knees shaking so bad, I wondered if I'd collapse. Still looking at me, he placed the gun on the table beside Maria's knife.

"Because we're old friends," he said, "I'm letting you go."

I stood up straight, stiff but no longer quite so jelly-kneed, and tried to speak. But my face felt like frozen meat, my entire body turned to stone. Larry slid over beside his wife and put his arm around her as she sobbed into his chest.

After a few moments, she began to get her breath easier, and I heard the snowplow approaching from a block away. Feeling had begun to flow back into my lower body, and I found my legs worked.

Quietly, unnoticed by either of them, I eased into the coat Erin had given me last Christmas, turned the lock and slipped out the door. A wave of wind sent me reeling backwards, but I righted myself and took one step, then another. Things were coming clear. I'd just punched my ex-best friend only yards from the Mound, where we played and dreamed. I clasped and unclasped my hand. Still sore, but I didn't think I'd broken anything. Shielding my eyes, I could barely make out the old school's columns and porticoes, nearly invisible in the swirling snow. I considered crossing the street and circling the building once, for old time's sake. But it was too cold; I couldn't stay here. Besides, I had a daughter somewhere.

My feet moved me forward, and I made the first tracks in new snow.

THE FINAL FLOAT

Kevin Brown

That it?" Kyson said.

He pointed at a wall of thickets and timbered old-growth dense as the rest of the woods surrounding them. An overgrown road disappeared inside it.

"Is what it?" Brodie said, raising his Oakley's and squinting through the back glass.

Kyson held the napkin up, slid his eyes from the scratched directions to the road and back. He angled it right, spun it left, then balled it up and dropped it in the floorboard.

Brodie shrugged and slipped his shades back down. Threw the pick-up in reverse, pulled onto the road, and started in.

The pitch was sharp, the truck bouncing over oak roots knotted in the road. Branches scraped the sides of the vehicle, the windows, the cab.

Slivers of sun-silvered river flared through holes in the canopied bush. Pieces of a building appeared and disappeared.

"Money," Brodie said.

"Ever any doubt?" Kyson said, gripping the "oh shit" handle. But he'd started to doubt. Began to think the place didn't exist. It wasn't on a map, not even close to another *road* on the map. And though he and Brodie had floated different rivers the last couple years, they'd never heard of this one. It was the weird old guy at Mason's Pub that told them about the place. The Rotten Oar. Overheard Kyson and Brodie talking about a two-day float and slid down to the stool next to them.

"You never had a float like it," he said, a wiry beard veined by a braid of scar along his jaw line. "Life changing."

He scrawled drunken directions on a beer damp napkin and three days later they were here.

At the bottom of the road it smoothed and opened to an old house and a large, weather-flaked barn. Behind the barn, a cluster of decrepit sheds.

"Rotten Oar Floats" was painted in red childlike letters above the open barn door. They pulled in, got out, and looked around.

The house was bowed in the middle. A dead maple had grown through the front porch, the top lying over the rusted tin roof. The breeze waved a shutter back and forth like a sleepy blinking eye.

"Don't look like much to me," Kyson said. He adjusted his Tilly Hat and said, "Anybody even here?"

Looking around, Brodie spat, leaned in the truck, and laid on the horn.

A soft echo.

He hit it again.

Cicadas screamed. There was a junkyard behind the sheds. Hollowed out vehicles, rusted through and gutted with weeds.

"Help you?" a scratchy voice said, from the dark of the barn. A large man appeared, staring as if he'd never seen customers before. He was bald except for a tuft of white hair above one ear. He wore an unbuttoned shirt, and a purple, rope thick scar ran from his naval over his breastbone. Up his throat and chin, splitting his bottom lip in a meaty wet V.

Kyson looked away. Said: "You rent canoes?" The man looked over his shoulder at the sign, then back at Kyson without speaking.

"We're gonna need one," Brodie said, slow. "And a shuttle upriver. 'Bout two days worth."

The man ran his eyes over them and looked out at the river. "Why don't you boys go somewheres else to do your floating?"

"Good sales pitch," Kyson said, to himself.

Brodie's jaw tightened. "We were told this is the float to take," he said. "Took us three days to find it, so."

The man breathed heavy, spittle whistling from his lip, and scratched at the scar. Shook his head and disappeared inside the barn. There was a loud thump, two slaps of wood-on-wood, and he reappeared, dragging a long oak canoe. It was warped and sun bleached, dark stains pock-marking the wood. One gunwhale was busted, and the hull was splintered and riddled with holes patched with sap. Inside were two bowed oars.

"Lives up to its name," Kyson said. "This thing even float?"

"It's a boat, ain't it?" the man said.

"Not really."

"It'll work," Brodie said. "What do we owe you?"

"Hundred a head," the man said.

"A *hundred*?" Kyson said.

Brodie held his hand up.

Kyson walked over and looked out at the river. The sun threw a million diamonds on the surface, and thirty yards up it ribboned off and out of sight, its skin wrinkled in the breeze.

Brodie paid and the man disappeared inside the barn.

"Two hundred bucks?" Kyson said.

"We're here," Brodie said, unloading the cooler. "Let's just *be* here."

Kyson grabbed the fishing rods. "Better be a hell of a float."

Brodie winked. "Always is."

The man pulled out in a truck with tattered screens bellied out for windows. He squeaked to a stop and stared ahead. Motor idling, brown exhaust streaming from the tailpipe.

"Hundred each," Kyson said, "and we load the damn canoe."

"I'm just ready to be on the water."

They loaded.

The cab floor was rusted out, the seat cushion-less, its springs shot.

"Guess we're in back," Kyson said.

They hopped in. The gears ground and they jerked toward the road they'd come down on, nosed up and disappeared into the landscape.

The truck rocked to a halt.

They dusted leaves from their laps. Exposed skin was red-welted from two hours of biting twigs, clawing briers.

It was five feet from the embankment to the water, and Brodie jumped in, knee deep, and extended an arm.

Kyson eased the boat over the lip, grunting as the weight took hold, and it dropped, smacking wings of water out the sides. He turned, and the man was standing a nose apart between noses, breath whistling through the lip. "Ten miles in, you'll come to a V," he said. "You're gonna wanna keep to the right." He sucked in a string of spit and swallowed, his Adam's Apple rolling up, then down beneath the scar. "That's the float you're here for."

"You bet," Kyson said. He stepped back and climbed down into the warm water.

The man stood over him, staring down.

Grabbing a tree trunk, they flung mud-slimed feet over the side and launched. It wobbled and they dipped their oars, bracing it. Eased out, absorbed by that first buoyant glide of a river's slither.

"Hear that?" the old man yelled. Kyson looked back. He stood facing the woods across the river. "Keep to the right!"

"Hell's that about?" Kyson said. As the thickets eclipsed the embankment, the man threw his head back, cupped his hands around his mouth, and screamed, "I told 'em!"

And he was gone.

The boil took them. Began to spin the stern perpendicular to the river, but Brodie dug left as Kyson pried the stern right, straightening it. A perfect cadence. The product of many miles and many currents.

The chop turned to foamy rapids that lifted the nose, then dipped it, a spray washing over them.

It rose and dipped. Smooth, rolling.

The landscape slid backwards. Opened up, then constricted.

The run pushed them around a bend and Kyson backwatered hard. Brodie threw his head back and howled.

"Hell *yeah!*" Kyson screamed, looking ahead at a grid of standing waves. The head troughed and the stern lifted, raising him off his seat, before the bow crested and sat him down. Then it calmed, the green water shoaling into an eddy.

Brodie palm-to-jaw popped his neck. "Not bad."

They coasted along, paddling in intervals. Boots submerged in a couple inches of water that had leaked through the resin. The surface went light green, then brown as the water shallowed over a riffle.

"Warm beer me," Brodie said. Kyson reached in the melted water of the cooler for a couple Blue Ribbons. He took a sip. Brodie bubbled his hard.

The water darkened again and they placed their oars across their laps. To the left, a fish rolled and disappeared.

"Let's get some dinner," Brodie said, and grabbed his pole. Baited the hook with a fly and cast, letting it drag.

The sun was wide and unblocked in the sky. Softshell turtles stuck to the banks like wet cobblestones, and loggerheads sat motionless on the trunks of downed trees. A water moccasin S'd past them upriver, its head raised. The soft current split around a boulder in the center of the river like white lace and the glassy surface of the water threw everything back on itself.

Brodie finished his beer, crushed the can, and peeled his wet shirt off.

Kyson stared at the U.S.M.C. tattoo in Old English across his back. He'd just gotten it a couple days ago and it was still puffy and red.

"You nervous?" Kyson said.

"Not looking forward to all those needles." He reeled in, cast again. "Can't wait for boot-camp, though."

Kyson knew this. Since Junior High, Brodie had been preparing for the Marine Corps. The last couple years it'd become an obsession. He read *Soldier Of Fortune*, quoted *Full Metal Jacket*, and worked out constantly, dieting until he was pads-on-pads of hard muscle roped in veins. He ran five miles before sun-up every morning, rain or shine, sick or well. He'd tried to get Kyson to enlist on the Buddy System. Even had a recruiter come see him. The Corps paid for college and you'd make good money and see the world. But Kyson did the math, and the good money he'd be making came out to about $350 a week. And the world he'd be seeing would be places the locals shoot at you. Plus, Kyson had been accepted at the University of Virginia, and that was world enough. So he passed. And though he'd miss his best friend since before *He-man* was wimpy, he wasn't about to go die in a desert for minimum wage.

Brodie was about to take a drink when the rod bent, the line whining.

He snagged back and worked it, and within a few minutes, the pale trout was beside the boat, thrashing. He palmed it, dislodged the hook, and tossed it in the bottom. It flopped upright in the crude-whittled keel line and tried to swim in the sloshing water.

"We'll eat tonight," Brodie said, and slipped his KA-BAR knife from its sheath. He smiled, and for a second, Kyson saw him as he used to—his buddy, wide-eyed and camo-ed with dirt. Who'd always be there tomorrow with some new idea or adventure to follow. Hard to believe this might be the last trip. Say a war doesn't get him, they'd both meet new friends, move on. It all felt like the end, like their river had reached the sea.

Kyson finished his beer, rigged his pole, and said, "Let me show you how a real angler does it."

They made camp on a rock bar with an oxbow lake arced behind it. It was the last flat bank before the landscape began to rise. The cliffs ahead were white, the tops limned with trees. The sun hovered just above, backlighting them.

Clouds the color of wet tissue stretched apart in the distance.

They each cleared a section of rocks for a bed and made small, makeshift lean-tos. They started a fire in a pit ringed with river stones, drank, and skipped shale. The water was dark except for a froth of small whitecaps that smoothed off and eddied on.

Kyson was drunk and seeing the world twinned. He cupped a handful of water over his face, the back of his neck. He was burnt, the skin on his nose and shoulders tight and sore. "Got warm."

"Gonna get chilly," Brodie said, and pointed at the clouds.

The sun flat lined over the rim of the cliffs.

After a while, they removed the fish from the stringer (Kyson had struck out, but Brodie landed another) and ran sticks through the bellies and out the mouths. Their red and green tint glimmered over the flames. They sat on rocks, sipping hot beers, and yawning.

A steady breeze kicked up, rattling the leaves. The smell of honeysuckle in its wake.

"Guess we might not get to do this again," Kyson said.

"I'll be back." Brodie took his fish from the flame, pinched a piece off. "It's only four years."

Kyson held his fish to his lips, blew, and took a bite, the fluffy white meat like cotton. "Remember *G.I. Joe*?"

Brodie smiled.

"You never admitted when I killed you?"

"You never did," Brodie said. "Cobra can hit a Joe, but he can't kill him." They laughed.

After a minute, Kyson stopped. "They drop you off over there," he said, "you *can* get killed."

"I can kill back, too."

They sat, fire popping and the river sliding by, black and fluid.

"Bout the eighth week of camp, your dick'll be so hard you can't blink."

Brodie smiled, said: "I get out, I feel sorry for the first mess hall *I* chow at. She'll see what one motivated Marine and his gun can do."

"Kristi Spark?"

"*Hell* no! Titties look like two raw eggs on a door nail."

"Like putty in panty hose."

"Marbles in a condom."

They laughed and Kyson raised his can. "To counting down but not counting out," he said. "Semper fi, motherfucker!"

Brodie raised his can. "Oorah!"

Heat lightning lit up the landscape. A distant rumble of thunder. The wind picked up, making a lip of waves crumble over the beach. A few drops of rain popped surfaces.

"Roughing it tonight," Brodie said.

"Any other way?"

Another flicker and the rain looked like ghost fingers thumping the water's surface.

It began to fall hard and they huddled under their lean-tos. The fire hissed and fluttered but didn't go out. After a half-hour, the storm slackened and moved on, its only evidence, the occasional wink of light and low grind of thunder disappearing upriver. The moon slid out.

They lay soaked in the mud, Kyson staring out at the fire.

"Brodie?"

He groaned.

"Who you think that old bastard was yelling at?"

"Don't know," Brodie said, voice dragging. "Bet he don't, either."

"Weird," Kyson said.

"Fuck him. He's miles off."

"More ways than one," Kyson said, and closed his eyes.

A distant scream snapped him awake. Moonlight filtered through the twigs of the lean-to, tiger-striping his face. It took a second to realize where he was.

There was a deep moan from the other side of the river.

Kyson rolled out, his insides novacained. Clothes wet and heavy.

"Brodie?" he said, but Brodie wasn't there. The embers in the fire pit glowed, and he stoked them and threw tender on, and it lit up Brodie's silhouette, shin-deep in the water near the end of the bar. Motionless, staring up at the cliffs.

"The hell is that?" Kyson said, running toward him.

Another scream broke, with a grumbled answer from the left wall, a wailed response from the right, zigzagging farther downriver.

"Animals?" Kyson said, and held his breath.

"Don't think so."

They heard the screams another few minutes.

They didn't sleep the rest of the night.

Light came, and the land began to form and take shape. One large Polaroid shaken until it developed. A natural chiaroscuro, mist smoked over the river. Somewhere in the distance, the sound of runoff.

After the screams stopped, they'd sat in silence. Brodie watching the cliffs. Kyson keeping the fire alive. His clothes gripped him, chilling him to the marrow, and his body ached from too much beer under too much sun. He washed his face and drank from the river, shivering.

"Hell with it," he said, voice sandpapered whet-rock. "Getting a hangover beer." The first drink was hard, but he put it away and began to feel better.

Brodie tipped the canoe, drained the water, and righted it. Following his lead, Kyson loaded the gear. He pissed on the coals, then swept stones over the pit with the side of his boot, and they slid the boat to the water's edge and pushed off.

The mist was a gauzy cataract around them. Brodie dug hard, cross-stroking in a scattershot rhythm, and Kyson struggled to control the yaw.

"You okay?" Kyson said.

No response.

"Brodie?"

"Just want some action's all."

The cliffs rose around them like a serpent's jaws. Large headwalls that cricked Kyson's neck when he looked up too long. The facing was pocked and pitted like acne scars.

"Could've been that old bastard," Kyson said. "Fucking with us."

"Maybe," Brodie said.

They wound on, Kyson drinking more and buzzing again. The sun burned the mist away. The water was deeper and a deeper shade of green.

After an hour or so, they came upon a spine of large boulders, dark and slick, that rose and disappeared in the water like a sea dragon's body.

"What you think?" Kyson said. "I don't trust that clit-lipped fucker."

"I'm here for a good float," Brodie said, over his shoulder. Kyson watched the delta slide by as he backwatered, and the left leg disappeared behind the grading landscape.

They rode the river, the dark water like gator scales in the sun. Then, the river constricted into a gorge and sped up in a loud hiss and burst. A gauntlet of boulders and banks, rushes and falls.

"Jesus," Kyson said, and, not looking back, Brodie yelled, "Unfuck yourself! This is hair rafting, baby!"

They hit the chute and the G-Force slid them up the right side of the S, then glided down and rode up the other side as the bend torsioned back. They stroked through a labyrinth of bony rapids that wrenched in a fall, and exploded through a curler, where the canoe boofed off the crest, spilling them. When they resurfaced, the boat was overturned and twisting in the wash, the gear and oars bobbing in the flat-water ahead.

Brodie threw his hands up and yelled, "*That's* what I'm talking about!"

"Sank in the drank," Kyson said, side-stroking toward the boat. He reached it and Brodie retrieved the gear.

They found a cavern at the foot of the cliff and swam to it. Got out and righted the boat, threw everything inside. A tongue of water curtained off the ceiling, and the river seen through it looked melted in molten glass. They climbed a large plate of limestone techtonic-ed against an end of the overhang, and dove and back-flipped from its pinnacle. Dubbed it "Memorial Rock" and, across its face, Brodie etched "MEMO" with the KA-BAR and they toasted it, then boarded the canoe and shoved off. Watched "MEMO" disappear behind them.

Brodie smiled at Kyson.

"What?"

His smiled widened. "Fun, wasn't it?"

"Damn straight," Kyson said.

Brodie dug them forward, back muscles rolling under the skin. The letters of his tattoo morphing: U.s.M.c.

Kyson's oar bit in harmony. They were here and they were now, and Brodie was right. It was fun.

Several miles down, they skirted a vein.

"Somebody needs art lessons," Brodie said.

Covering the cliff facing, a painting of a green stick figure, hands bound above its head. Five red figures surrounding it.

"How you get up there to paint that?" Kyson said.

"With a clinched asshole."

Kyson watched it pass behind them, out of sight.

Farther down, they saw a second image—the green figure gutted, red spraying from the bowels. Roped entrails held above the red figures' heads.

"The hell?" Kyson said.

Brodie stood in the canoe and scanned above. Shielding his eyes, he looked where they'd come from. Studied where they were headed. "Keep going," he said, and sat.

They rounded again and stopped at the same time. The canyon walls on both sides were blood red. Top to water, as far as they could see.

"Fuck *is* this?" Kyson said.

Brodie didn't answer. He plowed the oar in hard, and Kyson followed. They fought through a network of rapids, and Kyson's headache returned, his lung lining seared. His strokes began to slap off the water, and he stopped. "Hold on," he said, and spat.

"Don't stop," Brodie said.

"I need a minute," Kyson said, wrists draped over his knees.

Several more strokes and Brodie yanked his oar out. Glazed in sweat, he inhaled a single breath and heaved it out.

They drifted in circles but let it go.

Hear that?"

Brodie tilted his head.

The canoe whirled and the buzzing deepened, like the audible oscillation of a power line hum.

"Yellow-jacket nest," Brodie said.

"No," Kyson said, and pointed.

In the shade, lapping against the soggy bank was a dark mound in a swarming cloud.

They nosed toward it. Closer, they saw it was bloated at one end, the color of veins under pale skin. It was slick and coated with bluebottle flies.

Kyson put his face in the crook of his arm. Flies swarmed and landed on his head and ears and he swatted.

They scuttled over Brodie's face, circling off when he shook his head. He reached his oar out and pushed, and there was a release of gas as it rolled, and the fly cloud exploded.

Kyson leaned over and coughed.

It was half a human torso, split with precision up the sternum. The skull and a piece of the mandible attached and dangling, the soft tissue maggot-eaten away.

Brodie back-stroked, his lips tight. Tenting his shirt over his nose, Kyson spun them downriver and clawed forward.

"God," Kyson said, face bloodless. "We swam in that shit, man." He put a palm over his mouth. "I *drank* out of it."

"Just bury your paddle and keep going."

They rounded the next elbow and froze. Flanked along the right cliff top, not moving, were five nude figures holding what looked like handmade longbows. Their bodies the color of skinned muscle. The color of the cliffs.

"Brodie?" Kyson said.

"Don't," he whispered, "look." He knifed the blade of the oar into the water, barely slicing the surface. Extracted it just as easy.

Ahead, the muffled roar of rapids.

Kyson kept his paddle submerged, propelling with J-strokes, and in the mirrored ripples, he saw each figure draw its bow down in unison, and a scream erupted from the cliff top, so loud the air shimmied, the sound waves warbling the surface of the water. Droning moans ricocheted from cliff-to-cliff down the river.

He was reaching to cover his ears when Brodie was knocked off his seat as if yanked by a pulley. An arrow stemmed from his right side, the fletching of red feathers fluttering. His eyes wide, mouth open.

Kyson jumped toward him but his leg tethered. He looked down and an arrow had lodged in the meat of his thigh and stuck in the hull of the canoe. He wrapped a hand around each side of his quad and threw his head back, but his yell was drowned out by another scream above.

Arrows popped the side, punctured the cooler, strings of water tailing out. More flumped the surface around them and sank, yellow and refracted, in slow motion.

"Shit!" Kyson said, and felt a slap to the side of his head. He reached up, smeared two fingertips of blood from a gash.

The rapids were closer. He tugged the arrow pinning him and saw it was shafted in bone, feathered from a cardinal wing. A broad head sculpted from a shard of toothed jawbone biting into the wood. He gripped low where the head was buried and lifted in a twist, so hard a crown popped loose.

A dark wave of arrows funneled down.

Brodie gurgled. He was hit through the bicep and hand, his knee and groin.

Kyson torqued harder and the shaft squealed and snapped, and he bellied over the side for cover. The boil jerked the rod and, reaching to remove it, his feet buoyed out the other side of the boat. There was a snap in his ankle, and this one he felt full force. Dragging it back, he saw the blood like black smoke underwater. The arrow sunk to the feathers.

They were entering the runnel, and the figures lowered their bows in cohesion.

Brodie twitched on the canoe bottom, and Kyson thought of the trout.

"Hang on!" Kyson said, and the rapids took them. A submerged boulder rocked against his floating ribs, spun him in the undertow. The arrows through his limbs poled into the riverbed and vaulted him, and he almost let go.

They rode a wave, and Kyson saw a hole in Brodie's cheek with a single band of flesh stretched thin and tacked to the bottom. They troughed and Kyson lost grip and went under. Resurfaced, and the flow smoothed out.

He looked above and the figures were gone. The screams had stopped.

He vomited river foam. "They're gone," he said, whipping his head around.

"God," Brodie said, and coughed a string of blood. "They won't want me now."

Kyson tightened his grip, still watching above.

"They won't want me now."

"Who won't?"

Brodie's eyes were cut toward Kyson. His jaw locked in a grimace.

"Course they'll want you," Kyson said, and could see Brodie's back teeth through his cheek. "They *need* people like you."

Around the bend, the rush of another chute.

"They want survivors," Kyson said. He looked around for a bank, an overhang. Anything. "You're a survivor. A G.I. Joe," he said. "And Joes don't die."

Inside the canoe, the leak-water had crimsoned. The thwarts were splintered. The bottom and Port Side quilled with arrows. Kyson's Telly hat floated by and wedged in a bush, and he thought about the drunk at Mason's, a life changer, he'd said, and that old bastard yelling, "I told 'em!" and his face cinched in a cry but he did not.

"They won't," Brodie said, glassy-eyed.

The rapids louder, the water faster. A fallen tree tremored as if shaken by invisible hands. They were entering the cut.

"Know what?" Kyson said. "We get out of here, I'll join with you. Buddy System, how's that?" Hooking his elbow over the side, he tried to straighten the yaw with his other hand. "Cause they can hit us, goddamn it, but they can't kill us," he said, voice raised. "*Semper Fi!*" he yelled, throwing his head back. "*Oorah!*"

Brodie said, "Oorah," in a blood-drowned voice.

"Semper Fi!" Kyson yelled.

They rounded.

Brodie rolled his eyes from Kyson to the clouds above. "Oorah," he whispered, and a tear slid over his bloodied cheekbone and pearled down pink.

"*Semper Fi motherfuckers!*" Kyson said, flipping a middle finger to the world.

And above them, flanked along the left cliff top, not moving, were five nude figures. Bodies the color of skinned muscle. Longbows drawn as a scream pierced the land.

"Oorah," Kyson said, with what little breath he could.

THE VATICAN'S SECRET CABINET

Daniel Pearlman

Anyone who has ever been associated with the art colony in Rome will have heard of a certain "secret cabinet" hidden somewhere in the labyrinth of the Vatican Museums. It was the near-misfortune of one of the most renowned art dealers in Rome to have been exposed, recently, to the contents of that very real cabinet. The peculiar circumstances of his involvement are set out, in unflinching detail, in the following report.

Giuseppe Pennini had not done business with Cardinal Balducchione for three years now, and he had never liked doing business with Vatican curators anyhow. So what could it be—this "matter of utmost urgency" that had prompted the cardinal to summon him out of the blue? He directed his question at a pair of tight-lipped granite sphinxes as he passed through the Hall of the Greek Cross into the Museo Pio-Clementino. Though he knew the shorter way to the administrative offices, he took a longer route in order to revisit the Circular Hall, with its gigantic gilt Hercules, and the nine bronze Muses of the marble-columned hall named after them.

Ushered by a guard down a wide, dim corridor with a beautifully coffered ceiling, Giuseppe entered the offices of the curator of Greek and Roman antiquities. Instead of having to wait, as he had expected, he was led at once across plush Persian carpets and admitted by an elderly male receptionist through double oaken doors into the presence of the cardinal himself.

"Peppini!"

"Pennini, Your Eminence."

The cardinal's desktop was an enormous slab of antique inlaid marble and the feet were giant wooden claws clutching balls of milky chalcedony. The square-jawed, plump Balducchione, dressed in scarlet robe and skullcap, looked up from his computer terminal and waved Giuseppe toward a pair of armchairs arranged in front of his desk. Directly behind the cardinal was a section of chair-scuffed wall separating two long windows that gave a glimpse of the Belvedere courtyard. Balducchione did not smile. Giuseppe sat down, his stomach already atremble.

"Pennini, we are living through shameful times, do you agree?" And without waiting for an answer, the barrel-chested, ruddy-faced Eminenza continued: "Italy has not wallowed in such scandal since World War II!"

"Absolutely, Your Eminence. It's simply appalling!" And what did he, Giuseppe Pennini, grandson of the original Giuseppe Pennini, dealer in antiquities, who had opened his shop on the Piazza del Popolo even before World War I, have to do with crooked politicians, the Mafia, or homosexual clergy, that the cardinal should address him like this? he wondered.

"The level of morality in Italy befits the ninth circle of Hell. Imagine, the President of the Republic having an affair with the niece of the Mafia chief of Turin! Or the bribes accepted by our previous head of state from four competing corporations at once. Not one, but four!"

"Abominable," sighed Giuseppe, wiping sweat from his thin mustache even though the room was comfortably air-conditioned.

"Are there torments of Hell too severe for the man who betrays his own motherland, Peppini?"

"None that I can think of at the moment, Your Eminence."

"Of course not. And how about for the man who betrays his Mother the Church?"

"How's that, Your Eminence?"

"I'm talking about you, Peppini, you!" And the cardinal's hands slapped marble so hard that Giuseppe felt a sharp pain in the region of his old hernia scar.

"Me?" he said, clutching his groin. "But I can't ..."

"You can't imagine what I'm talking about? Remember that 'Head of a Warrior' you sold me for five million lire three years ago?"

"Second century B.C., showing Pergamene influence, an excellent example of its type, yes. And I assure you we made very little profit on that transaction."

"A fake, Pennini! It recently aroused the suspicion of a visiting international expert. On stylistic grounds. And subsequent chemical testing proved its fraudulent nature beyond question."

"But, Your Eminence, the Pennini family for generations has dealt with only the most respectable—" Giuseppe picked up a set of papers the cardinal shoved across his desk. As he glanced through them, his heart thumped loudly in his chest.

"The reputation of your House is about to fall, Pennini," the cardinal whispered hoarsely, leaning forward. "It is about to take a nosedive and join you down in that same subcellar of Hell which I've just referred to."

Giuseppe nearly blacked out from the rush of blood to his head. Never had anyone in his line been charged with fraud. The Penninis were the most conservative traders in Greco-Roman antiquities in Italy, and earnest—if somewhat irregular—churchgoers as well. And he himself was so expert in what he traded in that institutions and individuals everywhere clamored for his advice. ...So how now explain this turn of affairs to Delfinia, his wife of only six months and patroness of several galleries of modern art that ranked among the most elegant in Rome? Had she not chosen to unite her fortune—as well as her intoxicating person—to a Pennini for, at the very least, the cachet of generations of unassailable respectability? Like an insect tortured under a lens, Giuseppe squirmed beneath the cardinal's blistering stare.

"If the 'Head' is not genuine, Your Eminence, then I have been taken in as much as you, and I am prepared, to prove the integrity of the Pennini name, to make more than reasonable restitution to the Holy Church."

"The Santa Chiesa will not be mollified with mere monetary compensation, Pennini. Through my unwitting person you have stuck a spear in Her side. What I mean is that my reputation as curator has lately been smeared with calumnies, and you are in large measure to blame."

"But surely," said Giuseppe, "short of branding me in the public eye as a thief—"

"Just listen, Peppini, will you? ...For the past ten years I have tried my best to maintain and enlarge the most fabulous collection of classical antiquities in the world."

"And you've been most successful, too, Your—"

"But this has created jealousies, and jealousies have made me enemies, Pennini!"

"Enemies! Who could possibly—"

"In the battle for funding, the curator of the Etruscan Museum has never had qualms about shooting me in the heel... and now that the overall Directorship of the Vatican Museums and Galleries is soon to be vacant, and since he and I are the leading candidates for the post—an ambition which on my part is not personal, Parrini, but all the better to serve Mother Church—"

"Of course, of course, Your Eminence!"

"It appears that His Eminence of the Etruscan collection has been only too delighted to find 'proof' of my unsuitability for the directorship. As you know from the gossip of several years ago, said Eminence was himself duped by a bronze horse of dubious provenance—which I myself was unwise enough, when it was unmasked as a forgery, to call his 'Trojan Horse'..."

"And so he feels the score is finally evened?" said Giuseppe, wondering where all this could be leading.

"It pains me to reveal the pettiness of men who seem otherwise blameless, Pennino." The cardinal nervously patted his midriff.

"I understand, I understand," said Giuseppe, looking gravely down at his polished Gucci shoes, "but if Santa Chiesa is to be served..."

"Then She should be served by those most fit to do so. And to prove my fitness—which in a less corrupt world would be unnecessary—I must call upon your aid, Pennini."

"My aid, Your Eminence!"

"Your aid, Pennini, which I am sure will pour forth willingly from a heart so evidently bursting with contrition and the hope of doing penance—whether or not you tricked me intentionally—as yours is."

"My dear Cardinal Balducchione," said Giuseppe seeing a ray of hope in the offing, "whatever form of penitential assistance you demand of me, please consider my entire resources at your disposal."

"Thank you, Pannini. What you must help me do, then, is to counteract an insidious attempt on the part of his Etruscan Eminence to make me look as if I'm dragging my feet in the matter of certain ... delicate restorations."

"Restorations!" said Giuseppe, rubbing his hands together. "Now that's something I know a little about."

"Presumably you have heard the silly rumor that's been going around for years that somewhere in the Vatican there's a secret cabinet containing the lopped-off genitalia of a good many classical statues?"

"One hears such nonsense and discounts it as anticlerical fabulation, Your Eminence."

"You have spoken as one of the faithful. But there are those leftists—both without and within the Church—who use such a tale to deride the Vatican bureaucracy for its supposed prudishness and cultural ossification. They claim that, although it's been many years since His Holiness John XXIII admitted Modern Art to the Pinacoteca, still most of our museum staff think nudity is an offense against God."

"How ridiculous!" said Giuseppe.

"They say that by failing to correct the damage done by our predecessors to Italy's artistic heritage, we continue through the sin of omission to despise the beauty of Nature, God's own handiwork... We are accused of the deeper sin of Pride wrapped in the cloak of Morality!"

"No one can take seriously such stupid accusations!" pronounced Giuseppe. Scratching his head, he thought a moment. "But what is there to stop the ignorant and the prejudiced from snickering at the fig leaves worn by such world-renowned monuments as the Apollo Belvedere and others under your care, Your Eminence? Yes, I suppose it's easy to come under suspicion of—"

"Pennini," said the cardinal, throwing his hands up in the air, "if we were to remove those little bikinis from all the statues that wear them, what do you think we'd find underneath? ...In most cases, probably nothing! The private parts—gone. Jagged holes in their place."

"My experience in restorations fully supports what you say, Your Eminence."

Balducchione leaned far forward. "But if you do have such missing parts in some sort of secret armadio, Pennino, and your colleagues happen to know about it, then you do open yourself up to charges of being a reactionary— and this, in the post-Mapplethorpe era, could spell death to Your Eminence's ambitions in the world of the Vatican museums."

Giuseppe's jaw dropped. "There is truth to this rumor?"

"To the existence of such a, hm, 'reliquary'? Yes. To the motives imputed to us—to me, specifically, to be quite frank about it—for inaction in the matter for the ten or so years of my curatorship? No!"

"But what can I do to help Your Eminence in a matter of purely internal politics?"

"You, Pennini, are going to restore the exiled members to the monuments from which they were hacked."

Giuseppe could not believe his penance would be so light. "And will that make amends for ..."

"You have my word, Perrini."

"Your Eminence is far too merciful. During the course of my career I'm sure I've done far more difficult jobs of restoration. You may remember I supervised work on the damaged Pietà in—"

"You will not be 'supervising,' Peppini. You will be doing the work yourself. Discretion is of the utmost importance. Any publicity given to the project at this crucial time in my career can be of benefit only to my detractors. Do you understand?"

"Discretion is my middle name, Your Eminence." (And my last is Pennini! he wanted to shout.) "And I have not lost the skill of these hands!" said Giuseppe, wiggling all ten fingers at the cardinal. "You can already consider the job done."

Balducchione tapped on his desk and stared at Giuseppe through thick, horn-rimmed glasses. "Bennini, if the job were as easy as you think, it would have been done ten years ago."

"Excuse me, Your Eminence?"

"Do you think I've kept the lid on our little 'specimen cabinet' for all these years out of indifference, laziness, or the unfashionable morality of which I'm being accused?"

"I don't get it, Your—"

"You will when you see what confronts you. Come with me, Pennini."

Giuseppe followed the bouncing Balducchione through long, echoing corridors down twisting stone stairways until they arrived at the storage rooms, themselves a labyrinth which the cardinal navigated expertly, leading Giuseppe through dimly lit rooms full of shelves of framed paintings, frames without paintings, broken frames and fragments of canvas, terracotta potshards and bronze vessels, mildewed books and dusty old furniture, debouching at last into the statuary sector, where the walls and floors were lined with body parts—arms, legs, heads and torsos; chipped, battered and split; for all the world like the twilit scene after a battle in ancient Greece, after the corpses have been stripped of their armor and arranged in rough rows for burial. They stopped before a large, eighteenth-century wooden bureau badly in need of refinishing. Like a surgeon making a careful incision, the cardinal pried open one of the belly-like middle drawers.

"Eccoli!" He waved his hand over a collection of fragments that a moment's inspection revealed to Giuseppe to be a gathering of penises and scrotums, some together as a unit, some members separate, some removed with care, others evidently hacked off, some large, some small—a forlorn assortment as of spirits in Purgatory waiting for the Resurrection. They were lined up in careful rows, generally of the isolated virile members at the top, intact groupings in the middle, and orphaned testicles at the bottom. Giuseppe did not see any great problem. A little patchwork here and there... "Not in the best condition," he murmured.

"Oh, but these are the finest!" Balducchione picked up one large unit of the intact variety and began to blow the dust off. Giuseppe could not help the look on his face, and the cardinal, feigning a cough, quickly laid the piece down. "Gets to be quite filthy in here," he mumbled. "And if you don't think much of these, what do you think of this bunch?" The cardinal shut the drawer and opened the one just beneath. It disclosed a jumbled mess of stone fragments, evidently bits of genitalia, scattered about like the disassembled pieces of an elaborate three-dimensional jigsaw puzzle, or of a hundred small jigsaw puzzles all tossed together. Impossible! thought Giuseppe. He began to feel very uncomfortable.

"But don't worry about these fragments." The cardinal reopened the upper drawer. "Just reattach these, Peppino, and you'll have repaid your debt to the Mother you have so grossly abused."

Giuseppe sighed with relief, then looked more closely at the collection. "But how have they been catalogued?" They were neatly enough arranged in rows, but devoid of identifying labels. Categorized just by organ-type, then arrayed in size place! ...Overcoming an involuntary reluctance, he delicately reached in and turned a few clusters, one after another, over and over in his hands, then put each back in its place. One crudely Priapic grappolo seemed to belong to some old herm. Another set, more civilized, probably to some innocent Greek athlete or kouros. This other—to some Roman copy? Was there a stylistic difference between Greek and Roman ding-dongs? he wondered. A smile began stretching the corners of his mouth. Clamping his lips shut, Giuseppe loudly cleared his throat. "I don't see any identifying marks, Your Eminence. But as soon as I am supplied with all the needed information, I will immediately start—"

"They have not been catalogued, Peppini. They have been sorted—quite neatly, as you see. But no one has the faintest idea to which statues they belong."

"But, Your Eminence—!"

"Most of the dismemberments are believed to have occurred at various times during the nineteenth century, perhaps particularly under His Holiness Pius IX, and no one even knows if clergy were directly involved. What is amazing is that these fragments have been preserved at all! Perhaps it was due to some superstitious dread of the wrath of the pagan deities whose final marble resting places had been violated. ...So now you see, Pennini, that it is not an entirely easy task after all."

"But surely, Your Eminence, you have a list of the mutilated monuments? No? ...A list, then, of the collections in which they are to be found?"

The cardinal kept shaking his head.

"And the statues to which these members belong—they are, of course, all to be found in Rome, are they not?"

The cardinal shrugged his shoulders. "If I knew these things, I wouldn't need you, Pinnini."

"But you are giving me a damn near impossible task!" Giuseppe felt horrified at the language that had escaped him. What would Delfinia do, he wondered, if she saw herself cornered like this? A woman of the world, she had scratched her way up from the streets, whereas he simply carried on what he had inherited from his forebears.

"All I can suggest, rather strongly, Pennini, is that you'd be wasting your time to try matching them up with the sculptures in our collections. I've had experts come in here and try. You know Croce and Aldobrandini?"

"Among the best in the business," Giuseppe nodded.

"It put considerable strain on my budget, let me tell you. But the rumors that circulated afterward suggested that my efforts were merely 'perfunctory, suspiciously lacking in enthusiasm'!"

"We live among sharks," said Giuseppe.

"It is when they are dressed in robes that they are most dangerous," said Balducchione.

Giuseppe pulled at the hair on each side of his head. "So, if we eliminate the Vatican, that leaves me with only the rest of Italy to search!"

"I shall make it easier for you. Identify only twenty-five percent of the material in this drawer."

"Twenty-five percent of an impossible task is still an impossible task, Your Eminence."

"To the sinner given the chance to redeem himself, the task always appears impossible ... at first, Pennini, at first."

"Why me, Your Eminence, If even Croce—"?"

"That was a limited search, Pennini. None of today's so-called 'experts' wants to deal with a task... a challenge so global as yours. We could never pay them enough anyway, they say. Or else they'll tell me that life isn't long enough, ridiculously exaggerating the problem. The real problem is, however, that they are not sufficiently motivated. ...Now you, Peppini, are motivated."

Giuseppe carried pen and notebook in his inner jacket pocket. His brain spinning at the enormity of the assignment, he began to count the pieces in each row.

"I confess to you, Peppini, that this cabinet has been getting on my nerves. It has been causing me severe headaches."

"Headaches, Your Eminence?"

"Nightmares even, Pennino! If I were to describe to you — Forget it!" The cardinal covered his face with his palm.

"If I were Your Eminence, I would have tossed the whole lot of them into the garbage a long time ago."

"Don't you think I have dreamed of doing so, Pennini? Of smashing them all up into small, unrecognizable bits and adding them to the gravel in one of the Vatican gardens? ... But then, in my dream, overnight they reassemble, Pennini, and as I walk among the rose-bushes they point accusing ... Enough, Pennino!"

"Nothing would please me more than to rid you of such nightmares, Your Eminence," said Giuseppe, gazing at the drawer and slowly shaking his head.

"And I have such faith in your competence," said the cardinal, pointing his pressed palms at Giuseppe, "that I know you will be able to finish the job within exactly six months."

"Six months!"

"At that point, Peppini, I must parade my administrative accomplishments before the extremely critical eye of the Selections Committee for the next Director-General of the Vatican Museums."

When Giuseppe got home that evening he poured himself a double shot of brandy. His bride of six months remarked on the state he was in. "Mio Caro," she said, "you haven't kissed me once since stepping into the house."

Choking with outrage, Giuseppe spewed forth the whole tale of his encounter with Balducchione. Instead of wringing her hands in a show of compassion, however, Delfinia actually found his predicament amusing. Time and again she whooped with laughter, revealing distasteful glimpses of her rough-and-tumble background, a shadowy past cloaked in myth and rumor, a past Giuseppe knew little about and had no great desire to explore. What was past was past! Giuseppe preferred to ignore mere origins in the light of Delfinia's present command over the world of contemporary art.

"Mia Cara, you do not know wh-what it is like," he sputtered, "dealing in the world of antiquities." Her attempts to suppress a smile only irritated him all the more. "On the one hand I walk a tightrope over international politics, on the other I have the religious authorities to contend with, on still another there are the trackers of stolen war-booty..." What he wanted to say was that she had risen out of a far more slippery environment, a twilight world of flim-flam and hype where "the rules" were made and unmade as main-chance permitted. Although he did not know exactly how Delfinia had amassed her magnificent gallery holdings, he knew she had been the lover of some of the best-promoted names in current Italian painting, and friends of his even suggested that for a while she had run a most elegant upper-class brothel where artists of repute were encouraged to pay in canvas. As much sought-after for her Northern blond beauty as for her wealth and prestige, she had finally settled down at age forty-two to marry him, Giuseppe Pennini, one of the few men she could trust and admire—and who could also offer her entrée into the old Roman aristocracy.

"Men of the cloth can be difficult to deal with in the world of practical affairs, Peppino." Putting down her Cinzano, she arose from the sofa and embraced him, kissing his throbbing temples. "But remember that Balducchione is in at least as much trouble as you are, and that in fact he needs you more than you need him."

Delfinia's warm reassurances helped restore his lucidity of mind. First, he would focus totally on Rome, on the assumption that the puritanical zealots responsible for the dismemberments were locals whose crusades had been confined to a rather narrow geographical range. Second, the works they attacked must have been on public display, so that most must be still on exhibit in Roman museums, palazzi, and piazze. Third, he would photograph all statues wearing fig leaves (and also the leafless ones that showed mutilation) with special attention to close-ups, all taken from the same distance, of the area of the loins. These close-ups could then be compared with same-distance photos of the fragments stored at the Vatican. Fourth, by making plaster casts of the Vatican assemblage (the cardinal preferred that the originals remain in the armadio), he could put suspected matches to the test—with the cooperation, of course, of officials in a position to authorize the removal of fig leaves.

All this was far more easily said than done—even with a team of precisely-instructed photographers who pursued their quarry relentlessly around every crumbling corner of Rome. Two months had passed, thousands of photos had been taken, molds and casts had been made, but it began to seem to Giuseppe that only a supercomputer could run through all the permutations and combinations that the matching process entailed. The programming alone of a supercomputer would have taken several months, however, and Giuseppe had only four months left till the mid-September deadline that the cardinal had given him.

He began to spend both days and nights locked up with his collection of photos, dividing them into groups according to the suspected size of the genitals, laying transparencies of lopped-off members over fig leaf after fig leaf—in vain. The cardinal's 'experts' had been right to beg off. Everything was turning into a blur. He was plagued by severe headaches. He no longer seemed to know what he was looking for. He would wake up in the middle of the night terrified by a recurrent nightmare—that of a gigantic stone penis garbed in clerical attire, aiming at him like a cannon, and rushing up behind him on bouncing testicles for wheels. Not only were his nightly terrors also affecting Delfinia's sleep, but the lack of attention he'd been paying her recently was resulting in bitter quarrels. She accused him of becoming unhinged by "a mere threat" to his reputation, while he accused her of complete insensitivity to his plight.

"All right, then," she said one night after he had startled her up out of sleep again, "if you can't do the job, Mio Caro, then let me try it for a while!"

"That's absurd!" he said. "You have no training in antiquities."

"I won't need any!"

"And then I'll lose even more time explaining to you the search-procedure I've developed."

"I'll develop my own procedure."

"It's a scientific procedure!" he exclaimed.

"And where has it got you, Peppino?"

Muttering to himself in reply, he had to admit that to save both his sanity and his marriage, he must invite Delfinia to participate.

"Participate! ...I'm not going to merely 'participate,' dear. You are going to stay completely out of it. You are going to leave it all to me."

"I have less than four months to find the original proprietors of twenty-five percent of the material—exactly thirty-two orphaned penises!" he said.

"Thirty-three," Delfinia corrected him.

A meaningful silence ensued.

"This is getting to be insane!" shrieked Giuseppe.

"So are you, Peppino."

Giuseppe gave in.

Balducchione gave Giuseppe a brusque shake of the hand; then they sat down, as before, facing each other over the immensity of the cardinal's desk.

"You have news for me, Pennini?"

"A little, Your Eminence."

"A little? What little? You have less than three months left to finish your job."

"Progress is slow. You can imagine: a city the size of Rome, where you trip over a statue around every corner—"

"My dear man, I did not agree to see you today to hear a litany of excuses. What's in that leather pouch?"

Giuseppe could sense the cardinal's edginess. At their earlier meetings he had not had that tic at the corner of his mouth. "Affidavits, Your Eminence."

"Affidavits? Yes, yes, get on with it!"

"Proofs that I have managed to make eight positive matches to date."

"Eight? ...That is only twenty-five percent of the twenty-five percent to which I reduced your penance out of the goodness of my heart."

"From my point of view, however, it is already an amazing accomplishment, given the enormity of the task."

"Don't bargain with me, Peppini! I'm holding you strictly to the thirty-two you swore to. I can only hope that such a minimal number of matches will vouch for my industriousness and stop certain malicious tongues from wagging."

"But if your superiors knew what a Herculean labor you've taken upon yourself, Your Eminence—"

"No one wants to know about my problems, not in a politically charged atmosphere where no one listens to reason."

Giuseppe sighed and drew a handful of documents out of his pouch. "These are all, so far, from the curatorial staff of the Museo delle Terme—"

"The National Museum of Rome!" blurted the cardinal.

"The Terme, yes, a veritable labyrinth of antiquities. We have decided to work through one museum at a time."

"We, Pennini? Who is this we?"

"When I say we, Your Eminence, I mean of course mainly myself." Giuseppe fanned the papers out over the cardinal's desk. "Most, as you will see, are no great shakes: a scrotum paired to an otherwise uninteresting old herm, a full set of credentials restored to a satyr, a near-complete cluster to a sarcophagus."

"I am most impressed, Pennino. Continue."

"But they would not even have removed the fig leaf from the satyr, to which we matched its missing parts, had we not had luck first with the herm, which was leafless."

"Naturally," said Balducchione. "You had to prove yourself."

"Thereafter we scored a perfect hit under every fig leaf they removed for us."

"You must tell me sometime how you achieved such accuracy, Pennini, but right now—"

"But her greatest triumph, Your Eminence—my greatest coup to date, I mean—is the discovery of the missing member of a very special monument. It happened to fit precisely in the gouged-out depression above the testicles of one of the Terme's most precious statues, that famous Roman copy in marble of a bronze by the young Praxiteles himself—"

"Out with it, Pennigni! What in heaven's name are you slavering about?"

"I am slav—speaking of the virile member of the world-renowned statue of the Satyr Pouring Wine!"

The cardinal stared in disbelief. "Amazing! And to think that we've held the poor fellow's sex in captivity right here, practically next door, for over a century. ...And when is it to be refastened?"

"I don't know. The staff appeared ... embarrassed, Your Eminence, when they saw the perfect fit."

"Embarrassed to accept help from the Vatican?"

"I don't think so."

"Did they not show appropriate gratitude?"

"Formally, in this letter, Your Eminence, but in person it was clear they wished we had never darkened their door."

"You see, Pennini, it is we who are accused of prudishness, but when push comes to shove, it is the laiety who will always back down! ...Well, the important thing is that they have admitted, in writing, to you as agent of the Vatican Museums, that they have accepted from us the authentic missing etcetera, etcetera." The cardinal glanced quickly over the several affidavits all written within a day or two of each other.

"They seemed grateful enough," resumed Giuseppe, "to recover missing fragments of lesser statuary, but when it came to the famous Sàtiro versante..."

"Enough, Pennini! So far you excel in the quality of your identifications, but you lag far behind in quantity."

"We seem to be stepping up production, Your Eminence. As I've already hinted, I've enlisted a bit of help."

The cardinal looked sharply over the rims of his glasses. "Help? Nothing wrong with that, so long as the utmost discretion is maintained."

"My wife is the soul of discretion," said Giuseppe, blushing.

"Your wife! And what does she know about antiquities?"

"Very little, Your Eminence. And the 'hits,' of course, are being made largely by scientific means."

"Largely? You mean your wife is responsible for ..."

"A couple of the lesser matches. It is remarkable, how through intuition alone—"

"You mean pure chance, don't you, Peppini?"

Giuseppe just had to tell him. Who else could he speak to about it? "It's quite remarkable, Your Eminence. She'll spend a day wandering around the Terme, studying the mutilated statues, also studying those covered with fig leaves, and then she'll come home and start picking up plaster casts, at first seemingly at random, and then she'll close her eyes, dreamily—like so—and focus in on one or two and heft them around, and roll them in her hands, and sort of stroke them, one at a time—"

"Must you really be so graphic, Pennino? Before you compound one sin with another, just get out of here, will you, and rack up twenty-four new documented matches and we're quits!"

The living room where they sat together enjoying a glass of grappa had always struck Delfinia as too much like Giuseppe's galleries, with its terracotta figurines ensconced in alcoves and its pair of Roman lions, in beautifully restored bronze, upon the mantel of the great marble fireplace. So here and there she introduced a contemporary painting or sculpture, and Giuseppe found, to his delight, that they fitted in as harmoniously to the room as Delfinia fitted into his life.

"I still don't understand how you do it, Mia Cara! You are an illiterate when it comes to antiquities, and yet you have somehow acquired a magical feel for..."

"It just comes to me, Mio Caro. All of a sudden, I know. I seem to be guided by some unconscious store of nonverbal experience."

"I myself have been unable to make even one correct guess, whereas you—"

"Much good it does us, Peppino, with one month left and still ten identifications to go!"

Giuseppe took her hand, kissed it, and held it tenderly to his cheek. "The more evidence of success I present to the cardinal, the more the tyrant expects me to fulfill my part of the bargain to the letter—or should I say number. But whatever happens, my dear, even if his sclerotic conscience forces him to ruin me, I at least shall stand witness to the miracles you've wrought, and at the cost of taking you away entirely from your own demanding—"

"Listen, Peppino, we've ransacked every likely museum in Rome—the Capitolino, the Conservatori, the Museo Nazionale—not to mention the gardens, plazas, palaces, villas and galleries. We've done everything, in other words, but the Vatican museums."

"But they are off limits. The cardinal expressly said so!"

"But within that whole city full of antiquities lie the rest of our matches, Peppino. Where else could they be?"

"Anywhere, my dear. In Florence, in New York."

"No. They are in the Vatican, and right under Balducchione's stuffed nose!"

The glass began to shake in Giuseppe's hand. "You know what he said, dear, when I begged him for permission again, only two days ago. Apart from making him angry, and stiffening his resolve against me—"

"To hell with his 'absolute certainty' and his band of one-eyed 'experts.'"

"But what can I do, my dear, if the cardinal says no?"

Delfinia took a long sip of grappa, her beautifully manicured little-finger poised pensively in the air beside her glass. "I have a wonderful idea, Peppino. Together we can write a book. And whatever the cardinal causes you to lose in reputation, you can more than make up for in fame."

"A book? What sort of book, my dear?"

"Italy loves scandal, right? Well, why don't we kick up a stink over the reactions of museum staff when we show them we have what's missing from under their fig leaves?"

"But Cara, aren't we lucky enough to be able to extract affidavits? After all, they are under no obligation to replace the missing pieces, either in the immediate or distant future, or to dispense with the fig leaves once the lost fragments are restored."

"We are talking about Italy's artistic heritage, my love! As the curators of that heritage, they have no right to suppress any part of it. What will decent Italians think when they hear that Count Schiaverazzi chooses to put off restorations on the assumption that people won't believe they are genuine, or will make a laughingstock out of him even if they do, or that he will be accused in the popular press of indecency or morbid sexual preoccupations unbecoming a gentleman of his rank?"

"I've always thought well of Schiaverazzi," said Giuseppe, shaking his head. "He is an excellent after-dinner racconteur."

"And what about Bertolini's cheap excuses? He can't afford the cost of restorations right now, and besides, the little mealy-mouthed beggar fears that such repairs may bring 'negative attention' in a year when his budget is being decided on high. What negative attention could he mean?"

"Ah, yes," said Giuseppe, remembering. "The baron serves excellent champagne, but I have always sensed ulterior motives behind his every act of generosity."

"As to Prince Madrugore," said Delfinia, smiling wryly, "now his is one of the cleverest excuses for foot-dragging that we've heard. 'But, Signora Pennini, this great museum cannot afford the wave of feminist backlash that is sure to follow upon such one-sided restorations. They will march in the streets and castigate us for our neglect of damaged females!'"

"The Prince is the most accomplished hypocrite I know," said Giuseppe, adjusting his tie. "In fact, it is rumored that he purchased his title. A friend of mine who is acquainted with heraldry claims that he could not discover that family line in any of the records he consulted. ..."

"The book will be a bombshell, Mio Caro!" Delfinia ran her slender fingers over Giuseppe's narrow chest. "We will call it Removing the Fig Leaf from Italy's Major Museums. It is sure to be a smashing success!"

"Delfinia," said Giuseppe. He stood up and twirled his glass of grappa thoughtfully between his fingers. "I love you dearly and I have boundless respect for your extraordinary talents, of which I am discovering new ones every day. But..."

"But what, Caro?"

"Delfinia," said Giuseppe, sighing deeply, "Balducchione can only ruin me. But a book like that would destroy me!"

They both sat around in silence for a while, each drinking more heavily than usual of the excellent brandy.

Finally, it was Delfinia who spoke. "Very well, Peppino. There remains only one course of action. We must pursue our search in the only place where answers may still be found—in the Vatican museums, right under the cardinal's arrogant nose, and in spite of his prohibitions."

"And stiffen his back even further against any leniency he may still, at the last minute, be willing to show?" Giuseppe covered his face with his hands. "To me that does not sound like a very good idea, Mia Cara."

"He will not know you are involved because I will be working alone, dear."

"And how will you get authorization to... remove fig leaves, say, to test your hypotheses?"

Delfinia smiled at him. "As I have at the other places. I always manage to enlist the cooperation of subordinates. Through them, my sweet, I work my way to the top."

"All right, Delfinia!" Giuseppe threw up his hands. "Let's say you make a lucky 'hit' at the Vatican—as I have no doubt you will. How then do I approach Balducchione? How do I dare inform him without revealing that I have defied him?"

"We will cross that bridge when we come to it. It is amazing how people's attitudes change under the influence of facts."

"Yes, of course... but we are talking about the Vatican, Delfinia."

The Day of Judgment for Giuseppe had arrived. On that beautiful September morning, his legs quaking beneath him, Delfinia had insisted on accompanying him to the cardinal's office.

"Taking one's wife along on a business call? It's simply not done!" Giuseppe protested.

"You've already told him I'm also your assistant. My presence may be necessary if technical questions arise. The cardinal cannot possibly object."

"But look at you, Delfinia! Dressed for opening night of a new exhibition. Like no research assistant His Eminence has ever seen. Do you think your distracting presence is going to soften his attitude toward me?"

"This is just my normal business attire." They stopped before the outer office door, where Delfinia took one last look at herself, drawing her hands from her breasts to her thighs down her form-fitting black silk sheath. "Besides, I'm not here to make devotions."

When Giuseppe announced that he had arrived with his assistant, the dour receptionist, his face even paler than usual, beat a hasty retreat to the inner office. After an unduly long absence, the old flunkey emerged shaking his head but showed them in.

"Buon giorno, Signor Pennini. Buon giorno, Signorina," the cardinal trumpeted over his marble-topped barricade.

"Magari!" laughed Delfinia. "I am Signora... Signora Pennini, Your Excellency."

"'Eminence,'" Giuseppe croaked in her ear, nudging her with his elbow as he noisily cleared his throat.

The face across the desk, meanwhile, grew stony, the eyes retreating into shadowy grottoes beneath furrowed, bushy gray brows. "Signora, yes. Your reputation in the, ah, art-world precedes you, Signora."

Now what, precisely, did he mean by that? wondered Giuseppe. He could see by her deliberately blank expression that Delfinia was pondering that too. Excruciating seconds passed before the cardinal, with a sweeping gesture, finally invited them to seat themselves.

"You are here with your final progress report?" The cardinal stroked his jowls with thumb and forefinger. Giuseppe knew he should never have taken Delfinia along. Never had Balducchione seemed so lacking in cordiality. No mercy in those eyes! thought Giuseppe. Storm-clouds brewed in the prelate's Jovian brows.

"I feel, Your Eminence," Giuseppe began, "that in consideration of the difficulty of the task, which you admit that other experts you've consulted refused even to take on, a certain relaxation may be in order, that is, of the strict construction of our initial—shall I say overly optimistic? —agreement."

"Come out with it, Pennini? You are confessing to failure to hold up your end of the bargain?"

"I can hardly characterize my accomplishments to date," said Giuseppe, smiling weakly at Delfinia, "in view of the nature of the assignment, as in any sense a failure, Your Eminence."

"Are congratulations in order then, Pennini? You've come up with the last ten matches that you owe me?" The cardinal's eyes kept drifting toward Delfinia. Giuseppe glanced at her too. She kept fingering her magnificent pearl necklace as if counting the beads on a rosary.

"On the contrary, I was going to suggest to Your Eminence that the twenty I've delivered to date should be accepted as a sufficient number of pairings, given not only the inherent difficulty of the job, but the little time I was given, and that most of your colleagues would agree that—"

"Peppini, Peppini," sighed the cardinal, waving his hands palm down over his desk, "when you were a little boy did you bargain with the good Father in the confessional? Did you haggle over the number of Hail Marys he gave you to say?" Balducchione clucked his tongue and shook his head.

"In that case, Your Eminence, I do have some others to report that my research assistant came up with recently."

"Then why didn't you say so immediately?" The cardinal looked suspiciously at both of them.

"Because it may appear to Your Eminence that I have deliberately disobeyed your injunction against searching among the Vatican collections, and yet it is right here, during the last few weeks, among the sculptures in the Museo Gregoriano Profano, and even in the Pio-Clementino, where we now stand—"

"You have managed to make matches where I, with expert help for a decade, have failed?" The cardinal snickered and tapped his fingertips together below his chin. "You are making me quite angry, Perrini. Not only do you violate my trust, but now, out of sheer desperation, you are willing to make false claims about matches that I'm sure cannot be genuine."

"I beg to differ with Your Excellency," Delfinia broke in. "They are absolutely genuine."

The cardinal kept his eyes fixed on Giuseppe.

"Please understand, Your Eminence, that I did not deliberately violate your trust," protested Giuseppe.

"It was not my husband's decision to search at the Vatican," said Delfinia. "It was entirely my own. I did so against his wishes, in fact."

"Indeed!" said the cardinal. "And you, Signora, are suddenly such an expert in antiquities that you have managed to come up with what the best specialists—"

"Exactly! But not ten, Your Grace. Only three."

"I very much doubt that you've come up with even one."

Three? thought Giuseppe. But she had told him only of two. ...Giuseppe watched in terror as Delfinia opened her purse, picked carefully among its contents, and pulled out two documents, slapping them down under the cardinal's pinched beak with the sprezzatura of a baccarat dealer at Monte Carlo.

"I invite you to look at the verifying signatures," said Delfinia. "Your own curatorial staff. Father Maldonato at the Profano, who specializes in herms, and Father Crespini here at the Pio."

The cardinal turned red. "You might at least have come to me before informing my assistants of your... discoveries!"

"How could I have come to you, Your Worship, if not even my husband was permitted to lift the veil here at the Vatican?"

The cardinal appeared to be studying one of the documents. "How did you get Crespini to lift the—to remove the fig leaf from this Pergamene-style marble, simply on your conjecture, Signora?"

"I have always found my fellow connoisseurs the most obliging of people, Your Holiness."

"'Eminence'! 'Eminence' is quite enough," said the cardinal while Giuseppe felt his guts twisting into a helix. "Crespini might have consulted with me," mumbled the cardinal, speaking as if to himself. "But lately he's gotten chummy with some of the Etruscan staff, I hear..."

"I know nothing about all that," said Delfinia, "but Father Crespini was very impressed by my success with the Profano herm—as well as with the copies I showed him of the sheaf of affidavits that have already reached your desk through my husband, Your Grace."

"What do you mean, through your husband? Signor Peppini, what portion of all these matchings are you personally responsible for?"

Giuseppe clutched the arm-rests of his chair to prevent himself from sinking through the floor. "Personally, Your Eminence? ...Not one."

"Not one?"

"Not one. ...The Signora, from early on, began to reveal a remarkable gift—"

"This is a startling confession of the most flagrant irresponsibility!" The cardinal waved the two affidavits like scourges in Giuseppe's face. "Not only do you fail to do your own work, so that I might be assured of the utmost confidentiality, but you thereby fail to meet the quota we agreed to. Ergo, Pennino, you are hardly deserving of the mercy you came here to beg from me. ... So now, if you two will excuse me..."

"But I have not finished my presentation, Your Worship." Delfinia stood up and pressed catlike up against the edge of the cardinal's desk.

"For an amateur you have extraordinary talent, Signora," said the cardinal, picking at his collar as if plucking at imaginary beads, "but I do not wish to trouble you for any further demonstration of your exceptional..."

Giuseppe saw her reach into her magic bag and draw out the plaster-cast of a larger-than-life-size, full set of genitals. It was made from one of the most perfect clusters in the cabinet, and he had been sure that it had eluded even Delfinia's gift at match-making. Carefully, she plunked them down like a paperweight, right over the two affidavits.

"Because of my loyalty to my husband, and my own natural sense of discretion, Your Grace, I have decided to come directly to you with my latest discovery rather than request an affidavit from, say, the already-too-obliging Father Crespini."

The cardinal lurched backward horrified, like a vampire stunned by the Cross. "How dare you... What do you mean by..." he sputtered.

"These are the missing genitals of perhaps the most renowned classical statue in the world, Your Grace, and it stands here under Your Excellency's protection, right here in the Pio-Clementino—or should I rather say, out there, in the Belvedere courtyard, which houses the most precious antique sculptures in all the world."

"The Belvedere! Poppycock, Signora! Your behavior is absolutely—"

"You have before you, Your Grace, the exact replica of the intact member and undamaged testicles that should rightly replace the fig leaf on the Apollo Belvedere."

"The Apollo? Nonsense! I refuse to believe a word of it." Balducchione, visibly shaken, sat propped against the wall three feet behind his desk, one arm raised to his face as though warding off evil.

"Don't you think it will add immeasurably to the god's powerful pagan presence when his private parts are restored?"

"You are treading close on blasphemy, Signora. Please remove this..."

"It makes the perfect conclusion to our six months of investigations. My husband fully agrees, don't you, Caro?"

"Of course, Cara," mouthed Giuseppe.

"So I have come to you for our last affidavit, Your Excellency."

"This is all just a preposterous guess!" shouted the cardinal.

"So far I have never been wrong," said Delfinia. "Have I ever, Your Grace? ...I may not know a Polycleitos from a Praxiteles, but I can tell one penis from another." She stared at Balducchione meaningfully.

"Signora, this is highly irregular!"

"Irregular? No. Asymmetrical, perhaps, because of the pose of the figure. Otherwise perfectly proportioned, as befits a divinity." Delfinia turned the plaster model this way and that on the desk.

"Pennini," said the cardinal, ignoring her, "who in the world would believe such a preposterous claim?"

Giuseppe shrugged his shoulders. "All of Rome, Your Eminence?..."

"Hm! Peppini, we must try to be sensible. The world has known the Apollo... just as he is, for time out of mind. Can you imagine the reaction of a sentimental public to some sudden metamorphosis in an enshrined idol, an icon?"

"Tradition must bow to fact, Your Eminence," Giuseppe gravely intoned.

"Yes, yes, of course. But, responsible as I am for all our curatorial decisions, I am only thinking ahead to the reactions of my various constituencies, both within the Church—"

"However, Your Grace," said Delfinia, "if you prefer that one of your underlings shares in the credit for this discovery, instead of Your self-effacing Holiness, I shall return to Father Crespini, who will be amazed that this museum has kept hidden, during Your Excellency's entire stewardship..."

"I appreciate your coming first to me, Signora, but—"

"I am already preparing an article for the press on the coming restoration, Your Grace. How terrible to have to mention that the inevitable must be postponed because of the posture of the curator in charge, who puts his private sense of modesty over and above..."

"Now wait! ...Surely, Signora," said Balducchione, his tone suddenly unctuous (and in Giuseppe's estimation half an octave higher than a moment before), "given your tactful handling of this matter up to now, not to mention your connection with the prestigious name of Peppini, can you not think of some more tasteful way to settle our, ah, tactical differences?"

"Why certainly, Your Grace!" said Delfinia, blinking three perfectly spaced blinks while continuing to stroke her pearls. "What about an article which gives half the credit to you for this remarkable historic find?"

Balducchione, sucking his teeth, looked out toward the Belvedere courtyard. "That would be somewhat better," he conceded, "but to take so much undeserved credit, well..."

"No, no, I understand," said Delfinia, thinking. Well then, I suppose I could do the Christian thing, that is, relinquish my desire for the gratification that publicity would bring, and put the whole matter aside... indefinitely."

"Indefinitely, Signora?" Balducchione stared at her sharply over the tops of his sweat-rimmed glasses.

"However painfully, Your Eminence, I could forego my deep need for personal fame—in return for Your Eminence's own... equally generous... consideration." Delfinia's head turned slowly, first to Giuseppe, then to the cardinal, then back to Giuseppe.

When they were out of the office and halfway down the corridor, Giuseppe could no longer contain himself. Clutching in his fist the life-saving note, in the cardinal's own crabbed hand, that acquitted him of "any and all responsibility, moral, financial, or other, in the matter of" etcetera, etcetera, he turned, soaking with sweat, to Delfinia. "Why didn't you tell me, Mia Cara, that you had made such a monumental discovery? Why did you allow me to stew, for days, in agony?"

"Because, Mio Caro, I made no such discovery. I would like it to be true, but I predict that if and when the Apollo's members are recovered, they will be a fraction smaller, hang slightly more to the right, and appear more delicately contoured... with almost a feminine softness."

THE TRUTH AND DONNA DABRIZI

Leah Griesmann

One day the truth caught Donna Dabrizi. It wasn't her fault. She hadn't asked for it. If given a choice, she would have said no. But the truth, like the wind, couldn't be stopped. Once the truth had been let inside the apartment, it rushed through easy as breeze and cleared through everything in its wake. No corner was left unsullied by truth, no cranny unaltered.

It started with a chair. Donna had looked at that chair every day for twenty-two years and never noticed the truth. The chair had been given to her by her mother on the eve of her wedding, and occupied a hallowed position in the living room. They kept it covered and cleaned for seventeen years.

One day the thought came to her like a whisper. She and Greg had never liked the chair. This truth hit her like a sour piece of fruit. It made her purse her lips a little bit, but she swallowed it down. Since Greg had never complained about the chair, there would be no need to move it.

There were other glimpses of truth regarding her household items. Cutlery she never used. Blankets given to her as a present that stayed in the closet. A rug, Greg's favorite, that she thought was hideous. These truths were of the bitter, but painless variety. She noticed them, but did not cringe. Household items were useful or not, attractive or not, but in the end they were less than critical.

But truth didn't stop with the furniture. It was only a day later that truth moved on to the dog. She and Greg had taken Sadie in when she was a pup. They had really gotten her for Wesley when he was a boy. Wesley liked Sadie as any seven-year-old boy can like a pet, but he didn't bond with her the way she and Greg had expected.

When Wesley went off to college a year ago, he had told his parents that he couldn't keep a pet on campus, but that he would pick her up one day when he moved. In the meantime Sadie, now going on twelve years old, was blind and gaseous. Poor Sadie, she and Greg would say, giving her a sympathy pat. But the truth was, Sadie was decrepit and mostly unloved. She would probably be better off dead.

This was a thought that surprised Donna. This was the truth that one shouldn't speak out loud. How evil to wish death on a dog. But as she reflected on it, she knew that it wasn't actually morbid. It only sounded bad when she imagined other people hearing it. It was here her confusion began. If what was true could hurt others, or was embarrassing for her, then what good was the truth?

As truth continued to mount its campaign, Donna began spending more time at home, shunning the invitations of others. It would be horrible if, while working out at a healthclub, or drinking coffee with friends, she should have a truthful episode. She might offend her friends and embarrass herself. She began turning down all social calls in an effort to rebuff the truth.

But it was at home, in her relationship with Greg that she was having the most difficult time avoiding truth's seductions. Despite her best efforts to ignore it, the truth, bit by bit, was having its way with her. There was the matter of Greg's late returns from work once or twice a week. There was the silence between them some nights that she found unbearable, but which didn't seem to disturb him at all. On such nights, when she was crawling out of her skin, he would usually announce that he was tired and going to bed. The connection was gone, was the thought that truth told her.

That Wesley was gone now, in college, was a reality that seemed to linger in the emptiness of her days with Greg. The duties she had with Wesley, all the ferrying him around and his likes and dislikes, the minor calamities in the life of a child, the milestones of growth were all done now. She could ask for news about his progress and growth, but she was no longer directly involved. With that came an emptiness too, and a void of purpose. Without my son I have no life, came truth's whisper. It would echo through her day off the many walls in the well-furnished rooms of her comfortable home.

It was at this time that Donna began to walk. Every day she would walk from her house in the Excelsior through the outskirts of Golden Gate Park. The fog was low and heavy at this time of year, though the days were getting longer.

She would walk past coffeehouses and cinemas, past clothing stores and restaurants, past record stores and hospitals on her way downtown. Her walks were invigorating and always left questions in her mind. She wondered about the young people she saw, and the students, all of the social activity she saw on the streets. She wondered about their lives, and the lives of the well-heeled adults.

She would walk until she was exhausted and then hop on the Geary bus to go home again. She would come back to her house filled up by the experience, like a tourist in a far-away land. Her silent nights with Greg didn't bother her as much now that she had a secret life of her own.

Early one morning in late spring Donna decided to walk to the bay. It was the kind of morning San Francisco was famous for—cloudy, foggy, the sky a blanket of white. But by the time Donna had crossed Van Ness, the sun began peeking out from the brilliant blue blanket threaded with clouds. The sun lit up the grey and ivory of the buildings and cast shadows over Washington Street before disappearing again.

Donna paused to look down towards Market Street. The buildings were stretched out and gleaming before her, a tapestry of structure and light. Had she forgotten that San Francisco possessed such exquisite beauty? She had barely noticed it in many years.

At the top of the hill, Chinatown began its downward spill towards the water. There Donna felt a slight palpitation of her heart. The last time she had been to Chinatown was with Wesley when he was eight, to ring in the Year of the Boar. Grant Street, the entrance, would have the usual array of European tourists in letter sweatshirts, toting shopping bags and Japanese cameras. She would have to walk among them, but she was determined to keep her distance. It was not her Chinatown, she knew, but she was after all, San Franciscan, and not just some bargain-bound tourist.

Crossing Bush Street she steered away from the jade shops, restaurants, and souvenir stores. On the side streets were the genuine Chinese stores without the English lettering. Dirty sidewalks gave way to boisterous produce shops, butchers with hanging ducks, and the cramped and crowded herb shops with their barrels of fungi and ginseng. Here old ladies stooped with bokshoi cabbage would meet up with friends on the street.

When Chinatown's crowds and colors had their way with her, she crossed out the back into North Beach. At a café nearby she took a seat among newspaper-readers and youthful modern-day beatniks. A tattered array of posters covered an area of the wall by the restrooms. Next to the bulletin board, a young woman with black-framed glasses was flirting with a longhaired boy in a white T-shirt and jeans who looked about Wesley's age. He was drinking a foaming coffee in a tall glass, flipping his long mane away from his face with a laugh. He was pretty almost, and demure, whereas the girl was severe-looking and bold. The youth of San Francisco had often disturbed Donna with their hip attire and druggy lifestyle, but today they seemed darling to her, even innocent. She couldn't help smiling slightly when she accidentally caught the girl's eye.

Donna's early twenties had been carefree in their own way, though her lifestyle was conservative. Her dreams were of earning a good salary, getting married, and owning a home. She was not interested in the California counter-culture that so many her age were creating. Donna preferred to walk the straight and narrow path of forward movement, middle-class goals, and good hygiene. There was something in her today that envied the bohemian lifestyle of the youths in the cafe. She had missed out on something it was too late to acquire, and truth was now peeking in.

When Donna finished her coffee, she walked into the brisk air. It was late afternoon, and the financial crowd, the Fidi's, would be getting off rom their eight-hour day soon, rushing in ties and high heels to hit the subways and bridges back to their homes. Donna didn't feel like going home yet. The city was too exciting, too invigorating; she wanted to see more. She'd had enough of the respectable parts of town, of downtown and North Beach. For some unknown reason, while the truth was still blessedly avoiding her, the Mission District was calling her name.

The Mission Street bus was everybody's last resort. The jangly, smelly, crowded and yelling and don't-step-on-anyone's-toes bus was the one Donna wanted to ride. She welcomed the noise now, the smells even, the occasional smiles and politeness, the cry of the driver as he called out the streets. She felt like she was waking up for the first time in years.

In the Mission, excluding the drug trade that took place on the streets, the taquerias, the panaderias, and bars seemed to make up the gross neighborhood product. Donna was craving a margarita. A good, stiff, limey and salt margarita, of the kind that one should really only get in the Mission. She got off at 18th Street and walked up four blocks, taking stock of the restaurants and watering holes, hoping that one would beckon. She finally stopped in at Pancha's after reading a blackboard, upon which was written, "Happy Hour Margaritas."

Pancha's was dim and sour-smelling, but the bartender and the bar patrons were friendly. "Lime margarita, please," Donna said, taking a seat.

As the bartender fixed her order, she settled into her stool to look around. The place was wall-to-wall in mirrors, and the patrons were a mix of men, mostly Hispanic, and one or two women. The lighting was dim, which made it much more intimate, but harder to see the patrons' faces. Other than the fact that soccer was playing on the television, and not football, there was nothing particularly Latin about the place that she could note.

The bartender presented her with a salt-drenched, light green margarita. "Are you here to watch the show?"

Donna took a sip of her drink. "I didn't know there was a show."

"At 5pm, after the game. Latin Ladies."

"Oh," Donna said, distastefully.

"But not really ladies," the bartender said with a laugh.

"Oh," Donna said again, feeling relieved somehow, that men should be watching men in drag, rather than real women. Drag queens seemed quaint compared to real strippers. She hadn't seen a drag show in years.

The sour liquid mixed with the salt on the glass, refreshing what had increasingly become Donna's very staid sense of taste. She tried to sip her margarita slowly, to savor it, and the novelty of where she was. Still, within five minutes of ordering the margarita she found herself sucking the last drops from the bottom of the ice cubes. The soccer game was finishing up, in the final minutes, and most of the patrons had gathered around the bar to watch. After the final goal was kicked, there were some loud cheers and muffled sounds of disappointment as Argentina won the game against Bolivia.

Men at the bar chattered loudly about the outcome of the game, alternately patting each other on the back or giving high-fives. Donna took a seat to be closer to the stage area, a beer-stained floor with a curtained entranceway and a steel microphone stand. As she was taking her seat, a tall, muscular "woman" in a short red dress with an afro entered the bar.

"Hola!" the woman said prettily through painted lips to the bartender, and a few of the men, loud with liquor, greeted her back. She gave all of the men a big toothy smile and a kiss on the cheek, then went around through the bar to a back room. Men were starting to move toward the stage now to take seats, boisterous, and happily drinking. Donna, though the only woman in the room, felt comfortable with them, and some of them smiled in a friendly way in her direction.

In a few minutes the lights were dimmed, and mariachi music began playing on what sounded like a scratchy, old-fashioned turntable. The lights were turned on and the muscular "lady" in the red dress took the stage. Though her Spanish was basic, Donna gathered that the gist of the show was a history of famous Latin women through the ages. The women, who included Frida Kahlo and Eva Peron among them, were played by men who came onstage, paraded around in costume, and recited a monologue in an absurd high-pitched "female voice" which produced laughter from the crowd, and inevitably descended into a striptease. Donna enjoyed the show thoroughly, and when it was over, found herself along with the others placing a five-dollar bill in the bra cup of the red-dressed M.C.

Donna sat back after the show, sipping a second lime margarita. The Spanish emanating from the booths was starting to sound familiar now, and she enjoyed watching people reflected by the mirrored walls. She felt at home, happy to have the experience to herself. Her night at home would be so much easier now that she had her own adventures outside of the house.

Leaving Pancha's, Donna walked up 18th street towards the Castro, feeling the warmth from her margarita and the looseness in her joints. The sun was high, and the evening traffic and hustle of people were filling the colorful streets. Donna passed gay bookstores and rainbow flags, smoke shops and juice bars, the margaritas warming her in the encroaching chill of the wind.

The Castro was as crowded and colorful as she remembered. Pulsating disco music echoing forth from a dance club caught Donna's ears. She turned towards the music while stopping for traffic. The boom-boom-boom of the grating beat emanated from a black double-door under a silver sign that read, "Moonride." A man with a chiseled face and a hairy chest guarded the door.

Donna watched the club for a moment until the light turned, then stepped out into the street. As she did, she saw Greg, or at least a man who almost definitely was Greg, enter through the door of Moonride with another man.

Donna's first sensation was not one of shock. In fact, it was less a feeling than a thought process. What hit her primarily was an urgency to establish the certainty of whether the man she just saw had truly been Greg. She stopped in the street to see if she could get a better look, but the door that had closed did not open. Greg, or the man who looked like Greg, was not coming out of the door any time soon.

Her next instinct was to check the time. It was 5:47 according to her watch, and though it was still early evening, it was feasible that Greg would no longer be at work. When she finished crossing the street, she went into the first juice bar with seats available to sit down and think.

That had been Greg. It was certainly Greg, she thought — she knew her husband. But then a nagging second question. Could it possibly not have been Greg? She kept playing the memory back in her mind. The image of that fleeting second seeing the side of Greg's head as he opened the door to walk into Moonride. He had paused for just a moment to hold the door open for the other man. That was certainly Greg — unsmiling, and in work clothes still. You don't live with someone for twenty years and not recognize him from across the street. It had to have been Greg.

Having established with reasonable certainty in her mind that Greg was inside the Moonride club in the Castro early in the evening on a work night, Donna ordered a juice. She felt calm internally, as if the idea of Greg inside a Castro club had given her the confirmation she had been looking for. But the reason it did not sway her thoughts, or torque her reality too much was because she had been there to see it. She had been in the Castro to see Greg in the Castro. And before her recent encounters with truth, she would never have been away from home at this hour to see him.

She did not jump to any unnecessary conclusions because of the picture she had just internalized, the visual image of Greg going into the Moonride with another man. The distance between them was still theirs — it did not mean it was his distance, and his alone. She had been here on one of her secret afternoons to see him here. They were both out of bounds of each other.

That night in the Castro, the truth shone a light on her life with her husband. Their relationship was one of two people cohabiting. The vows had been exchanged, the child was born and had left, and their living together went on. When did a marriage become not a marriage, and merely the aftermath of a married situation, the twilight denouement of silly vows? What did the act of divorcing do besides stamp a letter that had already been sent? What did the purchase of juice have in common with soliciting gay sex at a disco? The boundary of intimacy was finite, not infinite; the secrecy in their souls was the same.

The walk home from Castro Street would be too long at this time of night. Her feet had the city-tired feeling that walking on pavement imparted. She would take the bus up to Geary through the Haight.

As the sun set, she watched her fellow passengers with a friendly detachment. The thought occurred to her that she wasn't reacting to the day's events appropriately. If this was a play, her role would be clear: she should be overwhelmed by the rawness of her experience. She should be crying bitter tears for the tragic irony of her situation as she pitifully rode a city bus home alone.

The scenario had no attraction for her. She was no more or less lonely than before the truth found her. And at least now she had San Francisco. Greg would be home from the Castro soon. And they would sleep.

ANOTHER PITTSBURGH BUS STORY

Linda Lee Harper

The only time I watched a man die was on the bus, 67 A Holiday Park Red Flyer Special. He was sitting almost diagonally across from me. But I had a real good view of his face. He had the kind of everyday face you wouldn't recall unless he did something to make you remember him. It's been a while, but he did, and I do.

This man was on the bus when I boarded it outside my downtown Walgreen's. He was in his mid-forties, not particularly heavy, about average height. He wore an ordinary neat brown suit and respectable white shirt. But his tie—his tie almost glowed with a dark blood-red, a kind of rich burgundy. Elegant small gold circles shone in an all-over pattern. Only expensive silk ties carry a sheen like that tie.

I never noticed what kind of shoes he wore. By the time I got a chance to get a good look, one of the do-gooders had taken the man's shoes off and was rubbing his stocking feet. Someone must have given the shoes to the ambulance attendant later.

I was loaded down with all the Christmas shopping that I like to get finished in September. I'm not as young as when my Harry was still alive, and the crowds are killers in

November. With the bad weather and the hills around here, well, September just seems to work out better for me. Lots of bargains, no rushing.

That time of year kids just have to have school clothes, and the shelves have choices, for once. My grandkids always have the pick of the crop though they don't get what I buy until December. Marge says buying that far in advance makes it hard to guess sizes, the way kids grow, but it's better than nothing, I tell her. Besides, I always ask her, who else do I have to spend money on?

So, here I was struggling to get on the bus with full shopping bags and the most convenient seats right up front—full. The only seat that wasn't clear back in the heel of the bus beckoned on the left. Nobody else sat there, so I struggled to it and settled the bags down next to me. If the bus got more crowded, I planned to put them on the floor. I like seats facing the aisle. I like to see what we're passing without getting a crook in my neck. Marge sits in the seats that face forward. She says where I sit makes her nauseous.

We passed through Squirrel Hill and stopped in Wilkinsburg proper. A thin, goateed black fellow carrying a guitar case and wearing one of those i-Things, climbed on. He looked happy, his earphones wrapped across the top of his head. He snapped his fingers to music turned up so loud you could still hear it over the sound of the bus' choking engine. He must have been partially deaf.

A scraggly older woman wearing a dirty pink beret had my favorite seat behind the bus driver. She stood up and tried to maneuver around the musician while he negotiated a transfer from the ticket box.

As she tried to step around him she said in a very loud and impatient voice, "Excuse me, pull-eeze." He probably didn't hear her with that music blasting into both ears. So when he didn't move, she poked his leg with the chrome tip of her umbrella. Lifting one earphone away from his head he turned around.

"Yes, ma'am?" he asked in a perfectly reasonable tone of voice.

The woman didn't answer him. She just pushed his hip with the side of her left arm as she forced her way past and got off the bus.

When the young man sat down in my favorite seat, he took his pocket stereo out of his pocket and adjusted the dials. Then he took the earphones off, folded them up and stuffed them into a side pocket of his blue leather jacket. He locked his upright guitar between his knees, closed his eyes and soon his head nodded with the rhythm of our bus as it started and stopped at what seemed to me, every corner in Wilkinsburg.

It was when we started up the hill, before Blackridge Court, that this ordinary man sitting directly across from the sleeping musician started to draw attention to himself.

First, he started to cough, hard. I noticed right away there was something strange about the way it came from his chest, a gurgling noise, followed by two or three loud barks. Then he sat there as if he were trying to clear his throat.

This went on until the bus reached the top of the hill. Way after he should have, he pulled a handkerchief from his pocket and coughed more into that. By the time we passed the Chalfont Apartments, he was practically choking. A rotund, pink-cheeked young man sitting next to him and dressed in a Macy's security guard uniform slapped him on his back.

"That's it. Get it up… get it all up!"

He continued to slap him on the back until the next bus stop. Somebody should have suggested the ailing man get off there and then. Afterwards, the woman behind me said it probably wouldn't have made any difference.

"His heart was in its death throes when he first coughed," she said shaking her head. "Just like my Harold. Only Harold coughed two or three times and dropped over like a cut tree. Just fell straight to the kitchen floor. Never said a word."

I didn't tell her my Harry did the same thing. Only he suffered his on the Captain's Midnight River Cruise last summer when Frank Olsen and Oswald McGruder came up from Morgantown for the Fourth of July. No wives allowed they said. I still regret that we all didn't go. If the wives had been along, at least my Harry would have eaten a better, final meal.

As it was, all he ate was a Riverdog, salty fries and lukewarm cans of Iron City. He complained all through the last can, Oswald told me at the funeral, that the beer was too warm, that it was making him sick. Poor Harry. I don't think he knew what hit him. I don't know. But it was a blessing, the speed, Rev. Haggarty said. Harry was with good friends and having a good time. I take comfort from that. I just wish I'd been there.

Anyway, the pink-cheeked Macy's guard was getting red in the face from slapping the man on the back. The coughing man, with one fist knotted in front of his mouth, tried to wave him away. Other people were craning their necks or half-standing to see what was going on. The poor man waved his free hand around in the air and caught hold of the security guard's red hair. The guard let out a whoop. It got sort of muffled because the coughing man had a good enough handful of hair to pull the guard's head down toward the lapel of the brown suit. It seemed as if he clutched the guard's head tightly to his chest. His other hand stretched straight out in front of him now, two fingers pointed at the black musician across from him.

The musician had opened his eyes and was in the process of rearranging the earphones back on his neatly groomed head. The coughing man pointed at him as if he wanted to say something. All that came out was a hiss, a raspy, strangled sound. The guard managed to loosen the man's grip on him.

"Driver, stop the bus, driver," yelled the guard, "Get help."

The driver took a few quick glances in the interior, rear-view mirror, checked the lane next to him and started to honk his horn. The bus lurched forward as he accelerated.

"Heart attack!" he boomed over his shoulder. "East Suburban's the closest. We'll get him there..." The driver continued to honk as the man's cough shifted into deep, sucking gasps for air. He had turned his head toward the back of the bus and his eyes focused on the colorful ad for a local radio station over my head. He looked scared.

The security guard with the help of a young woman in a gray worsted business suit tried to turn the man sideways so they could help him lie down. She looked like she knew what she was doing. Marge says to make it in business today, you have to know not only what you're doing, but what your boss is doing before he does, and probably be able to do a better job than he does. She says things haven't changed that much, no matter what the new generation believes. A woman is still a woman and should know that a man will better her every time he gets a chance. It's nature, Marge says. I don't know if she's right, but I haven't been in the work force since I cashiered at the Kmart eight years ago. I wanted extra money to buy Harry expensive casting rods and a tackle box. I never had much trouble with my bosses. Most of them were old enough to be a son, if Harry and I had a son. And they could run a register good as any of us women.

After the whole thing was over, I told the lady behind me it had been a good thing the young business girl's boss wasn't on that bus because just as she tightened her arm good and solid around the distressed man's shoulders, his body went to a spasm which locked his arms to his sides as if he were standing at attention. His gaze dropped and he stared right at me with the most panicked look I think I've ever seen. His chin dipped and his mouth gaped like a cored tomato.

Meanwhile, the bus was charging down the Parkway East on the Monroeville bypass, the engine grinding loudly, the horn warning cars and trucks out of its way.

Over all the noise we heard the man trying to force air into his lungs. We could all see the tremendous concentration on his face as he squeezed his eyes shut and swallowed one last gasp. He managed to twist a hand away from his side and to grasp at the young woman's jacket. His eyes rolled away from me towards her, and I could see that effort was too much. His face went pale, then his lips began to darken.

The young business woman pulled her arm from around his shoulders and tried to back away. But the man's hand bunched the bottom corner of her jacket tightly in his fist. He wasn't looking at her at all anymore. His glance settled slowly toward the ridge of where metal bolts scored the length of the bus.

A little girl in the back of the bus whose mother was holding her up high as if she were a small squirming sack squealed, "Mommy, Mommy...look...that man's doing like Granpa."

The business woman tugged at the pocket of her suit jacket , leaned over and pulled at the man's hand, uncurling his fingers from around the nice fabric.

"My god, " she said, "I think he's dying."

Well, I could have told her that just from watching reruns of ER. She did what the modern woman is never supposed to do—act like a woman. She pulled wadded Kleenex from her pocket and clutched them to her mouth like a microphone at a karaoke bar. Marge and I went to one once to hear her granddaughter.

The young woman started to sob.

"He's dead....oh God, look at him. He's not breathing." She clung to the chrome bar over head to steady herself as the bus pulled to the shoulder of the parkway. "DO-o-o-o-o something...Somebody...please..."

The bus ground to a halt on the gravel shoulder and the driver jumped up and hurried to the man whose eyes focused on something under his own eyebrows.

"Stretch him out on the floor. Get that tie off...open his shirt. " He took off his Port Authority coat and straddled the man's knees. "Come on! Somebody help me. NOW!"

That's when five or six people rushed toward the front end of the bus, and for a few seconds, I couldn't see a thing. But I did push my shopping bags over to the window side of the seat and coax the little girl back towards her mother. An older man in a safari jacket and open-necked flowered shirt handed me the beautiful silk tie with little gold circles all over it.

"Hold this," he commanded and stretched his arm across the aisle so nobody else could get closer.

I could see the driver's shoulders flex as he alternately bent over to force air into the man's mouth and then straighten to rhythmically pound the heel of his left palm over the man's heart. He did that for a while, probably two or three minutes until we heard a siren approaching from the Monroeville exit.

I realized the driver hadn't been talking to himself as he drove, but he'd been calling on his radio for help.

The black musician forced from his seat by all the commotion, reached across the space between the driver and himself. He touched the driver's shoulder as he labored over the still man.

"He's gone, man. Let it go." He pointed to the man's eyes. They had rolled back so far it looked like was trying to see under the bus seats.

The driver didn't answer but kept administering first aid that I read in the paper they trained all drivers to know. The little girl sat down with her mother. The man with the safari jacket moved to the step-well by the back exit door and the security guard stood like he was guarding Macy's fine jewelry counter, both thumbs tucked into his belt loops, his chest out, cheeks as pink as if they'd been rouged.

When the safari jacket moved toward the step-well, I could see the young business woman. She was kneeling on the floor next to the man's feet. His shoes were gone and she was massaging his left foot. Maybe she didn't really believe he was gone and was trying to help with circulation. I don't know, but it looked silly.

The ambulance attendants arrived and made a big fuss. They clamped an oxygen mask over the man's face. They ripped the sleeve of his suit coat in their haste to get if off. Into his right arm they jabbed needles attached by rubber tubes to a bag of clear liquid. The husky attendant took a long, fat, hypodermic and shot it directly into the poor man's exposed chest. That's all I got to see.

The EMT's lifted him up from the floor and carried him to a gurney set up outside.

Traffic on the parkway slowed down as it drove past our bus. The ambulance was parked in front of the bus, its red and white light beams swirling over the scene like a moonlight madness sale at Big-Lots. Some people in the slowest cars driving past, waved; so I waved back. The woman behind me said all of this was kind of exciting. I agreed but didn't tell her. I told her I thought it was a shame the little girl had seen so much, especially if she saw her grandfather get sick. Children are so impressionable, like Marge always says.

The ambulance screeched away with the dead man attached to an oxygen mask and needles. I always wonder why they do that, even though it's clear the person is gone. The bus driver stood outside the bus kicking stones at the guard rail close to where we had stopped. The safari jacket wondered when the hell we were going to get moving, and the Macy's man told him the driver had radioed for a replacement.. He couldn't continue the route.

About twenty minutes later, a Port Authority SUV rolled in behind us. A nice man in a plaid shirt with the sleeves rolled up apologized for the delay and hoped we would understand that a tragedy like the one we had witnessed is an upsetting occurrence. He ushered the musician out the front door, and the business woman and security guard joined them. They seemed to be talking all at once, shaking heads, nodding. The business woman got into the SUV with the driver and the guard and the musician climbed back on to the bus.

"They're bringing us a new bus," the guard announced as the musician once more adjusted his headphones. He sat down next to the safari jacket and tapped a quick beat on his knee with long, slender fingers.

I was beginning to wonder if I was ever going to get home when sure enough— a new bus chugged up behind us. We all disembarked through the emergency door. The smell of the poor man's urine and stool had completely fouled the bus. The EMTs had made a feeble effort to clean it all up. But even the open windows couldn't dispel it over the stench of disinfectant.

The woman behind me said it's a shame our bodies lose dignity so fast when we're dying.

She snapped her fingers.

"When I go, I hope it's as quick as him," she told me as she followed me down the aisle of the second bus. I turned in my seat to hear her better as she sat down, again behind me as if they were assigned seats. "That poor man never really knew what hit him. When you think of cancer and car wrecks and crime, all in all, it wasn't a bad way to go."

I didn't answer her. The new driver climbed up into place. Our first driver stuck his head in the door just far enough so we could hear him.

"Have a good trip home," he said as he zipped his coat. "And thanks to all who tried to help. It's just one of those things. "

He waved and stepped back down to the shoulder of the highway, turning back toward our first bus. The hydraulic doors heaved shut and our new bus pulled back on to the Parkway.

The woman behind me chattered down the parkway until we got to my exit, and then my stop. As I struggled with my two bags, some of the smaller things on top fell to the black rubber treads of the aisle. She leaned over and stuffed them back into my bag nearest her.

"Nice tie," she said as she carefully tucked the red burgundy necktie back into the shopping bag. "A present for somebody?"

I told her yes, good-bye and got off the bus the best way I could manage. Luckily, the rain Channel 4 predicted all day, held off until I was on my front porch. The newspaper I gathered from under the yews by the steps never got the slightest bit wet.

I unwrapped and stored all of the Christmas gifts in large plastic tubs with sturdy lids. I hung the tie on a wooden hanger in Harry's end of our closet and made myself a Weight Watcher's frozen dinner to eat while I watched the six o'clock news. They never mentioned our tragedy on the bus. I guess they know best what's newsworthy and what isn't.

I watched the papers for a few days to see if there would be any mention there. Nothing. Marge couldn't believe my bad luck to get stuck on a bus with a man dying in front of my eyes. I keep telling her, it was no big deal. It's nature, life taking its course. I didn't mention the tie. Why would I?

I never did find out what that poor man's name was. I guess I could have called the bus company. But it's been several years, and his widow may even have re-married by now. She may have moved. And besides, what would I say if I called her?

I'm sure others on the bus that day found out who he was and offered up their sympathies. And that's if he had a wife at all. My money's always been on yes. No man could pick out a tie as pretty as the one he wore that day. No man I ever knew.

BLUE WORLD

Andrew Bourelle

In the morning, the world is blue.

Most people consider sunsets in Montana more spectacular than sunrises. In the evening, a variety of clouds cover the sky: some mountains of thick white, some cottony wisps, some brush strokes as if from God's paintbrush. And as the sun descends, it bathes each of the clouds in different spectacular colors: reds and oranges, pinks and purples. Jason sits with Abby on their front porch in the evenings, watching the sunsets. But Jason secretly prefers the mornings. He wakes, boils a pot for tea, and sits at their oak kitchen table and watches the blue world become color. The sky turns from light blue to dark. The pastures and the mountains and the clouds, all shades of blue, slowly gain color and seem to become real. To Jason, watching the sunrise is like watching God create the world each morning. Sitting at the table and watching the blue world each day is his sanctuary. He never goes to church. But he says a prayer each morning.

He prays mostly about Abby, that she'll have a safe drive to and from town, that the children won't give her too much grief at school, that she'll continue to love him and be happy with their life here. But more than making such requests, he fills his prayers with thanks.

A fter Jason's accident, I watch him sometimes when he looks at his hand. He stares at it, as if to remind him of what happened. The pinky finger is missing from just above the top knuckle, his ring finger from just below the second knuckle, and his middle finger is all gone except for a tiny nub. The three stumps show the angle of the blade as it bit off one, two, three fingers before he pulled away, saving his thumb and forefinger. The skin across the stumps is scar-smooth, like melted wax, as if he held his hand to a fire and the tips of his fingers simply dripped off.

Ever since the accident, in the morning, as he watches the dawn, his gaze returns again and again to his left hand, with its missing fingers, and then to his right, where he wears his wedding band now.

When I see him like this, sometimes I ask him what he's thinking, the way he used to ask me when he noticed some melancholy to my expression, but he never answers.

It is spring, and Abby is planting her garden. When she plants each year, she tries a variety of crops. The hardiest—carrots, lettuce, onions, turnips—grow successfully. Others—potatoes, parsley, broccoli—are more difficult. And the more spirited attempts—corn, pumpkin, watermelon—are invariably failures. Some of her plants just don't take to the short growing season of Montana. Some are killed by late-spring frosts or early-fall snows. Some, for no obvious reason, simply don't grow to their full potential. She tries relentlessly each spring and summer.

"Corn won't grow here," he says. "Neither will—"

"I'm going to try anyway."

He kneels in the dirt with her, helping her, regardless of the fruitlessness of some of her vegetable choices. He reaches into the black soil, working the earth like a baker working dough, touching the insects and the worms in the damp dirt.

As he works, he feels as if he's reaching into the center of the planet, as if his ten fingers have turned into roots that stretch down beneath the topsoil and clay and into the crust of the world. He feels as if electricity—a low-level shock, pleasant and not painful—reaches up through his fingers and arms, into his elbows, shoulders, through his veins and arteries and capillaries, into the synapses of his brain. He looks at his hands, stained brownish black with dirt. He breathes in, breathes out, sharing the air with the breathing trees, the soil, the newly planted seeds, the elk and the wolves that run through the forests, the hawks, the crows, the atoms in everything beneath the canopy of the atmosphere. He looks at Abby, working in the same soil, breathing the same air, and he plunges his fingers back into the garden, feeling as if the electric life pulse of the earth connects him to her.

If divine forces didn't bring us together, then impossible luck did, a confluence of improbable circumstances. A month out of college, driving from Seattle to Chicago for a new job teaching high school, I pulled off the highway in Montana during an out-of-nowhere, rare-but-not-impossible August snowstorm. I turned left when I should have turned right, which took me away from town instead of into it, and I ended up lost on back gravel roads, cutting fresh tracks through the powder with no four-wheel drive or chains. When Jason found me, I was walking in the snow in a skirt and short-sleeved blouse, my car stuck in a ditch. He drove me to his house because it was closer than town and I was shivering violently. He handed me a pair of sweat pants and one of his old flannel shirts, pointed me to the shower and the tea pot, then grabbed a tow chain out of the barn and went back for my car. When he returned with it twenty minutes later, I was curled on the couch, wearing his clothes—about ten sizes too big—and holding a warm cup between both hands. I smiled, embarrassed and grateful, and something about the way he looked at me—the warmth in his expression—moved me. I told people later I fell in love with him right then.

All we did was talk that night. After midnight, he let me slip on a pair of his boots and a big down coat, and he took me outside. The sky was clear now, and the starlight made the snow glow a striking bluish-white, as if it was lit from beneath instead of above.

"I can't believe how beautiful it is," I said, staring out at the white fields, frosted hills, the branches of trees weighed down by wet snow.

I tilted my head back and looked upward. I gasped. I had never seen so many stars.

"Look there," he whispered.

A herd of deer, fifty yards away, tiptoed through the snow, their brown coats standing out against the white backdrop. I could hear the faint crunch of their hooves as they stepped through the snow, does and bucks alike.

"This is amazing," I said.

When I woke in the morning, I found him sitting at the kitchen table, looking out through the window. He seemed deep in concentration, lost in thought. He made me breakfast and talked for a while longer. I didn't want to leave, and I could tell he didn't want me to either. But staying just wasn't logical. By the time I started my car at noon, most of the snow had melted. I gave him my cell phone number, but he lived where there were no phone lines or cellular towers.

He told me later, as he watched my car drive away, leaving a cloud of dust behind on the gravel road, that he felt lonelier than he'd ever felt, even lonelier than when he'd retreated to Montana. He'd moved to this ranch to get away from people, to have his solitude and privacy, but now he felt like a ghost living in an abandoned homestead. Me, I felt like I was driving away from home. I hadn't been there twenty-four hours—and we hadn't so much as kissed—but I started crying like I'd just said goodbye to my longtime boyfriend. To the love of my life.

It's a warm, late-summer day, and they ride horses through the pastures and into the forest, the hooves clopping on the dirt as they ride among the ponderosa pine, the Douglas fir, and the Rocky Mountain maple. The tree branches move in the breeze. The mountains are alive. Jason and Abby take a break at the edge of a meadow overflowing with wildflowers. They sit on a log, eating sandwiches and sharing an apple. Jason thinks about the environment around him. Ants crawl through the duff on the ground, in and out of needles, along leaves, on branches, across the toe of his boot. Insects crawl on the log, which rots from the inside. The decomposition is part of the ecosystem's cycle, and Jason is filled with emotion as he wonders about the universe. Every pebble at his feet is as remarkable as a mountain.

"I think we're all one living thing," he says to Abby. "We're all separate living things, of course. But I think we're all part of a larger living presence, like the earth is an organism and we are just cells"

She smiles at him, and he senses sadness in it somehow.

She sits as he walks into the meadow, picking flowers: asters, bitterroots, poppies, dryads. He ties them into a bouquet with twine from the saddle bag, and he gives the flowers to Abby. She smiles, and her eyes shine in the sunlight as tears—just a hint of them—well up.

The school year starts, and Abby comes back one day and tells him about a new technological trend called Facebook.

"I remember e-mail," he says.

She explains that she's reconnecting with friends she hasn't talked to in years, from college, from high school, even from her childhood. He splits wood with an axe, repairs fences, builds bookshelves, wonders the woods with his bow, and he can't imagine whom he would want to reconnect with. But Abby reaches out—through computer wires and airwaves—with technological tentacles that stretch to Seattle and Chicago, New York and London.

He reads by the fire, old books by writers long dead, whose words still reach the minds of people living, and she asks why he doesn't feel the urge to connect with the world.

"I feel connected to the world in another way," he says.

A week after I left his house for Chicago, I got a call from an unfamiliar number, and I answered, just hoping it was him. When I heard his voice, my heart was beating like a high school girl getting a call from her longtime crush. He said he just wanted to make sure I was okay. He'd gone all the way to Missoula to buy a satellite phone. He tried to make it sound like he'd done it for other reasons, but I was touched, knowing he'd bought it just to call me. I asked him to call again soon.

We talked often, and eventually he drove to Missoula and then flew to Chicago to visit me. I took him to a Bears football game, took him to the lakefront, took him to eat deep-dish pizza. The crowded streets made him nervous, but he tried to hide his anxiety. He could tell I saw his discomfort and was self-conscious about it, but at my apartment, when we were alone together, he relaxed and was himself.

I drove back to Seattle for Christmas, rather than flying, so I could spend a few days with him in Montana. We made love the first night—I initiated it—and then again three times the next day.

As we lay naked, I touched the scars on his arm—horizontal slits, one after another—and asked what happened.

"I did that myself," he said. "A long time ago."

I didn't push it. I wanted him to tell me on his own.

"It was before I moved here," he added. "I'm a different person now." And that was really all the explanation I got. Or needed.

When I visited for my week of spring break, he asked me to come live with him and I agreed, smiling and crying. We hugged each other so tight our necks hurt.

"It's a hard life out here," he said.

"It's a hard life out there," I said, "without you."

W"hen you're in your early twenties, just out of college, you think you know who you are," she says. "But you don't. You really don't."

They sit on the front porch, watching the sunset. God has spilled buckets of red and orange and yellow paint onto the sky, mixing them together in abstract portraiture. Each moment, as the sun lowers and the clouds shift in the sky, the portrait changes. Each picture is unique, never to be seen again.

"I've really grown here," she says. "With you."

He nods. He's watched her grow, turn from a girl into a woman. She'd always been happy and embraced life in a way that excited Jason. She'd been eager for adventure, naïve about her inexperience, and fearless to live. Jason realized later that he didn't exactly fall in love with her but rather fell in love with the potential of her. He knew she was a good person—full of wonder and absent of cynicism—and he had known she would grow into an amazing person. He'd been right. She is more beautiful now than she'd been when he first saw her in the snowstorm; she's grown wiser and smarter, and yet she's never lost her wide-eyed wonderment.

"I love it here," Abby says, then pauses for a long time. "But I don't know if I can stay happy here."

Jason looks at her, saying nothing, showing her the concern on his face. He's expected this for a while now, expected it, in some sense, since the day she arrived. He'd expected it in the first few years. She'd been a twenty-three-year-old girl with her whole life ahead of her; he was a broken thirty-eight-year-old man who had retreated from the world. Nearly a decade has passed. How could she be happy?

"Could you ever leave?" she asks.

He thinks for a moment, really trying to consider her question. Then he leans forward in his chair, putting his elbows on his knees and looking at the ground, not at her.

"You're a different person now," she says. "You're not the same person who fled all those years ago. You've grown too."

"I don't know," he says, leaning back and looking at her. "I don't see it as 'fleeing.'" She looks beautiful, with the sun glowing against her like an angelic halo. "I see it as an escape. Like I was in prison and I tunneled under a wall through darkness and found freedom on the other side."

She nods, turns away, and faces the sunset. The sky is more purplish now, with varying hues: lilac, lavender, plum, violet. The two of them sit in silence, watching the transformations until finally the sky changes to a deep blood red.

Dawn is different when he's out in the woods. During bow-hunting season, he leaves the house early, while it's still pitch-dark outside. He walks through the fields, lit only by the light of the moon and the stars. So far from any light pollution, the stars brightly fill the sky. Star particles run through his bloodstream. He doesn't know much about physics and astronomy, but he knows everything is connected—the dewy blades of grass beneath his feet, the clothes that cover his body, his bones, his muscles, the air he breathes, the water in the clouds, the stars, the darkness, he and Abby. Everything is joined. He doesn't understand how, just like he doesn't understand God. But this lack of understanding doesn't bother him. He is a man, and the small batch of gray matter in his skull is too little for the universe to fit inside.

When he gets to the edge of the woods, he uses a headlamp to light his way. He doesn't like doing this—prefers instead the natural light of the moon or stars—but he can't see well enough to keep from tripping or running into trees. Through the glow of artificial light, he finds his way to where he wants to hunt. He turns off his headlamp, relaxes, lets his heartbeat, quickened from the walk, begin to slow. Blackness surrounds him. He can barely see his own hands as they set up his stool and cushion to sit on, nock an arrow to his bow so he'll be ready. Then the blueness comes, subtly at first, so subtle in fact that he is usually startled by how he can begin to see. Branches take form; the individual colors of leaves become distinct on the ground. Like a black-and-white photograph slowly developing, the land gains details. He understands that science would suggest it all has to do with light, refraction and reflection. But he can't help but feel that the world of darkness transforms each day into a world of lightness. The land loses its blue tint, comes completely into focus, and the woods are bathed in morning light. It is autumn and the aspen leaves are yellow and light up in the sun like shimmering yellow scales. But when he realizes the transformation is over, that the blueness has left and the day is here, he feels a pang of disappointment. He has to wait again until tomorrow to see God create the world anew.

Before I moved in, Jason explained that he'd bought his land when his first wife died in a fire. He used the insurance money to buy the house and surrounding woods and farmland. He'd wanted to retreat from his old world and live a life of solitude.

After that night, I brought up his former wife, Joyce, only occasionally. The first time, he held his head low and said, "The truth is, things weren't going so good for us. I think we were on the verge of divorce." He said that when he tried to think of her, he wanted to believe that perhaps they could have worked it out. As he mourned, he was disgusted with the thought that they'd been fighting, that they'd discussed splitting up. Now that she was gone and he couldn't have her back, he felt ashamed about his stubbornness toward the situation. Not stubbornness exactly, more like apathy. They'd drifted out of love and he hadn't cared if they drifted back. And she didn't seem to either.

He told me that the last time he saw her, they hardly acknowledged each other. She'd left for work as he sat at the computer in the morning. She'd said "Bye" like she always did, despite the troubles, but she did not say "I love you" and she did not kiss him. Nor did he try to do either. He didn't even look up from his computer, simply said, "Bye." That was the last time he saw her—a blurry image out of the corner of his eye, not even really seeing her at all. A ghost image in a memory he wanted to go back and change, so he could turn and at least see her clearly one last time.

A few hours later he received a call from the police. Faulty wiring had ignited a fire on the fifth floor of the building where she worked. She was on the sixth, and she and several coworkers burned alive before the firefighters could arrive to extinguish the blaze. It took the coroner's office two days to make an official identification, but he'd known by afternoon. It was easy math: Six bodies were found; six employees were unaccounted for. The police told him there was no reason for him to see her body; he would not be able to recognize her.

He told me, in the days after, he'd felt self-destructive, imagining wrecking his car on purpose, stepping deliberately into traffic, or jumping off a bridge into shallow water. He wasn't suicidal. He felt such pain inside that he wanted to feel pain outside, physical agony to equal his mental agony. He wanted to break his legs, crush his ribs, maim himself—scar himself externally the way he felt scarred inside.

After Jason arranged the funeral, hugged friends and his and her family, and watched as the casket was lowered into ground, he sold their house, collected the insurance, and fled.

When he told me this, I couldn't find the words to express my sympathy. "What a terrible way to…" I started to say, but then I trailed off.

"It wasn't so much grief that I felt," he said. "It's guilt."

I told him he didn't have anything to feel guilty for, but he said he felt it anyway—there was no stopping it.

I lived for one year with Jason before we were married in a small ceremony at the county courthouse. My parents came from Seattle, and he—after some deliberation—invited his parents, who attended without so much as a word said about his self-imposed banishment. I was twenty-four; Jason was thirty-nine. As we walked out of the courthouse into the bright sunlight, I thought Jason seemed to be aglow from the inside, as if energy was pouring out of him. He said he felt blessed to be this happy. I admit I wondered if Joyce was on his mind, somehow, and the look he had made me think that she was. But not in a way that should bother me. I think he was just very happy, and he had thought that he might never be that happy again after what had happened. So he wasn't longing for her or lamenting her loss—he was just happy, happier still because he had thought such happiness was forever out of his reach.

And what was I thinking? How was I feeling? I was in love. I wasn't exactly thinking of the future. I was young and naïve. So I can't say I was thinking of what life with Jason would be like in ten years. Or twenty. Or forty. But I was very happy and very much in love. Even during our hardest times, I always thought of that moment as one of the happiest of my life.

He sits reading by the fire when she comes home. She sits down next to him on the coffee table so she can face him.

He looks at her and she looks at him, and she says, "I'm not happy."

She's hinted at this, and he's long suspected it before the hints. But she's never come out and said the words.

He sets his book aside, sighs. "What can I do?"

"I don't know."

He waits.

"I don't know, Jason," she says, standing and beginning to pace. "I love you, and I love it here—sometimes. But I just feel…" She holds her hands up, gripping them, as if she can grasp the words with her hands that she can't find with her mind. Then she drops her arms, limp at her sides, and hangs her head.

"I hate to say it: I feel like I'm dying here."

Jason stands, walks to her, puts his arms around her and holds her close, like he did when she agreed to come live with him.

"I want you to be happy," he says. "More than anything."

She looks at him. Her face glows in the firelight; tears glisten on her cheeks.

"Can we leave?" she says. "Go live somewhere else?"

Her voice is hopeful and heartbreaking. Jason aches inside. She can't actually believe he would go, can she?

"Honey," he says, holding her shoulders, looking at her shining eyes. "You know I can't make it out there."

She breaks from his grasp and begins pacing. She says that she's going to apply to schools in Boise, Seattle, Portland, Salt Lake City.

"Just to see what happens," she says.

He stares at her, not knowing what to say.

"We could try living apart," she says. "I'd come here during my breaks. You could come there from time to time."

His body is cold on the outside, chill bumps rising on his skin, but he feels his insides burning, as if his heart could combust, igniting his organs and his muscles, and the fire would explode through his icy skin.

"Or we could find somewhere else, someplace we'd both be happy," she says. "It doesn't have to be a big city. Just… just… a city."

"Honey," he says, pleading, hoping that his tone will tell her not to keep asking.

Then her face changes. Her lips press together, her jaw muscles tighten, her brow wrinkles with strain.

"You can't make it out there?" she says. "Well I can't fucking make it here."

She stomps away. He stands, frozen for several minutes, staring at the wall. Then he exhales and walks to the door. Outside, he looks up at the sky. The bone-white moon shines like a bleached skull, casting pale light over the meadow and the road and the snowcaps of the mountains in the distance. He walks toward the woods. He breathes in the air, reaches out and touches the bark of trees with his fingers, listens to the hoot of an owl, wishes she could discover a way to find peace in this world the way he does.

He'd bought the land outright with the insurance money. When he told me how much it was, I was shocked that it was so inexpensive. But there are two Montanas. There are the types of places the tourists see: Bozeman and Whitefish and Glacier National Park, places like that, polished and pretty for the outsiders. And then there are the places no one visits, and despite their beauty, no one really wants to visit them. They are hard places, isolated, with long winters. And most people who buy the land in these places, with dreams of idyllic mountain living, only make it one winter before they realize what a mistake they've made.

Jason was different. He was at home with the hard mountain way of life. He made some money renting part of his land for cattle grazing and farming, and a little from his carpentry, which was more a hobby than a business. He made enough to get by, and he lived well off the land. He filled a freezer each fall with two or three deer and sometimes elk, moose, or antelope. His property contained enough dead or dying trees that he chainsawed enough firewood to get through the long winters. He drove the thirty miles into town—twenty-five on gravel roads—every month or two to stock up on supplies. He made longer trips to Missoula and Bozeman every now and then with a truckload of furniture and cabinets he tried to sell.

His house was well-kept, but it needed a woman's touch. I painted rooms, bought new curtains, cleaned, dusted, redecorated. I embraced the solitary lifestyle during my first summer, taking up gardening, canning, learning to ride Jason's horses. I even tried hunting that fall until I decided it wasn't for me. But I wasn't quite content to live a life of isolation, so I drove into town to work at the school. I volunteered at first because the school only had a handful of teachers and no vacancies. But the staff quickly liked me, and the kids quickly loved me, so the school board created a position for me. I didn't care that it was thirty miles away—a fifty-minute drive because of the roads, an hour and a half sometimes in winter. I became a part of the community, and Jason, therefore, became more than "that fella who owns the old Barnes' place" to the people in the town. He'd been there for six years before I came, but I had a bigger social network after one.

Still, that community wasn't usually enough. I wanted to take trips to Seattle to see my family and friends, or other cities for vacations. Jason went with me at first, but his discomfort was obvious to both of us and soon the trips became activities I did alone.

"Why do you hate it out there so much?" I asked once.

"It's not that I hate the world out there," he said. "It's that I hate who I am when I'm out there."

The circular saw blade spins toward him, the angled teeth—invisible in the blur—slicing into the wood as he pushes the board forward. The saw whines and a line appears in the board, a simple thin line where the saw cuts. Jason pushes the board forward until it is in two pieces. The cut is so perfect that it looks like the two boards were never together. Jason has the crazy thought as he works that he is the piece of wood and that time—not his own hand—is pushing him toward the saw blade. Whatever he does, he can't stop what's moving his life forward, and soon the saw will cut him and Abby in two, as if they were never together.

He sits in the forest on a small stool, watching as the blackness of night takes shape into the blueness or morning. Tree branches appear, a dark blue-gray. The thin frosting of snow becomes indigo. The trunks of pine trees are navy. Then the blue photo portrait of the world that God has taken for him develops before his eyes, and the blue becomes washed out with whites and browns and greens. It's fall and the world after dawn is gray.

Today, Jason doesn't take the same comfort from the dawn as most days. He is thinking about Abby. Her normally vivaciousness has faded into a state of ennui. They aren't talking much, aren't enjoying the sunsets together. He doesn't know what to do.

A doe walks along a stream bank fifty yards from Jason. Her brown fur stands out brightly in the gray morning light. The stream only contains sporadic puddles, and the doe stops at one, drops her head, and drinks. Jason pulls the bow back slowly. The sound of the string, pulling taut, is barely audible. He aims and waits as the deer walks closer. His left hand holds the bow at arm's length; his right hand grips the string with three fingers, bringing the arrow's nock to the corner of his mouth. The bow strains against his muscles. Normally he has inexhaustible patience, but today he feels frustrated that the deer isn't walking toward him fast enough. He almost lets the bow down—a movement that would scare off the deer—but then she steps closer and into a space where no tree branches obscure his shooting lane.

He releases and hears the thwack of the string. The doe jumps, falls onto her forelegs, jumps again, falls again, and then lies on the ground, one leg moving as if she still wants to run. One ear twitches for a moment. Jason sees the florescent green fletching of his arrow sticking out from the fur at her ribcage, just behind her front leg. He stands for a moment, staring at the doe. His chest heaves with heavy breaths that he can see in the cold air. He doesn't walk to the deer; he watches her.

Then he sees movement out of the corner of his eye and looks to see a buck walking down the same invisible path the doe took. The deer approaches the fallen doe, cautiously but not panicked. Jason moves slowly to nock another arrow without drawing attention. The breeze is in his favor, blowing his scent away from the animal. The buck steps up to the fallen doe, drops his head to sniff her. He smells the wound where the arrow—alien metal with plastic feathers—sticks out of her. Then he nudges her, as if to try to awaken her from a sleep. Jason has never seen this before. The buck should have run off at the first hint of trouble. But the deer acts like he's mourning, as if he's human. Jason's hands tremble. His eyes begin to water. He knows he is personifying the animals—that deer don't mate for life; that bucks mount every doe they can fight for—but it looks like the male is grieving for the female. It nudges her harder, like a dog pushing its owner's arm. Get up, the nudges say. Get up.

Jason's arms tremble, and he can't keep the bead of his sight on the deer. The deer freezes, tensing every muscle and turning toward Jason. The deer seems to look right at him; he will bolt in an instant. Jason releases. The arrow flies. The deer bounds through the trees. Jason blinks back tears, unsure of what happened. He hurries down to the dead doe, searching for signs of the other deer. He looks for his arrow and can't find it, then follows the deer's tracks for several feet, until he discovers a single drop of blood. He walks further, finding another and then another. It isn't much blood. He wipes his eyes, unable to keep himself from crying. This isn't the first time he's hit a deer that ran off. He knows if you let them go, don't track closely behind, they will lie down and die. If you track them too soon, if they know they are being pursued, they will keep running and running until they can't run any longer. The scarcity of blood worries him.

He kneels quietly next to the doe, putting his hand on her chest next to the protruding arrow. She is faintly warm. He's not sure what to do. Field dress her now, before going after the buck? Or leave her until he finds the other? He decides to dress her now, then drag her back to the edge of the woods, where he can pick her up with his truck.

The broadhead of his arrow pokes out her side, the shiny metal glistening blood, and he pulls the shaft all the way through, laying the bolt blood-coated on the pine needles. He rolls her on her back, and he skins back the fur at her abdomen with his knife, cuts her skin and opens up her body cavity. His hands are shaking and he accidentally hits the stomach with the blade of his knife. The stench of partially digested food bursts out. He splits her breastplate, pulls open her rib cage, holds her up by her front legs—her head dangling limp—and dumps her guts out, steaming in the snow. He stares at the viscera, looks at her liver, her intestines, her kidneys, the white lobes of the lungs, punctured from the arrow, and the heart, like a clenched red fist, with a black arrow hole through it. He begins to cry again. He can't wipe the tears away because both hands are bloody. He cries as he ties her front legs behind her head and drags her body through the trees, leaving a swathe of upturned dirt and spread pine needles. He cries as he walks to get his truck, and as he drives her into the barn and hoists her up on a pulley to drain and freeze. He has always had a healthy respect for the animals he shoots. He passes on difficult shots that might wound and not kill. He feels guilty when he hits a lung or the shoulder, instead of the heart, and prolongs the animal's suffering. He eats the meat, tans the hides for horse blankets, tries not to be wasteful. But he has never experienced emotions like this before. He knows he's not crying for the doe and the buck, but for something more, some internal ache inside himself. He can't stop thinking of the pile of guts he left in the woods—food for coyotes or wolves—and feels strangely as if he should be the one who is disemboweled, whose insides should be food for scavengers.

It's nearly noon when he returns to the woods to track the buck. He follows the prints at first. Once the tracks become more hidden, he looks for blood. Tracking is slow. Every time he finds a drop, he must search the area, starting in the direction the deer seemed to be going, and spreading his search out farther and farther. With the drops of blood tiny and scarce—sometimes twenty or thirty feet apart, sometimes no bigger than a seed—the search takes hours. He tracks the deer one hundred yards, then two, then three hundred. He loses the trail late in the afternoon. From the last drop of blood he's seen, he searches in a twenty-foot radius, then thirty, then forty and fifty. He looks for a drop of blood for an hour, then two.

The sun is descending when he walks back to where he shot the deer. He looks again for his arrow, thinking perhaps he only skimmed the deer, a minor cut, nothing fatal. But he can't find the arrow. It could have easily slipped beneath the underbrush and disappeared. But it could be in the deer too, wherever he is. As the sun sets, bathing the trees with an orange-red glow, Jason sits on a log and puts his head in his hands. His hands are still bloody, but the red has long since dried to his skin. He tells himself not to project human emotions on the deer, but he keeps thinking of the way the buck nudged the doe, as if refusing to believe.

God damn," Abby says one Sunday morning. "I'm freezing to death here." She kneels before the fireplace, putting more logs on the coals.

"I thought you'd get used to the cold." Jason stands by the stove, waiting for the water to boil.

She is wearing flannel pajamas and wool socks, and she pulls a heavy quilt around her shoulders like a shawl. He pours two mugs of tea to their rims, and then carries them to her—each hand gripping a mug handle, fingers locked in fists. Steam rises like smoke from the Seattle's Best mugs. Jason and Abby stare into the fireplace, sipping their tea, watching as the bed of hot coals heats up the new logs, blooming flames like flowers.

She leans against him, resting her head on his shoulder. "I'm sorry. I don't mean to complain about the house. The summers are beautiful and fantastic, but the winter is so long and cold."

"I like winter just as much as summer," he says. "Maybe more."

She laughs. "No you do not."

But he means what he said.

They're quiet for several minutes. When Abby finishes her tea, she says, "I know how you can help keep me warm."

He looks at her, his eyebrow raised, smiling. They haven't made love in weeks; they've been fighting instead about her wanting to leave. She opens the blanket up and wraps it around both of them, and then she leans in to kiss him. They make love, starting first wrapped in the blanket and then, when their bodies become too hot, lying on top of it, naked, their skin orange in the firelight. As he kisses her and presses into her, he runs his hands over her body, trying to touch as much of her skin as he can, as if his fingers might sink into her skin and they can become one.

"I still love you," she whispers.

He holds her like this is the last time they'll make love. He knows it's not—that it will be months before she leaves, years before she leaves him for good—but he clings to her as if this is the end. Afterward, when the perspiration on their bodies begins to chill, they cuddle naked in the blanket and watch the flames as the blue light of morning shines in through the ice-glazed windows.

I nursed him in the days after the accident, helping him to remember when to take his painkillers, making him meals, covering him with blankets. I would kiss him over and over, run my fingers through his hair. Hug him. Tell him I loved him.

We didn't talk about me leaving after that. I assumed he knew I changed my mind.

Finally, in the spring, when the streams were full and the brown grass was starting to turn green again, he asked if I'd heard back from any of the schools I'd applied to.

"I withdrew my applications," I said.

"Why?" He looked genuinely concerned about this, almost hurt. It wasn't the expression I was expecting.

"I've changed my mind," I said. "I want to stay here with you."

"You shouldn't stay out of guilt," he said.

"I'm not staying out of guilt."

"But if this hadn't happened," he said, holding up his hand, wiggling his shortened fingers, "then you would be leaving this summer."

I was quiet for a minute, looking at my hands, composing my words.

"You believe that God has a plan," I said, gesturing to the world beyond the window. "You believe that everything is connected. Every tree, every person, every molecule. Right?

"Well," I went on, "I believe that the accident happened for a reason. I believe it happened to show me that I can't leave, that I belong here, with you. Coming so close to losing you made me realize how stupid I was for thinking I could leave you. And I'm so sorry, Jason, that it took such a thing for me to realize that this is where I'm meant to be."

He reached out and took my hand with his good one. "You have nothing to be sorry for. It was just a stupid accident."

I knew that was true. The accident had nothing to do with my plans to leave. How could it? Not really. That wasn't what I was apologizing for. Not that I caused the accident somehow. I was sorry because it took the accident for me to see what I had to do. I was apologizing for ever thinking of leaving to begin with. Sure, I would still like to leave. I wish we could leave together. But if it's a choice between Montana with him or somewhere else without him, I have to choose Montana. I have to choose him. And I just have to try to be happy here. I think I can. I hope I can.

He watches the blue world as Abby gets ready for work. He thinks about her applications and her plans to live somewhere else. He tries to imagine sitting at the table, watching the earth be born each morning from inside an empty house. He did it once, but can he do it again? The temperatures have been low, not rising above freezing for weeks. Outside the window, snow covers the ground, and cocoons of ice have entombed the tree branches. In the blue morning light, Jason sees the world as if he is trapped under ice, looking out from beneath the thick glassy surface.

Abby, ready for work, kisses him goodbye. This is part of what makes her plans to leave so painful—they are still in love.

"Drive safely," he says.

"I will."

"I love you."

"I love you too."

He finishes his tea, not finding the solace and morning peace he used to. He pulls on his work boots and trudges out to the shed. Each step breaks the crusty surface before his feet sink into the powder.

He pushes boards, one after the other, into the table saw. The blade, spinning toward him, so fast the teeth disappear in a blur, bites into each piece of cedar, cutting through them in a thin line. He hurts inside, and he wants to hurt outside. He wants to feel physical pain that will mirror his mental pain. He knows it's a stupid idea. Selfishness again. His pain isn't the only pain that matters. But he shoves board after board into the blade, and as he does so, his anger becomes more and more enflamed. Today, the serenity he finds in carpentry is gone. With every board he cuts, he alternates, being angry at himself to being angry with Abby, hating himself to hating her.

Finally a rage takes hold of him unlike anything he's felt, superior even to what he felt in his previous life before his escape to Montana. The saw slices his first finger off painlessly. The sight of the severed nub from the tip of his littlest finger should be enough to stop him. He tells himself for a moment that he's done this out of carelessness. And maybe that's correct. But then he moves his hand forward, and he feels a pinch and vibration and the blade slices his second finger off at the center knuckle. Then another pinch, like a bee sting, and more vibrations, up to his elbow this time, and then his middle finger comes off nearly at its base. He stares at the severed fingers, lying next to the blade. Seeing them, disconnected from his body, seems illusory. The blade whirs as if nothing has changed. He holds his hand up, turning it in front of his face, looking for the invisible tips of his fingers. They must be there; he can still feel them.

Pain comes then and his knees almost buckle—he hurts everywhere, in his limbs, in his head, in his heart. He leans against the saw with his good hand, taking deep breaths. The saw is as loud as a jet turbine. Calmly, he reaches down and turns it off. His wedding ring sits among a splattering of blood at the edge of the table, as if he pulled it off and set it down. He reaches for the ring with his good hand, then cradles his injured hand to his body. Outside, the cool air embraces him, and the chill is a relief. A few drops of blood glide down onto the snow, burning a red shaft into the white.

In the house, he sits in his usual chair. He lays his hand on the table, letting the blood drip drip drip onto the wood. He sets his ring a foot or so away, but the growing pool enlarges until overtaking the band. It looks like a gold life raft floating in a sea of blood. He feels nauseous and he looks outside, breathing deeply. The bright light from the window—the sun reflecting off the snow—hurts his eyes. He's not used to sitting here this late in the morning, when the world is fully formed and burning from the sun's heat. He considers rising to pick up the satellite phone from the counter to call for help. 9-1-1 or Abby, either one. He decides not to. He told her he loved her this morning, and she told him the same. That would be a good way to leave things.

With his blood dripping onto the table, he watches the day—full-color, not the blue world of morning—and stays conscious for more than an hour. But then his face relaxes and his eyes keep trying to close. It is as if he is staying up late, trying to read, but he keeps nodding off, unable to finish the story. The blood has made a large puddle on the table now, congealing, turning into a red mirror through which he can see out the window. He stares into the blood, seeing the upside-down image of the trees and barn and mountains. A red lens instead of a blue one.

He falls off the chair. The collision with the floor wakes him for a moment. "I love you, Abby." He lays his head down on the wood, and dives into a black thoughtless sleep.

Then Abby is shaking him, waking him, and helping him to stand. The sun has set; the window is a black mirror. He doesn't recognize his pale reflection. He looks like he's already dead. Abby's face is panicked, but her actions are smart. He feels strangely proud that she can handle herself under pressure like this, but then he remembers what happened. He wishes he was dead.

She helps him to the car. Her breath comes out in thick white gasps that stand out in the darkness. He sits in her car, numb, as she runs to the barn, bounding through the deep snow, bringing back his fingers in a pail packed full of snow. Jason digs through the bucket with his one good hand.

"Don't do that," she says.

"I want to see."

When he finds the fingers, they are already blackish blue. He leans back to quell nausea.

She drives too fast over the gravel roads, still slick with snow and ice.

"I love you," he murmurs. "I want you to be happy. So if you have to go, if you have to leave, I want you to know—"

"Shhh," she says. "None of that's important now."

"I love you."

"I love you," she says.

But he keeps saying it over and over: "I love you. I love you. I love you." Each time, the words are an apology.

I think sometimes about Jason's previous marriage and our own. It's strange for me to think about how they were on the brink of separation before she died, which made him feel guilty and realize that he did still love her. It's almost as if that happened to me, only I didn't lose him and I was given a second chance to be with him.

How life works is strange, and it makes you wonder about fate and coincidence. If she had lived, they would have separated. But Jason would not have moved to Montana. And then I never would have met him. But because she died, I met him. And we fell in love. And while he never says it, I always feel that he probably loves me more than he ever loved her. Maybe not. Maybe he just doesn't ever want to let go of me because of how he lost her. But I prefer not to think of it like that. I prefer to think that he was ready to let her go and was averse to letting me go.

But how we got together... and what had to happen for us to stay together... it makes me think that perhaps Jason is right when he talks about God in the world, how things are meant to be. Maybe we are meant for each other. I didn't used to think that way. I used to just think that life was full of coincidence. But now I think things happen for a reason. Events far beyond our control, guided by God's hands, create blessings in our lives in the aftermath of tragedy.

I'm not convinced of this necessarily. I try to think that way. I have to think that way. To think otherwise might lead me down the path I was on before, the one that had me longing to leave here. It worries me though. I have to stay strong to stay here. I sometimes feel like I have to fool myself into never thinking about leaving. I'm like an alcoholic in a way. Just one drink doesn't seem like much, but it opens the door to a night of drinking, which leads to a week, and so on ... It's the same for me and leaving. If I open the door to even thinking about leaving again, well, I'm afraid of what that might lead to. And I'm happy now—happy enough—that I don't want to go down that road again. Jason was willing to let me go.

He wasn't excited about the idea, but he wanted me to be happy, in the end, so he endorsed the idea. He put my needs before his, and that makes me love him even more. So now I want to put his needs before mine. It pleases me to do so… but I admit I can't think too long about what else I'm missing out there in the world.

Jason and Abby take the horses riding, the first ride of spring. He rides the roan and she rides the bay. The hooves clap against the earth. The long pasture grass they ride through rustles against the horses' flanks. The two of them head toward the small, nameless range to the east, where the mountains stand like bald eagles, black bodies with white snowy peaks. The reins don't feel right in his hands; he hasn't adjusted to his missing fingers. Behind them, the sky is blue with a diffusion of white clouds. In front of them, the sky looms dark, like evening has already descended. Lightning flashes up ahead. Thunder rumbles. Neither he nor Abby suggests they should turn back. They are enjoying themselves too much. And with the sky blue behind them, the storm seems like something that's far away they don't need to worry about.

But then they feel the first drops of rain. The wind blows harder against them. The pasture grass moves like green ocean waves. The sunshine has been warm, but the wind chills them. Without a word, they pull the horses to a stop and turn them slowly around. More drops fall, and they spur the horses to a fast trot. The wind pushes at their backs. Without speaking, they push the horses into a lope, and then they are racing the storm. They lean into the horses, holding tight. Rain pelts them. Abby's hair, usually tied back on the rides, hangs loose, blowing behind her. She looks at him and smiles.

After several minutes, they race ahead of the storm and only feel the occasional sprinkle of rain, the tapering breeze. But they don't slow down. The storm is right behind them. They know this despite the brilliant blue sky in front. A patchwork of green and brown fields spreads out in front of them. The mountains and the sky look like paintings, like this can't be real. Like they've ridden off the earth and into heaven.

They trot into the barn, the familiar scent of hay enveloping them. Their horses' chests heave, and so do theirs. They have just enough time to stable the horses and walk to the edge of the big open barn door before the rain comes. The wind blows in the smell of the rain, overpowering the hay, and the water showers down in wet sheets. They stand together, just past the threshold, watching the downpour, mist on their faces. Even a quick run to the house would soak them. The sky is as dark as death. But the rain doesn't last long. Like most storms this time of year, it blows over quickly. In its wake, the storm leaves a bright, brilliant rainbow curving down through the distant gray. They describe to each other the colors they can discern: fuchsia, red, orange, yellow, green, purple, and a brilliant azure blue. The brightness of sunlight, now that the darkness has passed them, lights up Abby's face, and Jason looks at her, glowing like warm embers, as she looks at the rainbow.

"I love you," he says.

She exhales deeply, looks down now, at the grass instead of up at the arc of the rainbow, casting her face in shadow. "I love you too." She says it like she's helpless to change it.

"Are you happy?"

She nods her head slowly. "Yes."

She smiles at him, her face aglow once again, then she looks back to the sky.

Jason does too. A few beams of sunlight break through the gray clouds, spotlighting the hills, like God's radiance is shining down upon the land. But Jason doesn't feel the inspiration he used to feel, doesn't feel the connection he once felt with this land. It's as if, when he severed his fingers, he severed the communication lines with the mountains and the sky and the trees.

Jason turns and walks to the other side of the barn, looking to where the storm is heading. They stand like this for several minutes, Abby watching the rainbow and the sun breaking through the clouds from one side of the barn, Jason on the other watching the storm break against the mountains, dark like a shadow hanging over the landscape. Then Abby walks over to him and puts her arm around him. This is all he wanted, for her to stay, for her to by happy here. But he can't force himself to feel better, can't bring himself to find a blessing from God in all that has happened, not as he watches the black sky consuming the blue.

ABOUT THE CONTRIBUTORS

Rebeca Antoine, New Orleans, LA
Rebeca Antoine has an MFA from the Creative Writing Workshop at the University of New Orleans. Her fiction has appeared in *The Briar Cliff Review, Gulf Stream, Blithe House Quarterly,* and other publications. She is also the editor of the nonfiction anthologies *Voices Rising: Stories from the Katrina Narrative Project* (vols. I & II):

John Azrak, Douglastown, NY
John Azrak is the former chair of the English Department of Walt Whitman H.S. on Long Island. He was a finalist for *Glimmer Train's* very short fiction award, and a finalist in The Sonora Review's short-short fiction contest, judged by Steve Almond. He has poems in, among others, *Bryant Review, Court Green, Poetry East, The Hawai'i Pacific Review, Paddlefish, The Santa Fe Review, The Santa Clara Review, Coe Review, Oyez Review, Eclipse* and *The Comstock Review.* Short stories appear in the anthology *Bless Me, Father(Penguin), The Alembic, Another Chicago Magazine, Passages North, West Branch, Natural Bridge,* and *The Artful Dodge.*

Alex Baldwin, Logan, UT
Alex Ron Baldwin, autochthonous to Idaho Falls, currently works in Logan, Utah as a personal trainer and fitness instructor for Utah State University. In May of 2011 he earned his Bachelor of Arts in English with a Creative Writing emphasis from USU where his poetry, fiction, and nonfiction received various awards like 2011 English Student of the Year and Creative Writing

Student of the Year. His most recent poetry can be found in *Catfish Creek, Out of Our,* and *Sheepshead Review.* This is his first short story publication.

Michael Bigham, Portland, OR
Michael Bigham was a police officer in Oregon and graduated from Vermont College of Fine Arts with an MFA in Creative Writing. He lives in Portland, Oregon with his wife, daughter and a puppy named Pumpkin.

Andrew Bourelle, Albuquerque, NM
Andrew Bourelle's fiction has appeared in *Jabberwock Review, Red Rock Review, Rosebud,* and other publications. He lives in New Mexico with his wife Tiffany.

Kevin Brown, Cleveland, TN
Kevin Brown has had Fiction, Non-fiction, and Poetry published in over 100 Literary Journals, Magazines, Anthologies, and Best Of... Anthologies. His two collections of short fiction, *Ink On Wood* and *Death Roll,* were published in the Fall of 2010 by Virgogray Press and Lame Goat Press, respectively. He has won numerous writing competitions and was the recipient of several fellowships. He was also nominated for the 2007 Journey Award and three Pushcart Prizes. He co-wrote the screenplay *Living Dark: The Story of Ted the Caver,* that was made into a film in 2006. Recently, he completed a short novel, *Invisible Bodies,*

and a new collection of short fiction entitled *Pulling Wisdom From My Teeth.*

Glenn Cassidy, Carrboro, NC
Glenn Cassidy is a consultant and educator based in Carrboro, NC. He has a Ph.D. in public policy analysis and has taught public policy and public finance at several universities including UNC Chapel Hill. His poetry and short fiction draw on his formal study of human behavior and often address public policy issues. Editors at *The Main Street Rag, The Dead Mule School of Southern Poetry, Prime Number Magazine, Wild Goose Poetry Review,* and other journals have been entertained enough to publish forty of his poems and short stories. Works of his have been chosen as runner-up for the Analecta elegy competition and semi-finalist for the Brenda L. Smart Fiction Prize.

Ed Davis, Yellow Springs, OH
West Virginia native Ed Davis recently retired from teaching writing full-time at Sinclair Community College in Dayton, Ohio. He has also taught both fiction and poetry at the Antioch Writers' Workshop and is the author of the novels *I Was So Much Older Then* (Disc-Us Books, 2001) and *The Measure of Everything* (Plain View Press, 2005); four poetry chapbooks, including, most recently, *Healing Arts* (Pudding House, 2005); and many published stories and poems in anthologies and journals. His unpublished novel *Running from Mercy,* loosely based on the life of Bob Dylan, won the 2010 Hackney Award for the novel. He lives with his wife in the village of Yellow Springs, Ohio, where he bikes, hikes, blogs and meditates religiously. Please visit him at www.davised.com.

Michael Giorgio, Waukesha, WI

Michael Giorgio lives in Waukesha, WI, with his wife, author Kathie Giorgio, and their daughter, Olivia. After having audio dramas broadcast in markets from coast to coast, he turned his attention to prose fiction. His short stories have appeared internationally in magazines such as *The Strand* and *Criminal Class Review* and have been anthologized in *The Mammoth Book of Tales from the Road, It's That Time Again: The New Stories of Old Time Radio, Dark Things, Literary Foray, Who Died in Here? Twisted Cat Tales, Tales from the Cash Register, Dreamspell Revenge* and many more. He has also published nonfiction and poetry. In addition to writing, Giorgio teaches at AllWriters' Workplace and Workshop in Waukesha and for Writers' Digest University.

Nicki Gill, Victoria, Australia

Nicki Gill was born in Melbourne, Australia, where she practiced law, and dreamed of writing. She is a graduate of New York University's creative writing program, and has taught at New York and Marymount Universities. This is her first publication.

Leah Griesmann, San Jose, CA

Leah Griesmann earned an MA in Creative Writing at Boston University and was a 2010-2011 Steinbeck Fellow in Fiction at San Jose State University. She has taught writing and literature at Boston University, the University of Nevada, Las Vegas, and San Jose State University. Her stories have appeared in *Fourteen Hills, The Cortland Review, Litro Magazine, Union Station, Pif Magazine,* and *J Journal: New Writing on Justice.*

Gina Hanson, San Bernadino, CA
Gina Hanson earned her MFA in Fiction Writing at California State University, San Bernardino. Other short stories of hers have appeared in *The Ink-Filled Page, Red Clay Review,* and *ZYZZYVA.* Her work has been nominated for a Pushcart Prize. She currently lives in Southern California with her spouse and a menagerie of poorly behaved animals.

Linda Lee Harper, Lake Murray, SC
Linda Lee Harper has two collections of poetry and seven chapbooks. *Kiss Kiss* was selected as Cleveland State University Poetry Center's Open Competition winner. Two most recent chapbooks are *Small Waves* (Finishing Line Press, 2009) and *Driving Out* (Pudding House Publications, 2008). She has been the recipient of four Pushcart nominations, three fellowships at Yaddo, two at VCCA. Harper's work has appeared in *The Georgia Review, Nimrod, Beloit Poetry Journal, Southern Poetry Review, Rattle, Ascent, The Seneca Review, Crazyhorse,* and *Southern Humanities Review,* where she won the Hoepfner Award for Best Poem of the Year. She's served as faculty at USC-Aiken, the University of Pittsburgh, PA and regional writing conferences. Currently, she's working on a novella-in-verse Little Sugar, and written the libretto for an opera collaboration with composer Richard Maltz, based on the Boston Red Sox. She divides her time between Augusta, GA and Lake Murray, SC.

Toby Tucker Hecht, Bethesda, MD

Toby Tucker Hecht is a scientist and fiction writer from Bethesda, Maryland. Her previous publications include short stories in *The MacGuffin, Epiphany, The Baltimore Review, Red Wheelbarrow, RE:AL, THEMA,* and other print and online literary journals. When not writing, she can be found at the National Cancer Institute where she works in the Division of Cancer Treatment and Diagnosis, or taking swing dance lessons with her husband.

G. Davies Jandrey, Tucson, AZ

For many years G. Davies Jandrey taught in one of Tucson's most diverse inner-city high schools. Daily she eavesdropped on the Spanglish spoken in the hallways. These overheard conversations and experiences with her Mexican National and Mexican American students and their families inform her writing. Her work has appeared in *The Bi-Lingual Review, Calyx, Portland Review, Berkeley Fiction Review,* and *High Plains Literary Review* among others. Her first novel, *A Garden of Aloes,* was published by The Permanent Press in January 2008. Currently, she is working on a short story collection. "The Secret of Rain" is from that collection.

Nick Ostdick, Rockford, IL

Nick Ostdick is a husband, runner, and writer who currently resides in Rockford, Illinois. He holds an MFA in Fiction Writing from Southern Illinois University and is the editor and co-editor of the forthcoming anthologies *Hair Lit, Vol 1* (Orange Alert Press, 2012), and *The Man Date: 15 Bromances* (Prime Mincer, 2013). He's the winner of the Viola Wendt Award for Fiction and has been nominated for a

Puschart Prize, and his work has appeared or is forthcoming in *Annalemma Quarterly, The Emerson Review, Fox Cry Review, Pindeldyboz, Night Train,* and elsewhere.

Daniel Pearlman, Providence, RI
Dan Pearlman's fiction has appeared in magazines such as *The Florida Review, Spectrum, New England Review, Quarterly West, The MacGuffin,* and anthologies such as *Semiotext(e), Synergy, Simulations, The Year's Best Fantastic Fiction* (1996), *Going Postal* (1998), *Imaginings* (Pocket Books, 2003), and *XX Eccentric* (MSR Pub. Co., 2009). He has published over fifty short stories and novellas, most of which have been collected in three volumes: *The Final Dream & Other Fictions*(Permeable, 1995); *The Best-Known Man in the World & Other Misfits*(Aardwolf, 2001); and *A Giant in the House & Other Excesses*(Merry Blacksmith, 2011). His two novels to date are *Black Flames*(White Pine Press, 1997); and *Memini* (Prime/Wildside, 2003).

Maureen Pilkington, Rye, NY
Maureen Pilkington just completed her collection, *Float and Other Stories This Side of Water.* Her fiction has appeared in *Ploughshares, Puerto del Sol, Confrontation, Orchid Literary Review, Santa Barbara Review, Bridge: Art & Literature, Red Rock Review, Pedestal, Stone Table Review, SN Review, Marco Polo Quarterly, Miranda,* and numerous others. After working in book publishing, she received an MFA from Sarah Lawrence College, and is the founder of a writing program for New York City's inner city students. She is currently working on a novel, *Cry For Me,* and lives in New York with her husband and two children.

Gary Powell, Lake Norman, NC

Gary V. Powell's stories have appeared in *The Briar Cliff Review, Amarillo Bay, moonShine Review, The Thomas Wolfe Review,* and *Dogzplot Flash Fiction.* His story "Miller's Deer" was runner-up for the 2008 Thomas Wolfe Fiction Prize. Recently, "Trinity's," received an Honorable Mention for the Winter 2010 New Millennium Fiction Prize and "Fast Trains" placed in the 2010 Rick Demarinis Fiction Contest. He has work forthcoming at *Main Street Rag, The Newport Review,* and *The Blue Lake Review.* He lives near the shores of Lake Norman with his beautiful wife and amazing son. He recently completed his first novel, *Lucky Bastard.*

Rosemary Solarez, Tucson, AZ

Born in Tucson, AZ to Mexican-Lebanese parents, Rosemary Solarez is the consummate chola. Her family established one of the oldest and greatest Mexican restaurants in a city famous for great, old Mexican restaurants. She attended Catholic schools for 12 years, where, among other things, she learned the fear of hell. At her father's command, she earned her bachelors degree at the University of Arizona. Later, as a single mom with two young sons, she volunteered at a local soup kitchen, where she became politically awakened. A born again Buddhist, Rosemary has spent a lifetime in social services. One of her tattoos reads: *One people, one planet, one future.* Currently, she works with the homeless at the Primavera Foundation of Tucson.

John Struloeff, Thousand Oaks, CA
John Struloeff grew up in the mountainous rainforests of northwestern Oregon. His debut poetry collection, *The Man I Was Supposed to Be,* was published by Loom Press in 2008, with individual poems in *The Atlantic Monthly, The Southern Review, Prairie Schooner, ZYZZYVA, PN Review,* and elsewhere. His awards include a Stegner Fellowship from Stanford University, an NEA Literature Fellowship, a Sozopol Seminars Fiction Fellowship from the Elizabeth Kostova Foundation (Bulgaria), and both the Weldon Kees and Tennessee Williams Scholarships. He has taught at Stanford University and the University of Nebraska-Lincoln where he received both his MA and PhD in English. Currently he directs the creative writing program at Pepperdine University in Malibu, California.

Derek Tellier, Minnetonka, MN
Derek Tellier's work has appeared in *New Verse News, Ascent Aspirations, Pindeldyboz. com, The Pedestal Magazine.com, Poetry Motel, Blue Lit* and *Small Spiral Notebook. com.* He holds a Master of Fine Arts degree in Creative Writing from Minnesota State University, Mankato. He lives in the Twin Cities.

Katy Whittingham, Bridgewater, MA
Katy Whittingham has her MFA in Creative Writing from Emerson College, Boston. A poet, fiction writer, and photographer, her work has been published in numerous journals and magazines with a collection, *By a Different Ocean,* published by Plan B Press, Virginia in 2009. She teaches first year composition, poetry, children's literature, memoir and family narrative, and Creative

Writing at Bridgewater State University and the University of Massachusetts Dartmouth. Her other teaching and research interests include Irish American Studies, Children's Literature, and the incorporation of poetry in the early childhood classroom.

Abi Wyatt, Corwall, England

Abigail Wyatt lives and writes in the shadow of Carn Brea in Cornwall. Her poetry and her short and flash fiction have appeared in a range of publications. These include *Words with JAM, One Million Stories, Poetic Diversity, Word Gumbo* and *Poetry Cornwall.* Her poetry collection, *Moths in a Jar* (Palores, £4.00) became available in November, 2010 and she is now in the process of compiling a collection of a dozen or so short stories. Abigail is the founder member of the group Redruth Writers which meets at The Melting Pot Cafe, The Old Grammar School, Redruth. She is a keen amateur performer and appears with two drama groups. Contact via abigailwyatt.blogspot.com.

ABOUT THE EDITOR

Rayne Debski, Boiling Springs, PA

Born in New Jersey, Rayne Debski has lived in Florida and Virginia. She holds degrees from Rider University and Florida Atlantic University, and has been an innkeeper, college instructor, editor, and organizational development manager. She now lives and writes in central Pennsylvania, where she shares her life with her husband and their enthusiastic yellow lab. Her award-winning short fiction has appeared in several online and print journals and anthologies, including Main Street Rag's short fiction anthology *XX Eccentric.* Her work has been nominated for the Pushcart Prize and Best of the Net, and has been selected for dramatic readings by professional theatre groups in New York and Philadelphia. Between hiking, cycling, and kayaking adventures, she continues to work on a collection of linked short stories. She usually brings her fictional characters with her wherever she goes and hopes they'll continue to share their secrets.